The Infatuation Calculation

Susannah Nix is an award-winning and *USA Today* bestselling author of rom-coms and contemporary romances who lives in Texas with her husband. On the rare occasions she's not writing, she can be found reading, knitting, lifting weights, drinking wine, or obsessively watching *Ted Lasso* on repeat to stave off existential angst.

Chemistry Lessons Series

The Love Code
(formerly *Remedial Rocket Science*)

Dating and Other Theories
(formerly *Intermediate Thermodynamics*)

The Boyfriend Hypothesis
(formerly *Advanced Physical Chemistry*)

The Law of Attraction
(formerly *Applied Electromagnetism*)

The Best Friend Experiment
(formerly *Experimental Marine Biology*)

The Infatuation Calculation
(formerly *Elementary Romantic Calculus*)

SUSANNAH NIX

The Infatuation Calculation

PAN BOOKS

First published by the author 2021 as *Elementary Romantic Calculus*

This paperback edition first published 2025 by Pan Books
an imprint of Pan Macmillan
The Smithson, 6 Briset Street, London EC1M 5NR
EU representative: Macmillan Publishers Ireland Ltd, 1st Floor,
The Liffey Trust Centre, 117–126 Sheriff Street Upper,
Dublin 1 D01 YC43
Associated companies throughout the world

ISBN 978-1-0350-2603-6

Copyright © Susannah Nix 2021

The right of Susannah Nix to be identified as the
author of this work has been asserted in accordance
with the Copyright, Designs and Patents Act 1988.

All rights reserved. No part of this publication may be reproduced,
stored in a retrieval system, or transmitted, in any form, or by any means
(including, without limitation, electronic, mechanical, photocopying, recording
or otherwise) without the prior written permission of the publisher.

Pan Macmillan does not have any control over, or any responsibility for,
any author or third-party websites (including, without limitation, URLs,
emails and QR codes) referred to in or on this book.

1 3 5 7 9 8 6 4 2

A CIP catalogue record for this book is available from the British Library.

Typeset in Sabon by Six Red Marbles UK, Thetford, Norfolk
Printed and bound in the UK using 100% Renewable Electricity by
CPI Group (UK) Ltd

This book is sold subject to the condition that it shall not, by way of
trade or otherwise, be lent, hired out, or otherwise circulated without
the publisher's prior consent in any form of binding or cover other than
that in which it is published and without a similar condition including
this condition being imposed on the subsequent purchaser.

Visit **www.panmacmillan.com** to read more about all our books
and to buy them.

For everyone who has ever thought they were bad at math (like me).

Preface

Dear reader,

Although largely lighthearted, this book touches on certain subjects, including revenge porn and agoraphobia, that may be difficult or unpleasant for some.

I offer this warning so that those for whom these are sensitive subjects may make an informed decision about whether or not to proceed with the story.

Be good to yourself,
Susannah Nix

Chapter One

Mia Ballentine was lost. Metaphorically *and* literally.

She must have missed a turn somewhere. Surely she was not meant to be on this dusty farm road on the outskirts of some backwoods town in the middle of Texas.

And yet, here she was. Trying to find her way to an obscure regional university she'd never heard of before she'd applied for a visiting lecturer position in their mathematics department.

This wasn't how things were supposed to go. She'd earned her PhD from one of the top math programs in the country, for god's sake. Gotten her bachelor's at Princeton, where she'd won the Andrew H. Brown Prize before graduating with high honors. She'd laid out a twenty-year career plan for herself, and the next step was supposed to be a three-year postdoc at a top-tier university.

Not *this*.

Unfortunately, the economy had its own ideas. The country was coming off the biggest recession of the twenty-first century and higher education had taken a major hit. Budgets had been stretched to the breaking point as endowments shrank, grants evaporated, and enrollment dropped with the national employment rate. Postdocs were being cut, and hiring freezes were now the norm at most universities. Even low-paid adjunct contracts had become hard to get. It was the worst possible time to go on the job market with a brand-new PhD.

Most everyone in Mia's cohort was struggling—particularly those, like her, who'd done pure instead of applied mathematics. Some had put off defending their dissertations, some had taken temp jobs to make ends meet, and some had been forced to move back in with their parents when their fellowships ran out.

Mia had been scouring mathjobs.org and *The Chronicle of Higher Education* and everywhere else she could think of, applying for anything and everything she could find in academia. Up to now, she hadn't had a single serious expression of interest.

When Bowman University had invited her to come to Texas for an interview, she'd jumped at the opportunity.

At least it was a step up from an adjunct position, most of which were limited to part-time and only paid a few thousand dollars per semester. The Bowman job was full-time and paid enough that Mia wouldn't have to take a second job just to cover rent. It was only a one-year contract, but she couldn't imagine being stuck here in Podunksville for more than a year, anyway. Twelve months seemed like the absolute limit of what she'd be able to stand in a place like this.

Mia peered out the dusty windshield of her rental car and shuddered at the cow pastures around her. Country living had never held any appeal for her. She was a city girl through and through. A New Yorker by birth who'd found

THE INFATUATION CALCULATION

Los Angeles enough of a culture shock when she'd moved there for grad school.

Could she really survive in small-town Texas? Seventy miles from the nearest airport and who even knew how far away from a decent restaurant or grocery store. You probably couldn't even get food delivered here, except whatever passed for pizza in these parts.

They might not even have reliable internet. Or FedEx deliveries. She'd read the stories in *The Atlantic* and the *New Yorker* about all the ways rural America was being left behind by tech advancements, consumer monopolies, and crumbling infrastructure.

And now she might be living it firsthand.

She'd definitely missed a turn. This couldn't possibly be the road to the university, could it? There was nothing out here but pastureland, farmhouses, trees and—

Are those goats?

They were. There were freaking goats standing in the road up ahead. Three of them. And even more milling around the overgrown ditch that ran alongside the blacktop road.

Did people just let their goats roam freely out here?

Could they be *wild* goats? Did they have wild goats in Texas? Were wild goats even a thing? Mia had no idea. The closest she'd ever gotten to a goat was at a petting zoo.

She honked her horn as she neared the goats in the road, but they didn't seem interested in getting out of the way. They simply stared at her rental car as it rolled to a stop in front of them.

"Seriously?" Mia put the car in park, unclipped her seat belt, and shoved the door open.

The humid heat hit her like a slap from a hot towel. Her

weather app had predicted highs in the low nineties for Central Texas today—which had seemed ludicrously hot for May—but it felt more like a thousand degrees out here.

She took a few steps toward the nearest goat and waved her arms, trying to look menacing. "Shoo! Go on. Get out of here!"

Instead of moving out of the road like a reasonable creature should, the goat stood its ground, regarding her with its unnerving sideways cat-eyes. These goats weren't anything like the cute baby billy goats Mia had encountered at petting zoos. These goats were big and wide, almost half her height, with huge udders hanging between their back legs.

She felt a moment of trepidation as she remembered a video she'd once seen of a man getting knocked over by a rambunctious goat. The video had been hilarious, but it was probably a lot less funny if you were the person being attacked by the goat.

Maybe she should have stayed in the car.

She was dressed for her job interview and didn't fancy being butted into the ditch by an angry goat. Imagine explaining that to the hiring committee. *Sorry I'm covered in dirt and vegetation, gentlemen, but you see I was attacked by a wild goat on my way here.*

These goats didn't look particularly angry, fortunately. Or inclined to rambunctiousness. Mostly they looked bored—and hot.

Mia could relate.

"I don't think you're supposed to be here," she said to the goats in the road. "And I'm *definitely* not supposed to be here."

The nearest goat tilted its head at her and bleated. Though

it was almost more of a honk than a bleat. It had a big nose for a goat—not that Mia was any great expert on goat noses. But it seemed to have an unusually large, convex nose that gave it a distinctly comical appearance. It also had long, floppy ears that hung down past its chin like a lop-eared bunny.

It was pretty cute, actually.

Based on the bulging udder, she deduced it was female. It also didn't have any horns, which she hoped meant it wasn't the sort of goat who went around butting people into ditches.

It started walking toward her, and Mia stiffened in fear. But all it did when it reached her was nudge her hand with its head—the same way her friend Brooke's cat did when it wanted to be petted.

Mia gave the goat a tentative scratch between its floppy ears, and it closed its eyes in what was clearly an expression of ecstasy.

When it noticed its friend getting attention, one of the other goats wandered over and bumped its head against Mia's leg. She gave it a head scratch too. They seemed friendly and sweet as long as you gave them what they wanted. They reminded her of dogs, and she'd always liked dogs, despite never owning one herself.

A third goat wandered over, and Mia alternated pets between her three new friends. "You like that, huh? Just call me the Goat Whisperer, I guess."

This was certainly not how she'd expected today to go. She was supposed to be meeting with members of the Bowman University math department in fifteen minutes, not standing on a dusty farm road sweating inside her interview clothes while she catered to a herd of affection-starved goats.

"How do you guys stand the heat out here?" she asked her hoofed companions as a trickle of sweat puddled inside her bra.

"They're goats," a man's voice said behind her. "They're used to it."

Mia started and spun around.

A man in a cowboy hat stood in the road a few yards away from her. He seemed to have materialized out of thin air. There was no other car in sight, and no buildings within half a mile. She had no clue where he'd come from or how he'd managed to sneak up on her.

"Sorry." The man raised his palms in a placating gesture. "Didn't mean to scare you."

Mia had never encountered an actual cowboy before, but she assumed that was what he was. In addition to his cowboy hat, which was made of straw and fraying around the brim, he wore scuffed cowboy boots and dusty jeans. His arms were thick and deeply tanned, and his sweat-stained T-shirt pulled tight across broad shoulders. It was exactly the sort of hearty physique she imagined one developed from years of wrestling recalcitrant cows, lassoing horses, and hoeing crops.

Or whatever it was that cowboys did. Honestly, she had no idea.

The man nodded at her car. "You lost?"

"Is it that obvious?" Squinting, she lifted a hand to shield her eyes from the sun and nearly started again when she got a good look at his face.

She'd been so distracted by the whole cowboy thing, she hadn't appreciated how attractive he was. His strong, square jaw featured exactly the right amount of stubble to look manly and slightly rough, while his cleft chin added character to his face. But it was his eyes that struck Mia the most. Dark, deep set, and piercing beneath the brim of his hat, they regarded her with a startling intensity.

He scratched his stubbly jaw as those sharp eyes looked her up and down. "Well, you're not really dressed for a hike in the country. Let me guess: you're looking for Bowman."

"That's right," she said. "Am I close?"

"You're a couple miles off the mark. The GPS is wrong."

"How can the GPS be wrong?"

Pushing his hat back, he wiped the sweat off his forehead. "It just is. Been that way for years. I guess they don't care about getting it right out here, or they'd have fixed it by now." He pointed down the road behind her. "It's trying to direct you to the old Bowman Farm, which is on the far east side of the campus. The main entrance to the college is two more exits up the highway you came in on."

She turned to look in the direction he'd pointed, then back toward the highway she'd come from, resting her hands on her hips. "So you're telling me everyone just gets lost trying to find the university?"

The cowboy shrugged. "Most people going there already know where it is."

"Right," she said. "Of course they do."

He started toward the goats, who were watching him with interest. "I'll just get these fugitives out of your way so you can turn around."

"You mean they're not supposed to be wandering around loose?"

He let out a deep, throaty laugh. "Not so much, no. They're escape artists. Especially Alice. She's the mastermind.

Always leading the others into trouble." He made a kissing sound and the goats clustered around him.

"They're cute." *And so are you*, Mia thought, but fortunately refrained from saying out loud.

"Don't think they don't know it. They'll charm the pants off you and then start chewing on your shoes once your guard's down. Speaking of . . ." He nodded at Mia's feet, where one of her new goat friends was nibbling at the hem of her pants leg.

"Ack! Stop that!" She jerked back, out of the goat's reach, and it gave her an indignant look.

"Come on, Bell. Back where you belong." The man made another kissy noise and Bell trotted over to him, joining the others.

"Do they all have names?" Mia asked as she watched him lead the goats to a gap in the wire fence running alongside the road. She hadn't noticed it before, but it must have been where the goats had slipped out.

"Yep." He stooped to widen the hole in the fence and gestured the goats through. "That's Agatha," he pointed to each of the goats as he named them, "Zora, and Charlotte."

"Agatha Christie, Zora Neale Hurston, and Charlotte Brontë are all novelists." Mia read mostly nonfiction these days, but as a child she'd read a lot of classic literature because her father had told her it would make her smart.

The man nodded as he shooed the last goat through the fence. "That's right."

"Some people say *Jane Eyre*'s erotic masochism makes it the nineteenth-century *Fifty Shades of Grey*. But I think its complex depiction of female agency was profoundly feminist for its time."

The cowboy lifted his head and squinted at her.

"Charlotte Brontë is my second-favorite nineteenth-century author," Mia added, as if that could somehow explain why she'd said the words *erotic masochism* out loud to a total stranger.

"Are you an English professor?" he asked, frowning slightly.

"No, my PhD is in mathematics."

He accepted this information silently. At least he hadn't warily backed away from her. Yet.

Mia shuffled her feet, eager to end the conversation before she blurted out anything else embarrassing. "Thanks for, um . . . moving your goats."

The man's lips twitched in what she suspected was amusement at her expense. "If you head back the way you came and get on the highway heading east, you'll see a sign telling you where to exit for the college."

"Got it. Thank you very much."

Mia got back in her car, turned around, and drove back to the highway as fast as she safely could.

Chapter Two

Once she found the university, Mia's interview went well. So well they called her a few weeks later and offered her the job.

That left her with a difficult decision to make. On the one hand, it was the only decent job offer she'd received. On the other hand, she wasn't thrilled about the location, the school, or the job itself.

On the *other* other hand, she'd probably be so bored and lonely living in a small town that she'd have nothing else to do but spend her free time working on the proof she hoped to publish, which would go a long way to boosting her CV and helping her get a better job next year.

When it came right down to it, she didn't have a choice. It didn't matter how conflicted she was because she had no other options. None.

Mia called her boyfriend and arranged to meet him for dinner at their favorite Mexican restaurant to break the bad news. Paul worked at a tech company as a software programmer. They'd met via a dating app last year and hit it off immediately. They challenged each other, had deep, intellectual conversations, and were both focused on their careers and their mutual goals of financial independence. The two of them were ideally suited.

Except for the small matter of her career requiring her to move away from LA. She'd always known it was a possibility, but they'd never talked about it much. Every time she'd raised the subject, Paul had said they'd figure it out when the time came.

Well, the time was now.

Once they'd gotten their drinks, Mia moved straight to the bad news. "Bowman offered me the job. A one-year contract teaching three courses a semester. Starting in August."

Paul sat across the table from her picking through the bowl of tortilla chips. She watched his face carefully, but his ice-blue eyes betrayed no reaction as he selected a chip and used it to scoop up an implausible amount of salsa before shoving the whole thing in his mouth.

"Tell me again where this place is?" he said when he'd finished chewing.

She tucked her chin-length hair behind her ears. "Crowder, Texas. About seventy miles outside Austin."

"Wow. Okay." Was that a smidge of disappointment she detected in his voice? It was hard to tell. He reached for his michelada and licked some of the salt off the rim. "Are you going to take it?"

She took a long, deliberate sip of her margarita before answering. "I think I have to." She looked at him. "Don't I?"

He shook his head, pushing his drink away. "I can't tell you what to do."

She'd always appreciated that he never tried to exert influence over her life, but right now she'd give anything for someone to tell her what to do. "The way things are going, I might not get another offer this good. I think I have to take it."

Paul nodded and took a sip of his drink. "Then I guess we should probably break up," he said without any trace of emotion.

"What?" Mia jerked her head up. "Just like that? You don't want to—"

"Move to Texas?" His scoffing tone cut deep. "That's not on the table. I thought you knew that."

She hadn't known that. How could she when they hadn't talked about it? Was this what he'd meant all along when he said they'd figure it out? That they'd just break up?

Admittedly, rural Texas was a big ask. Paul's answer might have been different if she'd been offered a job in the Bay Area or New York City. It would be nice to think so, anyway.

Mia swallowed, trying to hide how much his reaction had hurt. "You're always saying how great it is that you can work remote from anywhere."

"Theoretically, yeah. But I've got a good job right now that's here, and they like to see my face in the office. This is where I need to be for networking and career advancement. There's nothing for me in wherever-the-fuck Texas."

"Crowder." Mia wanted to point out that *she* was the something for him there, but he clearly didn't consider that enough of an incentive.

"Whatever," he mumbled, as if the name of the place she'd be living wasn't important enough for him to remember.

"Okay but . . ." She struggled to find a solution to the problem. A way through that didn't mean the end of their relationship. "We don't necessarily have to break up. We could try to make it work. It would only be temporary."

He regarded her with a pitying expression. "This job's temporary, but what comes after? You'll have to move somewhere else in a year, right, to take another job? What are the odds it'll be here in LA? Or even on the West Coast? You'll be back in the exact same situation: at the mercy of whatever job you can get." He shook his head as he reached for another tortilla chip. "Even if you knew you were coming back here, a year is a long time."

"If you accept Einsteinian relativity, the passage of time is an illusion," she said. "Past, present, and future exist simultaneously with the three dimensions of space."

Paul rolled his eyes. "Don't go all weird on me now. This isn't a theoretical problem. I'm talking about real life."

The laws of physics *were* real life, but Mia didn't argue the point.

"You can't expect me to live like a monk for a year while you're half a continent away," Paul said.

It didn't seem like that much to ask.

Unfortunately, he didn't seem to agree. "A lot can happen in a year. We could grow apart, we could both become completely different people, I could meet someone . . ." His mouth twisted into a mocking smile. "Hey, maybe you'll fall in love with a cowboy and decide you never want to leave."

Mia would have laughed at the suggestion if she hadn't felt like crying.

Paul reached across the table and took her hand. She squeezed his fingers gratefully, comforted by his touch. But his next words offered only cold comfort. "I know this move isn't what you want, but you can't ask me to put my life on hold for you. We've had a good run. I think it's best if we call time of death now and move on."

Mia took the breakup hard.

She couldn't believe they were done, just like that. Everything had seemed to be perfect between them—right up until the moment it was over. The part that hurt most was how easily Paul had let her go. He hadn't even seemed upset. She'd seen him display more emotion over a Lakers game than he had over the end of their year-long relationship.

If he'd been torn up about it—acted even the least bit regretful—it might have been easier for Mia to accept. Instead, she felt like he'd pulled the rug out from under her. Everything she'd believed to be true—that he loved her, that they were a team, that he'd be there to support her through good times and bad—had turned out to be false.

Had she been deluding herself all this time? Overestimating the depth of his commitment? Or had he actively misrepresented his feelings? She couldn't stop rewinding her memories of every moment they'd spent together, searching for signs she should have picked up on before now.

A month after Paul had unceremoniously dumped her, Mia was still struggling to regain her footing. It didn't help that she was in the midst of uprooting her whole life, preparing for a move she didn't want to make in order to start a job she hadn't wanted to take. But at least it gave her something to focus on besides her broken heart.

She'd thrown herself into lesson planning for the three courses she'd be teaching, all of which were part of the university's core curriculum offerings: Calculus I, Foundations of Mathematics, and something called Math in Society, a math class tailored for humanities majors. Mia was expected to create her own lesson plans around the department's vague framework for the courses. In her previous teaching experience as a graduate student, she had been provided with a lesson plan by the professor she was assisting. This was the first time she'd ever had to come up with one on her own. To prepare for it, she'd been delving into educational resources online and brushing up on pedagogical techniques.

She was deep into a paper on active-learning approaches to post-secondary mathematics education when her phone rang on the table beside her. Seeing her sister's photo on the screen, she smiled.

Holly was basically a younger, cuter version of Mia. The same medium-brown hair and eyes that looked so plain on Mia were somehow much prettier on Holly, who was a full four inches shorter than Mia's six feet.

She and Holly had always been close, despite their three-year age difference, but Holly still lived with their mother in New York, and Mia missed her like crazy.

"Heya. How's it going?" Holly said cheerfully when she answered.

Mia leaned back and rubbed her tired eyes, forcing cheer into her voice. "Fine."

"You're not still pining over what's-his-name?"

"No way," Mia lied. "I'm *so* over it."

It was much easier to pretend she was taking it in her stride than admit she was struggling. And maybe, if she kept up the act long enough, it wouldn't be an act anymore. She *would* be over it.

"Good," Holly said. "I never liked him anyway."

"You didn't?" This was news to Mia. Holly had only met

Paul once, but they'd seemed to get on like gangbusters. Her sister had never voiced any criticism of him. "Why?"

"He never seemed to pay enough attention to you. You know all those little things guys do when they're head over heels in love? Like—I don't know—rubbing your back or checking if your drink needs a refill. Or gazing lovingly at you from across the room when you're talking to someone else. He never did any of that."

"Not all men do those things." What Holly was describing sounded like a fantasy rather than real life. They were the sorts of things Mia had assumed men only did in books and movies.

"They do when they're infatuated," Holly said. "You deserve a boyfriend who hangs on your every word. And that wasn't Paul."

It definitely was not. Maybe Holly was right. Maybe those were exactly the sorts of signs Mia should have picked up.

She squeezed her eyes shut, feeling like a fool. "You never said anything."

"Well, you know . . . you were so into him." Holly sounded regretful. "I didn't want to make waves."

"Promise me that the next time you don't like my boyfriend, you'll tell me. You could have saved me a lot of grief and wasted time."

"I promise," Holly said. "As long as you promise not to hold it against me."

"Deal." Mia reached for her coffee cup, which had long since grown cold. "So did you call just to check up on me?" She swallowed the dregs with a grimace.

"Not exactly. I have a question, although I think I already know the answer."

Uh oh. Mia recognized that tone, and it usually presaged something unpleasant. "What is it?" she asked, pushing her chair back to carry her empty mug into the kitchen.

"Have you told Dad about the job and your move yet?"

Mia hung her head with guilt as she set the mug in the sink. "Ummm . . . well . . ."

"Sis." For a younger sister, Holly was surprisingly good at sounding stern and disappointed.

"I know."

"You have to tell him."

"I will."

It wasn't entirely Mia's fault. She hadn't actually heard from her father in several months, which was par for their relationship. Sure, she could have called him herself to break the news, but it wasn't a conversation she was eager to have. So she hadn't.

Mia knew exactly how her father, a quantitative analyst who'd put his doctorate in statistics to work on Wall Street, would feel about her new job. He'd made his disappointment in her academic and professional choices clear enough already.

If she'd followed in his footsteps like he'd wanted, he could have helped her at every step of her career, smoothing the way for her to jump from the right schools into the right jobs with the right companies. Which might have been fine if she'd had any appetite for finance or the ambition to make ungodly amounts of money the way he had.

Mia preferred the creativity and challenge of pure mathematics—something her father had never been able to understand. Her choice of graduate school had been yet another disappointment. Choosing UCLA over his precious alma mater, Princeton? Was madness as far as her father was concerned. A deliberate choice to be mediocre instead of exceptional.

Mia had followed her heart instead of her father's advice, and now she was paying the price for it. She wasn't in a hurry to tell him it wasn't turning out as well as she'd hoped.

Holly let out an annoyed sigh. "I'm seeing Dad on Saturday and I don't want to have to cover for you."

"What are you seeing Dad for?"

Even though Holly only lived a borough away from their father, she didn't see much more of him than Mia did. Generally, his interactions with his daughters were confined to the winter holidays and odd special occasions—when he could be bothered to spare the time. Mia had lost count of all the birthday parties, recitals, and award ceremonies he'd missed over the years. He'd even missed Holly's high school graduation, canceling at the last minute because of a "work trip" they later learned had actually been a tryst in Hawaii with his mistress.

Holly sighed again. "It's his and Mindy's fifth anniversary, don't you know? So of course they're having a big party to show off how blissfully happy they are, and my presence has been commanded."

Mindy was their father's third wife. Not the wife he'd cheated on with the mistress in Hawaii, but the woman he'd cheated on his second wife with in Hawaii.

"Guess my invite must have gotten lost in the mail." Not that Mia would have wanted to go—or even been able to afford it—but she still felt salty about being excluded. No matter how many times she swore she wasn't going to let her father's chronic disregard affect her anymore, it still managed to hurt.

"I'm sure if you lived within commuting distance, you would have been summoned to make an appearance as well." She could practically hear Holly's eye roll over the phone. "But if you want to fly out here and take my place, by all means . . ."

"You don't have to go, you know."

"I know." Holly sounded defensive now. "But it's not worth the fight. I'd rather not deal with the bitching and moaning about how I've let him down—never mind that he's been letting me down my whole life and only ever remembers he has daughters when it suits him."

Mia winced at the familiar bitterness in her sister's voice. They'd had this conversation, or some version of it, hundreds of times before.

"Besides, it's free catered food and an open bar," Holly added. "That's worth putting up with Dad for the five whole minutes he'll spend talking to me."

"You know . . ." Mia chewed her lip. "If you're going to see him anyway, you could tell him about my new job for me."

Holly made a scoffing sound. "No way. I'm not your proxy."

"Fine. Be that way."

"Baby, I was *born* that way. You're going to have to deliver your own news."

Mia blew out a defeated breath. "I'll call him. No promises I'll actually be able to get hold of him by Saturday though."

"As long as you make the effort. Rip the Band-Aid off and

get it over with. You'll feel better when it's not hanging over your head anymore."

"Will I?"

"Maybe? Do it anyway. Today."

"Just be ready for him to complain to you about what a disappointment I turned out to be."

"You're not a disappointment. *He's* the disappointment." Holly spat the words like an overprotective yet adorable kitten. "And I'll tell him exactly that if he tries to say any shit about you."

"Don't get into a fight with Dad on my behalf. Please." The last thing Mia wanted was to be a source of even more tension in her family.

"It's on him if he can't behave. Don't start shit, won't be shit." Holly didn't share Mia's devotion to conflict avoidance. "Listen, I've gotta run. My lunch break's almost over. I'll talk to you soon, okay?"

Mia bid her sister goodbye and disconnected the call.

Before she could lose her nerve, she called her dad. Holly was right. Better to get it over with so it wouldn't be something else hanging over her head.

She got his voicemail, of course. He never answered his phone. Not when it was one of his daughters calling, anyway.

Chapter Three

"Are you sure you want to get rid of this?"

Mia glanced over at her friend Olivia, who was holding up a blank journal she'd found in the donation pile. "Positive. Take it if you want it."

She'd invited some friends over to pick through the stuff she was giving away before her move. The movers charged by the square foot, so she was determined to get rid of as much as she could stand.

Her other friend, Brooke, looked up from the box of old DVDs she was going through. "It's a really nice journal. Are you crazy?"

Mia turned back to flipping through the clothes in her closet. "Paul gave it to me for my birthday. And I prefer Moleskines anyway."

Paul was constantly giving her blank journals when they were dating. It was his go-to gift, and Mia had never used a single one of them. She was addicted to journals, but only to a very particular kind. They had to be a certain size, they had to have a flexible, plain black cover, and they absolutely, positively had to have graph lines on the pages. Paul had paid just enough attention to notice Mia's journal addiction, but not enough to ascertain her specific needs and preferences. Which pretty accurately summed up their entire relationship, now that she thought about it.

"Right." Olivia pursed her dark-red lips in distaste and dropped the leather journal back into the donation box. "Too bad LA's under a red flag warning, or we could have an ex-boyfriend bonfire before you go."

"He's not worth it," Mia replied. Although she had to admit the idea of a bonfire held appeal as a symbolic ritual.

She was trying to treat this move as an opportunity instead of a misfortune. This would be a rebuilding year for her. A chance to concentrate on her work without any distractions. Refocus on what she wanted from her career, figure out how she was going to get it, and adjust her twenty-year plan accordingly. And the first step was letting go of anything that might weigh her down.

Mia pulled her old winter coat out of the back of her closet. "How cold does it get in Central Texas in the winter?"

Olivia looked up from a box of Mia's old books that she was poking through. "Colder than here, but not cold enough for that."

"Won't you need it if you go home for Christmas?" Brooke pointed out.

"I guess." Reluctantly, Mia shoved the coat back into the closet.

"I can't believe you're moving to where we're from," Olivia said. "It's weird."

"*I'm* from Louisiana." Brooke's freckled cheeks dimpled as she made a face at Olivia. "Not Texas."

Olivia shrugged. "Close enough."

Brooke clasped her hands to her chest in mock offense.

"Better not let any of my Louisiana relatives hear you say that."

Olivia ignored her and turned back to Mia. "I'm having a real hard time picturing you in Texas. No offense, but you're such a New Yorker."

"None taken," Mia said, since she *was* a New Yorker and proud of it. "I'm also having a hard time picturing me there."

It had been a difficult enough adjustment when she'd moved to Los Angeles for graduate school eight years ago. But at least LA was a major metropolitan area with a large number of displaced New Yorkers like herself. Despite some of the peculiarities of West Coast living, Mia had found plenty of things to remind her of home and ease the transition.

"Especially Crowder of all places. Talk about culture clash. There's basically nothing there but cow shit and rednecks—and ice cream, of course." Olivia was originally from Houston, which was only two hours from the town where Mia would be living.

"Oh right! King's ice cream is headquartered there." Brooke slapped the heel of her hand against her forehead. "That's where I've heard of it before. I'm addicted to their Way the Cookie Crumbles flavor."

"I'm a Double Double Fudge and Truffle girl myself." Olivia finished with the box she was going through and pushed it closer to the door. "We used to take field trips to the creamery in elementary school. We always got a paper hat and an ice cream cone at the end of the tour. Best day of the whole school year."

Mia didn't like ice cream because it gave her brain freeze, which resulted when a rapid change of temperature in the mouth caused the blood vessels to constrict in an attempt to maintain the body's core temperature.

"The human brain doesn't like rapid change," she said, thinking about ice cream and brain freeze. But she supposed it also applied to her upcoming move. Unfortunately, in this case she didn't have a choice, and her brain would have to deal.

Brook gave her a sympathetic look. "Maybe a little culture clash is what you need. Stepping out of your comfort zone is supposed to be good for you, right? Self-actualization through new experiences—or whatever it was Julia Roberts was doing in *Eat, Pray, Love*."

Olivia snorted in amusement. "You're going to *Eat, Pray, Love* your way through Crowder, Texas? Good luck with that."

"What are you even going to do there?" Brooke asked. "Go cow tipping? Take up country-western dancing?"

"I'm going to work," Mia said firmly. "I'll have three courses to teach each semester, plus I need to get some papers published before I go back on the job market next year. That should be more than enough to keep me occupied."

Mia's primary field of concentration was knot theory, and she'd been obsessing over one specific problem since she'd finished her dissertation earlier this year. She was *so* close to solving it, she could practically taste the answer. If she could figure it out, it would be a game changer for her. The sort of thing that could open all the doors that had slammed shut in her face. It could be her ticket into the postdoc of her dreams, putting her twenty-year tenure plan back on track.

"How's your research coming?" Brooke asked. She was a

marine biology student in the last year of her PhD program. All she had left to finish was her dissertation, but she wasn't in a big hurry, given the current job prospects. Brooke had the advantage of living with a boyfriend who made plenty of money to support both of them, so she could afford to take her time before hitting the uncertain job market.

"Honestly, I've been so busy with my job hunt and move, I haven't had time for much else." Mia was ashamed to admit that she'd had trouble focusing on her work since Paul had dumped her.

Usually, all she had to do was close her eyes and she saw numbers and shapes dancing on the backs of her eyelids. It was how she used to put herself to sleep as a child. Some people made up stories; Mia thought about math.

But now when she tried it, all she could think about was Paul. Although it wasn't really Paul she was obsessing over so much as her own mistakes. Their relationship was a math problem she'd gotten wrong, and her mind couldn't stop trying to identify all the errors. Unfortunately, she was nowhere near as good at understanding people and their emotions as she was at math.

"But I'll crack it," she declared with more confidence than she felt. "A change of scenery should help." That was what she'd been telling herself. Once she'd settled into her new place and her new job, she'd be able to concentrate on her proof again. She'd have no choice, because she wouldn't have anything else to do.

The apartment door opened, and Brooke and Olivia's boyfriends strolled in.

"What's next?" asked Adam, who belonged to Olivia. "Any more stuff to go down yet?" He'd kindly offered his

SUV to drive the donations over to one of the local women's shelters.

"Those two boxes by the door." Olivia rose up on her toes to kiss his cheek. "Thanks, babe."

"Yes, thank you so much for doing this," Mia said, feeling an unexpected stab of melancholy. "I really appreciate the help."

One of the many things she was struggling with was leaving her friends here in LA. Sure, they'd all try to keep in touch, but realistically she knew they'd most likely end up drifting apart eventually.

She was about to be on her own in a strange place with no support system. Phone calls and texts were all well and good, but they couldn't help you move heavy boxes or come pick you up when your car broke down.

"No problem." Brooke's extravagantly handsome boyfriend, Dylan—who happened to be a model—tossed Mia a dazzling smile as he stooped to pick up one of the boxes. "We're happy to help."

Mia's phone rang as the guys carried the next load out.

Shit. It was her dad calling her back, finally. Three full days later, and just hours before his anniversary party was due to start.

Grimacing, she pressed the phone to her ear. "Hey, Dad."

Brooke and Olivia exchanged a quick glance, then grabbed two more boxes and followed the guys out the door to give Mia some privacy.

"I got your message," her father said in his usual curt tone. "I don't have a lot of time to talk. Mindy and I are hosting a party to celebrate our anniversary tonight. Five wonderful years."

"I heard." Mia rolled her eyes while trying to sound polite. "Congratulations."

"Thank you. I'll pass that on to her. I'm sure it will mean a lot."

Mia doubted that, since she and Mindy had never bothered to hide their mutual indifference. Other than the fact that they were only five years apart in age, their disinterest in one another was the only thing they had in common.

"Was that all you wanted?" her father asked, as if Mia would have called solely to wish him a happy anniversary. "Things are chaotic here today."

"Um, I guess I have some news to share." Mia spoke quickly to get it over with: "I got a job—not a great one or anything, just a one-year contract as a visiting lecturer, but it'll tide me over until I can find something better, hopefully."

"Congratulations." To describe her father's tone as lukewarm would be generous. "Where?"

"Bowman University."

There was a long, censorious pause. "Where's that?"

"It's outside Austin."

Her father made a faint grunting sound that managed to communicate how unimpressed he was. "So you're moving, I take it?"

"Next month."

"Email Mindy your new address so she can update our holiday card list, will you?"

Sure. Because that was definitely everyone's number one priority right now. Her father's Christmas card list.

"I will," Mia promised nonetheless. It was easier to play the part of the obedient daughter than make unnecessary waves. She'd learned that a long time ago.

"Good for you, Ace." Her dad's childhood nickname for her landed like a jab. He didn't even need to say how disappointed he was. The flatness of his voice said it all. "I'm sure you'll do well at . . . what was the name of the school again?"

"Bowman," she repeated through gritted teeth.

"Of course. Right. Good luck with the move. Let me know if you need anything. Sorry, kiddo, but I've got to run. Lots to do for tonight. I'll talk to you soon."

"Bye, Dad." Scowling, Mia jabbed her finger at the screen to end the call.

At least it was over with now. Her sister would be pleased, anyway. And Mia probably wouldn't have to talk to her father again until Christmas. Hopefully.

Chapter Four

Three weeks later, Mia drove into Crowder again. But this time it was to stay.

For the next year, anyway.

It was her first real look at the place. When she'd come for her interview, she'd skirted the center of town to get to the university, then driven straight back to Austin afterward. She probably should have explored it more, but she hadn't seriously expected to end up taking the job.

It's not that bad, she told herself as she drove through the quaint town center, past an antique store, an old-timey ice cream shop, and a cozy-looking cafe. According to her research, Crowder sported a number of restaurants and most of the major fast-food chains. There was also a Walmart and a couple of decent-sized grocery stores, so it wasn't as if she'd left civilization behind. You could get all the essentials here, if not necessarily all the luxuries she'd grown accustomed to in the city.

While she waited at a red light, Mia peered in the window of a boutique clothing shop. It appeared to carry a lot of brightly patterned dresses and filmy scarves of the sort favored by flamboyant grandmothers and eccentric spinster aunts.

Next door was a western wear store displaying all manner of cowboy boots, hats, and plaid shirts in the window. A few of the people walking on the sidewalk looked to have gotten their clothes there, but not all. Not even most. Aside from a few men wearing cowboy boots and jeans, most people were either dressed business casual for work or attired to beat the summer heat in flip-flops and shorts. Honestly, the fashion wasn't that different from what you saw in LA during a heat wave.

The light changed, and Mia drove on past a yoga studio, a pizza place, and a library. Beyond that, a grassy town square with a band gazebo sat across from an unremarkable town hall building.

After a few more blocks, the charming downtown area gave way to less picturesque commercial ventures: an auto parts store, a pawn shop, and a seedy-looking bar. There was even a feed store to drive home the fact that she was in the country now.

Beyond that, retail properties gave way to more residential ones. Modest ranch-style houses squatted on generous lots shaded by the arms of spreading oak trees. As she drew nearer to the university, the neighborhood shifted to older bungalows with a few larger Victorians scattered here and there.

The GPS directed Mia through a maze of shady streets to the address on her new residential lease. When her phone announced she'd arrived at her destination, she parked on the street behind a dusty pickup truck and stared at the property with a sinking feeling.

THE INFATUATION CALCULATION

She'd picked it out online, sight unseen. The listing had included photos of the garage apartment she'd be calling home for the next year, but not of the main house it sat behind.

There certainly had been no photographic evidence of the old denim couch that sat on the house's front porch, the patch of knee-high weeds growing in the open ditch running alongside the street, or the chickens wandering around the gravel driveway.

Live chickens.

Hanging out in the driveway as if that was a perfectly normal place for chickens to be.

What have I done? Was she really supposed to live here? In this place that had forgotten the chic part of shabby chic, where livestock roamed freely and the nearest Sephora was two hours away?

As Mia sat in the car mustering the courage to unfasten her seat belt and take her first steps toward her new life, the front door of the house opened and a woman came out. She had short, spiky gray hair and wore Birkenstocks with a flowery muumuu that looked like it had come from the clothing boutique downtown.

"Hellooooo!" she called, waving as she approached the car. "Are you Mia Ballentine?"

Mia forced herself to get out of the car. Her sunglasses fogged up as soon as she stepped into the sweltering air, and she pushed them up onto her head.

"That's me," she said with a pasted-on smile. "Helen Fishbaugh?" It was the name that had been on her lease, and the only piece of information she had about her new landlord.

The woman's nose wrinkled. "I haven't been Helen since

grade school. Everyone around here calls me Birdie." Her smile grew wider, and her round, friendly face crinkled around her eyes. "My goodness! Aren't you a statuesque beauty?"

Mia wasn't accustomed to being described so generously. More commonly, her six-foot height had earned her nicknames like Gigantor, She-Hulk, and Bigfoot. She'd never thought of herself as particularly statuesque either—unless you were talking about statues of thick-thighed Greek soldiers. She was built less like the Venus de Milo and more like a tree trunk: sturdy and straight-up-and-down

Flustered by the unexpected compliment, Mia turned back to the car to retrieve her purse.

"I'm glad to see you," Birdie said, sounding every bit like she meant it. "I've been worried about you making that long drive by yourself. I hope you didn't run into any trouble."

"None at all. It was smooth sailing all the way." Mia had never had a landlord express concern for her before. Or claim to be glad to see her. Glad to see her rent money, sure. But not her.

"Oh, that's good," Birdie said. "I'll bet you're relieved to be home, finally."

Home.

Mia looked past Birdie to the driveway that presumably led to her new apartment. She didn't want this place to be her home, but here she was. It was too late to turn back now.

Birdie rested her hands on her hips. "Texas just seems to stretch on forever, doesn't it? I remember taking a trip to the Davis Mountains to visit the McDonald Observatory when I was a girl, and I couldn't believe how wide the state was.

THE INFATUATION CALCULATION

Texas is so big you can drive for twelve hours and still be in Texas." She laughed to herself, patting her chest. "Anyway, I expect you're eager to see your apartment. There's a space for your car in the garage, but it's a bit tight, so I suggest you park in the driveway while you're unloading your things."

"Okay." Mia was feeling overwhelmed by this social interaction. She'd assumed she'd be given her keys and left alone to fend for herself, not expected to make small talk in one-hundred-degree heat.

Birdie cupped her hands around her face and squinted in the window of Mia's car, which was packed to the roof with boxes and suitcases. "Is this all the stuff you've got?"

"No, the movers are bringing my furniture this afternoon."

"Oh good. We can't have you sleeping on the floor."

"That won't be a problem," Mia assured her. "Hopefully the truck won't be in your way long."

"Don't you worry about that." Birdie pulled a set of keys out of the pocket of her dress and jingled them. "Come on, then. Pull your car up in front of the garage, and I'll show you your new home."

Mia cast an uncertain glance at the chickens in the driveway. "Do we need to move them first? I don't want to hurt your chickens."

Birdie laughed. "Oh honey, don't worry about them. They'll scram when they see you coming."

Mia got back in her car and pulled it into Birdie's driveway. Sure enough, as soon as they saw the Toyota hatchback creeping toward them, the chickens scattered onto the grass with a flurry of indignant clucks and flapping wings.

At the end of the long driveway, a two-car garage loomed behind the one-story house. The double garage door stood open, and inside sat an old Subaru station wagon with just enough space next to it to fit her car in. A wooden staircase on one side of the garage led up to the second-story apartment Mia had rented.

Birdie's backyard offered a clue as to why she was called Birdie. Bird feeders hung from every available surface. They lined the eaves of the back porch, dangled from the lower limbs of a huge tree beside the house, and graced multiple shepherd's hooks and poles positioned around the yard.

The yard itself was huge by Mia's standards. Off the back porch of the house was a shady concrete patio populated with rusty furniture. Beyond that was a shed, a chicken coop, and several rows of raised vegetable beds along the back fence, with a grassy open space leftover for the roaming chickens.

Birdie waited at the foot of the stairs while Mia grabbed her overnight bag from the car. Both the house and the garage were painted an unattractive salmon pink with dingy white trim that was peeling in a few places. It had looked much nicer online, but it also wasn't as if there had been many choices. The Crowder real estate market wasn't exactly expansive.

Girding herself for the worst, Mia followed Birdie upstairs to her new apartment. It was as small as she'd expected but nicer than she'd feared. The interior was impeccably clean and smelled of fresh paint. The kitchen appeared to have been recently renovated with new white ceramic tile and gleaming silver fixtures. Both the stove and fridge looked relatively new, and the hardwood floors were in excellent condition.

"You like it?" Birdie asked, looking around proudly. "I

had it fixed up a few years back so I could rent it out. Before that it was just storage."

"It's great," Mia said, feeling more optimistic.

"Good. Here's your key and the clicker for the garage. I'll leave you to get settled in." Birdie handed Mia a garage door opener and a freshly cut house key on a keychain in the shape of Texas. "You said you've got movers coming this afternoon?"

"Between one and three, allegedly."

Birdie nodded as she started for the door. "I'll keep an eye out for them. You let me know if there's anything you need. My back door's always open."

Mia wasn't sure if she meant that figuratively, as in visitors were always welcome, or literally, as in she didn't bother to lock her door. Either way, Mia wouldn't be letting herself into Birdie's house without knocking, and she'd be keeping her own door locked.

Once Birdie was gone, Mia set herself to the task of unloading her car. It took her the better part of an hour, and by the time she was done she was a sweaty mess, and her calves were aching from trudging up and down the stairs.

While she was unpacking her toiletries in the bathroom, there was a knock at her door. She went to answer it, hoping the movers had shown up early, and instead found Birdie holding a tote bag and a tray covered with a dish towel.

"I made you a little lunch," she said, bustling inside.

"You really didn't have to do that," Mia said, although her stomach rumbled at the mere mention of food. It occurred to her she hadn't eaten anything since the Egg McMuffin she'd wolfed down that morning in Fort Stockton.

"It's just some snacks to tide you over until you can get

yourself to a grocery store. I hope you like cheese." Birdie whipped the towel off the tray and Mia's eyes nearly bugged out of her head.

Birdie's version of "some snacks" was a full-fledged platter featuring a selection of hard and soft cheeses, crackers, cherry tomatoes, and assorted pickled vegetables.

"Wow. This is amazing." Mia gaped at the mouthwatering selection of cheese, which happened to be her favorite food. "Thank you so much."

Birdie waved her hand as if it was nothing. "Most of the veggies are from my garden, and the cheese is from my nephew's goat farm."

"Your nephew has a goat farm?" Mia recalled the handsome cowboy she'd encountered on the way to her interview and wondered how many goat farmers there were around Crowder.

"Redbud Farm belonged to his parents," Birdie said as she carried her tote bag over to the fridge. "Josh took it over when my sister and her husband retired to Maine a few years ago." She began transferring bottles of water from her bag into Mia's fridge. "This should keep you hydrated through the afternoon. It's supposed to break a hundred again today, so make sure you drink plenty of water. Heat exhaustion can sneak up on you."

"Thank you," Mia mumbled around a mouthful of the most incredible feta she'd ever tasted. "That's so thoughtful."

"I also left some of the herb chèvre and a jar of goat milk yogurt in there for you." Birdie moved to the counter and proceeded to pull several more jars from her bag, which seemed to be bottomless and possibly of magical origin. "And here's some of my homemade pickled okra and a jar of honey. Did you know neighborhood honey is the best thing in the world for hay fever? Arlo who lives next door, he keeps bees, and I trade him vegetables from my garden that his bees help pollinate, for some of the honey his bees make with nectar from my garden. So it all works out perfectly."

Mia didn't know how to respond to Birdie's kindness. The concept of a landlord who brought lunch and housewarming presents was completely alien. Also, holy crap, her nephew's feta was practically orgasmic.

"You didn't have to do all this," she told Birdie around a mouthful of cheese.

"Oh honey, I'm up to my eyeballs in okra this time of year. I can't pickle it fast enough, and my pantry's overflowing with the stuff. Believe me, you're doing me a favor taking it off my hands. And at least now I know you won't starve before you can get to the grocery store."

Mia thanked her again and invited her to stay and share the lunch she'd brought, but Birdie refused, insisting she had too much to do that day. On her way out the door, she wished Mia luck with the movers and told her to call if she needed anything.

Once she was alone again, Mia attacked the snack platter with enthusiasm and wonderment. Nothing about this experience so far had been what she'd expected. She still wasn't sure how she felt about sharing a yard with chickens, didn't know how to handle a landlord who treated her more like a guest than a tenant, and had no idea if she even liked pickled okra, which she now had three large jars of.

One thing she did know: she was a *huge* fan of this goat cheese.

Whoever Birdie's nephew was, he was a freaking cheese artist.

The movers arrived only an hour late, and within forty-five minutes they had carried all of Mia's furniture up the narrow stairs to her apartment and driven away again.

She spent the rest of the afternoon unpacking and organizing her new apartment as the mercury climbed higher and the air-conditioning unit in the window struggled to keep up. Occasionally, she caught sight of Birdie working in the yard or coming and going in the old Subaru wagon. Every time the garage door opened or closed, the floor of Mia's apartment vibrated. She dearly hoped Birdie wasn't prone to going out late at night.

By seven o'clock, Mia was sweaty, exhausted, and ready to throw in the towel for the day. She'd managed to make up her bed, put away all her clothes, and unpack enough of the kitchen that she'd be able to fix herself a cup of coffee in the morning. That was enough for now.

What she needed was a shower, clean pajamas, and a night's sleep in her own bed.

The bathroom was cramped, as one would expect from a garage apartment, with just enough space for a sink, toilet, and shower stall. She stepped into the stream of cool water and sighed with pleasure as it hit her skin, washing away the layers of sweat and dust that had accumulated during the day.

At least the water pressure was good. Maybe this place wouldn't be so bad. Maybe she could get used to country living and country people. She liked Birdie. If the rest of the town was anything like her, it might not be half bad living here. Maybe the next twelve months would pass quickly and pleasantly, a temporary but not completely miserable detour on a career path that would eventually get back on track and lead her to a tenured position at a better school.

Mia closed her eyes and let the water run over her short hair before lathering it up with shampoo. After she'd finished rinsing it out, she opened her eyes and noticed an odd black-and-yellow splotch on the ceiling of the shower.

Weird.

As she blinked the water out of her eyes, the splotch came into better focus, and she let out a panicked squawk when she realized it was a spider.

The *biggest fucking spider* she'd ever seen in her life.

And it was only inches away from her head. The thing was nearly the size of her fist and perched in a web that stretched across the ceiling of the shower stall.

Not only was it enormous, it was staring at her like it had skipped lunch and she was a big, juicy fly. She could swear the thing was actually licking its lips. Or it would have been, if spiders had lips.

As she stared in horror, the repulsive thing raised its front legs to expose a pair of terrifying fangs and *came at her*.

A scream tore its way out of Mia's throat, and she threw herself out of the shower so violently she clipped her forehead on the edge of the fiberglass enclosure. With her adrenaline spiking and her head throbbing, she only barely managed to grab a towel in her mad rush to flee Shelob's lair.

Once she was safely out of the bathroom, she wrapped the towel around her dripping torso, reached up to push back her soaking wet hair, and froze when her fingers touched *something that was not her hair.*

Something chitinous and creepy.
OHMYGOD, IT'S ON ME!

Mia screamed again and ran out of the apartment, clutching the bath towel around herself. She careened down the stairs in a blind panic, coming to an abrupt and unexpected stop when she collided with someone in the yard below.

Chapter Five

"What the hell?" a male voice grunted as Mia slammed into him. He grabbed onto her arm as she started to fall backward. "Are you okay?"

"Spider," Mia gasped, shaking her head like a cartoon character. "There's a spider in my hair!"

"Hang on. Be still." Two hands grasped her head, tilting it from side to side as fingers threaded through her wet hair.

Squeezing her eyes shut, she tried to calm her racing heart as she clutched her towel to avoid flashing the helpful stranger inspecting her for arachnids. She had no idea who he was, but she didn't care as long as he *got the fucking spider off her*.

"As far as I can tell, you're spider-free." His voice was deep and slightly raspy, with a pronounced Texas drawl. "Your head's bleeding though."

Mia reached up to touch her forehead. "I must have hit it when I ran out of the shower." Her fingers came away stained with blood.

"How hard?" The stranger's tone sounded teasing.

Mia raised her head, looking into the man's face for the first time. "It's you!" she said, realizing he was the very same goat rustler she'd encountered on the way to her Bowman interview.

He seemed to flinch, his previously friendly expression shuttering. "Do I know you?"

"You're the goat guy." She crossed her arms to hold her towel more firmly in place. "You gave me directions to the university a few months ago when you were recapturing some runaway goats named after female authors. Agatha and Zora, if I remember right."

"And Charlotte." The corner of his mouth twitched, and he seemed to relax again. "You're the *Jane Eyre* fan."

Mia reddened at the reminder of her embarrassing attempt to make conversation, but she couldn't help being pleased he remembered their encounter. She smiled, noticing for the first time how tall he was. His striking brown eyes were exactly level with hers.

"Did I hear screams?" Birdie burst out of the house and hurried toward them, her eyes widening as she took in Mia's soaking wet, towel-clad appearance. "Oh my word! What happened? Are you all right?"

"I'm fine." Now that the initial spike of fear had receded, Mia felt foolish about her panicked reaction—not to mention her state of near nakedness. She hiked her towel up higher in an attempt to maintain a modicum of dignity. "There was a huge spider in my shower—the biggest I've ever seen. I thought it had jumped into my hair." She darted a sheepish look at Goat Guy. "But I might have been wrong."

Birdie's face lit up, her concern shifting to excitement. "What kind of spider? What did it look like?"

"Yellow and black," Mia said, wishing she didn't have

such a clear memory of the wretched thing. "It was almost as wide as my palm."

"A banana spider, I'll bet." Birdie looked delighted. "Do you think it's still inside your apartment?"

"I don't know." Mia shivered at the thought of it waiting upstairs for her. "I guess if it wasn't on me when I ran outside, then it might be." She snuck another glance at the man she assumed was Birdie's cheesemaking nephew, hoping he'd offer to perform a search and destroy mission.

Either that or they could just burn the whole garage down with all her worldly possessions in it, because there was no way she'd be able to sleep up there until she was certain it was one hundred percent spider free.

It was Birdie who leaped into action, however, collecting a pair of gloves and an empty mason jar from her potting bench. "I'll go see if I can catch it. She'll make an excellent addition to my garden!"

As Birdie hastened upstairs, Mia cast a dubious look at the garden. As much as she was in favor of Birdie catching the spider, she didn't love the idea of it taking up permanent residence in the yard right next to her apartment.

"We should do something about that cut on your head," the man said.

Mia's gaze darted back to him, and she remembered she was bleeding in addition to being wet and clad in nothing but a damp towel.

"Let's go in the house so I can take a closer look." He was without his hat tonight, and he ran his hand over his head, ruffling his dark-brown hair as he politely averted his gaze from her state of undress. "And maybe find you something to wear."

"That'd be great." Mia followed him toward Birdie's back porch, picking her way through the grass in her bare feet and trying not to think about all the chicken poop she was probably walking on.

The man threw a look over his shoulder, slowing his gait to match hers. "I'm Birdie's nephew, Josh Lockhart."

"The cheesemaker, right? Birdie brought me some of your cheese. Your feta is exquisite." Mia stumbled as she stepped on something sharp. "Ow!"

"Watch out for the pecan shells." Josh offered her his elbow. "Here, hold on to me for balance."

She gripped his arm with the hand that wasn't holding her towel up, feeling her cheeks redden further as her fingers squeezed his substantial biceps. "I'm Mia Ballentine, Birdie's new tenant."

"You work at the university?"

"Starting next week. I'm a lecturer in the math department."

"Should I call you Dr. Ballentine, then?"

"Mia's fine unless you're one of my students. You're not a student, are you?" He didn't look that young, but you never knew. Better to find out now, before she accidentally went and developed an inappropriate crush on a student.

Not that she was crushing on Josh. But the potential was certainly there. Hot goat farmer. Master cheesemaker. It was a dangerously alluring combination.

Josh's expression turned wry as he shook his head. "My college days are long past."

"You can't be that old." If she had to guess, she'd put him in his late twenties, close to her own age.

They'd reached the house finally, and he held the back

door open for her. "You don't look old enough to be a college professor."

"I'm twenty-eight. This is my first full-time teaching position after finishing my PhD." She let go of Josh's arm and preceded him inside, grateful to put her bare feet on solid floors.

The interior of Birdie's house was as eclectic as the exterior. The furniture was mismatched and comfortably worn, nearly every surface covered with clutter. Books mostly, but a variety of projects also lay scattered about—a disassembled bird feeder on the dining table, a basket of knitting on the couch, a TV tray by the window covered with seedlings growing in tiny paper cups.

"Sit down." Josh gestured her to a stool at the breakfast bar. "I'll get the first aid kit."

Mia sank onto the stool while he disappeared into the back of the house. On the bar next to her sat a bowl of newly harvested okra and bright red and green peppers of various shapes and sizes. Beside the sink were rows of empty mason jars and a drying rack full of dishes. Pots full of fresh herbs lined the windowsill. More herbs that had been cut hung in bunches from clips suspended by a length of string above the sink.

Despite the clutter, the house was clean. There were no dirty dishes in sight and no visible dust on the surfaces. Everything in Birdie's house looked cared-for and loved.

Josh returned shortly with a silk kimono-style robe. "Here, you might be more comfortable in this." He handed it to her and turned his back, offering her privacy while he busied himself with the first aid kit.

"Thank you." Mia stood and slipped the floral turquoise

robe on, turning away before letting the towel drop and tying the robe closed. Once she was more decently attired, she sat on the stool again, balling up the damp towel in her lap. "It's safe to turn around now."

Josh faced her, his gaze flicking downward briefly before homing in on her injured forehead. "Let me see that cut." He moved closer, peering at it as he tore open an alcohol wipe.

Mia flinched when he dabbed at the wound.

"Sorry," he said, brushing her damp hair back. "I'll try to be gentle."

"It's okay. It just stings a little." She cast her eyes down as a shiver traveled through her. "Is it bad?

Touching a finger to the underside of her chin, he tilted her head up and leaned in closer. "No, it looks pretty shallow."

"That's good. I'd hate to end up in urgent care on my first night in town. Wait—" Her gaze darted to his face. "There is an urgent care in town, right?"

It was hard to see him clearly when he was this close to her—and he was *really* close, his face only inches from hers—but she was almost certain he rolled his eyes. "We've actually got *two* urgent care centers in addition to a hospital with an emergency room."

She blew out a breath between her teeth. "That's a relief."

"Where'd you move here from?" he asked as he continued to clean the blood off her forehead. "I'm guessing not a small town."

Mia smiled wryly. "How could you tell?"

He shrugged as he exchanged the alcohol wipe for a tube of antibiotic ointment. "You give off a pretty strong city girl vibe."

"I've been in Los Angeles for the last eight years, but I grew up in Brooklyn."

"Crowder must be a big change for you." His teeth bit into his lower lip as he applied medicine to her cut. For someone with rough farmer's hands, he had an incredibly gentle touch.

"You could say that," she murmured as the earthy scent of his warm skin enveloped her. The nearness of him was overwhelming as he leaned over her, cradling her face in one of his large hands.

"Why'd you take a job at Bowman?"

"Because they offered it to me. Beggars can't be choosers." She winced. "Sorry, I don't mean to sound bitter. I'm sure it's a very nice school and a very nice town."

Josh let go of her and turned back to the first aid kit. "No need to apologize. Times are tough. I get it."

"It's definitely a challenging time to be entering the academic job market as a new PhD."

"So you wound up here." He ripped open a bandage as he faced her again.

"For the next year, anyway." She stared at his collarbone as he moved toward her. A hint of dark chest hair peeked out of his T-shirt beneath the strong, stubbly column of his throat.

"Lucky us."

Mia swallowed, trying to hold still as he applied the bandage to her forehead, but she was oddly lightheaded and her heart was thudding so hard it made her feel wobbly. She wondered if she could have given herself a concussion and that was why she felt so weird.

Or maybe it was simply her proximity to an attractive

cheesemaker causing abrupt changes to the blood flow in certain parts of her body.

Josh gave the bandage a final tap and drew back to survey his work. Now that he wasn't so close, it was easier for her to see his eyes, which were the color of warm milk chocolate. His lips parted, drawing her attention to the way they formed a perfect Cupid's bow that practically demanded to be licked. Honestly, lips like that should be illegal on a man.

Mia realized that she was staring at his lips and he was watching her do it. Her gaze sprang back to his eyes, which were no less mesmerizing than that gorgeous mouth of his, especially when those eyes were looking right into hers.

For a moment neither of them moved. It might only have been a second, but it felt like an eternity. Like nothing else existed in the world but Josh's eyes gazing into hers.

The back door banged open, causing them both to startle, and Birdie came in with her mason jar held aloft in triumph. "I got her!"

Josh turned toward his aunt, and Mia could swear he looked rattled before he fixed a pleasant expression in place. But maybe it was just her imagination working overtime.

Birdie marched up to them and held the mason jar in front of Mia's face. "Ta da! Isn't she a beauty?"

Beauty was not the word Mia would have chosen to describe the creature inside the jar. Words like odious, vile, and loathsome leaped to mind as she came eyeball to eyeball with her uninvited arachnid roommate once more.

It was every bit as large as Mia remembered, at least three inches in diameter to the spiny tips of its yellow-and-black striped legs, its hideous spotted body nearly the size of a quarter. Truly, it was a horrifying specimen.

Josh took the mason jar from his aunt, graciously moving it out of Mia's face as he held it up to the light for a better look. "That's a banana spider all right. One of the bigger ones I've seen." He threw Mia a look that seemed to be apologizing for doubting her.

"Do you have a lot of them around here?" she asked, afraid of the answer. Of all the things she'd worried about prior to moving to Texas, *giant honking spiders* hadn't even made the list. Which clearly had been a serious oversight on her part. She should have realized that when people said "Everything's bigger in Texas," that included the massive goddamn spiders.

"I wouldn't call it a lot." Josh handed the jar back to Birdie. "You see 'em every once in a while, mostly out in the woods. It's rare to find one inside."

Thank god for that. Hopefully Mia wouldn't have any more terrifying visitors. At least not of that particular species.

Birdie stroked the jar like it contained a beloved pet. "Poor thing must have been lost to make a web in the shower like that." Mia gave a full-body shudder, and Birdie glanced at her, seeming to notice her injury for the first time. "Oh honey, what happened to your head?"

"I bumped it on my way out of the shower and Josh was kind enough to bandage it up for me." Mia gingerly touched the Band-Aid on her forehead. "I hope you don't mind, he loaned me your robe since I wasn't exactly dressed."

Birdie's smile took on an enigmatic twist. "I'm glad you two have made each other's acquaintance. You're in good hands with Josh." Her eyes twinkled with affection as she patted her nephew on the arm. "Now, if you'll excuse me, I'm going to introduce Imelda to my bean patch."

As Birdie took her new prize outside, Mia turned to Josh with her eyebrows raised. "Imelda?"

He shrugged. "Birdie loves all god's creatures, great and small."

"She seems like a real character."

"Yeah, she's great." A fond smile curved his lips as he watched his aunt through the window.

"She lives here alone?" Mia hadn't seen any evidence of anyone else around the house.

Josh nodded. "Always has. It was her parents' house—my grandparents on my mother's side. I try to come by as often as I can to help out with odd jobs around the place."

"Is that what you were doing in the yard when I crashed into you?"

"I was dropping off some leftover fertilizer." His lips pressed together, as if he was suppressing a smile at the memory. "Can't say I expected to run into a screaming woman in a towel." He stopped fighting it and let his smile break free.

"Believe me, it wasn't how I'd planned my evening to go either." Mia's cheeks burned as she basked in the warmth of his smile. "Thanks for saving me."

"You saved yourself just fine." He inclined his head. "Other than some minor head trauma, that is."

She clutched her balled-up towel and slid off the stool, deciding now was a good time to make a graceful exit—before she said anything to embarrass herself. "Thank you for the first aid."

"You're welcome," he said. "It was nice to meet you, Mia."

"Likewise," she mumbled and headed for the door, her pulse jumping at the sound of her name on his lips. She paused on her way out, glancing back one last time from the doorway as she hugged her towel to her chest. "I guess I'll see you around."

"I guess you will." The look on his face made her stomach swoop.

Outside, Mia waved good night to Birdie as she took herself back up to her apartment—hopefully now spider-free.

As she hung her towel up in the bathroom, she realized she'd probably left the shower running in her panicked flight. Birdie must have turned it off for her when she'd come up to retrieve the spider. Warily, Mia peered into the shower and saw that the web was also gone. Birdie must have taken care of that for her too.

Thank god for Birdie. She'd already earned the title of Best Landlord Ever.

Mia took off the borrowed robe and hung it on the outside of the closet door so she'd remember to take it back tomorrow. After changing into a comfy oversized T-shirt, she flopped down on the bed.

It was still light outside, the late summer sky just beginning to turn dusky at eight o'clock. As she stared at the ceiling, her hands clenched the familiar comforter beneath her. The air conditioner hummed and chugged across the room, drowning out all other sounds as it labored to cool her one-room apartment.

I'm lucky to be here, she reminded herself. *I'm lucky to have this job, and this apartment, even if it's not where I ever pictured myself.*

Besides, it's only temporary.

That had become her mantra since she'd accepted the Bowman job.

It was only for a year. It wasn't forever. She could stand anything for a year.

Truly, today hadn't been so bad—gargantuan spider attack aside. Birdie's unexpected kindness had made it better.

And Josh's.

Mia thought about his elusive smile and his gentle touch. His deep, husky drawl. His arresting dark eyes, which managed to be both piercing and soft.

She kept thinking about him until her own eyes drifted shut and her exhaustion overtook her, pulling her down into sleep.

Chapter Six

Three days later, Mia drove to the university for her first day on campus. New faculty orientation didn't start until the following day, but she had a mountain of HR paperwork to fill out first, and she was anxious to familiarize herself with her new place of work.

She was pleasantly surprised to discover the math department had an office for her, although it wasn't so much an office as a closet. Literally, she'd been given a corner of a storage room that had been cleared out enough to fit a desk and two chairs—one for her and one for any students who might come to her office hours. Which meant that occasionally other faculty members or the department admin would show up and squeeze past her in order to get more printer paper or whiteboard markers. But it was fine. It was better than no office.

She was in the midst of trying to get her laptop to talk to the department printer when there was a knock at her office door. Mia looked up, hoping for someone from the IT help desk, but instead found a young woman standing in her doorway.

"Are you Mia?" She was dressed in khaki pants and a

forest-green polo shirt with an official-looking patch on the sleeve. Although her expression was friendly, everything about her bearing said she was the sort of person who meant business.

Mia offered an uncertain smile, wondering if she'd done something wrong already. "That's me."

The woman stepped into the office and stuck out her hand. "I'm Andie Lockhart. My aunt Birdie's your landlady."

"Oh!" Mia got to her feet to take Andie's hand. "You must be Josh's sister."

Andie's gaze narrowed. "You know Josh?"

"I met him the day I moved in. I think he was dropping off some fertilizer for your aunt." Mia elected not to mention that she'd been mostly naked, shrieking about spiders, and had crashed into him at full speed. It hadn't exactly been her finest hour.

"Right, of course." Andie's smile returned to its full warmth. "Birdie told me you were coming to campus today, so I thought I'd drop in and say hi while I was here."

Mia made a mental note not to tell Birdie anything she didn't care to have repeated to her landlady's social circle, which—based on Mia's several conversations with her the last few days—seemed to be extensive. "Do you work here?" she asked Andie.

"Part-time lecturer in the college of forestry and agriculture. The rest of the time I'm a resources specialist for the state parks and wildlife service." That explained the patch on Andie's shirt and the practical, outdoorsy attire.

"Does that mean you take care of the trees and animals?" Mia asked, unable to remember the last time she'd set foot in a state park. She generally preferred to view the outdoors from indoors. Preferably through thick glass.

"Something like that, yeah." Andie glanced around Mia's storage closet. "Nice digs they've got you in."

"Honestly, I'm just glad to have an office at all."

Andie hooked a thumb over her shoulder. "I was gonna go grab some coffee. Wanna join me?"

"God, yes," Mia said, grabbing her bag. "I'd love that."

The campus coffee shop was located in the student union building, which wasn't too far from the math building. Andie pointed out various campus landmarks along the way, including the giant new ag building where she taught, which was much grander than the buildings that housed the college of science. The entire college of forestry and agriculture took up one whole half of the campus, including a large swath of farm and pastureland stretching to the south.

"It's a nice campus." Mia wiped a trickle of sweat off her forehead, hoping the coffee shop was air-conditioned.

So far, she'd found the oppressive heat and humidity the most challenging part of living in Texas. Other than the banana spiders, of course. Fortunately, she hadn't encountered Imelda or any of her brethren since her first night—although she did give Birdie's garden a wide berth.

"Even nicer when it's empty like this. Once the students arrive on Friday it'll be chaos. Enjoy the peace and quiet while you can." Andie pulled open the door to the student union and a blast of arctic air hit them.

"God that feels nice." Mia sighed with pleasure as she stepped into the freezing cold building. "When does the weather start to cool off around here?"

"Not for another couple months, at least." Andie eyed

Mia's short-sleeved blouse. "Piece of advice: bring a sweater with you to class. They keep most of the lecture halls at sub-zero temperatures—except in the winter when they're like a sauna. But also sometimes they like to mix it up to keep things interesting, so you never know what you're going to get from one day to the next."

"Noted."

The coffee shop was deserted except for a young woman with a pink streak in her hair who was sitting at a booth staring at her phone. She jumped up and ran behind the counter when they walked in, greeting them with a smile. "Hi! What can I get you?" she asked in the Texas twang Mia was still getting used to.

Andie ordered a large iced coffee for herself. Mia considered doing the same, but she was already starting to get cold as the powerful air-conditioning chilled the sweat on her skin. She went with a hot soy latte instead.

"Have you met the rest of your department?" Andie asked when they settled into a booth with their drinks.

"When I came for my interview," Mia said. The math office was empty today except for the chair and the admin. Most of the department wouldn't be in until the all-university faculty and staff meeting on Thursday.

Andie sucked on her straw. "What'd you think?"

"They seem nice." Mia shrugged. "They're mostly older. And male." That wasn't unusual for her field, but the department at Bowman was a particularly antediluvian bunch.

"The forestry department's the same. Maybe not quite as old as you guys in math, but it's basically wall-to-wall penises." Andie made a face. "And not in a good way."

Mia snorted into her latte and reached for a napkin to

wipe the coffee off her chin. "So you teach *and* work full-time as a park ranger?"

Andie explained that she taught one course a semester, plus a co-requisite lab, on forest insects and diseases. Her students did some of their lab work at Gettinger State Park, the thousand-acre forest north of town, and in exchange the university gave Andie the use of a lab to do her research for the park service.

She wasn't actually a park ranger as Mia had assumed—the rangers were the ones who managed the state parks' recreational operations and facilities. Andie was an ecosystems biologist, so her job consisted primarily of research and fieldwork: sample collection, data analysis, and writing environmental impact assessments.

It was fascinating, but far outside Mia's wheelhouse. Nature was fine in theory, but in actual practice it was always either trying to bite you, give you a rash, or outright murder you.

Like spiders, for instance. The spiny, murdering bastards.

Mia had to assume Andie didn't mind spiders and other creepy crawlies, given that she studied insects for a living. And not just in the lab—in their natural environment in the woods. Andie probably ran into spiders all the time—quite literally—and calmly begged their pardon for disturbing their habitat.

"You should come see the state park sometime," Andie suggested. "It's pretty gorgeous up there, especially in the fall once the temps cool down a little."

"Yeah, maybe," Mia replied, sipping her coffee.

The thought of wandering around in the woods with all those bugs and snakes gave her the shudders. And what about bears? Did they have bears in Texas? Or mountain lions? No thank you. She'd prefer not to take her life into her own hands for the sake of some leaf-peeping, no matter what Henry David Thoreau had to say for it.

"Thoreau's mother brought him food and did his laundry while he was allegedly communing with nature in Walden Wood." Mia winced, realizing too late that she'd done it again. She had a bad habit of speaking in non sequiturs. It always made sense in her head, but the problem was that other people couldn't see what was going on in her head.

Andie tilted an eyebrow but seemed otherwise unfazed by the abrupt subject change. "He was also a self-obsessed misanthrope who considered sexuality a contaminant. So, you know." She shrugged, regarding Mia as she sipped her coffee. "You don't have to hike the trails if the woods aren't your bag. There's a lake with a wide path around it and a nice, civilized picnic area. And of course, the springs are really popular this time of year."

"The springs?"

"The springs that feed Cooper Creek. There's a few natural swimming holes up there. Including the Holler, which is clothing-optional if you're into that."

Mia stared at her in surprise. "There's a nude swimming area?"

"Been here for years." Andie took her ponytail out and raked her fingers through her thick, glossy hair that was the same shade of dark brown as her brother's. "The area was settled by Czech and German immigrants who brought nude sunbathing over from the Old World." Gathering her hair up again, she refastened it into a bun as she spoke. "Then in the sixties, the hippies discovered the Holler when old Earnest

King started up a folk festival to promote the dance hall here. They started coming down from Austin for the music, and a lot of them put down roots and never left."

"Hippies? Really?" Mia hadn't expected to find hippies in a place like this.

"Hell yeah. A whole bunch of artists and musicians moved here in the sixties and seventies. Between the music festival and the ice cream factory, there was enough tourism to support a decent living." Andie grinned as she leaned forward, resting her arms on the table. "Birdie's parents—my grandparents on my mother's side—used to own a head shop right on Main Street."

Mia's mouth fell open. "You're kidding?"

"Nope." Andie shook her head as she leaned back in the booth, crossing her arms. "They sold other stuff besides weed paraphernalia, of course. New age crap like crystals, incense, candles, and whatever else stoners were into. My grandmother used to make the candles herself. And my grandfather made these hand-carved pipes and incense holders. They did pretty well in the seventies and eighties before internet sales became a thing."

Mia found Andie's stories about the town and her family's history fascinating. She didn't have any interesting stories about her own straitlaced and upwardly mobile family. "So where'd the goat farm come from?" She remembered Birdie saying it had been in Josh's family for years.

"That was my dad's brainchild. He was a geologist for one of the big oil companies. He came here to do a survey, met my mom, and fell in love with her and the town."

"So he just stayed here? Did he have to give up his job?" Mia couldn't help thinking about her last conversation with

Paul. She'd hoped he would offer to move here with her, but only because he had the option of working remote—he could have done it and still kept his job. As crushed as she'd been by the breakup, she'd never once been the slightest bit tempted to sacrifice her own professional ambitions in order to stay with him.

"Not at first," Andie said. "My mom moved to Dallas after they got married and worked as a bookkeeper for a while, but Dad traveled so much she was miserable all the time. After Josh was born, my parents moved back here and bought a piece of land to raise dairy goats."

"Wow." Mia couldn't imagine doing something like that. Giving up your career for the person you loved and moving to the country to become a farmer? It was unfathomable. Her parents had never given up anything for each other. Or for their kids, for that matter.

"Everyone thought they were off their rockers. My dad was a city boy and neither of them knew the first thing about goats." Andie shrugged. "But they ended up loving it, so I guess it was the right choice."

"You grew up on a goat farm?" As she sipped her coffee, Mia tried to picture what that must have been like. Very different from the Park Slope brownstone where she'd spent her youth.

"Yeah, I knew how to milk a goat before I could ride a bike." Andie eyed Mia as though she were sizing her up. "Aunt Birdie said you moved here from California?"

"I was in Los Angeles for graduate school, but I grew up in Brooklyn."

Andie arched an eyebrow. "A New York City girl. Wow. This place must feel like you've landed on Mars."

"A little." Mia was self-conscious about seeming like an outsider. She knew she *was* one, but she hated the idea of sticking out like a sore thumb. Life was much easier when you could blend in with the crowd—which didn't take as much effort in a city of millions. She steered the subject away from her own upbringing and back to Andie. "I gather you're not involved with the goat farm anymore?"

"Nah, it's my brother's thing," Andie said. "He was happy to take over after our parents retired, and I was happy to let him have it. The goats have to be milked every twelve hours, so you're basically married to the farm. You can't ever go on vacations or take a day off. I'd lose my mind if I had to live like that."

It sounded awful. Mia could understand why Andie had wanted something else for herself. "But your brother doesn't mind it?" Mia couldn't resist asking about him. He'd been on her mind ever since their last encounter. She was dying to know more about him.

"No, he does not." Andie shot Mia an appraising look. "I don't know how much you actually talked to him, but Josh is sort of a recluse."

"Really? We only chatted for a few minutes, but he seemed normal to me." Both times she'd talked to him, in fact. Friendly, even. He certainly hadn't struck Mia as antisocial.

Andie's eyebrows shot up. "My brother *chatted* with you? For a few minutes—as in more than one? That's impressive."

"I sort of bumped into him," Mia explained. "Like literally, in Birdie's yard. Crashed might be a better word. There was a spider in my apartment and . . ." Once again Mia skipped over the part about being half naked. "And I'd hit my head and was bleeding, so Josh offered to get me a

Band-Aid while Birdie went to save the spider and . . ." She trailed off, reddening as she noticed the look of amusement on Andie's face. "Anyway, he seemed nice."

"He *is* nice." Andie said. "He's just—" She hesitated, and Mia got the impression she was choosing her words carefully. "I think he likes being tied to the farm a little too much. When he came back from college, he—" Andie pressed her lips together and shook her head. "He sort of threw himself into it, to the exclusion of everything else. And he had a good reason, I guess, but now I think he uses the farm as an excuse. He avoids going into town and doesn't have any kind of social life. The guy talks to his goats more than he talks to real, actual humans."

"That sounds like a lonely life."

"That's what I keep telling him, but what do I know? I'm just his little sister." Andie glanced at the watch on her wrist. "Shoot, is that the time? I've got to get back to work." She got to her feet and chucked her empty cup at the trash.

Mia knocked back the last few drops of her latte and followed Andie to the door. "It was really nice talking to you."

Andie threw a smile over her shoulder as they stepped outside into the sunlight. "We should go out for a drink or something. I can introduce you to the highlights of Crowder nightlife—such as it is."

"I'd really like that," Mia said.

"Dope. I'll get your number from my aunt." Andie waved goodbye as she headed for the parking lot. "See ya!"

Mia watched her go, feeling more optimistic about her one-year sentence in Crowder.

And more intrigued than ever about the reclusive Josh.

Chapter Seven

On Friday, after an interminable week of deadly dull orientation sessions and tedious faculty meetings, Mia came home to find a jar of pickled okra sitting by her door with a note taped to it.

If you're free, come for dinner Saturday night at 6:00. I'm making my famous chicken fried steak.

—Birdie

Mia carried the okra inside and set it next to the three unopened jars already in her pantry, which was beginning to look like it belonged to one of those end-of-the-world preppers. At least she'd be well supplied with spicy okra in the event of a food shortage.

After maneuvering her bra off through her sleeve and tossing it onto her bed, she poured a glass of wine and made herself a peanut butter and jelly sandwich for dinner. While she ate it, she thought about the really good Hawaiian place she used to order from back in Los Angeles, and how much she missed their kettle corn.

She was halfway through her sandwich when Birdie called. Mia still had her listed as "Helen Fishbaugh" in her contacts, and she made a mental note to update it.

"Did you get my note?" Birdie asked.

"I did," Mia said, swallowing a mouthful of peanut butter sandwich. "Thank you for the okra."

"Are you free tomorrow night?"

Andie's invitation to take Mia out for drinks had never materialized, so Mia's social calendar was wide-open. "Yes. I'd love to come to dinner." She was getting tired of peanut butter and jelly sandwiches.

"Perfect. I'll see you at six."

"Can I bring anything?"

"Only your lovely self," Birdie said. "Enjoy the rest of your evening!"

After she hung up, Mia stared at what was left of her peanut butter sandwich in dissatisfaction. Birdie's parting advice made her feel like she ought to be doing something more enjoyable with her evening.

It was Friday night, and Mia was young and single. Theoretically, the world was her oyster. Or at least this small corner of the world.

Today marked her one-week anniversary in Crowder, and she'd hardly seen any of the town yet. She'd learned her way around campus and grown familiar with the route between her apartment and the faculty parking lot. There had been two trips to two different grocery stores and one stop at a Starbucks in town. But that was it.

She could go out, she supposed. Explore the town by herself instead of waiting for Andie to call. Drive down Main Street and find a restaurant. Somewhere with a counter, maybe, where she could sit and talk to the waiter or waitress while she ate.

They probably had somewhere like that around here. A diner where the locals gathered to trade gossip over cups of unlimited coffee refilled by waitresses who knew every customer by name. The kind of place reporters from *The New York Times* would go to find "real Americans" to interview for their perspective on current events.

Although most of what Mia had seen driving through Crowder was the same stuff you'd see anywhere else in America. Strip shopping centers filled with the same stores and restaurant chains that occupied strip shopping centers everywhere else. Walgreens and Bank of America and Mattress Firm. Subway and Pizza Hut and Chili's. The sprawl wasn't entirely unlike Los Angeles, actually, just . . . less urban. With fewer palm trees and more pickup trucks per capita.

To a lot of people, it was probably comforting, knowing they could travel anywhere and still find the same familiar favorites. Mostly it made Mia feel sad. The things she missed about Los Angeles and New York were the things you couldn't find anywhere else. The dragon roll at her favorite hole-in-the-wall sushi restaurant on La Cienega. Or the Italian bakery back in Brooklyn where you had to go early before the best bomboloni sold out.

Maybe there were gems like that to discover here too. Probably there were. Maybe not sushi or bomboloni, but other things she'd yet to experience. Uniquely Crowder things.

The thought didn't thrill her. It had already been an exhausting week of orienting herself to campus culture.

Learning the names of buildings and new coworkers. Memorizing logins and searching for room numbers. Being lectured on school policies, faculty guidelines, and departmental procedure.

She was sick of navigating unfamiliar spaces and feeling lost and out of sorts. All her exploring energy had been depleted.

Instead of going out, Mia went into the bathroom and washed her makeup off. She applied the various serums that were part of her bedtime skincare routine, following them up with a non-oily moisturizer. She'd found her skin wasn't nearly as dry here—an unexpected bonus of the merciless humidity. After that was done, she changed into her softest, comfiest pajamas and made herself some microwave popcorn.

Getting to know the town could wait. Tonight, she was going to sit on her couch and watch Netflix documentaries.

And then first thing tomorrow she'd get back to work on her proof. The whole weekend lay ahead of her, gloriously empty and free of obligations, and she planned to spend it untangling her knot problem.

Except for tomorrow night, when she'd take a short break to have dinner with her middle-aged landlady.

What an exciting life she led.

When she woke up in the morning, Mia performed her a.m. skincare routine and made a full pot of coffee. While it finished brewing, she had a breakfast of farm-fresh goat's milk yogurt and raw local honey that was worthy of an Instagram lifestyle blogger. If only she'd had any Instagram followers. Or an Instagram account where she could post artistically staged photos of her farm-to-table breakfast for her non-existent followers to admire.

She'd never had goat yogurt before this week, but it had turned out to be delicious and only subtly different from cow's milk yogurt. A large part of that deliciousness was undoubtedly due to the full fat content, but she wasn't complaining.

Once she'd been adequately caffeinated, she sat down with a fresh black Moleskine notebook and her favorite mechanical pencil, and tried to think about the eleven-crossing knot that had been haunting her for months.

Unfortunately, her brain had other ideas. Instead of helping her visualize the knot problem in four-dimensional space, it instead chose to think of things she should add to her lesson plans or include in her class lectures next week. It suggested items that should be added to her grocery list. It reminded her that her sister's birthday was coming up and deliberated over gift ideas for her.

An hour later, Mia was on Etsy trying to decide if her sister would prefer a vintage tea set or a vintage glass decanter set.

It was the same thing that had been happening lately every time she tried to concentrate on a theoretical problem instead of a concrete one. She'd been able to focus just fine when she was researching apartments, working on her lesson plans, and pulling together the syllabi for her classes.

But as soon as she tried to think about abstract math, her brain stopped cooperating. She couldn't seem to find her groove anymore.

She tried the meditation exercises she'd learned on You-Tube. When that didn't work, she tried doodling. Seifert surfaces. Apollonian gaskets. Her favorite equations, like Euler's identity, which she had tattooed on her foot.

She tried getting up and moving around the apartment. She tried opening all the window blinds, and then she tried closing them again. She tried three different music playlists, and then white noise, and then finally silence.

None of it helped. No matter what she did, her brain threw roadblocks up, wandering off on random tangents instead of focusing on the task at hand. It tempted her to shop for new work clothes on sale, or to make a new focus playlist that would be better than all the other focus playlists she'd already made.

She tried taking a shower, which sometimes helped trigger her creative thinking. Then she tried washing dishes, which also sometimes helped.

After that, she gave up and spent the rest of the afternoon watching Netflix.

At six o'clock, Mia knocked on Birdie's back door. She was taken by surprise when Josh opened it. "Hi," she said, trying not to appear flustered. "I didn't know you'd be here." She wished she'd bothered to put on makeup.

His eyebrows arched slightly. "Disappointed?"

It felt like he was teasing her. Mia knew that sometimes when people teased you it was because they were making fun of you, but also sometimes it was because they were flirting. And it wasn't always easy to tell the difference.

Josh's affect was extremely dry, which made it even harder to decipher his intent.

Andie appeared beside him. "Hey! Birdie invited the whole gang for dinner tonight."

"There's a gang?" Mia asked as she stepped inside.

"Usually it's just the three of us," Andie said. "It'll be nice to have a fourth."

"Hellooooo!" Birdie waved from the kitchen. "Welcome! Make yourself at home and whatnot."

"It smells delicious in here," Mia said. In addition to hot cooking oil, Birdie's house smelled like fresh-baked bread. It reminded her of the bakeries back home.

"That's Birdie's homemade yeast rolls." Andie was putting the finishing touches on what looked to be another snack platter. "Best part of coming to dinner on Saturdays."

"Hey!" Birdie exclaimed in faux indignation, shooting a smile at her niece. "What about me?"

"Besides the company," Andie added affectionately, swatting her brother's hand when he leaned in to steal a pickled okra.

"Can I help with anything?" Mia offered.

"We've got it under control," Birdie said from the stove, where she was supervising a cast-iron pan that sizzled and spat hot grease. "We're like a well-oiled machine."

Mia was relieved not to be needed in the kitchen. She didn't have any experience frying things in hot oil, and she found it intimidating and a little frightening. For that matter, she didn't have much experience with any kind of cooking. Or with family dinners where everyone chipped in. Her mother was a workaholic cardiac surgeon, so her family had always relied heavily on takeout, even at holidays. Mia wasn't certain her mother even knew how to turn on her expensive digital oven.

Consequently, Mia was useless in the kitchen, aside from a few basic skills like boiling pasta and making grilled cheese sandwiches. Although she always offered to help when people had her to dinner, because she knew it was the polite thing to do. But then she usually got embarrassed when she was asked to perform tasks beyond her abilities.

"Josh, get her a drink," Birdie ordered.

"What'll you have?" Josh asked Mia as he stole a slice of the bell pepper Andie was cutting. This time his sister let him get away with it.

"What are my choices?" Mia said.

"Sweet tea, lemonade, bourbon, or beer."

She didn't think it was wise to go straight for the hard stuff, so she requested a beer. Although both Andie and Birdie appeared to be sipping bourbon.

Josh got two beers out of the fridge and twisted the caps off before handing one to Mia. "Cheers." He clinked his bottle against hers before taking a long swig.

"Dig in." Andie set the platter on the breakfast bar in front of Mia.

Mia didn't need to be told twice when there was cheese on offer. She went straight for the feta, which she'd been craving since the day she moved in. She was on her third piece before she noticed Josh watching her. "What?"

"Nothing." His gaze skated away, and he took another swig of beer.

"I like cheese," Mia said. "And I really like this feta."

One side of his mouth quirked. "I seem to recall the word you used before was 'exquisite.'" He was definitely teasing her, but she decided she didn't mind.

She reached for another piece of cheese. "So if a person wanted to buy some of this feta for herself, where would she have to go?"

"She could just ask." His dark eyes met hers and held, causing her stomach to do a flip. "I'm happy to drop some by for you next time I'm here."

She lowered her gaze to the cheese board, feeling slightly dizzy. "I'm trying to be a paying customer, not asking for a favor."

"You can get it at the farmers' market in Austin every Saturday," Birdie said, sipping her bourbon with one hand as she flipped steaks with the other.

Mia lifted her eyebrows as she looked back at Josh. "I have to drive all the way to Austin to buy cheese made here in town?"

He shrugged. "I don't have a store at the farm or anything."

"There's not a farmers' market here in Crowder?"

"There is," Andie volunteered as she was setting the table. "First Saturday of every month in the town square." She threw a pointed look at her brother. "But someone doesn't think it's worth his time."

His mouth turned down at the corners. "I earn five times at the Austin market what I'd be able to make off a booth here. It doesn't make financial sense to miss the one for the other."

Andie rolled her eyes as if she'd heard this explanation before. "Yeah but Ray does the market in Austin every week, so you could run the booth here yourself."

"I don't have time," Josh said. "I've got to do the milking by myself while Ray's in Austin."

"You could make time, if you wanted to."

"I don't want to." Josh's tone had gone flat.

Mia sensed she'd reopened an old argument between them and regretted it. "I guess I'll just have to drive to Austin, then." Her voice had gone extra chirpy in an attempt to smooth over the tension.

Josh's gaze flicked back to her. "Like I said, I'm happy to drop some off for you."

"I don't want to be a freeloader. You'd have to let me pay you for it."

"If you want. It's twenty dollars a pound."

Mia choked. "Twenty?"

"That's the retail price. Ten dollars per eight-ounce container."

"People in Austin have more money than they know what to do with," Birdie said. "Can you imagine paying that much for cheese?"

Andie leaned between Mia and Josh for a pickled okra. "They'll pay through the nose for anything with the word 'artisan' on it. They love all that locally made, pasture-raised shit."

"It's why I don't sell the milk," Josh said. "I make three times as much if I turn it into cheese."

"Maybe we can work out some sort of barter arrangement," Mia offered, only half joking. Josh's artisan cheese wasn't a luxury she could afford.

"Can you do anything useful?" Josh's tone was so dry it was hard to tell if he was being earnest or teasing her again.

Mia thought about it. Practically speaking, she wasn't good for much. "Math?"

"I've got a calculator for that. And an accountant." Definitely teasing.

Did that mean he was flirting? She considered the possibility and decided she liked it. Her stomach did another flip to register its concurrence.

"I'm hopeless at accounting," she said. "I can barely do my own taxes. But if you need help with 4-manifold topology, I'm your woman."

"There's always plenty of work to do on the farm." Andie grinned at Mia as she pulled a tray of rolls out of the oven. "Teach her to milk the goats."

"Dinner's ready!" Birdie announced, carrying a large platter of chicken fried steaks to the table. "Josh, honey, grab the potatoes, will you?"

"Yes, ma'am."

Mia found it endearing that Josh called his aunt ma'am. Especially since Birdie was so easygoing and unpretentious, she seemed like the last person who'd demand that sort of deference.

They all sat down and started passing plates around the table. In addition to the chicken fried steaks, there was mashed potatoes drenched in butter, and cream gravy to pour over everything. Plus, Birdie's homemade yeast rolls, still warm from the oven. It was a giant, marvelous carb fest, with nary a green vegetable in sight.

Mia had only ever encountered chicken fried steak in school lunchrooms or frozen dinners. She'd never had it homemade before. It had never even occurred to her it was something people made at home.

After one bite of Birdie's chicken fried steak, she realized she'd been missing out by living a life devoid of homemade chicken fried steak. Birdie's crispy, light breading bore no resemblance to the soggy crust Mia had assumed was standard practice. Even better, the steak inside tasted like actual steak instead of some bland mystery meat. Birdie's mashed potatoes were just as good, and so rich Mia suspected they were at least fifty percent dairy fat.

"This is amazing," she said. "It's the best chicken fried steak I've ever had."

Birdie beamed and offered her more gravy.

"What kind of math do you do?" Andie asked.

"I wrote my dissertation on knot theory," Mia said.

Birdie looked up from the roll she was buttering. "Knot theory? Like the kind of knots sailors and Boy Scouts learn?"

"Sort of," Mia said. "Except mathematical knots are closed polygonal curves. Rings, basically," she added off Birdie's blank look. "Like a string with the ends tied together. One of the things I study is all the possible ways you can configure and deform a closed curve. It's like looking at a tangled-up jumble of string and trying to work out if it can be untangled without cutting it."

"Oh!" Birdie nodded with understanding. "I do that with knitting when my yarn gets tangled."

"Or with necklaces," Andie said.

"Exactly," Mia said. "That's just one part of it though. We also look at knotted spheres in extradimensional space. A loop is one-dimensional, just like a geometry point or line, and in order to untangle it you have to move it around in three-dimensional space—like you do with your yarn or a necklace. But a sphere has two dimensions, and it can be crumpled up and twisted into a knot too. So we have to examine it in four-dimensional space in order to unravel it. One of the questions we ask is what you see when you slice through a knotted sphere—do you see a knotted loop or an unknotted loop? Any knot you can make by slicing through a knotted sphere is considered a slice knot."

When Mia finished, she realized everyone was staring at her blankly, which was what usually happened when she started talking about her work around non-math people.

"I didn't understand a word of that." Birdie shook her head as she cut another bite of steak. "I never got past trigonometry at school."

"I think I understood maybe half of it," Andie said. "And I'm feeling pretty good about that. You lost me once you moved into four dimensions though."

"I think it's impressive." Josh's gaze met Mia's across the table. "I don't have to understand any of it to know that much."

Mia felt her cheeks heat and looked down at her plate. "It'd be more impressive if I could crack this one particular knot I've been stuck on for ages. It's starting to make me think maybe I picked the wrong field." It was the first time she'd ever put into words the fear that had been lurking in the back of her head.

"I'm sure you'll get there," Birdie said. "Inspiration usually strikes in its own sweet time. Sometimes when you least expect it."

Mia nodded, forcing a smile. "Anyway, it's all pretty theoretical, but it has applications in things like the study of DNA and polymers."

"Very cool." Andie grinned as she passed Mia another roll. "I feel like I'm having dinner with Einstein."

After dinner was over, Mia insisted on doing the dishes, rebuffing Birdie's attempts to talk her out of it. Dirty dishes, at least, were something she could handle. "Go sit down and leave the cleanup to me."

"I'll help," Josh offered, and this time Mia didn't argue.

Andie left them to it, pouring more bourbon into Birdie's glass before following her into the living room.

Mia and Josh worked together to clear the table, then he packed up the leftovers while she loaded the dishwasher.

"Does Birdie have you over for dinner a lot?" Mia was wondering how often Josh came by—and how often she might hope to run into him.

"Once or twice a week, usually. Birdie loves to cook." He threw a grin her way. "And I love to eat her cooking."

"I can certainly see why. Is the detergent under the sink?" Mia opened the cabinet and squatted down to examine the collection of cleaning supplies.

Josh's hand settled warmly between her shoulder blades as he bent down next to her, reaching into the cabinet for the dishwasher soap. His warm, earthy scent filled up her lungs and set her pulse pounding as he leaned in close. His head was perilously close to her face. Close enough to lick his ear without hardly moving at all.

As soon as she had the thought, it became impossible to think about anything else, and she became consumed by fear that she might actually do it. Panicking, she lurched upright and ended up whacking her head on the edge of the counter.

"Careful," Josh warned too late. "You okay?"

"Yep, fine." She couldn't tell if the stars in her field of vision were a result of hitting her head or from being so close to Josh.

He stood and looked her in the eye, which did nothing to improve her lightheadedness. It was all she could do to stand still as his gaze swept over her face, lingering on the half-healed cut on her forehead. "You seem to hit your head a lot."

"Only when you're around." After the words left her mouth, she realized how they sounded. She'd as good as admitted that his mere presence turned her into a swooning klutz.

Josh didn't smirk like she expected. Or flush. Or move away. He stayed right where he was, his eyes serious and steady as they stared into hers.

"Hey, let's go to the Rusty Spoke!" Andie said, joining them in the kitchen. "I promised to show you the nightlife, remember?"

Mia tore her gaze away from Josh and tried to pretend she hadn't just been thinking about kissing him. "What's the Rusty Spoke?"

"It's an icehouse."

"A place you buy ice?" Mia asked, confused.

Andie laughed. "Originally, yeah. They were neighborhood stores where you could get a block of ice for your icebox—or pick up some cold beer and cigarettes and hang out for a while. After modern refrigeration came to Texas, they evolved into outdoor beer joints."

"Sounds like fun." Mia turned to Josh and was disappointed to find that his expression had gone flat.

"I'll pass." He turned away and started stacking the leftovers in Birdie's fridge.

"Don't be a party pooper," Andie said. "It's our obligation as good citizens to show Mia around town. She's new. We have to do it."

"I'm sure you can handle it." He didn't look at them as he rearranged the contents of Birdie's fridge to make room. "I've got an early morning."

"Fine." Andie seized Mia's hand and pulled her out of the kitchen. "We'll have fun without you."

Mia tried to hide her disappointment as Birdie hugged Andie good night and told them to have a good time. When Mia thanked her for dinner, Birdie surprised her with a hug too. Not a brief hug either. A long, firm hug, the way Mia's grandmother used to hug her when she was a kid.

She hadn't realized how much she'd missed being hugged like that. Neither of her parents were big huggers. Her mother gave hugs like she couldn't wait for them to be over. A quick squeeze was all Mia ever got before she was turning away to do something else. And her father, on the rare occasions she saw him, had always been a stiff peck on the cheek sort of person rather than a hugger.

"Let's roll." Andie was impatient, rattling her keys. Of course she was; she got hugs from Birdie all the time. She couldn't know what it was like to live most of your life with only minimal hugging.

Mia let go of Birdie and threw one last glance at Josh on her way out the door. He didn't even look at her to say goodbye.

Apparently he hadn't been flirting with her after all. Mia was disappointed but not surprised. It wouldn't be the first time she'd misinterpreted something like that. She'd always been better with numbers than people.

"I told you my brother was antisocial." Andie sounded annoyed, and not the least bit concerned Josh might be able to hear her as they walked to her car. In fact, she might have been speaking intentionally loud, hoping it would carry to the house. "Don't take it personally," she said more quietly.

But Mia already had, and nothing Andie could say would change that. Antisocial or not, if Josh had wanted to spend time with her, wouldn't he at least have been tempted to say yes? Or suggested they do something more to his liking? Or even just looked disappointed? The fact that he hadn't done any of those things had to mean he wasn't as interested as Mia thought.

Which was fine. Mia was supposed to be taking a break from men. She certainly wasn't about to go pinning her hopes on an indifferent goat farmer.

No matter how much she liked his cheese.

Andie's car was a Jeep Cherokee that smelled like coffee and insect repellent inside. Possibly because there were several empty travel mugs on the floor at Mia's feet, along with a can of Deep Woods Off.

"Sorry about the mess," Andie said, sounding not sorry at all. Country music blasted out of the speakers when she started the ignition, and she turned it down to a more reasonable level.

Mia wondered if they were going to a country-western bar. She'd never been to one before. She couldn't say she was a fan of country music, although she also couldn't say she'd heard much of it. She'd always just assumed she didn't like it, in the same way she'd assumed she didn't like men in cowboy boots and hats. She'd already had reason to reconsider her opinion on the latter, so perhaps she could give the former a chance as well.

The Rusty Spoke was only ten minutes away, on the outskirts of downtown. As she got out of the car, Mia was greeted by the sound of a Lizzo song. So not a country bar, then.

She wondered how many of the patrons standing around

the large patio and sitting at the dozen or so picnic tables would turn out to be students of hers. Then she told herself to stop thinking about it, because she was already nervous about classes starting Monday.

She followed Andie into a wooden building that could only be described as a shack. Inside, they wove through a smattering of tables to reach a bar at the back.

"What do you want?" Andie asked as she waited for the bartender's attention.

Most of the bars Mia had frequented in grad school specialized in either craft cocktails or wine, but neither of those seemed like a good bet here. "Whatever you're having is fine," she told Andie.

When the harried bartender made her way over to them, Andie greeted her by name and asked for two Shiners. With their beers in hand, they made their way out to the patio and claimed the empty end of a long picnic table occupied by a couple who appeared to be on a date.

"Evening." Andie raised her bottle to them in greeting as she and Mia sat down.

"How's it going?" the man said as his date offered a friendly smile.

"Better now," Andie replied and took a long swig of beer.

They all laughed, and the couple turned back to their conversation.

"Do you know them?" Mia asked, wondering why Andie hadn't introduced her.

"Nope."

Mia was confused by the interaction. Why would you greet someone you didn't know or ask how they were doing? Wouldn't it be more polite to respect their privacy and not interrupt their conversation? She put it down to one of those regional peculiarities she'd probably need to get used to.

Mia clutched her beer bottle. "I thought everyone knew everyone in small towns." Condensation dripped down her fingers in the heat. There were big fans all around the patio, but they only stirred up the soupy air. She wondered, not for the first time, why people chose to live in places that were this hot so much of the year.

"Crowder's not *that* small," Andie said. "Especially with the university and King's Creamery bringing people in."

"Do a lot of people who live here work at the ice cream factory?"

"Eighteen hundred and sixty-five. It's the single largest employer. Second place is Ballard County government at fourteen hundred ninety."

"That's an oddly specific set of facts to have in your head." Especially given that Andie didn't work for King's Creamery or the county government.

Andie grinned. "I have a lot of odd facts in my head."

"Why is that?" Mia asked, since Andie seemed proud of it.

"I guess because I read a lot and I have a good memory," Andie shrugged. "I like trivia. I kill at Trivial Pursuit."

Mia was terrible at trivia because the facts she had were always the wrong facts. She knew this because Paul had once dragged her to a pub trivia night and not a single one of the questions had been about Euclidean geometry but instead had been about football players and the cast of *Friends*. She assumed she'd be just as bad at Trivial Pursuit, but she'd never played it. Her family hadn't done board games. Or many of the other traditional activities of childhood, for that matter.

"I never learned to ride a bike," Mia said.

Andie smiled at her. "You're a weird duck."

Mia felt her face redden, although it was already probably red from the heat. "Sorry."

"No, I like it." Andie's expression was open and friendly, and it eased some of Mia's self-consciousness. "Weird's a compliment."

"Is it?" Mia had been called weird a lot, but it had never felt like a positive thing.

"In my book it is. Who wants to be normal? Normal's boring."

I do. Mia had spent most of her life wanting to be normal. She worked hard at trying to be more like everyone else. It was one of the reasons she found socializing exhausting. She was constantly studying the people around her and trying to guess what they expected from her.

It was impossible to imagine moving through the world without expending all that effort trying to conform. What else would she be able to do with her extra energy? Publish more often probably. Or even take up a hobby.

"Do you have any hobbies?" she asked Andie.

"Needlepoint."

"Really?" Mia had expected Andie to say something more rugged and practical, like archery or cabinetmaking. Something that would be useful in a post-apocalyptic world. Andie seemed like she'd be a good person to have around during an apocalypse. "I can start a fire with a magnifying glass," Mia said. "As long as the sun's out."

Andie nodded like this was a totally normal thing to say. "Is that your hobby?"

"No, it's just something I learned when I was a kid. I don't have any hobbies."

"I mostly do subversive embroidery."

Mia had never heard of this, but she was intrigued. "Subversive how?"

"Rude or snarky phrases surrounded by needlepoint flowers. Like 'Fuck off and die,' or 'Whatever, bitches.' It helps me channel my anger."

"That's kind of . . . weird," Mia said cautiously. "But also cool."

Andie smiled again. "I'm telling you, this town's full of weirdos. We've got a dude who roller-skates up and down Main Street every day in a tie-dyed tank top and super-short jeans shorts singing Dolly Parton songs."

"I think I've seen him," Mia said, although she hadn't recognized the song he'd been singing.

"His name's Pete. He's really nice." Andie took a drink of her beer. "And look at my aunt Birdie. She's always done whatever the fuck she wants. When she was in her twenties, she left a guy at the altar—pulled a literal runaway bride—and spent the whole summer following Lilith Fair around the country. She also chained herself to a tree in someone's yard a few years ago to keep it from being cut down." Andie paused to shake her head. "And of course my brother's a total weirdo."

Mia didn't really understand Josh, but she didn't find him weird. Inscrutable? Definitely. Private? Sure. Weird? Not so much.

"Even people who seem normal on the outside always turn out to be secretly weird when you scratch the surface. My mailman collects vintage Barbie dolls. He's got like four hundred of them in his house. And that chick in there who sold us our beers? She's a flat-Earther—do not ask her about it. Even the mayor—she dresses her French bulldogs up in costumes and takes pictures of them re-enacting famous scenes from movies. She's got a whole Instagram account devoted to it. I'm pretty sure it helped her get elected, actually."

"That is weird," Mia agreed.

"My point is," Andie said, "I think you're going to fit in just fine here."

Chapter Eight

To say Mia was nervous about her first day of class at Bowman would be an understatement.

Talking about math was one of her favorite things to do, and talking about it with other people who loved math as much as she did? There was nothing better. But teaching required her to develop a rapport with people who didn't necessarily love math—or even like it—and she wasn't exactly brimming with confidence in her oral communication skills.

Upper-level classes were easier, because they were populated by math majors who were there because they wanted to be and were actively engaged with the subject matter. But the core curriculum classes like Mia was teaching at Bowman tended to be full of students who didn't care about the subject and were only in the class because they needed the credits to graduate.

She'd TA'd enough intro classes at UCLA to know what those students could be like. Bored. Distracted. Disengaged. Sometimes even downright hostile to the material.

Mia didn't know how to relate to people who weren't interested in learning. She didn't know how to talk to them when they only wanted the bare minimum amount of information required to pass the class. Mia didn't know how to do the bare minimum, so they sometimes got frustrated when they came to her office hours for help, because she wanted them to understand the concepts, not just be able to fake it enough to earn a passing grade.

Sometimes it felt like she was speaking a completely different language. But she supposed maybe it felt that way to her students too.

Additionally, Bowman was a teaching-focused university, which meant smaller class sizes to allow for more one-on-one interaction between students and instructors. There would be no teaching assistants to help with grading or offer additional assistance. Mia was on her own.

When she walked into her Calculus I class on Monday, she didn't know what to expect. She didn't know what her students' secondary education had been like or what they hoped to do after they graduated. She didn't know how many suffered from "math anxiety"—a persistent and almost always false belief that they were naturally bad at math—but it was sure to be a nonzero number. Some might have even failed previous calculus classes and already developed a strong aversion to the course.

Nerves roiled Mia's stomach as she watched her first batch of students file into the classroom Monday morning. They appeared evenly balanced between male and female. Most were typical college age, but she noted a few older students in the mix.

Once they'd settled, Mia pasted on a smile and introduced herself, pleased that her voice only shook a little. Once that was out of the way, she launched right into her first lesson.

THE INFATUATION CALCULATION

A lot of professors started the first day by going over the syllabus and outlining what would be expected of their students over the semester. Mia chose not to do that, because she felt there was no faster way to make undergrads' eyes glaze over than reviewing a list of topics that didn't mean anything to them yet.

So she started off by throwing out a deceptively simple question to the class. "Who can tell me what sixty miles per hour means?"

Before they tried to start learning calculus, Mia wanted them to understand why it was useful. Otherwise, they'd just end up mimicking the techniques without actually knowing what any of it meant.

After a moment's hesitation, several hands shot up, and Mia called on a young woman in the front row, asking her to introduce herself before answering the question.

"I'm Madison," the student declared with a confidence Mia envied. "Miles per hour is a British Imperial unit of speed based on the number of miles traveled in one hour—which in this case would be sixty."

"Thank you, Madison." Mia rewarded her with an approving smile and mentally cataloged Madison as a type A overachiever.

She'd found it useful to identify different personality types in order to tailor her approach to people. Overachievers, for instance, thrived on praise. But their enthusiasm needed to be tempered so they didn't monopolize class discussions.

"We use a combination of distance and time to express speed," Mia continued, addressing the class again. "If you keep going at the same speed for one hour, you'll have traveled sixty miles. Pretty simple, right? But when we're driving our cars, do we always go the same speed the whole time?"

She was pleased to see lots of heads shaking around the room, which indicated they were actually listening to her.

"No, of course we don't. Speed can be inconstant, so our speedometer might read thirty miles per hour when we set out at nine o'clock, and eighty a minute later after we've gotten on the highway."

"Speed limit's only seventy heading out of town," piped up a male student in the back row. "So you'll be going zero after you get pulled over by the state trooper hiding behind the Buc-ee's billboard."

He smirked proudly as several of his classmates laughed, and Mia put him down as the cocky class clown. Class clowns could be useful for keeping the other students engaged, but they could also pose a distraction if you let them derail the conversation.

"What's your name?" she asked him.

"Cody, ma'am."

She winced inwardly at being called ma'am as she gave him an approving nod. "That's a great point you've brought up. When the police set up a speed trap, they don't care about your average speed over time, do they? They use a radar detector to clock your speed at the moment you happen to be passing them. In calculus, we call this instantaneous speed, which is speed at one specific instant in time."

The nods were a little less vigorous now that she'd introduced the first new mathematical term, but most of the class seemed to still be with her. Good, because they were about to jump right in—hopefully before most of them noticed it was happening.

THE INFATUATION CALCULATION

"What if your car didn't have a speedometer?" she asked. "But it did have an odometer to tell you how many miles you'd traveled. Using just your odometer and a clock, could you figure out your speed?" Madison's hand shot up again, but this time Mia pointed at a young Latino man who'd only tentatively raised his hand. "What's your name?"

"Antonio." He looked as nervous as Mia was, and she felt an immediate sense of kinship with him.

"Tell us how you'd do it, Antonio."

His gaze darted around the room before he answered. "I'd subtract my starting mileage from my ending mileage and divide that by the time it took to get there."

"Excellent." Mia gave him her most encouraging smile. "Antonio's just described the formula for calculating rate of speed, which you may remember learning in one of your previous math classes. It's expressed mathematically as r, for rate of speed, equals d—distance—over t for time." She wrote the formula on the chalkboard behind her, circled it, and then wrote it again as an equation, filling in the variables. "So if, for example, between nine o'clock and nine thirty—a period of one half-hour—you'd traveled thirty miles, your average speed would be sixty miles per hour."

She turned around to make sure everyone was still with her. This was middle school math, but it was good to review it before introducing the next concept, which would be their first real calculus lesson. Mia was pleased to see most of the class was still with her, aside from one or two who seemed to be reading their phones. Overall, not a bad engagement rate.

Now it was time to do some calculus.

"What if I wanted to know the car's speed at exactly

9:05?" she asked the class. "Is there a way to estimate that using only our odometer and a clock?"

The question was met by silence, but Mia was gratified to see a lot of furrowed brows and other evidence of mental wheels turning as they contemplated the problem. Several students shifted in their seats, sitting up straighter or leaning forward in concentration.

Now that she had them hooked, she showed them how to do their first approximation, writing out a formula for estimating the miles per minute for a five-minute interval. Once they seemed to have grasped that, she walked them through a second approximation, reducing the interval even further, and then a third, using a fraction of a minute.

By the end of the first fifty-minute class, she'd introduced them to limits, derivatives, and functions, which would form the basis of much of their work over the upcoming semester. Even better, most seemed to have followed along, judging by their body language. There were some groans when she assigned homework to reinforce the lesson they'd just learned, but that was to be expected. Overall, it felt like a success.

After the students had all filed out, Mia felt both drained and exhilarated. She practically ran back to her office, where she closed the door before collapsing into her chair in an exhausted heap.

She'd done it. She'd survived her first class.

And it had actually gone . . . well?

Maybe this job wouldn't be so bad after all. She *liked* teaching, and furthermore she was good at it. She'd needed a reminder of that. The relentless disappointment of her job search and the breakup with Paul had both sapped her confidence these last few months. But now she knew. She could do this.

Mia spun her chair in a circle, grinning. She felt like celebrating.

Unfortunately, she didn't have anyone to celebrate with. Although she'd gotten to know her new colleagues in the department a little better over the last week, none were candidates to become the sort of friends she could confide in or hang out with for fun.

She had no one to share this small triumph with. At the realization, a pang of loneliness punctured her euphoria.

But then she remembered Andie. It felt like they were on the way to becoming friends. She'd be at work now, but Mia could call her later. Maybe they could go out for dinner.

And there was Birdie, of course. She always seemed happy to talk, and she'd probably love to hear about Mia's first day of class.

Mia's mind leaped to Josh next. But her feelings about him were confusing and doused with uncertainty.

Better not to think about him at all. She didn't need another man in her life distracting her from her goals or undermining her confidence.

She didn't need another man in her life, period.

Mia's routine quickly fell into a manageable pattern. Teaching and office hours, trips to the grocery store, occasional chats with Birdie in the yard. Phone calls with her sister and her friends back in LA. She even got together with Andie a couple more times.

If only she could bring the same energy to her knot problem. She remained stuck and couldn't seem to get unstuck.

Meanwhile, the end of her employment contract loomed on the distant horizon like a mushroom cloud. A year sounded like a long time, but university hiring cycles could be lengthy, and new positions were often posted up to nine months in advance. Before she knew it, it would be time to go back on the job market. And with nothing to show for herself, she was unlikely to have any better luck than she'd had this year.

There was a possibility Bowman might offer her another contract. But it wasn't something that could be counted on. Another year at Bowman wasn't something she wanted, anyway. It was one thing to put up with a place for a year, and another altogether to let yourself get stuck there. Career momentum was hard to get back once you let inertia overtake you. You had to keep moving if you wanted to get anywhere.

It was nearing the point where she needed to either crack this proof or admit defeat and move on to something else. Already she'd begun considering other topics for publication. The problem was none of them were anywhere near as good. But something would be better than nothing.

That was her plan for the evening as she headed home, a little over a month after moving to Crowder. She was going to make a list of potential papers she could throw together quickly. Once she'd done that, she would pick two, write them up, and start submitting to every journal she could think of.

Unfortunately, her air conditioner had other plans.

When she walked into her apartment, the temperature was stifling. So hot it felt like it was singeing the hair on her arms.

Normally, she left the AC on energy saver while she was gone, which kept the apartment at a barely tolerable eighty degrees. But tonight it was like an oven inside. You could probably bake a cake by leaving it on the countertop.

She went to check the AC, which was rumbling and blowing as usual, but the air coming out of it was hot and humid. Switching it from energy saver to max cool had no effect. Neither did adjusting the temperature. She could barely breathe in the apartment, it was so hot. She opened all the windows, but the air wasn't that much cooler outside, and there wasn't enough of a breeze to penetrate the swelter inside.

By that point so much sweat had collected in her bra that it had soaked through to her shirt. Mia went downstairs and knocked on Birdie's back door for help.

When she explained the problem, Birdie invited Mia into her blissfully air-conditioned house and made a lovely, comforting fuss over her. Mia was given a glass of sweet iced tea and a seat under the ceiling fan in the living room while Birdie went up to investigate the AC problem.

A few minutes later, Birdie came back, shaking her head. "Something's wrong with it all right—not that I didn't believe you. I'll have to call in an expert."

Mia sipped her iced tea, finally starting to cool off a little, while Birdie called someone named Wyatt and explained the problem.

"Good news," Birdie said when she got off the phone. "Wyatt's coming right over."

It didn't surprise Mia that Birdie knew someone who did AC repairs and was willing to drop everything and come over straight away. Birdie seemed connected to nearly everyone in town through an elaborate barter economy. Much like her arrangement with her beekeeping neighbor, Arlo, there was a dairy farmer named Buzz who kept her in fresh cow's milk, a woman named Jeanette who dropped off lemons and limes from her trees, and a guy named Dwight who'd come over last week to give Birdie's Subaru a tune-up.

Wyatt the AC guy was as good as his word, because fifteen minutes later Birdie's front doorbell rang. By then, Birdie was in the middle of making dinner, which she'd insisted on sharing with Mia. So it was Mia who went to answer the door.

She had carelessly assumed Wyatt would be middle-aged, pot-bellied, and balding. Possibly with BO and a case of plumber's butt. It was an unfair stereotype, but one supported by most of her previous experiences with repairmen.

Wyatt was none of the above.

Au contraire. This AC repairman was, as the kids liked to say, a total snack.

He was not only young but fit enough to give any Hollywood star a run for his money and blessed with the sort of face that probably caused women to spontaneously ovulate when he walked into a room. Eyes as blue as a tropical ocean, cheekbones straight out of central casting, and a jaw fit for a comic-book superhero.

He reminded Mia of her friend Brooke's model boyfriend, Dylan—except for the tattoos that covered most of Wyatt's arms, disappearing under the sleeves of his T-shirt. Mia was too nervous to study them carefully, but she caught glimpses of twining flowers and birds and a skull amidst the colored patterns.

Wyatt was so good-looking, it was hard to believe he was a real repairman. He looked like a fake repairman you'd hire to strip at a bachelorette party. Or the kind of repairman who turned up in a pornographic movie to show off his hammer for the lady of the house.

He was the sort of repairman Mia had always assumed didn't exist in real life. And yet, here he stood in front of her with a leather utility belt slung casually over one shoulder and a battered toolbox in his hand.

And here Mia was with visible boob sweat and her makeup half melted off.

Perfect.

Wyatt's face split into a grin so resplendent it was like standing in a beam of actual sunlight. It made Mia's pits break into a sweat all over again.

"You must be Birdie's new renter," he said.

"Mia," she managed, her voice coming out a little froggy.

His eyes glinted as if he knew exactly what effect he had on women and enjoyed every bit of it. "I'm Wyatt, and I'm here to solve all your problems." Every word was laden with innuendo as if he was intentionally leaning into the porn cliché.

"Birdie's in the kitchen." Mia turned on her heel, leaving the unnervingly gorgeous Wyatt to follow in her wake.

Birdie beamed when she caught sight of him. She wiped her hands on a towel and greeted him with a hug. "Thanks for getting here so fast."

"Anything for you, Birdie. You know I'm always at your beck and call. You just say the word, anytime day or night, and I'll come running with my heart on my sleeve." Wyatt's manner remained flirtatious with Birdie, but more playful, as if it was grounded in genuine affection.

"Oh stop." Birdie waved him off as if she'd heard it before. "I might be tempted if I hadn't helped potty train you."

He draped an arm around Birdie's shoulders as he turned to address Mia. "Birdie was my preschool teacher. I've been in love with her since I was three."

Mia hadn't known Birdie used to be a teacher. As far as she'd been able to divine, Birdie's only job was as a school crossing guard. Mia had driven past her a few times, holding her stop sign and shepherding elementary school children across the street.

Birdie chuckled. "Yes, you were quite the charmer with your saggy drawers and that filthy stuffed duck you carried everywhere."

"Her name was Gertrude Ducky," Wyatt said with absolute seriousness. "And I was your favorite student. Admit it."

"All my students were special to me," Birdie replied diplomatically before returning to the crisis at hand. "Tell me honestly, do you think you'll be able to get that old AC running again so poor Mia can sleep in her apartment tonight?"

Wyatt's gaze landed on Mia and the glint returned to his eyes. "I promise I'll do my best to get Mia into bed tonight."

"Behave," Birdie commanded, giving him a gentle slap on the arm.

"Yes, ma'am." He tipped an imaginary hat at her. "I'll just go take a look at that AC, shall I?" On his way out the back door he gifted Mia with a wink that left her feeling dizzy.

"Don't pay him any mind," Birdie told Mia after Wyatt had gone. "His bark is worse than his bite."

An image popped into Mia's head of Wyatt's teeth biting her skin in a decidedly sexual context. *Thanks for that, Birdie.*

"Wyatt's a good boy." Birdie glanced out the kitchen window and Mia followed her gaze. They both watched

Wyatt disappear into the garage apartment. "He comes on a little strong," Birdie continued, looking down at the pastry dough she was cutting into bite-size squares, "but it's all for show."

"Is it?" Wyatt's flirting hadn't felt like a bluff. It had felt calculated and purposeful.

"Well . . ." Birdie threw a wry smile over her shoulder. "No, not really. He's full of wild oats and he likes to sow 'em. So you know, mind your heart."

Mia appreciated the warning, but since she wasn't looking to form any serious attachments, she thought her heart was probably safe. The rest of her, however, might be open to temptation . . .

Birdie began dropping squares of dough into the simmering chicken stew on the stove. "It's a shame, because what that boy needs is to settle down with a nice girl who isn't impressed by all his swagger. Wyatt's mother died when he was ten—sweetest woman in the world, god rest her soul. But his father . . . well." Birdie's lips pressed into a thin line. "Let's just say George King isn't the nurturing type. Kids need love as much as they need a firm guiding hand, and Wyatt didn't have much of either. Underneath all that cockiness is a little boy who's starved for any kind of attention he can get."

Mia hadn't expected to find herself relating so much to someone like Wyatt. Her parents were both still living, but she'd also lacked parental attention during her formative years. It was interesting that in Wyatt's case it had manifested in extreme extroversion, while Mia had gone the opposite direction.

She supposed it came down to the source material. Nurture

could only exert so much influence over nature. You could pound bread dough into any shape you liked, but when it came out of the oven it would still be bread.

"I often wonder how Wyatt would have turned out if Kathleen had lived." Birdie stirred the chicken and dumplings, seeming to get lost in her memories for a moment before she shook herself out of it. "Anyway, dinner's ready. Get out some bowls and spoons, will you?"

Mia set the table while Birdie took a tray of reheated rolls out of the oven. Then she carried the pot of chicken and dumplings to the table and they sat down to eat.

When Wyatt came back twenty minutes later, Mia was on her second helping. She looked up as the back door opened and froze with her spoon halfway to her face.

Wyatt had taken his shirt off.

It was obvious why. His naked torso—covered only by more tattoos and a small gold medallion hanging around his neck—was dripping with sweat. Of course it was, because he'd just spent the last half hour in her apartment, which was currently one zillion degrees. All that naked, glistening skin—not to mention the newly revealed rock-hard abs and chest—was a sight to behold.

"Any luck?" Birdie asked, seemingly unfazed by the sight of Wyatt's nipples. As was to be expected, since she'd participated in his potty training.

Mia stared, unable to tear her gaze away as Wyatt set his toolbox inside the door and used his discarded shirt to wipe the excess sweat off his face and neck. He'd fastened his leather toolbelt around his waist, and both it and his jeans hung extra-low on his hips, exposing the black waistband of his underwear and what felt like an indecent amount of his pelvis.

"'Fraid not," he said draping his damp T-shirt around the back of his neck. "The coil's toast and you might as well buy a whole new unit for what it'll cost to replace it."

"Oh dear. I was afraid of that," Birdie said.

Wyatt strode to the kitchen sink to wash his hands. "The good news is, I found you a good deal on a replacement. But it's in Austin, so I won't be able to pick it up until tomorrow."

Mia finally recovered the power of speech. "Tomorrow?" What was she supposed to do in the meantime? Die of heatstroke?

"Drat." Birdie looked at Mia. "You'll just have to sleep here tonight."

"Oh no," Mia said. "I couldn't do that." Maybe Birdie could loan her a fan. She might be able to tough it out for one night.

"You'll have to." Birdie's tone left no room for argument. "I certainly can't let you sleep up there."

"It's ninety-two degrees in that apartment right now." Wyatt leaned in next to Mia and grabbed a dinner roll off the table, putting his glistening nipples directly in her eyeline. A tiny bead of sweat slid down his pec and over the rippled muscles along his rib cage. "And don't expect it to cool off much overnight."

Mia exhaled as Wyatt straightened, but he stayed where he was, casually resting a hand on the back of her chair as he bit into his roll.

"You can sleep in my spare room tonight," Birdie said. "It's not the Ritz, but it'll have to do."

All Mia could do was nod numbly as Wyatt's cologne

mingled with the heady scent of his sweat-soaked skin, fogging her senses.

Birdie clapped her hands with pleasure and pushed her chair back. "Who wants dessert?"

"I do," Wyatt said, letting his gaze fall heavily on Mia.

Chapter Nine

Wyatt inhaled two bowls of Birdie's banana pudding before bidding them good night. Mia couldn't decide if she was more relieved or disappointed to see him go.

He certainly made things more interesting. But did she actually want more complexity in her life? She was supposed to be avoiding distractions, and Wyatt was someone who oozed distraction out of his pores. Flattering as it was to be the focus of his attention, she felt drained after half an hour in his presence.

After Wyatt had left, Mia went up to her apartment and packed an overnight bag, hastily grabbing pajamas, toiletries, and a change of clothes before fleeing the sweltering apartment. It had been foolish, she realized, to think she could tough it out up there overnight.

Living in New York and LA, Mia had considered air-conditioning a luxury rather than a necessity. None of her last few apartments had it, and she hadn't missed it except for a few weeks in the summer when temperatures became truly intemperate. But even during a heat wave it cooled off enough overnight to offer a temporary reprieve.

Not here. The temperature outside had barely dropped at all

since the sun had dipped below the horizon. Mia blamed the humidity, which hung in the air like a miasma, trapping the heat under its oppressive weight. There was no breeze to speak of either. The air here was brutally still. How did anyone survive a Texas summer without air-conditioning?

Birdie was still clearing off the bed in the spare room when Mia came back. Like many a guest bedroom, it mostly seemed to be used for storage, and Mia helped her move the last few boxes onto the floor.

Underneath the clutter, the twin-size mattress was covered with a patchwork quilt and sheets dotted with tiny pink roses. There was a ruffled mint green bed skirt to match the ruffled gingham valance above the window. It was a little like standing in the cottagecore Holy Land.

Birdie surveyed the room with a faint look of distaste. "This was my bedroom, once upon a time."

Mia could easily picture a teenaged Birdie in here listening to records on the dusty old stereo in the corner as a precursor to her Lilith Fair groupie days. Several of Mia's friends back home would kill to get their hands on a vintage record player like that. Eighties throwbacks were all the rage right now.

Birdie pulled the chain on the ceiling fan to switch it on. "Bathroom's right across the hall. I set out fresh towels for you. Just let me know if you need anything at all."

After Mia bid her good night, she took her bag across the hall and got ready for bed in the pink-tiled bathroom. It was only nine thirty, but she was strangely exhausted.

Back in Birdie's old bedroom, she turned down the quilt and lay on the bed, letting the ceiling fan cool her off from head to toe. Like the rest of the room, the mattress seemed to date from the eighties. It was rock-hard with a body-shaped divot in the middle. Mia wondered how long it had been since anyone had slept on it.

Nevertheless, she was grateful to be there, lying in an air-conditioned room under a ceiling fan rather than fending for herself in a ninety-degree apartment. Which was exactly what all her previous landlords would have left her to do.

She was lucky to have Birdie.

She could deal with an uncomfortable bed for one night. It wasn't that bad.

In the morning, when Mia woke with a ferocious crick in her neck, she reconsidered her opinion of the bed.

It *was* that bad.

She could barely move her head at all. A hot shower loosened it up some, but it still hurt like a son of a bitch.

Birdie had left her a half-full pot of coffee in the kitchen and a note saying she'd gone to do her crossing guard shift. Since Mia's first class didn't start for an hour, she headed up to her apartment in search of some Advil.

When she reached the top of the stairs, she was startled to find the door open and Wyatt in her kitchen. "What are you doing?" she asked, pausing in the doorway.

He didn't look up from the caulk gun he was using to draw a perfect bead around the edge of the kitchen sink. "Recaulking your sink. I noticed some of the old caulk was wearing away."

"You're a real jack of all trades, aren't you?" It wasn't wrong to admire his butt as he bent over her counter, was it? She thought not, since Wyatt so clearly enjoyed being looked at. Hopefully not, because that was exactly what she was doing.

He finished his task and set the caulk gun down with a grin that said he knew she'd been staring at his ass. "That's me, the helpful handyman." He gestured around the small apartment proudly. "I did most of the work on this place for Birdie when she decided to start renting it out." As he said it, he dug his wallet out of the back pocket of his jeans and handed Mia a business card.

Wyatt King, The Helpful Handyman it read, along with a phone number.

"That's my cell number," Wyatt said, leaning in close to tap the card in her hand. "Feel free to call me anytime you have a need."

Even Mia couldn't miss the implicit suggestion in his words. But she chose to believe the sweat she was breaking into was due to the temperature in the un-air-conditioned apartment and not because of Wyatt. "I've got a Cody King in my calculus class. Is he related to you?"

Wyatt grabbed his caulk gun off the counter and carried it over to his toolbox. "That'd be my youngest brother."

"Any connection to the ice cream company?" She'd been wondering about Cody since she first saw his name on her class roll, but she hadn't found an opportunity to ask him about it.

"You could say that." Wyatt's mouth took on a wry twist. "Our dad's the president and CEO."

Mia's eyebrows lifted. "And you work as a handyman?"

"I never cared much for ice cream," Wyatt said with a shrug. "Or being under my old man's thumb."

Given what Birdie had said about Wyatt's childhood, Mia could understand why he might not want to join the family business. Still, working as a handyman seemed an unusual career choice for someone who must have grown up with money.

"How did you learn how to do all this stuff?" she asked as she got a bottle of Advil out of the cabinet by the sink.

"My uncle, mostly. He takes a lot of pride in doing things for himself." Wyatt's eyes narrowed as he watched her dry-swallow two pills. "What's wrong?"

"The mattress in Birdie's spare room didn't agree with my neck." Mia reached up to massage the sore muscles. "It's fine though."

"I can fix it for you," Wyatt said casually. "If you want."

She threw him a look conveying her skepticism. "You fix sore muscles in addition to houses?"

Smirking lewdly, he held up his hands and wiggled his fingers. "I have magic fingers."

Mia rolled her eyes. "Sure you do."

"Seriously, I can probably help." The smirk faded to something slightly more sincere, and he held his palms up in a gesture of submission. "If you'll let me."

She chewed on the inside of her cheek as she considered his offer. It might just be a ploy to put his hands on her, but getting a free massage from a hot handyman wasn't the worst thing she could imagine. And what if he was right? What if he could help the pain in her neck?

She decided it was worth the risk. "Fine. No funny business though."

"Excuse you, I'm a professional. Now turn around." He twirled his index finger in a circle.

Mia did as he asked, tensing as Wyatt stepped close to her.

"Try to relax." His breath tickled the back of her neck.

It was a struggle not to jump when he touched her. A

trickle of sweat traveled down between her breasts as his calloused hands moved experimentally over her neck, tracing the length of her cervical spine before he grasped both her shoulders.

She let out an involuntary groan as he began kneading the muscle, gently at first and then increasing the pressure.

"That's better," he said when her shoulders started to unclench. "Gotta let go of all that tension." His thumbs dug in next to the rim of her shoulder blades, causing her to flinch at the sudden flare of pain. "There it is. That's what I thought."

His thumbs eased up, then dug back in mercilessly while his fingers held her shoulders to prevent her from edging away. "A lot of the time, what we think is neck pain actually originates in our shoulders and upper back."

Already, Mia's neck was feeling better. Wyatt moved down lower and dug into a new spot, releasing a fresh burst of discomfort.

"People spend so much time hunched over their computers and their phones and their car steering wheels," he said. "You've got to get in there nice and deep and work out the kinks." He moved lower still, digging his thumbs under her shoulder blades.

She let out a moan as the pain started to morph into something closer to pleasure. It still hurt, but it was the good kind of hurt. The kind that brought relief.

"It's the right side that's worst, isn't it? I can feel the knot. Right. Here." His thumb pressed harder and she let out a yelp. "Sorry. Let me just—" He let go of her and reached around so her collarbone lay against his left forearm with his hand gripping her right shoulder. Then he used the knuckles of his right hand to dig into her back, working at the knot in the muscle with his fist.

"That feels amazing." Holding on to his forearm for support as his fist ground into her back, she let her head slump forward. Her neck pain was almost completely gone. "Where did you learn to do this?"

"Dated a physical therapist once." She could hear the smile in his voice. "I learned a few tricks of the trade before we parted ways."

"Wooooowww." She exhaled a deep, contented sigh. "I apologize for doubting you. You really do have magic fingers."

He laughed. "You don't know the half of it."

There was a tread on the steps outside, and Mia looked up as Josh walked into the apartment. His face froze when he saw them.

"Hey, man," Wyatt said cheerfully. "Have you met Mia?"

Josh's expression remained flat as he nodded. "Sorry if I'm interrupting."

Mia slid out of Wyatt's grasp. She felt like she'd been caught doing something wrong. And that made her annoyed at herself for feeling that way. Josh hadn't shown any interest in her, so why shouldn't she enjoy the fact that Wyatt had?

"I had a crick in my neck, and Wyatt was just helping me with it," she explained, nevertheless. As if she owed Josh an explanation for some reason.

"I'll bet he was." Josh's sharp tone caused Mia to bristle.

"You know what Birdie's spare bed is like," Wyatt said, giving him an odd look.

"What are you doing here?" Mia asked Josh. Her

apartment had suddenly become hot guy central, and it wasn't nearly as much fun as it ought to be.

Josh's gaze landed coolly on Wyatt. "Wyatt asked me to help him get the old AC down and into his truck."

"Are you two friends?" Mia looked from Josh to Wyatt, confused. They weren't acting like friends. Well, Wyatt was. But Josh certainly wasn't. If anything, he seemed angry at Wyatt for some reason.

Wyatt strode over to Josh and threw an arm around his shoulders, giving him a friendly shake. "*Best* friends. Been that way since first grade."

"Gosh," Mia said, confused by the dynamic between them.

Josh tolerated Wyatt's embrace for a second before pulling away. "I don't have a lot of time, so if we're gonna do this, we better get to it." The kind, helpful Josh she'd met before had been replaced by someone hostile and withdrawn.

"I've got to get to campus," Mia said, grateful for a reason to excuse herself from whatever was going on between the two men. They could work out their interpersonal difficulties without her. She turned to Wyatt and offered a grateful smile. "Thank you for fixing my neck. You saved my whole day."

"My pleasure," he replied without any flirtatious overtones for once. His smile was friendly but subdued, a far cry from his usual smirking grin.

Josh was still lingering by the door, watching them sullenly. Mia offered him an uncertain smile. "Thank you for helping Wyatt out with my AC. You're both lifesavers."

The only response she got was a vague nod.

Fine. He could be that way if he wanted. Whatever had crawled up his ass, she hoped for his sake it extricated itself.

In the meantime, she was going to work.

Mia's sister called that afternoon on her lunch break from her graphic design job. "How are things going with the hot cowboy? I want an update."

Mia had made the mistake of telling Holly about Josh, and her sister had read way too much into a couple of casual encounters. Holly had repeatedly tried to get Mia to take the initiative and make an overture, and Mia had repeatedly told her that wasn't going to happen. For a number of reasons. Not least of which being, Josh didn't seem to like her anymore.

"It's not going anywhere," Mia said, pushing aside the stack of grading she'd been working on.

"Boo," Holly replied. "Have you seen him at all?" There was street noise in the background, which meant she was probably eating lunch in Madison Square Park, which was close to her office in Manhattan.

Mia felt a pang of homesickness at the familiar city sounds. "This morning, actually." She rubbed her forehead, thinking of all the places around Madison Square Park she missed. Eataly. Wagamama. The National Museum of Mathematics.

"And?" Her sister's voice rose an octave in excitement.

"Hang on." Mia grabbed her keys and let herself out of her office, heading for the nearest exit. "Let me go outside first." The building that housed the math department had been built in the seventies, and the walls were annoyingly thin. She'd overheard too many snippets of her colleagues' personal conversations already and had no desire to make her romantic travails—or lack thereof—public.

As she pushed out the door, the heat outside hit her like a sledgehammer. It couldn't be good for a person, repeatedly going from arctic cold to blistering heat all day, yet that was what everyone here did.

Once she was clear of a group of students passing by, she said, "He acted like kind of a jerk, actually. So I was right, he's definitely not interested."

"Sometimes guys act like jerks *because* they're interested."

"Or maybe they act like jerks because they *are* jerks, and no amount of projecting nobler motives onto them will change that essential reality." Mia strolled away from the math building, following an aimless path through campus. What little breeze there was blew in an unfortunate direction today, carrying the stink of animals over from the ag barns.

"You said this guy didn't seem like a jerk," Holly reminded her.

"Obviously I don't know him very well."

Holly made an impatient sound. "Tell me what happened and let me be the judge of that."

So Mia did, because as much as Holly occasionally got swept away on flights of fancy, she was still often better at understanding human behavior than Mia. Not to mention, she had a lot more experience on the dating battlefield. Mia told her sister about the broken air conditioner, and about Wyatt and his aggressive flirting, and about Birdie's neck-breaking mattress. Holly listened quietly until Mia got to Wyatt's shoulder massage.

"I'm sorry," Holly interrupted. "Hold up. Did you just say a hot handyman gave you a back rub this morning?"

"He totally fixed my neck pain."

"Sure, I'll bet he did. *Oh my god, Mia!*"

Mia winced and rubbed her ear at Holly's screechy outburst.

"Why didn't you lead with that?" Holly demanded. "Or call me immediately after leaving his presence? At the very least that should have been the first thing out of your mouth. You should have answered the phone with, 'Hi sis, guess what? This morning I got a neck rub from a porn star handyman.'"

"He's not a porn star," Mia said, casting a wary glance around to make sure no one was in eavesdropping range. "He just sort of looks like one. Only not, because he's much more attractive than most adult film actors."

"Right. Of course," Holly said dryly. "So? What happened next?"

"Nothing, because Josh walked in." Mia glanced up and realized her meandering had inadvertently brought her past the King Food Science Building. A building no doubt paid for by Wyatt's wealthy family. She turned the other direction and kept walking.

"What? In the middle of the back rub?"

"Yes." Something uncomfortable tightened in Mia's stomach at the memory of Josh's expression.

"And? What did he do?"

"Nothing. He just acted really cold. To both of us, even though allegedly he and Wyatt are friends."

"That is so awesome!"

"It wasn't," Mia said. "It was the opposite of that."

"You've got two hot men fighting for your attention! Girl, maybe I should move to Texas."

"They're not fighting." Mia frowned. "There was no fighting. Neither of them care enough about me to fight."

"Okay, first of all, hot handymen do not just go around giving innocent neck rubs."

"Some of them might."

"Shush. That dude was interested in you."

"Maybe," Mia was willing to allow. "But he seems like the kind of guy who's interested in every woman with a pulse."

"Be that as it may, the fact that your hot farmer didn't like seeing you get a neck rub from the hot handyman means something."

"He's not *my* farmer."

"But it sounds like maybe he wants to be." A loud bus rumbled by in the background, and Holly paused until it had passed. "You know what this means, don't you?"

"No."

"You're in a love triangle! Oh my god, I'm so jealous. This is so much better than *Twilight*."

"You're reading way too much into all of this." Mia had begun to regret telling Holly anything.

"You said it yourself: the hot farmer guy got all salty when he walked in on you getting a back rub from the hot handyman. It's obvious he was jealous."

"Is it?" Mia hadn't found it obvious. Did jealousy look the same as disinterest?

"Yes! My god. *He* wanted to be the one giving you a sexy

back rub." Holly let out a theatrical sigh. "I'm so envious. What even is your life?"

Mia honestly had no idea. She'd never been in a situation like this before. Assuming she was even in one now, which seemed like an awfully big assumption.

"Okay, but here's the big question," Holly continued. "Which one of them do you want?"

Mia bit her lip as her stomach tightened again.

"Don't think about it," Holly said. "Just listen to your gut. In a perfect world, if you could have your choice of either of them, which one would you want?"

Josh.

There was no contest. As stunningly good-looking as Wyatt was, he didn't stir anything in Mia but shallow lust.

It was Josh who made her stomach alternately flip and clench up, and Josh who had been haunting her thoughts for the last month.

"This is pointless," Mia said, reluctant to admit she had feelings for either of them. "This isn't a movie, and it certainly isn't a love triangle."

"Everything's a love triangle when you love triangles!" Holly trilled in a singsong voice.

"You're ridiculous," Mia said, but couldn't help laughing. She wished Holly had more time off work so she could come visit. Her sister would find a way to make even a place like Crowder seem fun.

"Just promise me you'll *do something*. Make the most of this amazing, once-in-a-lifetime opportunity and pick one of them before they both decide you're not interested and give up."

"I'm not promising anything," Mia said.

She didn't entirely trust Holly's assessment of the situation. Not enough to act on it.

And she definitely didn't trust her own instincts.

When Mia came home that night, it was to an air-conditioned apartment. In her absence, Wyatt had removed the old unit and replaced it with a brand-new and much quieter one. It hummed efficiently, cooling the apartment to a pleasant seventy-six degrees without sounding like an overburdened steam engine chugging up a hill.

She sent Birdie a text thanking her and asking her to pass her gratitude on to Wyatt as well.

Mia slept exceptionally well that night in her cool, quieter apartment on her own comfortable mattress. She awoke in the morning feeling refreshed and newly resolved to put both Wyatt and Josh firmly out of her mind.

She didn't need the distraction. Keep it simple, that was her mantra from here on out.

At least for the next eleven months.

Friday was one of the days Andie was on campus for her class, and she texted Mia to suggest they meet for lunch. They went to the student union as usual and got in line for hamburgers.

Mia had been thinking about the Shake Shack in Madison Square Park ever since she'd talked to her sister yesterday. The burgers at the student union were nowhere near good enough to satisfy her craving, unfortunately. There was a Shake Shack in Austin though. Maybe tomorrow she'd drive up and spend the day in the city. She needed some things from Sephora anyway. She could even go early and check out the farmers' market Josh had mentioned. Possibly even splurge on some cheese.

"I heard you met the famous Wyatt King," Andie said while Mia was eating her unsatisfying burger.

Mia took a drink of iced tea to wash down the stale, dry bun. "Is he famous?" she asked, wiping her mouth.

"Around here he is." Andie's lips twisted. "Famous for leaving a string of broken hearts across three counties."

"Is this you trying to warn me off?" Mia asked, wondering if Andie's had been one of the hearts he'd left broken.

"I wouldn't dare," Andie said. "Just so long as you know what kind of man you're dealing with."

"What kind of man is that?" Mia was curious to get Andie's take on Wyatt. If he and her brother had been friends most of their lives, she must know him pretty well.

"Wyatt can be a great guy." Andie shrugged as she reached for a french fry. "As a friend, he's as loyal as it gets. But as a boyfriend? He's basically the worst. He treats women like outfits to try on and discard whenever the mood strikes him. The guy's got serious impulse control issues and the attention span of a squirrel. The second a tastier-looking nut comes along, he goes scampering after it."

"Are you speaking from personal experience, perhaps?"

Andie laughed. "Me and Wyatt? Hell no. I've known him way too long to go barking up that tree. But I have a few friends who've had their hearts stomped by Hurricane Wyatt. Just wanted to make sure you didn't end up one of them."

"I appreciate the heads-up," Mia said. "But you've got nothing to worry about. Wyatt's not my type."

She'd made up her mind about that for sure. Wyatt King wasn't the kind of trouble she needed in her life right now.

Andie looked at her like she'd just announced that she despised puppies. "What, hot and charming aren't your thing?"

Wyatt might be hot, but Mia hadn't found his smarmy approach that charming. She'd been more charmed by Josh's understated solicitude—until he'd withdrawn it, anyway.

But she wasn't supposed to be thinking about Josh either. He was no more her type than Wyatt. Honestly, what was she thinking? The idea of her dating a goat farmer was too ridiculous to contemplate.

"Wyatt's good-looking," Mia allowed. "But the rest of it . . . the aggressive flirting and the constant . . ." She hesitated, searching for the right words.

"Neediness?" Andie suggested.

"I was thinking attention-seeking, but that works too. It's exhausting, but also it strikes me as sort of—"

"Desperate?"

"Sad, actually."

Andie snorted. "Sure."

"Birdie told me about his mother dying when he was young. And I gather he doesn't get along with his father."

"Yeah, his dad's a real piece of work." Andie sucked on the straw in her diet soda. "But don't buy too hard into the 'poor little rich boy' narrative. Wyatt grew up with pretty much every advantage a person can have, and he's a hundred percent living the life he wants to live. He came out just fine."

"Who told you I met Wyatt, anyway?" Mia couldn't resist wondering if Josh had mentioned her to his sister. But also, maybe Andie knew why he'd started acting so cold around Mia.

"Birdie," Andie said, dashing Mia's hopes. "She told me

about your bum AC. My condolences. I know what her guest bed is like."

Mia's neck gave a phantom twinge at the memory. "It was nice of her to let me stay."

"I gather Josh and Wyatt drove to Austin yesterday to get you a new air conditioner."

Mia hadn't realized Josh had gone to Austin with Wyatt. "Are they really best friends?"

"Since first grade."

"Huh."

Andie looked up from picking through her french fries. "Why?"

"No reason." Mia paused. "It just seemed like Josh wasn't very happy when he showed up yesterday. I had the impression he might have been mad about something."

"Is that right?" Andie looked thoughtful for a moment. Then she shrugged and popped a fry in her mouth. "My brother can be a moody-ass bitch sometimes. I wouldn't worry about it."

"It was probably nothing," Mia said. "We all have our bad days."

"Hey, you know what we should do?" Andie sat up straight and smacked her palm on the table. "We should go to the Rusty Spoke tonight. Wyatt's band is playing."

Mia's eyebrows lifted. "Wyatt's in a band?" Not only was the guy hot, rich, and handy around the house, he was in a band too? Talk about an unfair advantage.

"It's just him and a few guys from high school goofing around, but they're pretty decent." Andie grinned. "Especially after you've had a few beers."

"Sounds like fun," Mia said.

She could certainly use a night out. And maybe it would help take her mind off Josh, who'd been occupying far too much of her thoughts.

"Great," Andie said. "I'll pick you up at eight."

The Rusty Spoke was hopping when Mia and Andie got there. The band hadn't started playing yet, but the patio was nearly full and there was a line to order drinks at the walk-up bar window outside.

After they stood in line to buy a bucket of beer, Andie dragged Mia over to the low stage where Wyatt was standing around with a group of guys. His face split into a wide grin when he caught sight of Andie, and he bellowed her name, flinging his arms wide. Over her laughing objections, he lifted her off the ground and spun her around. It was a good thing Mia was holding the bucket of beer, or they'd have been left with a bucket of undrinkable beer grenades.

After Wyatt set Andie down he turned his attention to Mia, hugging her like an old friend instead of someone he'd met for the first time two days ago—though considerably less boisterously than he'd hugged Andie.

He helped himself to one of the beers from the bucket Mia was holding, earning a swat from Andie, though she didn't actually seem to mind. While Wyatt threw his head back and guzzled a truly impressive amount of beer, Andie introduced Mia to his bandmates, Tyler, Matt, and Corey. She learned their band was named Shiny Heathens, and Wyatt was the lead singer.

"Thanks for getting my new AC up and running," Mia told Wyatt once he'd finished chugging half his beer.

"De nada." His gaze flicked over to Andie, who was

chatting with the other guys, before returning to Mia. "It's Josh you should thank. I got paid for my labor, but he was there out of the goodness of his heart."

Mia didn't want to think about Josh tonight. He inspired too many contradictory feelings. It had been easy to talk herself out of her attraction to Wyatt, but Josh was another matter. Despite his hot-and-cold attitude—or maybe because of it—she hadn't been able to stop thinking about him all afternoon.

She took a swig of beer and surveyed the crowd around them. "You guys seem to be quite a draw."

Wyatt shook his head in an uncharacteristic display of self-deprecation. "This is just the regular Friday night crowd. No one comes just to see us." He relieved her of her beer bucket and set it on the edge of the stage next to them.

"Are you any good?" Mia asked, watching a man in a backward baseball cap tinkering with the sound equipment.

"We're all right." Wyatt shrugged and took another drink of beer. "It's just for fun."

He wasn't being nearly as flirty as before. Mia suspected it was because there were so many other women here. If what Andie had said about him was true, he'd want to keep his options open. Which was fine by Mia. He was easier to talk to when he wasn't laying the charm on so thick.

"You never wanted to pursue it seriously?" she asked him.

He dragged his hand across his mouth. "I don't have the discipline to take it seriously." His lips took on a bitter twist. "Besides, one rock star in the family is enough."

Mia raised her eyebrows. "There's a rock star in your family?"

"You heard of Ghost Ships?"

"Yes." Everyone had heard of Ghost Ships. Even Mia, whose favorite playlists consisted mostly of ambient noise to aid her concentration while she was working. She didn't pay a lot of attention to music, but Ghost Ships had been an inescapable fixture of the pop culture landscape for the last ten years or so.

Wyatt stared at the ground as he dug the toe of his work boot into the gravel. "Brady King, the lead guitarist—he's my dad's oldest spawn."

It seemed like a peculiar choice of words to describe a brother. Mia inferred from it, and from Wyatt's sudden interest in the ground, that his incredibly successful rock star sibling wasn't his favorite topic of conversation.

"How many siblings do you have, exactly?" She knew about Cody—and now Brady—but she got the sense there were even more.

Wyatt rubbed his temple as if he was doing a complex equation in his head. "Nine?"

"You don't sound sure about that."

"It's complicated. My dad's had three wives and my mom had a son before she married him, so I've got five half-brothers, two half-sisters, and an adopted brother, plus Tanner, who's my only full-blood sibling. And don't even ask me about my cousins, because I can't count that high."

"Wow," Mia said. "Your family's huge." Both her parents had been only children, and neither had any other kids after their divorce. Her family was minuscule compared to Wyatt's expansive clan.

He snorted into his beer. "Yeah, it's not so much a family as a nest of rattlesnakes."

"You aren't close with any of them?"

"I get on with a few of them great. Others, not so much. But that's families for you." He eyed her over the top of his beer as he took another swig. "What about you? You have any siblings?"

"Just a sister."

"You close?"

Mia smiled. "We are, yeah. Our parents weren't around much, so we had to rely on each other."

Wyatt nodded. "That's me and Tanner. We've always been close. You older or younger than your sister?"

"Older."

"So you took care of her, I'll bet."

"I guess I did, yeah. I mean, we had nannies to feed us and get us to and from school, but sometimes it felt like I was more of a mother to her than our mother was."

Wyatt picked at the label on his beer bottle. "Tanner's older, so he always looked out for me. Or tried to, anyway." He flashed his trademark smirk, but it felt half-hearted. "I was too much of a hellion. He could never keep up with me."

Before Mia could ask him anything else, Wyatt's bandmates beckoned him to the stage. The sound guy had finished final checks and they were ready to start their set.

"I gotta do this thing," Wyatt said, gesturing at the stage with his beer bottle.

"Yeah, of course. Break a leg or whatever." Did you say that to musicians? Or was it only actors? Maybe she should have just wished him luck.

"Thanks." Wyatt inclined his head. "Enjoy the show."

Mia grabbed their beer bucket and rejoined Andie, who steered her over to a spot next to the fence at the side of the patio. There was a ledge all along it for setting drinks on, and Mia set the bucket down before opening a fresh beer.

She hadn't been sure what to expect from Wyatt's band, but they seemed to play mostly radio-friendly hits from the last several decades. Mia didn't know enough about music to judge how technically adept they were, but Wyatt had a great voice and they managed an enjoyable approximation of the original songs.

"They're really good," she told Andie when they launched into a Fleetwood Mac cover. The speakers were dialed down enough to allow conversation over the music, and most people seemed to be talking more than listening to the band.

Andie looked up from her phone, which she'd been checking intermittently through the last three songs. "Yeah, they're not bad, right?"

"You said they all met in high school?"

Andie nodded, slipping her phone into her pocket. "They used to cut class to go practice in Matt's garage when his parents were at work."

"Couldn't people hear them? I would have thought they'd be found out playing in a garage in the middle of a school day."

"Oh yeah, they got caught all the time." Andie laughed as she took a swig of beer. "I think getting caught was half the fun." Her gaze caught on something on the other side of the patio, and her eyes widened. "Holy shit, he actually showed."

"Who?" Mia craned her neck, trying to see who Andie was talking about.

"My brother."

Mia's stomach did another one of those annoying flips as she caught sight of Josh, who supposedly never went anywhere.

Chapter Ten

As if the stomach flip hadn't been enough, Mia's heart stuttered when Josh's gaze met hers—which was how she knew exactly how far gone she was.

Dammit. The last thing she needed was to go losing her head over some emotionally unavailable cowboy. He was a complication she didn't want right now.

Except she did want him. In her bed, in her life, or just in front of her face as much as possible. Which was probably why she'd begun bouncing on her toes as he made his way toward them.

He looked uneasy as he ducked through the crowd, but when he reached them he flashed a smile that banished all the shadows. The warmth in his expression was unexpected, especially after their last encounter. Mia could almost believe he was happy to see her.

"You made it!" Andie threw her arms around Josh's neck and whispered something in his ear before letting him go.

Whatever she said made him grimace a little, but his smile came back as he turned to greet Mia with a nod of his head. "Hey."

She returned his understated greeting, secretly wishing he

was more of a hugger like Wyatt. She sure wouldn't mind feeling those arms around her. Or getting a sniff of his hair.

Oh no, things were definitely bad if she was fantasizing about the smell of his hair.

"Here, have a beer." Andie thrust their last bottle into her brother's hand. "I'm going to go get us some more."

And then she was gone, leaving Mia alone with Josh.

He uncapped his beer and tipped the bottle to his lips. Mia's mouth went dry as she watched his Adam's apple bob.

"You look nice tonight," he said, letting his gaze travel downward.

"Thanks." She'd worn a thin sundress, which sweat had long since plastered to her body. But if the look in Josh's eyes was any indication, he didn't mind a bit.

They stared at one another as the band played the final bars of "Go Your Own Way." There was a smattering of applause and Mia joined in, turning her gaze toward the stage. After a second Josh followed suit.

Wyatt thanked the audience and introduced himself and the other members of Shiny Heathens. As he was going through his patter, his gaze lit on Josh and he raised his hand in a friendly greeting.

When they launched into The Killers' "Mr. Brightside," Josh leaned over to speak in Mia's ear. The feel of his breath on the side of her face raised goose bumps on her arms despite the heat. "Are you enjoying the show?"

She turned to look at him, appreciating the fact that their eyes were on the same level. "Yes. I had no idea Wyatt was in a band."

Josh's extremely lickable lips pressed into a wry expression.

"Like a lot of things Wyatt does, it started out as a way to get girls."

"Why aren't you up there with him?" she asked teasingly. She'd assumed Josh would never in a million years set foot on a stage, so his response took her by surprise.

"I used to be. I was one of the founding members, in fact."

Her jaw dropped. "You're kidding." He was so dry sometimes, it was hard to tell, but he didn't look like he was joking.

"I was the lead singer before Wyatt." He winced slightly. "And I'm the one who came up with the name."

"So why *aren't* you up there with them?" She'd give anything to hear him sing. With that deep voice of his like a warm, velvety blanket, it was guaranteed to be sexy. Heat pulsed between her legs just thinking about it.

Josh shrugged and stared down at his beer. "I quit when I left for A&M. The rest of the guys stayed here and kept the band going in their spare time."

"But you're back now. Why not rejoin? They'd take you, wouldn't they?"

"Probably." His mouth had pulled into a tight line. "But it's not something I'm interested in doing anymore."

"Why not?"

He gave another shrug. "I don't have time with all my other responsibilities."

"Andie told me you don't like to go out. She called you a recluse, actually." Mia hoped she wasn't getting her new friend in trouble by saying that, but she suspected Andie had said as much to her brother's face before—and more, probably. In typical sibling fashion, she didn't seem to pull her punches with him.

Josh shook his head, frowning a little. "The farm's a twenty-four hour a day responsibility. She knows that, but she could never get on board with it."

"She told me that too." Mia felt obligated to stick up for Andie, but also she couldn't help needling Josh. "She said you like having an excuse to keep to yourself."

His lips twitched. "Y'all seem to talk about me an awful lot."

Mia's cheeks flushed, but she refused to let him change the subject. "Is she right? Don't you ever want to get away from it for a while and have some fun?"

"I'm having fun right now."

Pleasure bloomed in her chest as his eyes gazed into hers, dark and hot and unambiguous. Something that looked like hunger flashed across his expression, and the warm, glowy feeling in her chest traveled down to her thighs in a molten rush.

She dropped her gaze, the energy between them making her feel unsteady. *What happened to no distractions?* Was she really going to lose her head over a man in cowboy boots?

Yes.

She wanted him to touch her so badly she might actually explode with longing. Josh made her feel weak in a way that scared her—but also somehow oddly brave too. If he didn't kiss her, she might have to grab him and take the initiative herself. Which wasn't like her at all, but he made her feel strong enough—or maybe just needy enough—to do it. He made her feel a lot of things. Shaky. Eager. Beautiful. Reckless. *Safe*.

The toe of his boot tapped the gravel next to her foot. He

leaned in close to her ear, and a shiver rolled through her as he asked, "Is that a tattoo?"

"Yes." She pointed her toe, rotating her ankle to give him a better look at the ink visible between the straps of her sandals.

"What is it?" he asked. "Is that math?"

"It's Euler's identity. The most beautiful equation in mathematics." She shrugged, slightly embarrassed. "I got it in high school."

"You got a math tattoo in high school?" There was a smile in his voice, but it wasn't mocking. He almost sounded impressed. "What makes it beautiful?"

Her gaze lifted to his, and he met it with earnest curiosity. Mia felt herself grow even braver. "Because of its perfect simplicity, and the fact that it contains five of the most important mathematical constants: zero, one, pi, the imaginary number i, and Euler's number, which is the base of natural logarithms." She looked down at her foot, remembering the youthful exuberance that had inspired the tattoo but now felt a bit corny. "It's been compared to a Shakespearean sonnet. I guess I thought it was romantic."

Gently, Josh's hand touched hers. A shower of sparks traveled up her arm as his fingers slowly curled around hers. He didn't speak. Just stood there lightly playing with her fingers as they watched Wyatt's band play a Blink-182 song.

It was one of the most erotic things she'd ever experienced. Which was funny because she didn't even like Blink-182.

"Hey, it's Waldo!" someone shouted drunkenly at one of the tables on the patio, breaking the mood.

Josh's whole body went rigid and he dropped her hand.

"What's wrong?" Mia asked.

"Look, everyone, I found Waldo," the drunk guy shouted. "I should get a prize." The other people at his table laughed along with him.

Josh didn't answer her. All the blood had drained from his face. The hand that had been holding hers a moment ago was clenched into a fist.

"Hey, Sexy Waldo, where's your hat?" The guy seemed to be shouting in their direction. Some other people had joined in, chanting "Waldo" and banging on the table.

Mia touched her fingers to Josh's arm. "Is he talking to you?"

"Ignore him." His eyes were focused on the stage, but they burned with barely controlled anger.

"Come on, Waldo, do a dance for us." The drunk guy had gotten up and was staggering toward them, egged on by his friends. "Show us your sexy Waldo dance."

The other people near them began edging away. Mia had a similar instinct. She wanted to grab Josh's arm and drag him as far away from here as possible. But something told her it wouldn't work. Josh wouldn't let himself be dragged, and the drunk guy wouldn't just let them walk away undisturbed.

Josh still hadn't moved or even looked at his heckler. "Give it a rest, Aaron." His voice was pitched low, but loud enough to carry and dangerous-sounding.

"Or what? What are you gonna do to me, Wallldooooo?" Aaron dragged out the name in a mocking, singsongy voice. "You gonna make me?"

Everything seemed to have gone quiet around them, and Mia realized the music had stopped. All the other conversations had stopped too.

Josh slipped his beer into Mia's hand with an apologetic look and turned, stepping forward to confront the drunk Aaron.

The air seemed to crackle with tension as the two men stared each other down—one grinning smugly and the other emanating cold rage. Mia had never seen a bar fight before, but she was absolutely certain she was about to.

Wyatt appeared beside them and shouldered his way past Josh. He marched up to Aaron, getting right up in his face, and shoved him hard enough to make him stagger backward a few steps. "How about if I fucking make you, you shit-smeared pencil dick?"

Aaron spat on the ground and lunged at Wyatt. But Wyatt already had his arm cocked back. His fist shot out and slammed into Aaron's jaw.

Mia flinched as Aaron collapsed to the ground. She'd never seen anyone get punched in the face before. Not in person and up close like this.

A few of Aaron's friends gaped—and a few others snickered—as he moaned in pain. No one moved to help him.

"Anybody else got a smart mouth that needs a lesson in manners?" Wyatt demanded, scowling at the crowd of onlookers.

Andie materialized beside Mia with the bouncer not far behind her. As soon as he arrived on the scene, the crowd melted away in an impressive imitation of Homer Simpson backing into a hedge.

"You okay?" Andie asked, squeezing Mia's hand, and Mia managed a nod.

"Get him out of here," the bouncer ordered Aaron's friends. "All of you, get the hell out." He was stout and square with a long, scraggly beard and a bandana tied around his head. No one argued with him.

Aaron's companions dragged their buddy upright and herded him out toward the parking lot. He seemed to be okay, if a little unsteady on his feet. Okay enough to throw a hostile look in Wyatt's direction, anyway.

The bouncer turned on Wyatt with an angry glare. "I can't even take a damn leak without you starting some shit."

Wyatt held up his hands in supplication. "I didn't start it. I just finished it."

The bouncer shook his head, his gaze alighting on Josh briefly before he stalked back to his post by the door.

Josh hadn't moved since Wyatt's intervention. He was still standing stock-still with his back to Mia. She wished he would turn around so she could see his face. Her instinct was to run over and hug him, but she was afraid he might pull away from her.

"Son of a bitch." Wyatt shook his hand out, grimacing. "That fucking *hurts*. I'm not gonna be able to play for like a week now."

"Idiot." Andie took Wyatt's injured hand and shoved it down in the beer bucket she was holding.

"Ow! Who are you calling an idiot? Me or Aaron?"

"Both of you."

Josh turned around finally, but his face was devoid of expression. There was nothing there but this awful, cold blankness that made Mia's chest ache.

No one had even asked him if he was okay, which was the only thing Mia cared about. Why weren't they asking him if he was okay?

She started to move toward him, then stopped herself,

feeling more like an outsider than ever. People didn't get into bar fights in the world she was accustomed to. They didn't get into any sort of physical altercations anywhere. They dealt with their hostilities like civilized adults—with passive-aggressive remarks, cold silences, and talking about one another behind their backs.

"He had it coming," Wyatt said. "Tell me he didn't have it coming."

Josh's gaze flicked to Mia, and for a second the blankness was replaced by raw anguish. She started toward him again, but he turned away from her to address his sister. "Can you please take Mia home?"

Andie looked over at her. Then back at Josh, giving him a nod. She thrust the ice bucket at Wyatt, brushing a quick kiss against his cheek before moving to Mia's side.

"Come on." She slung an arm around Mia's shoulders. "Let's go."

As Andie led her away, Mia threw one last look at Josh over her shoulder, but his gaze was fixed firmly on the ground.

Andie didn't say anything until they were in the car. "I swear to god, those fucking assholes." She threw the SUV into gear and spun out of the gravel parking lot. "One of these days I'm going to put my foot so far up all their anuses they'll have to shit through their noses."

"Who were they?" Mia still had no idea what had happened. She felt like she'd missed the first part of the movie and was lacking some important chunks of exposition.

Andie's jaw clenched. "No one. Just some local dickheads."

"What were they even talking about? What was all that Waldo stuff?"

"It's better that you don't know."

"What does *that* mean?" Mia was starting to freak out a little, in what was probably a delayed reaction to adrenaline. She'd just witnessed her first bar fight, which had been stressful enough, but the fact that she still didn't understand what it was about wasn't helping her calm down. She had the unsettling impression there was some big, mysterious secret about Josh that no one wanted to tell her. And the more they didn't want to tell her, the worse her mind imagined it to be.

Whatever it was that guy had been taunting him about, she assumed it was the reason Josh lived so much like a hermit. She wouldn't want to go out either if being jeered at like that was a regular occurrence.

Andie shook her head as she checked her rearview mirror. "It's nothing bad, I swear. It's stupid. It's one of those dumb, embarrassing things that only idiots like to laugh about. But people won't let it go, and Josh is really sensitive about it. Not that you can blame him when he has to deal with shit like that." She glanced over at Mia. "I'm sorry. I thought people would have gotten tired of it by now. I didn't think that would happen when I talked Josh into coming out tonight."

"Tired of *what*?"

Andie pressed her lips together. "I really don't want to tell you."

"Why?"

"Because Josh wouldn't want me to."

"But why? I don't understand."

"I'm asking you to trust me and leave it alone."

"Are you kidding?" How could Mia leave it alone when

she had so many unanswered questions? Especially when everyone else around her seemed to be in on the secret. There was no way she could forget about it. Was she supposed to act like nothing had happened the next time she saw Josh?

Assuming there was even a next time. After this, he might go back into hiding and never leave the farm at all.

"I *promise* you it's not bad," Andie said. "He's not a pervert, or a criminal, or whatever else you're worried about. I wouldn't keep something like that from you."

"Then what is he?" Mia asked.

"Just a regular guy who had a cruel trick played on him."

"Cruel how?"

Andie sighed. "Okay, look. Imagine something really embarrassing—like, say, your diary or a super sappy love letter you'd written—had been made public, and everyone you knew had seen you at your most vulnerable and all had a big laugh about it."

"Is that what happened?"

"No. But it was sort of like that." They'd reached Birdie's house, and Andie pulled into the driveway, rolling to a stop in front of the garage and putting the car in park. She didn't turn off the engine.

Mia stared out the window at Birdie's house. The lights were all off except for the back bedroom, which meant she was still awake. "Will Birdie tell me if I ask her?"

"I doubt it. She's even more protective of Josh than I am."

Mia unbuckled her seat belt and turned toward Andie. "You realize how unfair this is, right? Everyone knows but me."

"I'm sorry. I know it sucks. But if you knew, you'd understand."

Mia threw her hands up in frustration. "But I don't know!"

Andie's voice grew soft. "That's one of the reasons Josh likes you. Because when you look at him, you don't see his most embarrassing moment the way everyone else does."

Mia's brain filed away the information that Josh liked her, but it was hard to get excited about it because she didn't know who Josh really was. She couldn't, when she was missing what felt like a huge piece of information.

She stared at Andie and shook her head. "That's seriously all you're going to tell me?"

Andie sighed. "If you absolutely have to know more, you'll have to ask Josh yourself." She paused. "But if you care about him as much as I think you do, you won't ask him."

Mia gave up and got out of the car. Andie waited until she had gotten upstairs and unlocked the door. Then she backed out of the driveway, leaving Mia alone and frustrated and very confused.

Chapter Eleven

Josh visited Mia in her dreams that night.

In her dream, he knocked on the door of her apartment in the middle of the night. She answered in her rumpled, oversized T-shirt, not the least bit embarrassed for him to see her half-dressed.

He didn't speak, but his eyes told her everything she needed to know. What that was, exactly, was difficult to discern in the dream world, but it left her with a feeling of absolute trust in him.

She invited him inside without speaking herself. He entered, inexplicably barefoot, and shut the door behind him.

"I love you," he said, speaking at last. The roughness of his voice touched her like a warm caress.

"I know," she replied in the grand tradition of Han Solo.

Josh's gaze remained fixed on her face as he moved toward her with purpose. His hands slid into her hair, tilting her head as his mouth met hers. She melted into him, squeezing her eyes shut against the glaring light that seemed to have filled the room. She felt his arms envelop her like a blanket, wrapping her in his secure embrace.

Distantly, she was aware of another knock at the door,

but she refused to acknowledge it. She was too busy kissing Josh, who didn't seem to notice it. It was probably her imagination.

She kept on kissing Josh, letting her hands wander over his chest and shoulders, then down to his stomach. His hands meanwhile had traveled down her body to the hem of her T-shirt.

The knocking grew louder, and Mia's brain registered the fact that she was dreaming. But she didn't want to wake up. She'd rather stay in her dream. With Josh.

The knocking continued. Whoever was at her door clearly had no intention of letting that happen.

It occurred to her that it might be Josh, come to see her in real life and not just in her dream.

Mia jolted upright. Running a hand through her hair to tame it, she staggered out of bed, staring around her for something to wear. In desperation, she dragged on a pair of discarded work slacks and a cardigan before answering the door.

"Oh, I've gotten you out of bed," Birdie said.

"No, I was awake." Mia clutched her cardigan around herself, embarrassed to have been dragged out of a sex dream about Josh by his aunt.

"You've got some dried drool on your face."

"Shit," Mia blurted, scrubbing at her cheek, then felt bad for swearing. "Sorry."

Birdie smiled. "I thought you might like to come to my yoga class this morning."

"You take yoga?" This was new information to Mia, who couldn't imagine why Birdie would think she'd want to join her with no notice.

They hadn't had a conversation about it, had they? And she'd somehow forgotten? She racked her brain but could swear Birdie had never mentioned it before.

"I *teach* a yoga class," Birdie corrected. "Goat yoga. Every Saturday morning at ten."

"Goat yoga?" Mia rubbed her eyes, convinced she must have misheard her.

Birdie nodded. "That's right."

"What's goat yoga?"

"You practice yoga alongside goats." Birdie said it as if this was a perfectly normal and rational thing to do.

"And what do the goats do?" Mia asked.

"Stand around mostly. Sometimes they jump on you. Also, they poop. A lot, unfortunately."

"Why?" Mia was not awake enough for this conversation. The words Birdie was saying sounded nonsensical, like something your brain made up in a dream. Was it possible she was still asleep in bed and having another dream? She cast a nervous glance at her bed, but it was empty.

"All animals poop," Birdie said. "They can't help it."

Mia blinked at her. "No, I mean, why practice yoga with goats?"

"Because they're cute, I suppose. It's one of those fads everyone suddenly wants to get in on. My classes are booked up weeks in advance, mostly with people driving down from Austin." Birdie gave a shrug that seemed to say city folk were strange and incomprehensible, and in this case Mia had to agree. "I used to teach an afternoon yoga class at the community center, but when I heard about this goat yoga craze on NPR, I figured why not get in on it? I could offer goat yoga if people want to pay for goat yoga. And they do. Quite a lot, as it happens."

"Gwyneth Paltrow sells a vagina-scented candle for seventy-five dollars." It was a fact Mia regretted knowing.

"There you go," Birdie said with a nod.

"That's very entrepreneurial of you."

Birdie looked pleased. "I'm leaving in thirty minutes if you want to come. As my guest, free of charge."

"Ummmm . . ." Mia searched for a polite way to decline her generous offer to exercise in a barnyard while being pooped on.

"It's at Josh's farm," Birdie added.

"Oh?" Mia tried to sound offhand, although her interest had definitely been piqued.

A shrewd twinkle came into Birdie's eye. "If you wanted to see his farm, this would be your chance to do it."

Mia was far less interested in seeing the farm than she was in seeing Josh, and she had a feeling Birdie knew it. But there was no way she was passing up an opportunity like this. "Thirty minutes, you said?"

Birdie nodded, looking smug.

"I'll be ready," Mia told her. "Thank you for the invitation."

She was going to goat yoga.

More importantly, she was going to see Josh.

Mia tugged at the shelf bra in her yoga tank and cast an uncertain look at Birdie in the driver's seat beside her. She wanted to tell Birdie about the incident at the bar last night and ask her what Josh's big secret was. She was dying to do it, actually.

But she suspected Andie was right. Birdie wouldn't tell her. Not if it would hurt Josh somehow. And she couldn't help feeling Birdie might think less of her for even asking about it.

Ugh, what was she doing? Why was she so eager to throw herself into the middle of someone else's personal drama when her focus was supposed to be on her work?

Birdie glanced at Mia. "You all right, honey?"

Mia offered a weak smile. "Just a little sleepy still."

"Some exercise and fresh air will fix you right up, I promise." Birdie gave her an encouraging pat on the knee. "We've got to pick up my friend Renée on the way. You'll like her, she's a teacher like you."

Renée turned out to be a friendly Black woman around Birdie's age who lived a few streets away. Mia did like her, especially when she learned Renée taught trigonometry and pre-algebra at the local high school. For the rest of the drive, Mia peppered her with questions about the district's math curriculum, which Renée answered candidly, highlighting what she considered the curriculum's strengths and weaknesses, as well as the particular challenges they faced following state guidelines. It was an enlightening conversation, and Mia planned to use what she'd learned from Renée to tailor her approach to her own students, many of whom had come through the local school system.

"We're here," Birdie announced as she turned off an asphalt road onto a gravel one.

Mia had been so caught up in her conversation with Renée that she hadn't been paying attention to the scenery. But now she recognized the farm road they'd just left as the one where she'd gotten lost on her first visit to Crowder. The one where she'd first met Josh.

At the memory, her stomach gave a little lurch which was amplified as the car bounced over a cattle guard.

An artistic metal sign arching above the gate identified their destination as Redbud Farm. She pressed her forehead to the car window, curious to see where Josh lived and worked. Off to one side lay a broad field dotted with goats—the same kind of floppy-eared ones she'd met in the road. Some of them came over to the fence along the driveway, following the car's progress as if eager to see who'd come to visit.

Birdie pulled into a dirt clearing surrounded by fences. It was empty except for a lone dusty pickup truck sporting the same "Coexist" bumper sticker she'd noticed on a few cars around town, including Birdie's. On the other side of the fence stood a huge oak tree with a picnic table beneath its shady arms. Beyond it was a modest farmhouse with a wraparound porch. Arrayed to the side and behind it were barns and outbuildings of various sizes, materials, and ages—some shiny and new-looking while others were older and more rustic. A giant peace sign with a rainbow background had been painted on one of the older buildings, its colors slightly faded in the sun.

They got out and retrieved their yoga mats and water bottles from the back of the wagon. Birdie led them through a gate and around the side of the house, to an empty pen in a grassy field. Mia gazed around the farmyard, spying chickens, pigs, and a shaggy dog lolling in the sun. That was in addition to the goats, of course, who seemed to have free rein of the place. Some were milling around close to one of the big barns, while others grazed in a nearby pasture.

She hadn't set foot on a farm since . . . She searched her memory banks and decided it must have been an elementary school field trip to a pumpkin farm. Her parents certainly hadn't gone in for family apple-picking excursions upstate or other such things, like some of her school friends' families had.

This farm was somewhat less picturesque than that long-ago pumpkin farm that had been designed for tourists. Redbud Farm was clearly a working farm, meant to be practical rather than pretty. But it had its own sort of appeal.

The view was stunning, for one thing. Rolling green hills dotted with wildflowers stretched out under a wide blue sky as far as the eye could see. What a sight to wake up to every morning. Mia's gaze returned to the farmhouse, and she tried to imagine what it would have been like for Andie and Josh to grow up here.

Not so bad, she decided. It felt like a home. A place where a family lived.

Had lived.

Josh lived here alone now, she reminded herself. All this space for only one person. It seemed lonelier when she thought of it like that.

"You won't see him," Birdie said, coming up beside her.

"What?" Mia blinked at her, startled out of her thoughts.

"Josh. He never comes out while the class is here. He hates it." Birdie's mouth twisted into a satisfied smirk. "He didn't want to let me use his farm, but he couldn't bring himself to say no to me. So he stays out of sight until all the paying customers are gone."

A door slammed behind them, and Mia spun around, hoping Josh had come out after all.

A young man was coming toward them from the nearest barn, carrying a large plywood sign. Mia's heart sank when she saw it wasn't Josh. But as he drew nearer she realized she knew him.

"Antonio?" she said in surprise. He was one of her Calc I students. One of her best students, in fact, though he was still a little shy about speaking up in class.

Antonio grinned at her, appearing much more confident and relaxed than in class. "Hey, Dr. Ballentine. Fancy meeting you here." His gaze moved to Renée with a deferential head bob. "Morning, Mrs. Robbins."

Renée paused her warm-up exercises long enough to give him a wave as he passed by with the sign, which had been hand-painted with the words *GOAT YOGA*.

"Thank you, Antonio, you're a dear," Birdie called after him.

"He's one of my students." Mia watched him carry the sign out to the end of the drive. "Does he work here?"

Birdie nodded. "His father worked for Josh's dad, and now they both help Josh out around the place." She pointed out a small red house farther back on the property. "They live in that house back there. Ray, Antonio's father, is a sculptor. Metalworking, primarily. Josh let him convert one of the empty sheds into a studio."

As Antonio finished propping the sign against the fence, a car pulled into the drive.

"Oh, they're starting to arrive." Birdie rubbed her hands together gleefully, and Mia could swear she saw dollar signs shining in her eyes. "Better claim your spot."

Mia laid her mat out on the side of the pen farthest from the house, just in case Josh happened to look out one of his windows. She didn't relish the thought of him watching her try to do yoga while being pooped on by his goats.

As she slipped off her flip-flops and set them beside her mat, her gaze drifted to the goats grazing nearby with their giant udders hanging between their back legs. By Mia's estimate they had to weigh close to a hundred pounds. Surely Birdie had been kidding about the goats standing on you. They'd break your back if they tried it. Not to mention the gouges those hooves would leave behind.

More cars were pulling in now, and Antonio waved them into parking spaces and pointed the groups of spandex-clad women toward the field where they were setting up. Birdie greeted them, checking their names against a list on her phone, and showed them where to lay out their yoga mats.

Once they'd all arrived, she gave Antonio a thumbs-up, and he carried the sign back to the barn he'd emerged from. Birdie started off the class by telling them a little about the farm, including a plug for Josh's cheese, which she advised them could be purchased at the farmers' market in Austin.

She then proceeded to give a little orientation, letting them know what to expect from the goats. First of all, she said, goats liked to chew on things. That included hair, clothes, and shoes, apparently, and she advised all the long-haired women to tuck their hair into a bun. Then she told them about the pooping, which inspired a few wrinkled noses, but she assured them goat poop was clean and compact like rabbit pellets, and easily brushed away.

"Goats can't control their bowels," she explained, "so they can't be housebroken. They poop when they're comfortable, so take it as a compliment if they're comfortable enough to poop on you."

There was a chorus of nervous laughter among the gathered students.

"Other than that, you'll find goats are a lot like dogs. They can be shy of strangers at first, but eventually their curiosity will get the better of them and they'll come over to check you out. Let them approach at their own pace and you'll soon find yourself with a new best friend. They also love to climb and stand on high surfaces, so they'll jump on you if they get a chance."

Mia could only hope there were smaller goats somewhere that would be joining the class, because no way was she letting one of those milk-filled behemoths climb onto her back.

After she'd finished her orientation, Birdie started them out with some simple warm-up poses. Mia wasn't a big yoga aficionado, but she'd been to enough classes that she was easily able to keep up.

While they were moving through a series of sun salutations, Antonio emerged from the barn again with a small flock of baby goats at his heels. Everyone gave up on their warrior poses to exclaim over the adorable little things, who capered around Antonio, acutely interested in the bucket he carried. He coaxed them all into the pen and closed the gate behind him, leaving the bucket outside.

There were a dozen kids of varying sizes, most of them barely knee height. They milled around, snuffling at the grass as Birdie introduced them all by name. Like the goats Josh had introduced Mia to before, she recognized most of them as belonging to novelists. By the time Birdie had gone through all the names, the goats had begun to wander among the yoga mats, checking out the students, submitting to pets, and—yes—pooping.

There were a few horrified squeals and peals of laughter as the first yoga mats were fouled. But everyone quickly got used to flicking the poo away, which seemed a small price to pay for the opportunity to commune with such adorable and friendly creatures.

They really were like puppies, Mia marveled, as one of the kids climbed into her lap, begging for attention. Slobbery, bitey, lovable puppies. Its little tail wagged as she scratched its head, and it anointed her with several pellets of poop.

Once the goats and people had all gotten used to one another, Birdie started the class back up, leading them through a series of poses designed to give the goats plenty of surfaces to jump onto. As the students assumed tabletop, downward dog, and cobra pose, Antonio moved among them, plying the goats with treats to encourage them onto people's backs and behinds. There was a lot of laughter—a lot more laughter than actual yoga practice—but everyone seemed to be having a blast, including the goats.

Mia honestly couldn't remember when she'd had so much fun or laughed so hard, which was exactly what she'd needed today.

Birdie ended the class by having everybody line up, side by side in tabletop pose, while she and Antonio coaxed all the goats to leap from person to person along the ridge formed by their backs, and then underneath them through the tunnel made by their arms and legs. After that, everyone was given a handful of goat treats to dole out and an opportunity to cuddle the goats for the next ten minutes until the hour was up.

"Guess I don't have to ask if you enjoyed yourself," Birdie

commented, joining Mia after the last of the students had been pried away from the goats.

Mia looked up from the goat she was petting. Her name was Zadie, and she was Mia's favorite. "I have to admit I was skeptical, but it was so much fun."

"Yeah, there's something to it." Birdie smiled. "Gives you a real serotonin release."

"I guess I should probably say goodbye to this little one now." Mia picked Zadie up and gave her a hug. The little goat snuggled into her and then proceeded to pee all over her chest.

Mia yelped as warm goat urine soaked into the front of her yoga top. She held Zadie away from her, but the damage had already been done.

"Oh dear." Birdie covered her mouth to smother a laugh.

Antonio didn't bother to hide his amusement. "She really must like you."

"Great." Mia set the goat down and examined her pee-covered top. "That's fantastic."

Of course that was the moment when Josh came out of the house. When Mia was covered in fresh goat pee.

Of course it was.

He lifted his hand in greeting as he came toward them, stopping outside the fence that surrounded the yoga pen. "How'd it go?" The corner of his mouth twitched as he took in Mia and her wet shirt.

"I got peed on." She tried to hold the damp fabric away from her skin. "Other than that, it was really fun."

All the kids had gone over to greet Josh, clamoring for his attention and trying to jump up on the fence to get at him.

He leaned over to pet them. "Pee happens when you handle animals."

"Do you think you could take Mia inside to clean up?" Birdie suggested. "And maybe loan her a clean shirt."

"Sure, I can do that." Josh straightened and inclined his head toward the house. "Come on, I'll get you squared away." He didn't seem unwilling, but neither did he betray any sense that he was especially happy to see her. He didn't betray anything at all, as per frustrating usual. The man was like a sentient android without an emotion chip sometimes.

Which possibly went a long way to explaining Mia's fixation on him, given her longstanding crush on Data from *Star Trek: The Next Generation.* Apparently she was doomed to fall for emotionally unavailable men.

Mia let herself out of the goat pen and fell into step beside Josh as he headed back to the house.

"I'm sure she'd love a tour of the farm while you're at it," Birdie called after them.

Josh glanced over at Mia, his expression dry as ever. "Is she right? Would you love a tour of the farm?"

"I wouldn't want to be an imposition," she said, feeling like Birdie had put him on the spot. "But if you've got time, then yes, I'd love to see the farm."

"I can probably squeeze you in." As he held the screen door open, gesturing for her to precede him inside the house, he allowed the faintest hint of a smile to curve his lips. "But first, let's get you out of those clothes."

Chapter Twelve

Mia did her best to wash all the pee off in Josh's downstairs half bathroom. He'd provided her with a clean washcloth, towel, and a bar of what smelled like Zest soap, as well as one of his T-shirts to change into. She scrubbed her chest and stomach until the skin turned pink, then washed her pits for good measure. An hour of yoga in the Texas heat had left her sweaty and a little stinky, even before the eau de goat urine.

She peeked inside the medicine cabinet, hoping to find some deodorant, but it was empty except for a bottle of aspirin and a box of tampons.

Who were the tampons for? Could Josh have a girlfriend? It seemed unlikely that Andie wouldn't have mentioned it before now.

Possibly an ex had left them behind. Or even Andie herself. She did used to live here, and probably still visited sometimes.

It doesn't matter. Mia shut the medicine cabinet. Whoever the tampons belonged to was no business of hers. She had more pressing problems . . . like the state of her hair.

Not only was it sweat-soaked and disheveled from exercising in the sun, but there were sticky patches of what could only be goat spit.

Super attractive.

Scrunching her nose, she tried to run her fingers through her gunky hair. Gross. It was a miracle Josh had even admitted her to his house in her current disgusting state. No wonder he hadn't seemed thrilled about it.

Dunking her head under the faucet, Mia did her best to rinse most of the goat saliva out. After toweling off her head, she combed her hair back into place with her fingers. That was the beauty of short hair at least—easy wash-and-go style. She wouldn't be winning any beauty contests, but at least she was no longer actively repulsive.

The T-shirt Josh had left was a soft charcoal gray with the farm's logo on it. She slipped it on, feeling better as soon as the fresh detergent scent enveloped her.

Once she'd made herself as presentable as possible she slipped out of the bathroom, carrying her wet yoga top, which she'd done her best to clean in the sink. She found Josh in the kitchen, pouring two glasses of iced tea.

"Is there somewhere I can hang this to dry?" she asked, holding up the wad of damp fabric in her hands.

His gaze lingered on her, taking in the sight of her in his shirt before he answered. "You can drape it over the front porch railing."

"Thanks." She stepped onto the porch and found her yoga mat and water bottle sitting beside the door. Someone must have brought them over from the pen where she'd left them. As she draped her top over the porch rail, she noticed the parking area was now empty except for the one lone pickup truck.

Birdie's car was gone.

Mia went back inside the house. "Where's Birdie?"

Josh handed her a glass of iced tea. "She left."

"Is she coming back?"

"Not as far as I know."

Mia wrapped both hands around the cold iced tea glass. "How am I supposed to get home?"

"I think she assumed I'd drive you."

"Oh." Mia blinked. "I didn't realize—"

"I can take you now if you're in a hurry to get back."

"No, I'm not in a hurry." She bit her lip. "I just don't want to be an inconvenience."

"You're not an inconvenience."

Those four simple words, spoken with a matter-of-factness that left no doubt of their truth, sent a flush of warmth coursing through her. Mia had spent a lot of her life feeling like she was in the way. A burden. Unwanted. Trying to mitigate the imposition of her presence by making herself smaller, more invisible.

But Josh had just told her that wasn't necessary. He made it sound like he actually wanted her here. Coming from him, she took it as a high compliment.

"I was thinking I could make us some lunch and then do the tour after." His eyelashes lowered and for a second he looked almost shy. "If you like."

Mia smiled. "I'd like that a lot."

Josh made them sandwiches. Thick slices of wholegrain bread slathered with herbed goat cheese (of course) and piled high with tomatoes, cucumbers, and avocados.

"How'd you like Birdie's goat yoga class?" he asked after they sat down to eat at the round oak table in the kitchen. It was a cheerful space with a long butcher-block island and a bay window accented by fabric shades in a bright floral pattern.

"It wasn't what I expected." Mia wiped a stray smear of cheese off her lip. "I'll be honest—it sounded crazy when Birdie described it, but I ended up having a lot of fun."

"It's hard not to fall in love with the kids."

Mia smiled ruefully. "Until they pee on you."

"I've been peed on plenty of times, believe me." Josh's gaze dropped to her borrowed shirt.

Profoundly conscious of the fact that she wasn't wearing a bra, Mia reached for her iced tea as she felt her face heat. "Don't you think it's twisted that people convince children there's a fairy who sneaks into their room while they're asleep to steal their teeth?"

Josh stared at her, blinking in confusion, and she realized she'd done that thing again where she jumped from one subject to another without warning.

"Sorry." She shook her head. "The goat that peed on me is named Zadie, which I assume is for Zadie Smith, whose debut novel was *White Teeth*, which made me think of the tooth fairy. It all made sense in my brain."

He smiled. "I guess the tooth fairy is pretty dark when you think about it."

Mia looked down at her plate, embarrassed. Why couldn't she just have a normal conversation like normal people did? Instead of randomly bringing up teeth over lunch.

"Although she doesn't steal them," Josh continued thoughtfully. "She leaves money behind, so it's a financial transaction. You could make a case that it's meant to indoctrinate children into capitalism the moment they start to leave infancy behind."

Mia looked up at him. "Are you saying the tooth fairy is capitalist propaganda?"

He shrugged. "You could make a case for it."

She smiled, and he smiled back at her. He had the most incredible smile when he cared to show it. It reminded her of a sunbeam breaking through a cloudy sky. Warm and sweet and a little lopsided. But then as she watched, the clouds rolled back in.

"Listen, I . . ." He paused, shifting in his seat. "I owe you an apology for last night." It clearly pained him to raise the subject.

"It wasn't your fault." She almost reached for his hand, but the look on his face stopped her.

"I'm sorry anyway that you had to see it."

"I don't really understand what happened." She paused, hoping he'd volunteer an explanation, but he looked away and said nothing. "Andie wouldn't tell me what it was about," she continued. "Or why that guy was hassling you like that."

Josh got up and cleared away their empty plates, leaving her implied question unanswered. Mia waited while he put them in the sink. With his back turned, she could see the lines of tension radiating through his shoulders and neck.

She thought about the last thing Andie had said: *If you care about him as much as I think you do, you won't ask him.*

Mia did care about him. The thought of causing him more distress kept her from demanding an answer outright.

Finally, he came and sat down again. Forced himself to look her in the eye. "If you ask me, I'll tell you." His expression was pained but also resigned. Sadly so.

"I have to ask?"

He nodded.

"You can't just tell me?"

His jaw clenched. "It's humiliating." He lowered his gaze, focusing on a random spot on the table. "Someone I thought I could trust played a cruel trick on me a few years ago. She made something public that should have been between us. Made me a laughingstock."

Mia's mind raced through different possibilities, trying to imagine what it could have been. Like a diary or a love letter, Andie had said. But something else.

Nude photos, maybe. Or screenshots of a text conversation. A *dirty* text conversation.

All the likeliest scenarios seemed to involve sex. When else were we more vulnerable than when we were being intimate with another person? Mia thought about all the celebrity nude leaks, phone hacks, and revenge porn incidents that were forever making the news, and the glee with which people seemed to latch onto the sordid details of someone else's sex life.

Of course it could have been something else. A secret about himself that he'd shared in confidence. Something that people might hold against him in a closed-minded small town.

Mia had a sudden thought—one she perhaps should have considered sooner. "You're not gay, are you? Or . . . something else?" There was a whole spectrum of related possibilities, but she didn't want to start taking stabs in the dark. "Because it's fine if you are," she hastened to add.

Except for the part where I got my hopes up for nothing. Could she have read him so wrong? Possibly. It seemed like he'd been giving off encouraging signals, but it certainly wouldn't be the first time she'd made *that* mistake.

He met her eye. "I'm not gay. I wouldn't be ashamed if that's what it was."

"Okay." Mia tried not to look relieved.

Not barking up the wrong tree after all. Whew.

He'd said it was a "she" who'd betrayed his trust, so her mind leaped to the next logical conclusion. "Was it an ex-girlfriend who did it?"

He nodded. "She got angry when I broke up with her and decided to get revenge in a very public way. Pretty much everyone I know saw it, and people around here have long memories." The scowl on his face made her stomach clench in sympathy. "Just when I start to think maybe everyone's finally forgotten about it, someone like Aaron makes sure to remind 'em."

Mia gave in to the instinct to reach for his hand. "I don't care what some drunk jerk like that thinks of you."

Josh let her interlace her fingers with his on the tabletop. "I appreciate that. I know I shouldn't let it bother me so much, but I guess I've got too much pride. It's hard to face people when you know all they're thinking about is the most embarrassing thing that's ever happened to you. So I end up keeping to myself a lot. Too much, probably."

It tore her heart open to see him so vulnerable and in so much pain. What kind of person could do something like that to him? Mia wasn't ordinarily prone to homicidal thoughts, but seeing Josh like this engaged her protective instincts and made her want to do brutal, violent things to the woman who'd hurt him.

His eyes fell closed for a second, and when they opened

again he seemed more even-keeled. "But I don't want you to think I'm hiding anything." He met her gaze steadily. "So I'll tell you all the sorry details if you want me to."

Mia didn't want to know anymore. Not after everything he'd already told her and after seeing how hard it was for him to talk about it. He'd offered to tell her and that was enough of a show of trust. More than enough. She didn't need him to rip open the wound all over again to satisfy her curiosity.

"Don't tell me." She squeezed his hand. "It doesn't matter anyway. I don't need to know." Whatever embarrassing incident haunted him, it wouldn't change what she thought of him. It couldn't change how she felt.

He looked so relieved she wanted to cry. "Thanks for letting me off the hook."

"Whatever." She shrugged like it was nothing. "I've already forgotten about it. What were we talking about again?"

He looked down at their hands and smiled. "Do you want that tour of the farm now?"

"Do I get to see how you make cheese?"

"If you want."

She tapped her lips, pretending to deliberate over it. "And is there a cheese-tasting included in this tour?"

"There can be," he said, his smile growing even wider.

"Then heck yeah I do."

They exited the house by the back door, where they were met by the dog Mia had seen earlier. Her name was Biscuit and she was a foster, Josh explained. While Mia was petting her, they were joined by two other dogs, who snuffled at her, wagging their tails.

"And here's Smoky and Clyde," Josh said. "They're supposed to keep predators away from the goats, but they mostly just sleep and beg for treats."

Mia had never been allowed so much as one dog. Three dogs seemed like an unimaginable bounty of dogs. Josh waited patiently while she got her fill of petting them. When she was thoroughly covered in dog hair they moved on, and he showed her the vegetable garden where he grew a lot of his own food.

"Are your chickens . . . dead?" Mia asked fearfully when she spotted several of them lying on their sides in the yard nearby with their feet sticking out at odd angles. She'd never seen Birdie's chickens lie on the ground like that.

Josh laughed. "No, they're just sunning." Sure enough, as they drew nearer, the dead chickens hopped to their feet and started walking around, perfectly alive.

While he was showing Mia the chicken coop he and his father had built together, one of the chickens came over and pecked at her toenail polish.

"Ow!" she yelped, jerking her foot back.

Josh made a shooing motion to drive the chicken away. "That's one of several reasons why you always wear closed-toe shoes on a farm."

"I thought I was just coming to yoga," Mia said. "I wouldn't have worn flip-flops if I'd known I was going to be attacked by tiny, feathered velociraptors."

Smiling, Josh took her hand and they strolled over to the pigpen, where six huge hogs were lying in the sun. When he leaned on the fence, two of them got up and waddled over to greet him. Mia had never seen pigs that large up close, but she decided they were still pretty cute despite their intimidating size.

"Is it true that pigs are the smartest domesticated animal?" she asked.

Josh nodded as he bent down to pat one of them. "They make their own latrine area to keep their food from getting contaminated, and they have excellent long-term memories. People have even taught them to play video games."

"What do you do with the pigs?" She had a feeling she wouldn't like the answer.

"Send them for processing once they reach full size."

"Processing . . . to be eaten?"

Josh glanced over his shoulder at her. "Does that upset you?" There was no judgment or ridicule in his question. He merely seemed curious.

"A little," she admitted. "If I let myself think about it. I'm not used to looking my food in the eye." She'd flirted with vegetarianism in college, but in the end she'd liked bacon and hamburgers too much to give it up for good.

Josh nodded. "When you get your food at grocery stores and restaurants, you don't have to think about where it comes from or what it took to get it in front of you."

"How do you keep from getting attached?"

"Who says I don't get attached?" he said, shooting her a sideways glance.

"But you can still raise pigs to be butchered for food?"

He pushed himself upright and wiped his hand on his jeans. "I can't afford to let anything go to waste if I want to keep the farm afloat. I need the pigs to eat the whey leftover from making the cheese so I can sell the pigs and use that money to pay for feed for the goats."

"It's an interdependent system," Mia said. "If one part of the system breaks down, the whole thing fails."

Josh nodded. "Exactly."

"You don't ever get tempted to keep one as a pet?"

"That's a thousand-dollar pig you're looking at."

Mia stared at the pig with newfound respect. "So that's a no, then."

"That's a no."

After they moved on from the pigs, he led her inside the large doe barn. That was where all the youngest kids were, in a pen all their own. Beside it was another pen for the does who were about to give birth. The rest of the barn was a big communal loafing area where the goats could wander freely in and out to eat hay from a long manger.

The goats followed Josh around the same way the dogs did, nosing their way under his hands begging for pets. It was utterly adorable, the way all the animals vied for his attention like he was their human dad.

The goats nosed at Mia too, and as she petted them Josh rattled off their names for her. *Octavia. Eudora. Shirley. Madeleine. Dorothy. Willa. Pearl.*

She was impressed he could not only tell the goats apart but remember all their names. "What are you going to do when you run out of authors?"

"Scientists," he answered without hesitation.

"What about mathematicians?" she asked.

"Them too." He flashed her a smile. "You can give me a list if you want."

A covered walkway from the doe barn led to a separate building where the goats were milked. "The goats hate rain,"

Josh explained. "The cover makes it easier to coax them into the milking parlor on rainy days."

Inside the milking room were rows of aluminum platforms for the goats to stand on. The milking was done by machine while the goats were fed grain to keep them happy and distracted.

Mia eyed the suction tubes connected to long hoses. "Does it hurt them?"

"They seem okay with it," Josh said. "It hurts them a lot less than not milking them, which can cause a lot of discomfort, not to mention infections like mastitis."

Next door to the milking parlor was the part of the tour Mia was most excited about: the cheese kitchen.

Inside they found Ray, who'd just returned from the farmers' market in Austin and was unloading a big Igloo cooler. Josh made the introductions and explained that Ray was his right-hand man who, along with his son Antonio, helped him keep the farm running.

"I teach math at the university," Mia said as she peered into the large walk-in fridge where Ray was putting away leftover stock. "Antonio's in my calculus class."

"I hope he works hard," Ray said.

"He does. He's one of my top students."

Ray looked pleased.

The fridge shelves were full of different kinds of cheeses—some packaged in plastic containers and others wrapped in butcher paper. At the back stood a rolling rack that held at least a dozen uncovered wheels of cheese. Mia's mouth watered at the sight of all that naked cheese sitting around, begging to be eaten.

"How'd we do this morning?" Josh asked.

"Good," Ray said. "I sold out of the cajeta."

"I should make more. We're running low." Josh eyed the stock Ray was returning to the fridge. "Looks like the cracked pepper chèvre isn't selling."

"It's the least popular. You should think about replacing it with one of the new ones you've been experimenting with."

"I will when we run out of labels. The question is which one?"

Ray finished emptying his cooler and came out of the fridge. "You know my vote."

"The Anaheim chili?"

"That's it." Ray smiled at Mia on the way out the door. "It was nice meeting you."

After Ray was gone, Josh shoved his hands in the back pockets of his jeans and gazed around the kitchen. "Anyway, this is where I make the cheese. I'm afraid it's not very exciting."

It looked a lot like a typical commercial kitchen. There were stainless steel prep counters and sinks, a stove, a heavy-duty mixer, and of course the large walk-in fridge that held a veritable treasure trove of cheese.

"Do you make it all yourself?" Mia asked.

Josh nodded. "Most weekdays I let Ray handle the morning milking while I'm in here making yogurt or cheese. It takes a few hours to pasteurize, cool, and culture the milk, then I've got to scoop and drain the curd, and later there's the salting and packaging. It all varies depending on the product I'm making."

She liked listening to him talk about cheesemaking. There was something incredibly sexy about the air of comfortable authority he got when he was talking about something he was good at. "How many kinds of cheese do you make?" she asked so he'd keep talking.

"Depends on the season. I'm always experimenting and swapping them out. There's usually about five different flavors of chèvre at any given time. That plus the feta, yogurt, and cajeta all sell well at the farmers' market. The soft-ripened and aged cheeses I mostly sell to a few cheese shops and grocery stores in Austin. Right now, I've got a Crottin, a Sainte-Maure, and an Añejo. I've been experimenting with a bleu, but I'm not satisfied with it yet."

Mia didn't know what all of those cheeses were, but she was dying to find out. She rubbed her palms together in greedy anticipation. "Do I get to taste some or what?"

Josh's mouth quirked in amusement. "As soon as we wash our hands."

Sound advice after they'd petted so many animals. He showed her which sink to use, and they both lathered up their hands and dried them on paper towels.

When they were done, he went to the fridge and heaved the heavy door open. "Do you have a favorite kind of cheese?"

"All of them?"

Josh threw a look over his shoulder, one dark eyebrow arching to say she wasn't being helpful. But beneath the feigned exasperation, his gaze held a warmth that sent Mia's heart skittering in her chest.

Josh came back with an armful of different cheeses for her to try. He got out knives and crackers, and cut samples of every kind of cheese for her. As she tasted each one, he explained the origin of it and a little about the process involved in making it.

Mia's favorite ended up being the Crottin, a nutty aged cheese with a rippled rind.

"It's not too strong for you?" Josh seemed surprised she liked it so much.

"No, not at all. I like complex flavors."

"The longer a cheese ages, the more character it develops."

She popped another sliver of Crottin in her mouth. "Like people."

A smile hovered on his lips. "This one's about two weeks old, but it can age for a lot longer, depending on how strong you want it to get. The body of the cheese will become drier and denser as it loses moisture, and the flavor will become more robust and full-bodied."

"I love it when you talk cheese." She was practically drooling, she was so turned on by his cheese talk.

"You do?" He looked skeptical. "It's not boring?"

"No, it's totally sexy." She hadn't meant to say *sexy*. It had slipped out in place of a more innocuous word like *fascinating*. But it was true. And now it was out there and there was no taking it back.

Josh's eyebrows lifted. "Is that right?"

Mia swallowed, refusing to break eye contact.

He gazed at her for a charged moment, his dark eyes thoughtful and intent. She wondered if he was about to kiss her. Were they allowed to kiss in here? Would it be some sort of health code violation? Sex was probably a major no-no in food prep areas, but what about an innocent kiss?

Or a not-so-innocent one, even.

Josh turned, breaking the spell, and reached up to retrieve a jar from the cabinet. "You should try the cajeta. It goes surprisingly well with a strong cheese."

Mia sucked in a breath, feeling dizzy. "What's cajeta?"

"It's a Mexican caramel. Like dulce de leche but made with goat's milk." He twisted the lid off the jar and held it out to her. "Try it."

Their fingers brushed as she took the jar from him, sending a shower of electricity zipping down her spine. "Do I just use my finger?"

"I can get you a spoon if you prefer." His voice was teasing, like he was daring her.

"No, it's fine." She dipped her finger in the dark, creamy syrup and popped it in her mouth. Her eyes fell closed, and she couldn't help moaning a little as the flavor settled on her tongue. "Oh wow, that's amazing."

It was sweet and rich, with a hint of the tartness characteristic of goat's milk. Josh was right, the flavor complemented the Crottin perfectly, the same way honey and blue cheese made a perfect match.

When Mia opened her eyes again, he was staring at her with a smile curving his mouth. She licked the caramel off her lips, and his pupils grew wider.

Slowly, he reached up and settled his fingers under the curve of her jaw. She inhaled a shuddering breath as his thumb stroked across her lower lip, catching a stray smudge of cajeta. Without breaking eye contact, he lifted his thumb to his lips and licked the caramel off.

It was so erotic that Mia's knees threatened to buckle beneath her.

Josh watched her carefully, his gaze steady and unblinking. He was close enough that she could feel the heat radiating off him, mingling with her own elevated temperature. So close he could probably sense her trembling.

His lips only a whisper away from hers.

She felt herself sway, and his hands grasped her hips. Squeezing. Pulling her gently closer until their noses brushed.

His head tilted, and she closed her eyes.

Pleasure rolled through her as his lips met hers in the sweetest of kisses. Soft as a whisper. Barely any pressure at all, and yet enough to send a shock of arousal through her nervous system. Like touching a live wire.

She whimpered, craving more of that raw electricity. At the sound, he seemed to hesitate, but she slid a hand around the back of his neck, pulling him closer. Her mouth pressed against his, and he responded the way she'd hoped he would.

Cupping her face in both his hands, he teased her lips apart with the tip of his tongue. His mouth tasted sweet and salty, rich and dark. Mia melted against him, losing herself in the sensation as Josh's thumbs swept over her cheekbones, his thick calluses dragging across her skin with the best sort of friction.

Desire pulsed through her veins like a drumbeat. Her fingers curled into his hair, pulling him closer. Their bodies pressed together as he claimed her with his mouth, every demanding sweep of his tongue increasing the pressure building between her thighs.

A loud crack of thunder rattled the windows, startling them apart.

The sky had clouded over outside while they'd been lost in each other. The steady patter Mia had blamed on her heartbeat was actually rain. Heavy rain.

Josh regarded her with slightly glassy eyes. His face looked flushed, and she realized he was trembling almost as much as she was. He shut his eyes for a moment like he was pulling himself together. No longer did he seem confident and unfazed. He looked more like a man on the verge of losing control. A man who could make an absolute mess of her if she let him.

But then he opened his eyes and seemed more like himself. Contained. Whatever lay hidden beneath his serene surface had been safely put back in the bottle.

Pity.

Lightning streaked across the sky, and he strode to the door and pulled it open. Rain pelted the ground outside, rattling on the metal roof of the walkway. A gust of moist air blew into the room as another crash of thunder boomed.

Moving behind him, Mia peered out the door at the rain-drenched farmyard. "Will the animals be okay? Do you need to do anything for them?"

"They've all got shelter. They're fine."

The wind blew a spray of rain at them, and he closed the door again, turning toward her. Their eyes caught and held, both of them conscious of what they had been doing moments before. Involuntarily, her gaze dropped to his mouth.

"We can try to wait out the storm here," he said. "Or we can make a run for the house."

"How long do you think it will last?"

He pulled out his phone and thumbed through his apps. His brows drew together. "Looks like a few hours at least."

Mia glanced around the cheese kitchen with all its cold, hard surfaces. Ample supply of cheese notwithstanding, it wasn't the most comfortable place to hang out for a few hours. "Make a run for it?" she suggested.

He nodded. "All right, then. Get ready to get soaked."

Chapter Thirteen

Josh held Mia's hand as they splashed across the yard—until one of her flip-flops got stuck in the mud. Then he surprised her by picking her up, throwing her over his shoulder, and carrying her and her errant flip-flops the rest of the way to the house.

Mia was still laughing and protesting when he deposited her on the back porch, and she clutched at his arms—his strong, capable arms—for balance while she caught her breath.

A smile tilted his lips as his gaze settled on her rain-streaked face, and he reached up to push a lock of damp hair off her forehead. His eyes had gone soft and liquid in a way that made her knees feel weak. She lowered her gaze and quickly got distracted by his wet shirt pulling tight across his broad chest.

"Stay here," he said—unnecessarily, since her legs were incapable of taking her anywhere just then. "I'll go get us some towels."

He took off his muddy boots before he went into the house. While he was gone, Mia sat on the porch steps and let the rain wash the mud off her feet and legs. A minute later,

THE INFATUATION CALCULATION

Josh came back with an armful of mismatched towels and draped one around her shoulders.

Once they'd dried themselves off as best they could with their clothes still soaking wet, he led her through the tiled kitchen and up the family-photo-lined staircase. Mia waited outside his bedroom, taking in the plain navy comforter and unadorned walls while he dug in a dresser for yet another clean T-shirt for her to borrow, along with a pair of sweatpants.

Then he led her to a bathroom down the hall and left her alone to get cleaned up. It was a Jack and Jill style bathroom that connected the two spare bedrooms, which she presumed had belonged to him and Andie growing up. Finding the shower stocked with essentials, she helped herself to a quick shampoo to wash away the last traces of goat spit and mud from the morning's adventures.

Five minutes later, feeling considerably fresher, she emerged from the bathroom attired in the sweatpants and Texas A&M T-shirt Josh had loaned her. She heard his voice downstairs and followed the sound to the kitchen, where she found him at the back door talking to Ray.

The rain continued to pour down in buckets outside. Josh was barefoot and looking unfairly sexy as he stood inside the door in fresh jeans and a clean T-shirt. Ray stayed back on the steps, attired for the weather in a dripping cowboy hat, rubber boots, and a long yellow rain slicker. When he caught sight of Mia, he touched the brim of his hat in greeting.

Josh threw a glance over his shoulder and thanked Ray before bidding him goodbye.

"Is everything okay?" Mia asked as Josh closed the kitchen door.

"Fine. Ray was just letting me know he'd checked on all the animals." He moved to the sink. "Do you want some coffee? I was about to make a pot."

"I'd love some." The rain had taken the edge off the heat outside, and the damp had left her feeling chilled in the air-conditioned house. She lingered at the edge of the kitchen, admiring the rear view while Josh started the coffee. The strong, broad lines of his shoulders formed a perfect V as they narrowed to an ass that looked like a million bucks in his old Levi's.

"How long have you lived here by yourself?" she asked.

"A little over three years now. Since my parents retired."

"Birdie said they moved to Maine?"

He nodded as he scooped coffee grounds into the filter basket. "They stuck around for a few years after I came back from college. Just to make sure I could handle the place on my own before they retired."

Once he'd started the coffee brewing, he indicated they should go into the living room. Mia peered around curiously as she followed him. Most of the furnishings seemed to be old—left there by his parents, she assumed.

"Why Maine?" she asked. It seemed like an odd choice for retirement—somewhere a million miles away from Crowder, Texas. But maybe that was the point.

Josh sank down at one end of a worn leather couch. "It's where my dad's family is from. He inherited a house up there from his parents."

Mia claimed the other end of the couch. A crocheted blanket lay draped over the back of it, and she ran her hand over the multicolored wool loops, admiring the intricate pattern. "Do they like it?"

"They seem to." Josh's mouth curved in a wry smile. "I think they're both relieved not to be milking goats anymore."

She could only imagine, after doing it twice a day every day for twenty-plus years. "But you like it? Running the farm by yourself?"

"I'm not by myself. I've got Ray and Antonio. I wouldn't be able to keep this place running without them."

She noticed he'd sidestepped the question of whether he actually liked it, but she didn't press him on it. "What are Antonio's plans after college? Stay here and work on the farm with his father?"

"I don't know. I'm not sure he knows yet, but he's still got time to figure it out. I guess we'll see in three years what he decides to do." Josh's gaze settled on Mia, lingering in a way that made her mouth feel dry. "What about you? Did you always want to be a mathematician?"

"Always. Ever since I was old enough to know what a mathematician was."

"Why?"

"Because math makes sense to me, more than most other things in the world do. Certainly more than people do." She glanced down at her lap self-consciously.

"Math follows rules," he said. "People, not so much."

She darted a look at him, pleased that he seemed to understand. "Exactly."

His brow creased as if he was thinking hard. "Math never made all that much sense to me, but I can see how it would be appealing if you had a gift for it. Like that knot you're working on. Being able to take something complex like that and break it down to its component parts until you've untangled it. Imposing order on chaos." He winced apologetically. "That probably sounds dumb."

"No, not at all." She smiled at him. "That's exactly what it's like."

"How's that going? Have you cracked it yet?"

Her smile faded and she looked down at her lap again. "Not yet. It's probably time to give up and move on to something else. My ambitions may have been too lofty for my abilities."

"I don't believe that. Some things just take time. Maybe you're putting too much pressure on yourself."

"Maybe." She rubbed at a tiny snag in the borrowed sweatpants she was wearing. "The problem is I don't have infinite time. I need to publish something soon. If it's not going to be this, it'll have to be something else."

"I'm sure you'll figure it out."

She looked up. His eyes were so clear and bright, his expression so absolutely certain, she could almost believe he was right.

The coffee maker beeped in the kitchen, and he pushed himself to his feet. "Stay put," he said when she tried to follow. "How do you take your coffee?"

She requested cream and he went into the kitchen. While he was gone, her gaze wandered to the window. Rain spattered against the glass, turning the world outside to a smeary gray haze. It didn't look likely to let up anytime soon.

This was the first rain they'd had since Mia had moved here over a month ago. Before today, she'd heard several people remark on the drought conditions that had necessitated a burn ban in the county. It was one of the few things that had felt familiar to her after moving from Los Angeles.

"It's a real gully washer." Josh held a steaming hot mug in front of her.

She thanked him for the coffee. "Does it rain like this a lot?"

He settled onto the couch again with his own mug. "I wouldn't say a lot. We don't get a ton of rain in general. But when it does finally rain, it can sometimes feel like it's trying to make up for lost time."

They both fell silent as they sipped their coffee and listened to the rain beating against the house. Mia slid a sideways look at Josh, admiring his strong profile and the way his dark hair had curled slightly as it dried. He raised his mug to his lips, and she was reminded of the way those lips had felt on hers. The way his large hands had cradled her face.

He glanced over and caught her staring at him. "Coffee okay?"

"It's great, thanks." She felt her cheeks redden and looked away.

The couch shuddered as he shifted position, turning to face her more. "What do you think of Crowder now that you've been here a while?"

She lifted her coffee to her lips as she tried to decide how honest she should be. "It's not what I expected."

"How so?" He lounged back against the cushions with his mug resting on his knee.

She considered her words carefully. "I'd always heard that people were friendly in Texas, but I guess I hadn't really understood what that meant."

"Not everyone's friendly all the time." His tone held a note of warning—and more than a little bitterness.

"No, but the people who are—like Birdie and Andie . . ."

She met his gaze pointedly. "... and you—have gone out of your way to make me feel welcome here. It's made the transition easier."

"But still not easy." He was too perceptive. He'd called it the first time he'd ever laid eyes on her. She'd been lost then, and she was still lost now, despite her attempts to pretend otherwise.

All the friendliness in the world couldn't change the fact that she didn't fit in here and didn't particularly want to. This wasn't where she wanted to be—geographically or professionally. Since she'd arrived, she'd felt like she was spinning her wheels. Moving backward instead of forward. With each passing day, her goals felt a little farther out of reach.

She inclined her head. "I'd be lying if I said this job was my first choice."

"I guessed as much. Not many people are dying to move to Crowder."

"You moved here. Back here, I mean. After college."

"That was always the plan." He drained the last of his coffee and got to his feet. "You want some more?"

She shook her head, and he carried his mug into the kitchen. This time she followed him. "Whose plan was it?" she asked. "Yours or your parents'?"

"Both." He set his mug in the sink and turned around, resting his hands on the edge of the counter. "It's all I've ever wanted to do. Run the farm and make cheese. Ever since I can remember. Just like you and math. It felt like my calling."

Her hands tightened around her own mug. "And now that you're doing what you wanted? Are you happy?" She genuinely wanted to know, after chasing her own dreams for so long, if finally getting what you'd worked for was all it was cracked up to be.

He appeared to consider his answer carefully. "Can anyone truthfully say yes to that question? Happy's a state of mind that changes as much as the weather. Am I happy every day? No. But I guess I'm content." He paused. "Mostly."

It was on the tip of Mia's tongue to ask what was lacking, what would make his contentment complete. But before she could say anything, his phone rang.

He fished it out of his pocket and smiled at the screen before holding it to his ear. "Hey, Birdie. What's up?" His gaze flicked to Mia. "No, she's still here."

As he listened to his aunt speak, Mia finished the last of her coffee and leaned around him to put her mug in the sink.

His gaze followed her as she entered his personal space, but he didn't move away. "Sure," he said into the phone. "Yeah."

She could hear Birdie's voice on the other end, but not well enough to make out what she was saying. She seemed to be talking an awful lot.

Josh's expression told her nothing. "Okay." He rubbed the phone against his temple. "I will." Pause. "Sure." And finally: "Okay, you be careful. Thanks for calling."

"Is everything all right?" Mia asked as he disconnected the call.

"Fine." He shoved the phone back in his pocket. "She was calling to let us know her street's flooded."

"Oh no! Is she okay?" Mia's mind conjured images of Birdie stranded as floodwaters raged around her, seeking shelter in her attic, requiring a rooftop helicopter rescue.

Although she gathered from Josh's calm demeanor that none of her panicked imaginings were imminent.

He smiled and gave her arm a reassuring squeeze. "She's perfectly safe. It happens sometimes when we get a hard rain like this. Her street might fill up, but there's no danger of the water rising anywhere near high enough to make it into her house."

"That's good." Mia's skin tingled where Josh had touched her. She fought the urge to rub the spot with her fingers.

"It's not drivable though." He paused, his gaze settling on her meaningfully. "She thinks you should spend the night here." Another heavy pause. "Just to be safe."

"Oh." Mia swallowed as her heartbeat quickened. "And what do you think?"

Josh shifted closer, and his eyes locked onto her. "I don't think you've got much of a choice unless you want to swim for it. Which I don't recommend on account of the snakes and floating fire ants."

She frowned, trying to figure out if he was messing with her. "Floating fire ants?"

Nodding, he edged even closer. "Whole colonies of them floating on top of the floodwaters." His mouth quirked. "So it's probably best that you stay here."

Her head was swimming, but she forced herself to hold his gaze. "You know, I have this funny feeling that your family might be conspiring to push us together." For all she knew, Birdie had lied about the street being flooded. After the way she'd abandoned Mia here this morning, it didn't seem beyond the realm of possibility.

Josh's hands settled on her waist. Tugged her against him so their knees bumped together. "They like you."

There was nowhere for Mia to put her hands but on his chest. She flattened her palms, letting them slide over the front of his T-shirt. Wantonly caressing the muscles that lay beneath. "Their opinion isn't the one that matters."

He lifted a hand to her face. Traced his fingertips over the curve of her cheek. "I like you too." Bending his head, he trailed his lips along her jaw. "Did I not make that clear enough?" His hot breath seared the words into her skin.

She inhaled sharply, letting her eyes fall closed. "It could probably be clearer. You know . . . just to be sure."

He backed her up against the counter, fitting her against him as he encircled her with his arms. Surrounding her. Claiming her. Not trying to hide his arousal as he pressed his weight into her.

His head dipped again, and his teeth tugged at her earlobe. "Clear like this?"

"Well . . ." Her legs parted, letting one of his thighs ease between them. Welcoming him against her growing ache. She fisted her hands in his shirt, pulling him closer, her whole body straining for more contact.

His fingers slid through her still-damp hair as he pressed his mouth to her throat, sucking at the delicate skin hard enough to make her breath hitch. Then he lifted his head, gazing at her with heavy-lidded eyes. His thumb dragged across her cheek and along her jaw. Tipped her chin down. Traced her lips. "Or like this?"

His mouth settled over hers.

She gave in to the plush slickness, her lips parting as her tongue sought his. The release of tension buckled her knees and she sank against him.

His thigh pressed between her legs as his mouth claimed

her. He sucked on her tongue, then nipped her lower lip. She arched into him with a low moan, rubbing against him, so turned on she could hardly stand it.

The intensity of it overwhelmed her, and she felt a moment of doubt. A warning echo in the back of her mind.

She didn't need any complications in her life right now. She couldn't afford to let herself get attached. To let herself be hurt again.

She pushed all her doubts aside. This didn't have to be complicated. He couldn't hurt her unless she let him. And she deserved a little pleasure. Wanted it. Wanted *him*.

Josh hummed low in the back of his throat and cupped his hands under her ass, rocking her against him. She bit off a moan as he hitched her against his leg. Clutching at his shoulders, she let her head loll back, and he licked a path down her throat as she ground against the bulge in his jeans.

His fingers tightened on her, digging into her hips before he stroked his palms up under her shirt. They roamed over her back, up her sides, to the swell of her unrestrained breasts. Kneading gently, he swept his thumbs over her tight nipples, circling her areolas before stroking his hands downward again. Over her stomach. To the waistband of her sweatpants.

One of his hands slid around to spread over her back, fingers splayed wide. The other slipped inside her pants.

She hadn't been wearing underwear with her yoga pants, and she wasn't wearing any now. He encountered no resistance as his hand slipped between her trembling thighs. She whimpered, arching against him at the first electric contact.

"I like it when you make that sound." He smiled against her throat as he kissed his way back to her lips. His tongue plunged into her mouth at the same time his fingers plunged inside her.

Quivering in his arms, she spread her legs wider, her fingernails digging into the back of his neck as he stroked her, slow at first, then faster and faster. He was holding them both up, pressing her against the counter as his hips rocked against her and she shamelessly ground against his hand.

She panted into his mouth as the pressure built and built. She was so close. So unbearably close she could almost scream.

His free hand tangled in her hair, tugging her head back. She was dimly aware of his gaze on her face, drinking her in as he drove her to the edge, increasing the pressure as he found the exact right rhythm. And then she was breaking, falling apart in his arms with a ragged cry as pleasure exploded through her.

Trembling, she pressed her face into his neck. He held her, stroking her hair while she found her breath again.

"Was that clear enough for you?" His voice was husky, even rougher than usual.

She lifted her head and he smiled, looking pleased with himself. Smug, even.

He'd certainly earned it. That had to be a record for the fastest she'd ever come without battery-powered assistance.

"Not bad," she allowed, returning his smile. "Although I might need a few more reminders. If I'm going to be stuck here, we may as well make the most of it."

The corner of his mouth twitched. "That's the spirit."

She reached up to run her fingers through his hair. Bit her lip as she considered all the things she wanted to do with him. "Do you have work you need to do today?"

He pressed a kiss to her temple. "I asked Ray to handle the milking tonight. I'm all yours."

His choice of words sent a fresh spike of arousal thrumming through her. "A whole night together, hmmm?" Her fingers curled possessively in his shirt.

"And most of an afternoon," he pointed out.

"However will we pass the time?"

His lips curved into a libidinous smile. "We'll have to improvise, I guess."

She liked the sound of that.

She liked it very much.

Chapter Fourteen

Mia rolled over, encountering empty space where she'd expected to find a warm body. She'd fallen asleep next to Josh last night. She was sure of it.

Hadn't she?

Her sleep-befuddled mind pieced together hazy memories of the night before. Extremely pleasant memories. So pleasant, for a second she feared it had all been a dream, like the one Birdie had woken her from yesterday morning.

She cracked a bleary eye and was relieved to find herself in Josh's bedroom, where she remembered falling asleep with her body tucked against his. As she peered around the semi-dark room, he appeared in her field of vision. Smiling, he bent over the bed and kissed her.

"What time is it?" she mumbled against his lips.

"Time for me to do chores. Go back to sleep." He started to pull away and she grabbed the front of his shirt.

"Wait." She tugged him down for another kiss, taking her time with this one. "Are you coming back?"

"In a while. Plenty of time for you to get some more sleep." He kissed her forehead before pushing himself upright. "I'll be back later to make you breakfast." This time, she let him go.

Mia curled up on her side, feeling happy. Content, even.

She listened to the sound of Josh's footsteps going down the stairs, followed by the screen door slamming shut behind him. Outside, a dog barked a greeting, and Josh spoke to it in a low voice. A rooster crowed, sounding exactly like the See 'n Say toy she'd had as a kid. She could hear the hens too, singing the way Birdie's always did in the morning, along with the honking bleats of the goats.

It wasn't exactly quiet, but it was peaceful. A different world than the city noises she'd awakened to almost every other day of her life. Even Birdie's quiet neighborhood sounded more citified than this, with its garbage trucks and school buses and lawn mowers.

Mia rolled onto her back, letting the tranquility wash over her. Feeling satisfied and comfortable. Letting her mind wander. Thinking of things she needed to do this week. Changes she wanted to make to her lesson plans based on her conversation with Renée yesterday.

An image floated through her mind of the eleven-crossing knot she'd been trying to untangle. She pictured its curves and whorls, as she had so many times before. Visualized its trace, a more complex four-dimensional rendering associated with every knot. If she could just figure out how to construct a knot with the same trace, she might be able to use an invariant to ascertain its slice status, and thereby the status of its trace sibling.

It was the step she'd been stuck on for months. She lay there turning the problem over in her head as she'd done so often before. But this time, instead of hitting a wall and giving up in frustration, her drowsy, relaxed mind kept needling at it, teasing around the edges of the puzzle.

Until suddenly, like a match flaring in a dark room, she saw the solution.

Holy shit.

It was only a glimpse. The beginnings of an idea.

But it was the piece she'd been missing.

Mia bolted upright, trying to hold on to the image in her head before it slipped away.

Paper.

She needed paper. Something to write on.

She had to get it down before she lost it.

For once in her life, she hadn't brought a notebook with her, because she'd thought she was coming here for yoga. Panicked, she cast around the room for something to write on. She couldn't bring herself to rifle through his bedside drawers, but she remembered seeing an office downstairs. There had to be paper in there.

Mia ran out of the room, desperately hoping she could find something before she lost the first breakthrough she'd had in months.

Two hours later, when Josh came back, Mia was seated cross-legged on the floor of his bedroom, surrounded by notes and diagrams she'd hastily scribbled on pieces of plain white printer paper.

He stopped in the doorway, holding a tray. "I was going to bring you breakfast in bed." His gaze traveled over the chaos of papers fanned out around her. "But I guess you're up."

She scrambled to her feet, ignoring the kinks that had formed in her back. "I think I figured it out!"

"Figured what out?" The tray he'd brought held a plate of bacon and eggs and a mug of steaming coffee.

She'd been so focused she hadn't heard him come back to the house. Or start cooking. Nor had she noticed that the whole house smelled like bacon.

Picking her way through the papers on the floor, Mia went to give him a kiss. "The knot problem I've been working on." She claimed the coffee, cradling it in both hands as she turned to survey her notes. "The solution came to me when I was lying in bed. I know how to prove whether it's smoothly slice. Or I think I do."

Josh turned to her, his mouth stretching into a grin. "Hey, that's great. Congratulations."

She offered him a wavery smile before biting down on her lower lip and looking back at her notes. "I haven't done it yet. But I can see the path in my head."

"You'll get there. I believe in you." He carried the breakfast tray to the bed and set it down.

"I hope you don't mind, I got some paper out of your printer downstairs."

"I don't mind. Let me know if you need anything else." He squatted down for a closer look at the papers by his feet, his brow creasing as he squinted at her indecipherable scrawl. "I've probably got some spiral notebooks somewhere."

She stretched her back, wincing as her vertebrae popped. "What about butcher paper?" She'd seen some yesterday in the cheese kitchen. It was exactly what she needed to give her back a break.

Nodding, he got to his feet again. "I'll go get it."

"And tape?" she added. "And Sharpies, if you have them."

He kissed her cheek on his way out the door. "Be right back."

A few minutes later, he came back with a commercial roll of butcher paper, a box of black Sharpies, and a roll of masking tape. At Mia's direction, he tore off big sheets of paper and taped them to the walls of his bedroom, creating a makeshift whiteboard for her to use.

"Thank you! That's perfect!" She threw her arms around his neck and kissed him.

His hand cupped the back of her head, his fingers tangling in her hair as his lips lingered on hers, reminding her of their long afternoon and evening of passion yesterday, and everything they'd shared—and done to each other.

She'd hoped to spend as much of today with him as he had to spare. He'd offered to teach her how to milk a goat, and she'd been oddly looking forward to it.

But now . . .

She looked at the papers on the floor. They beckoned to her. Demanding her attention. Her absolute focus.

Turning back to Josh, she lifted a hand to caress his cheek, running her fingers over the prickly stubble. "You don't mind, do you? If I keep working on this?"

"Of course I don't mind." He pressed a kiss to the tip of her nose. Her forehead. Both her cheeks. "This is important." His eyes were steady and warm as they gazed at her. "You need anything else?"

She shook her head, relieved that he understood. "I think I'm good. I just need to get it all down before it slips away."

"Then I'll leave you to it." He lifted her hand to his lips, kissed her knuckles, and cast a meaningful look at the tray on the bed. "Make sure you eat something though."

Josh left her alone for the rest of the day, ceding his bedroom to her and popping in only occasionally to bring her more coffee, or a glass of water, or a sandwich. And once to grab a clean shirt after a situation with a pregnant goat that he assured her she did not want the details of.

Otherwise, he let her work undisturbed. At one point late in the day, she heard him singing to himself downstairs. As alluring as that was, she held strong and refused to let herself get distracted.

By evening, she was certain she was on the right track. There was still a lot to do, but she knew how she was going to do it. Could see the solution glowing in her mind like a beacon, lighting the way ahead.

She stepped back, hands on her hips, and surveyed her work with a sense of pride that had been missing in her life for too long. Pride that had been stolen from her by her disheartening job search and compounded by Paul's abandonment at her lowest moment.

It seemed silly now that she'd invested so much in someone who'd never exhibited more than a passing attachment to her. It was embarrassing that she'd allowed him to hurt her. To damage her sense of her own self-worth.

She didn't need him or anyone else to validate her. She didn't need an impressive academic position to prove she was a gifted mathematician either. Not once she'd published this proof. It would stand on its own as a testament to her worthiness.

A mathematical proof, but also proof that she was good enough.

And she'd done it on her own, without institutional support.

Take that, Princeton. What do you think of my CV now?

She was feeling confident enough to pack it in for the day, and made her way downstairs, in search of Josh. She found him in the kitchen, newly returned from milking the goats and in the middle of making dinner. For the two of them.

He looked up, smiling at the sight of her, and she threw herself into his arms, kissing him until he gently untangled himself so he could tend to the food that was in danger of burning on the stove.

Mia wasn't used to people doing things for her. But she might be able to get used to it, she decided, standing in that farmhouse kitchen filled with the fragrant sizzle of cooking food.

"Do you like cooking?" she asked, grabbing two beers out of the fridge.

He shrugged as he pushed ground beef around a skillet. "I like to eat. It's hard to do one without the other."

"I never learned to cook." She twisted the caps off both bottles and handed one to Josh.

He eyed her as he sipped his beer. "What do you eat?"

"I can make pasta. Grilled cheese sandwiches. Canned soup."

"That's cooking."

"Not like this." She nodded at the skillet of beef and onions he was stirring.

"Beef stroganoff is easy. Anyone can make it." He tipped

some beer into the pan. Stirred it some more. "I could teach you."

"Could you?"

He shrugged. "If you want to learn."

"Maybe? My brain's pretty fried tonight though."

"I'll bet." He took another swig of beer. "Doesn't have to be tonight."

"Does that mean I'm invited back?"

He set down his spatula and his beer. Abandoning his post at the stove, he took her in his arms and gave her a kiss that made her whole body light up. His hands cupped her face as he gazed at her. "You can come back anytime you want."

She inhaled a shaky breath, in real danger of swooning dead away. "Careful, I might take you up on it."

"I wouldn't have said it if I didn't mean it."

She believed him. He wasn't the most effusive man she'd ever met, and he didn't speak frivolously. If he said he wanted her here, it was because he did.

He went back to the stove and picked up his spatula again. "Hand me those mushrooms, would you?" She brought him the bowl of sliced mushrooms on the butcher block and he dumped them in the skillet. As he stirred them in with the meat and onions, he pointed at a bag of noodles on the counter. "Think you can use your cheffing skills to cook those noodles?"

There was already a pot of water boiling on the stove. Mia dumped the noodles in and Josh handed her a wooden spoon to stir them with.

Ten minutes later, they sat down to eat. He'd mixed goat's milk yogurt in with the meat to make a creamy sauce.

THE INFATUATION CALCULATION

Secretly, Mia had been a little skeptical, but it turned out delicious.

After dinner, she helped him do the dishes, and then he surprised her by asking if he could see what she'd been working on all day.

She took him by the hand and led him upstairs. Together, they stood in the middle of his bedroom looking at the sheets of butcher paper she'd covered with notes and drawings.

"What does it all mean? Explain it to me."

"It's pretty technical," she said. "It won't make any sense to you unless you've studied differential equations, algebraic geometry, and combinatorics." Even then, it'd be difficult for anyone without a background in advanced topology to fully understand.

"That's okay. I don't expect to understand any of it. I just want to hear you explain it."

So she walked him through all her notes and calculations, showing him the original knot diagram with its eleven crossings, and explaining four-dimensional spheres, concordance, positive mutations, abelian and metabelian sliceness invariants, diffeomorphic traces, and manifolds.

He listened carefully to every word, seeming to follow along at first. But as she retraced her hypotheses and calculations, getting deeper and deeper into abstract math, a crease formed in his brow. By the time she'd started to describe the trace sibling she proposed to construct in order to prove her theorem, she could tell she'd lost him completely.

"I'm sorry," she said. "Once I start talking about this stuff I tend to get carried away."

"You're passionate about it." He wasn't teasing her the

way Paul used to do sometimes when she got fired up talking about her work. Josh said it like it was a compliment.

"I guess I am." It was nice to be able to feel that way again. She'd been putting so much pressure on herself that the thing she used to love more than anything else in the world had turned into a source of anxiety. The competition and uncertainty of the job market, the need to distinguish herself from her peers, publish more, do more, be better than everyone else, had stolen most of the joy out of it.

She'd almost forgotten how fun it could be to work at a problem. The endorphin high when the solution finally clicked into place.

Josh was still staring at her notes, scratching his head as he tried to decipher what must look like an alien language to him, and it inspired a warm surge of affection.

Slipping her arms around his waist from behind, she rested her chin on his shoulder. "I warned you it wouldn't make sense. You're probably feeling sorry for my poor students now, having to listen to me ramble in class."

"Are you kidding?" He laid a hand over hers where they were clasped across his stomach. "That made way more sense than any of the lectures in my business calculus class."

She nuzzled at the skin behind his ear. "Sure." He was only saying that to be nice. Humoring her. She appreciated it, but she didn't for a minute believe it.

"I admit I lost you a bit with the exotic four-dimensional spaces. And I didn't really get any of the stuff about manifolds." He pointed to the page showing her handle calculus for the four-manifold, proving he actually had been following along. "But I understood a lot more than I thought I would. You've got a gift for teaching."

She let out a soft snort against his neck. "I don't know about that."

"I do." He twisted in her arms so they were face-to-face. The crease had returned to his forehead and his tone was lightly chiding. "Antonio said the same thing."

She blinked in surprise. "He did?"

"He said your class was his favorite. That he never felt like he was good at math before, but you've helped him realize he actually likes it."

"Oh." Mia bit down on her lip as she felt herself smile. "That's nice of him. I'm glad he's gaining confidence." Antonio's compliment inspired a wholly new sense of pride, bringing an endorphin high that rivaled the one she'd gotten from her breakthrough this morning.

Teaching had never been her priority in grad school. You couldn't get ahead in academia just by being a good teacher. It was the scholarship you produced that mattered most for getting hired. You only had to be *good enough* at teaching, rather than the very best.

As a PhD student, she hadn't had much to do with the master's students pursuing a teaching degree. Perhaps she'd even looked down on them a little, if she was being honest. One of her father's favorite asshole refrains had always been, "Those who can, do, and those who can't, teach." Although she'd recognized it as elitist, contemptible bullshit, it was possible she'd unwittingly internalized a little of his attitude anyway.

Certainly teaching was a noble profession, but it wasn't exactly prestigious. Noble endeavors weren't supposed to bring prestige. They were for people without ambition driving them to less selfless markers of success.

Teaching MAs were destined for a lifetime of underfunded

classrooms, teaching to standardized tests, and chaperoning school dances. Mia had her sights set on the ivy-covered halls of academia, research grants, and symposia.

As far as she'd been concerned, teaching was a side gig. One she'd never much enjoyed when she was teaching someone else's lesson plan. The discussion sections she'd taught in grad school had been limited to clarifying lessons the instructors had presented in their lectures, working through examples to illustrate the material, and answering questions on the homework.

While there had been isolated moments when she felt like she'd connected with some of the students or helped them reach a breakthrough in the material, she'd also experienced a lot of frustration, boredom, and impatience—both on her own behalf and coming from her students. Maybe she should have tried harder to engage them, but as a grad student she'd been spread thin between her two discussion sections, office hours, and student math center shifts on top of twelve units of graduate coursework per quarter, not to mention the research and work on her dissertation that had been her top priority.

At the beginning of this semester, she'd struggled to find her feet, lacking confidence in her teaching abilities. Ideally, her postdoc fellowship would have been where she'd honed those skills as she took on more mentoring and teaching responsibilities alongside her research. Instead, she'd been thrown straight into the fire.

And it turned out she'd done okay. Better than okay. For the first time, Mia allowed herself to sit with the idea that she was good at teaching.

Turning in her arms, Josh stroked his hands up Mia's back.

"I wish I'd had a math prof like you. And not just because it's sexy as hell when you talk about sliceness invariants and diffeo-whatevers."

"Diffeomorphic traces," she murmured, thrown off-balance. "You think it's sexy when I talk about math?"

He gave a shrug, his lips curving. "You like it when I talk about cheese. I like it when you talk about math."

How was he even real? Never, ever would she have believed a man like this existed in the world. A man this gorgeous and sexy who made cheese and got turned on when she talked about math? Ridiculous. It was like he'd been conjured into existence by her deepest desires.

Mia pressed her face into his neck, inhaling his clean, earthy scent deep into her lungs. She slid her hands under his blue plaid shirt and smoothed her palms over the firm planes of his stomach, luxuriating in the feel of his warm skin. "So you'd get turned on if I started talking about Seifert matrices?"

Josh grunted. "*Get* turned on? Shit, I'm already hard." His arms tightened around her, pulling her against him to demonstrate the truth of his words.

Heat flooded her body, pooling low in her abdomen, and she felt her lips tug into a smile. "For any known knot, the Seifert algorithm produces an orientable surface with only one boundary component, such that the boundary component is the knot in question."

Squeezing her ass, he let out a thready laugh that sounded like he was having trouble getting enough oxygen.

"The signature of a diagonal matrix is the number of positive entries minus the number of negative entries." Her hands worked his shirt open—god bless the snaps on western-style work shirts—and she pushed it off his shoulders.

His tongue slid across his lower lip as he watched her, his eyes going from brown to nearly black.

She pressed an open-mouth kiss to his chest. "Two diagonal matrices are congruent if and only if they have the same number of positive, negative, and zero entries."

When she sank to her knees he sucked in a shuddering breath. His hands curled into her hair, but they didn't tug, although they spasmed briefly as she began to unbutton his pants.

After that, her mouth was too busy to talk about math anymore.

Chapter Fifteen

Early the next morning, as the rooster crowed the start of a new day, Josh drove Mia home. She took her notes with her and hung them up on the walls of her own small apartment before heading to campus for her first Monday class.

For the rest of that week, Mia spent every free minute working on her proof. She didn't see Josh at all, although they texted every day. Working in her cramped office between classes and office hours, and at home late into the night every night, she successfully constructed a trace sibling for her knot and began testing it against invariants.

By Friday, she had her solution. She'd found an invariant that showed her new knot wasn't smoothly slice, thereby proving the original knot wasn't either. After double-checking her calculations, she wrote up a summary of her breakthrough and emailed it to her former advisor at UCLA.

Then she texted Josh.

> **Mia**: I solved it! It's done!
> **Josh**: CONGRATULATIONS! I knew you'd get there.
> **MIA**: I can't believe it. I'm actually shaking I'm so happy.
> **Josh**: Are you done working for the day?

Mia: Yes. My brain is totally fried. I feel like celebrating.
Josh: Want to come over here?

She'd been thinking more along the lines of going out somewhere for celebratory drinks, but she could understand why Josh might not be into that. And she didn't care that much where they went or didn't go. What mattered was that she had someone to share this moment of accomplishment with.

Thirty minutes later she knocked on the door of Josh's farmhouse. He swept her up in a congratulatory hug, lifting her clean off the floor. Kicking the door closed behind them, he spun her around before setting her on the floor and kissing her hard enough to make her dizzy. Then he took her by the hand and led her to the kitchen where he'd set out a bottle of champagne and two glasses.

"I bought it this week," he told her. "I figured I should have some on hand for whenever you solved your proof."

He really had believed in her. Enough to spend almost a hundred dollars of his hard-earned money on an expensive bottle of champagne. But it wasn't only that. All week he'd been supportive and encouraging, checking in on her but understanding her need to focus. Letting her know he cared without placing demands on her.

The pure excitement on his face—excitement for *her*, over an achievement he didn't even fully understand—inspired a giddy, tender rush of feelings. She threw herself at him, peppering his face with delighted kisses until he let out a warm, throaty laugh.

All thoughts of champagne fled from her mind as she captured his still smiling mouth with hers. He kissed her back hungrily, letting her know without words how much he'd missed her. When his teeth tugged at her bottom lip, her body lit up like Times Square and she let out a lustful moan.

Her backside hit the counter, his hands grabbed her thighs, and he picked her up, spinning her as his mouth continued to devour her. She wrapped her legs around his waist, and he carried her upstairs to his bedroom.

They didn't get around to drinking the champagne until much, much later that night.

Naked.

In Josh's bed.

Mid-October brought the first cool front of the season, dropping the humidity and temperature to something approaching pleasant for a few days. It wasn't exactly the sort of crisp autumn weather Mia was used to seeing this time of year, but it at least made her want to spend more time outdoors.

"It won't last," Josh warned her as they watched the sunset from his porch swing.

And of course, he was right. Summer came raging back a few days later, nearly as hot and sticky as before.

By then, they'd settled into the habit of spending weekends together at the farm. They saw less of each other during the week when Mia was busier, but sometimes on weeknights Josh would come over to her apartment for a couple hours after he'd finished the evening milking.

Mia's advisor had emailed her back almost immediately and encouraged her to submit her proof to the *Annals of Mathematics*, one of the discipline's top journals—if not *the* top. Now that she had independent confirmation that she wasn't completely off base, she'd begun writing up her paper for submission. On top of that, midterms were upon them, and her office hours were busier than usual. At night she brought home stacks of exams to grade while Josh sat next to her on the couch reading.

He eventually got around to teaching her how to milk a goat. Even better, he let her bottle-feed some of the newborn kids, which she liked much better than milking. As she got more comfortable at the farm, she even started helping with a few of the chores. *Her*. The New York City girl. Collecting eggs. Feeding the pigs. Settling into farm life.

Everything was easy and comfortable with Josh.

Maybe a little too comfortable.

As the end of their first month together approached, Mia realized they hadn't been anywhere other than dinner at Birdie's a couple times, which hardly counted as going out. She knew Josh preferred to stay in rather than go out, but she also knew he went into town regularly for groceries and supplies for the farm. It wasn't like he never went anywhere.

Surely a date wasn't too much to ask? It wasn't like they were hiding the fact that they were spending time together. Andie knew, and so did Wyatt. And of course Birdie knew, which probably meant half the town knew as well.

Wouldn't it be fun to get dressed up and go somewhere nice for a change? Somewhere quiet where no one would disturb them. The more she thought about it, the more excited Mia got about the idea.

But when she suggested it to Josh that evening as they cleaned up the dinner dishes, his expression grew pinched and his lips pressed together in a thin, flat line. She could tell immediately that she'd asked for too much.

He raked a hand through his hair and dropped his gaze to the floor. "I'd rather not. If it's all right with you."

Clearly she'd underestimated his aversion to going out. Why hadn't she realized before how bad it was for him? When Andie had called him a recluse, Mia had assumed she was joking. But this was no joke. Not if he looked this upset at the mere prospect of going to a restaurant.

Worry tugged at her gut, but she tried to put on a cheerful face. "Of course it's all right." Her fingers smoothed over the front of his shirt. "We don't have to. It was just an idea."

He seemed almost painfully relieved. "Thank you." His gaze darted away from her and he cleared his throat. "For understanding."

Impulsively, she wound her arms around him, resting her chin on his shoulder. "It's all right," she said, although it didn't seem all right. It felt like something much bigger and more serious than she knew how to handle.

His hand cupped the back of her neck. "You're disappointed. You wanted to go."

"Not that bad." Not enough to make him this unhappy. "It's really fine."

He turned his head and kissed her hair. "I'll make it up to you. We'll do something else special."

Her throat tightened. She felt like she had to say something. "Have you ever . . . talked to anyone?"

"What do you mean?" His whole body had tensed up like he was expecting a blow to the stomach.

She clasped her hands behind his back, refusing to let him move even an inch farther away. When she spoke, she tried to make her voice as gentle as possible. "Like a therapist."

His chest expanded and contracted against hers with

short, shallow breaths. Angry breaths. "I don't need therapy." His voice sounded oddly flat and quiet.

Mia resisted her instinctive urge to drop the subject in order to smooth things over. As much as she hated conflict, and as hard as it was for her to speak up, this was too important. She couldn't say nothing. "I think you might have agoraphobia."

Josh's hands dropped to his sides. He unwound her arms and stepped away from her, pacing to the other side of the kitchen. He stood with his back to her, staring out the window. "It's not a phobia." The words came out sounding like they'd been dragged over sharp rocks. "This isn't some irrational fear. You think I haven't tried to forget about it and move on? I'd love to. But people can't seem to let me do that. Not when it's so much fun to rub my humiliation in my face. Therapy isn't going to change that."

Maybe not, but it might help him cope with it. Mia opened her mouth to say that, but he spoke again before she had the chance.

"I'm fine, okay? I promise." He turned around, his jaw set and his mouth hard. "I don't want you to worry about me. That's not your job."

It felt like a warning. Josh's way of setting a boundary. Telling her how far she was permitted to push. It was fine to spend all this time together, but his mental well-being wasn't hers to manage.

Fair enough.

She wasn't an expert on this stuff. Far from it. And maybe he was right. Maybe he was fine.

But somehow she didn't quite believe it. This didn't feel like what *fine* looked like.

It must have showed on her face, because his expression hardened further. "I'll show you. Then you'll understand." He pulled out his phone and tapped the screen.

Mia's chest constricted as she watched him. Dreading what he was about to show her, but also wanting to know. To finally understand the scars he bore.

He walked toward her and held up his phone so she could see the screen. He'd pulled up a video titled "Sexy Waldo Gets Busy." It had almost seven million views. He tapped the play button.

At first all Mia could see was the inside of a bedroom. Then Josh came into view, dressed up like Waldo from the *Where's Waldo?* children's books.

"It was Halloween." He spoke in a dull, strained voice. "The costume was Kayla's idea. She was dressed like Carmen Sandiego, but you can't see that in the video, just like you can't see the way she was egging me on."

Music started to play, superimposed over the video. Something electronic with a pronounced, throbbing beat. On screen, Josh began to dance. Slowly and seductively.

"We'd been to a party," he said. "I'd had a few drinks. Then we went back to her place. She told me she'd always had a—*fetish*." He stumbled a little over the word, like it hurt him to say it. "For Waldo."

In the video, Josh had started doing a striptease for someone off camera. Pulling up his red-and-white-striped shirt a little bit at a time to expose his stomach. Thrusting his hips. Someone had used video editing tricks to match Josh's movements to the music for maximum comedic effect.

"I didn't know the camera was there." The muscles in his jaw contracted. "Obviously."

His shirt was hiked up to expose his whole chest now. Pelvis gyrating, he licked his thumb and trailed it down his torso to his waist. It was incredibly sexual—and nothing at all like the Josh she knew. Even at the height of passion or in the most intimate moments they'd shared, Mia had never seen him so uninhibited. So loose and easy. She wondered if it was the effect of the alcohol, or if he'd been that much more carefree before the betrayal.

"This is the edited version that went viral." He wasn't looking at the video or at her. His eyes stayed focused on an empty spot across the room as he held the phone. "All over social media and on most of the entertainment sites. Even a few local news shows. People made gifs of it."

Mia had seen the gifs before, she realized. She'd never seen the original video, hadn't known the context or where they were from, but she remembered seeing sexy dancing Waldo gifs on social media.

"For about a month, I was everywhere, doing a striptease in a Waldo costume. Until something else came along for everyone to laugh at. It still gets used as a reaction gif though. I'm a classic." He sounded so bitter.

She couldn't blame him. If the whole world had seen her doing something so . . . overtly sexual. So clearly meant to be private. If her parents had seen it. Her exes. Her professional colleagues. She'd curl up and die of embarrassment.

On screen, Josh-as-Waldo was unbuckling his pants. Mia's hand covered her mouth in horror as he shoved them down, exposing himself. A black bar had been superimposed over his genitals, preserving at least that much of his dignity in order to bypass the adult content filters. The video ended with him doing a sort of flourish as he bared himself to the world, his nudity comedically censored.

What kind of a monster could do something like this? Record him in private without his consent. Take a moment so intimate and . . . and *generous*, and make a public mockery out of it. Out of Josh.

"That's not even the worst part." He lowered the phone and walked to the opposite side of the kitchen again. "The original video, the unedited one, didn't stop when I got naked."

Oh. Oh *no*.

She could guess what was coming next, and it made her feel sick on his behalf.

He leaned against the counter, arms crossed, refusing to look at her as he spoke. "She didn't just record my little dance for her. She recorded us having sex. All of it. And I never knew." His mouth twisted in a scowl. "Until we broke up, and she decided to send the video to everyone we knew as some sort of revenge for rejecting her. I guess she didn't care that people were looking at her too, although you couldn't see her face the way you could see mine." He paused, like he was trying to find the strength to say the last part. "The video made its way all over campus before ending up on a bunch of porn sites. It's still out there as far as I know. I tried to get it taken down, but it'd just get re-uploaded again. Last I looked, it had millions of views racked up."

Mia went to him, uncrossed his arms, and fitted herself against him. "I'm so sorry. I can't imagine how awful that must have been." She held him as tightly as she could. As tightly as he'd let her.

Josh's body remained rigid as she pressed herself against him. Resistant to her comfort.

But then he finally exhaled a long, shaky breath and sagged toward her. His arms constricted around her as his head dropped forward.

Stroking his hair, she pressed her lips to his temple. "I can see why you didn't want to show me before. I wish I'd never seen it."

"I needed you to understand. My last semester of college was a living nightmare. Then I came back here, hoping to get away from it. Only it was just as bad, because the internet is everywhere. Everyone in town had seen it—or at least heard about it."

As he spoke, she ran her hand over his back, trying to caress away some of the tension knotting his muscles. Hurting for him so much it felt like she'd been stabbed.

"The thing about small towns is they're short on entertainment." He spoke quietly, his forehead pressed against her neck. Leaning on her. "People talk about the same shit over and over again for years, because they've got nothing better to do. Nothing else to talk about. Even though most decent people were too polite to say anything to my face, I couldn't look them in the eye anymore knowing they were talking about me behind my back and thinking about that video every single time they saw me."

He lifted his head and fixed her with an anguished look that begged for her understanding.

"Imagine knowing your kindergarten teacher and your dentist and the waitress at your favorite restaurant had all seen a video of you like that one. Maybe even the other one. The uncensored one."

Mia couldn't bear to imagine it. It would be unspeakable.

Josh's face was close to hers, so pained and so dear. She touched her hand to it. Leaned up to kiss his cheek.

His eyes fell closed and he blew out a long breath. "And of course all the assholes I went to high school with, like those guys at the bar, can't keep their goddamn mouths shut. They think it's so fucking hilarious that they can't ever let me live it down."

He was vibrating with anger. She could feel his body trembling with it. She was shaking with anger too, on his behalf, now that she understood exactly what they'd been mocking him for.

But then he seemed to take hold of himself. Straightened his spine. Unclenched his jaw. Bent his head to kiss her forehead. "Most of the time it's easier to stay home than take a chance that I'm going to have to deal with their shit."

It was hard for Mia to understand why he'd stayed in Crowder given all that. Wouldn't he have been happier someplace he was a stranger? Somewhere he had a better chance of blending in, unnoticed?

But she supposed there wasn't really anywhere he could go to escape his notoriety once the video had gone viral. He would always run the risk of being recognized anywhere the internet reached.

And the farm was here. His family farm that he'd said was his calling. The only thing he'd ever wanted to do. He couldn't just pick it up and move it. So he'd stuck it out here, doing the work he wanted to do, and hiding from everything else.

No wonder he hadn't been able to call himself happy.

Josh lifted his head, his gaze steady as it met hers. Most

of the pain tucked neatly away. "So I hope you can understand now why I feel the way I do. Why I don't ever just go out for a beer or to grab a coffee. Why I'd rather not eat out at a restaurant with you. I wouldn't be able to enjoy myself, because I'd be worried the whole time that someone was going to act like an ass."

"Of course I understand." How could she not? She'd seen the ruthlessness with which the guy at the bar had taunted him, callously cheered on by his friends. Who would want to deal with that when you could simply avoid it?

Josh appeared to absorb her words with relief, a little more of his tension draining away. "But all the same, if it's important to you—"

"It's not," Mia said firmly.

"If it's important to you," he repeated, cocking an admonishing eyebrow at her, "I'll go. We can do whatever you want."

"No." She shook her head. "I don't want to. Forget I ever suggested it."

"I meant it when I said I'd think of something else special for us to do." He cupped her face in his hands and bent his lips to hers in a soft, tender kiss. "I like being with you. I don't want anything to ruin the time we have together."

His choice of words struck straight at her heart.

The time we have together.

It was a reminder that her time with him was limited. Her employment contract would end next year, and she'd move on to her next job. Some other school. Some other city.

It was what she wanted.

A month ago, she would have said she couldn't wait to

leave this place. But leaving Crowder meant leaving Josh. The thought of it settled in her stomach like a lead weight.

She put a hand on his chest, needing the reassurance that he was still here for now. Neither of them was going anywhere yet. Not for a while.

"I like being with you too," she said, her throat suddenly dry.

He covered her hand with his, holding it in place over his heart, his expression betraying a hint of uncertainty. "Still? Even after you've seen that video?"

She gazed into his eyes as his heart beat against her palm, steady but vulnerable. Fragile. Precious. "Nothing in that video changes how I feel about you."

It might be better for her if it had.

As it was, her feelings were in danger of running away with her. And once that toothpaste was out of the tube, there was no cramming it back in there. No easy way of letting him go.

So much for not letting it get complicated.

She could feel things changing—feel *herself* changing—the more time they spent together. Feel the pressure slowly contracting around her heart.

Like someone squeezing the toothpaste tube.

Things were getting very complicated indeed.

Josh smiled at her and lifted her hand to his lips. "Good."

"Can I ask you something?" she said as he kissed her knuckles.

He turned her hand over, opened her fingers, and placed a kiss in the center of her palm. "Shoot."

"Why did you show up at the Rusty Spoke that night? If you don't like to go out?"

His fingers tightened around hers. "Because Andie told me you'd be there. I wanted to see you." He said it simply, but the words etched themselves into her heart. He inclined his head and brushed his lips across hers. "You were worth the risk."

Mia closed her eyes and held him as tight as she could.

Josh kept his promise.

He wouldn't tell her what he'd planned, but he planned it for the following Monday. All he would tell Mia was to change into comfortable, casual clothes when she got home and wait for him to pick her up.

When she climbed into his truck, she noticed a duffel bag and a small cooler stowed in the cab behind the seats.

"Are we going on a picnic?" She tried to keep the disappointment out of her voice. Sitting on the ground eating with all the bugs and dirt wasn't exactly in her top ten list of romantic dates. But if that was what he'd planned for them, she'd smile and pretend to be having a great time.

His gaze slid over to her, his lips tilting slightly. "Try to keep an open mind."

Apparently she hadn't hidden her disappointment well enough. *Oops.*

"I'm sure it will be great," she said with forced cheer. "Whatever we're doing." She didn't want to seem ungrateful when he'd gone to all this trouble.

Dropping his hand to her thigh, he gave a gentle squeeze. "All will be revealed soon enough."

As he drove through town to wherever he was taking her, Josh sang along with the country song on the radio. Mia had heard him singing before, around the house or when he was working on the farm. He had a Bluetooth speaker in the cheese kitchen and another in the milking parlor, so he could play music while he worked, and he'd often sing along. He'd even told her singing to the goats made them happier, which made the milk taste better. She still wasn't sure if he was kidding or not. He'd seemed pretty earnest when he said it.

Regardless, she'd gotten her wish to hear him sing several times over, and she still loved it every time. Mia couldn't hold a tune to save her life, but she loved the sound of Josh's voice. It was every bit as sexy as she'd imagined and then some. He seemed to favor a mix of classic rock and country music, but she'd caught him singing an Ariana Grande song in the shower once, so clearly he had range.

Mia leaned back in her seat, smiling as she watched him sing.

She liked looking at his profile, the strong, straight lines of his nose and jaw. She liked his thick, suntanned forearms, and the fine layer of dark hair that covered them. She enjoyed his chest hair too, and had become addicted to running her fingers through it. She'd never dated a man with this much body hair before. It was a pleasure she hadn't even known she was missing.

Josh tapped his thumb on the steering wheel, keeping time with the Tom Petty song he was singing now. He was wearing shorts and sneakers today, which he didn't often do since they weren't practical for work on the farm. Mia liked being able to look at his legs, which were muscular and covered with the same dark hair as his arms and chest.

Impulsively, she reached over and laid her hand on his thigh. He threw a sideways glance at her, smiled without missing a note, and switched hands on the steering wheel to cover her hand with his.

He got onto the highway and headed north of town. Just when Mia was wondering if they were headed to Austin, he got off at the exit for Gettinger State Park. Lowering his window, he pulled the truck up to the booth inside the park entrance. "Are you Carlos?" he said as he leaned out to talk to the ranger. "I'm Josh, Andie's brother. She said she'd leave a pass for me."

"Got it right here." Carlos passed Josh a hangtag, which he affixed to his rearview mirror. "You know where you're going?"

"I do, thanks." Josh gave Carlos a wave and drove into the park.

Andie had said Mia should see the park where she worked. And now Mia was seeing it.

The scenery was nice. There was the lake Andie had mentioned, and the picnic area next to it. Josh kept driving, deeper into the park. This late in the day on a Monday it seemed to be mostly empty. Mia only saw one or two people out walking around the lake, and only a few RVs and cars parked at the campground they drove past.

There were lots of trees, and . . . even more trees. Mia wondered again about the possibility of encountering bears or mountain lions as they wound their way through them, following a narrow paved road. There were signs along the way pointing park visitors toward various recreational activities. Camping and hiking. A turnoff for fishing and another for boating. A couple different ones for swimming.

Then Mia saw a wooden sign that was different than the others. It was faded and clearly handmade. Someone had written *The Holler* on it in black paint, with an arrow pointing down a narrow gravel lane she might have missed if it hadn't been for the sign.

That was the turnoff Josh took.

Her mouth fell open. "We're going to the *nude* swimming hole?"

Chapter Sixteen

Never in a million years would Mia have guessed Josh would go in for public nudity. Not voluntarily, anyway.

He glanced at her in amusement. "Who told you about this place?"

"Your sister."

His amusement turned into an eye roll. "Of course she did."

"Is that really where we're going?" Mia didn't know whether to be anxious or excited. At the moment she was feeling equal parts of both.

"That's where we're going." Josh pulled into a small parking area and cut the engine. Mia was relieved to find theirs was the only car in sight. She wasn't ready to come face-to-face with a bunch of aging hippie nudists. Or *any* nudists, for that matter.

They got out of the truck, and Josh slung the duffel over his shoulder before retrieving the cooler. There was a trailhead leading away from the parking area, and next to it a big sign warning that they were about to enter a clothing-optional area restricted to visitors age eighteen and up. Next to it was a long list of rules, but before Mia could read any of them, Josh took her by the hand and led her down the mulch trail that wound through the trees.

A few moments later she caught a glimmer of water ahead, and not long after that they stepped out into a clearing. A sparkling swimming hole lay before them, carved out of the natural rock formations by the creek that fed into it. The ground sloped down to the water, the leaf-covered forest floor giving way to a patchy grass clearing, and the grass giving way to a broad, smooth shelf of flat stone that ran alongside the water and would probably be perfect for sunning. If it were still sunny. It was edging toward sunset now, the sky awash with shades of twilight orange and pink.

Josh set his load down on the stone shelf and began unpacking the duffel bag. While he spread out a blanket for them to sit on, Mia ventured down toward the water.

It was dark and deep. And quite possibly teeming with snakes.

But it also looked appealingly cool. The temps had been hovering just below brutishly, improbably hot all week, and even with the sun sinking it was uncomfortably warm. But not in the water, probably.

"Feel like taking a swim?" Josh's arms wrapped around her from behind, his chest pressing against her back.

"Are you serious?"

He nuzzled against her neck. "It's a swimming hole. It's for swimming."

Mia had never swum anywhere that wasn't man-made and chlorinated. She eyed the gloomy water with suspicion. "Is it safe?"

"Can you swim?"

"Yes."

"Then it's safe."

"What about snakes?"

He turned her in his arms and kissed the tip of her nose. "Snakes are as eager to steer clear of you as you are of them. They're not going to come anywhere near a full-grown adult splashing around in the water."

"Do you promise?"

"I promise," he said solemnly. He bent his head to kiss her cheek before his lips moved to her ear. "I'll even jump in first." He let go of her and yanked his T-shirt over his head.

The sight made her pulse jump and her stomach feel tingly. He had a legit farmer's tan and she liked the way it emphasized his biceps. But the rest of his torso was tasty as well. His broad shoulders, firm pecs, and hard stomach could have been sculpted out of marble.

He winked at her and the tingle in her stomach moved lower. "That way I'll be sure to scare off any snakes who might be loitering in the vicinity."

Still, she remained unconvinced as she watched him toe off his sneakers. "Are we really supposed to swim nude?"

The prospect of getting naked in what was technically a public space was daunting enough—even if there wasn't currently anyone else around. But when she thought about getting in that untreated water without so much as a thin layer of spandex between her and whatever wildlife lurked in its depths, an unsexy shudder ran through her.

"That's the idea." Josh grinned at her and shoved his shorts and underwear down to his ankles.

"Oh. Okay. Wow. That's—you just went for it." She hadn't expected him to be so casual about getting naked outdoors.

"You don't have to take your clothes off if you don't

want to. It's clothing optional. That means it's totally your choice."

Mia chewed on her lower lip, distracted by the sight of him stooping to pick up his clothes in his resplendent altogether. "But I don't have a swimsuit."

He balled up his clothes and tossed them toward the blanket like a basketball. "You can swim in your underwear if you'd be more comfortable."

"Hmmm." She sidled closer, intending to squeeze that perfect ass of his, but he dodged away from her with a smirk. "If you want some of this, you have to come and get it." Before she could make another grab for him, he cannonballed into the water.

Shrieking, she leaped backward to avoid getting drenched by the splash. Josh disappeared under the water for a moment before his head broke the surface again. Shaking the water out of his hair like a dog, he grinned up at her. "Did I get you wet?"

"No. Thanks to my catlike reflexes."

"Why don't you bring those catlike reflexes over here?" His eyebrows tilted seductively as his arms sliced through the water, keeping him afloat. "Come on in, the water's fine."

"Is it cold?" She kicked off her sandals and edged toward the water, intending to dip a toe in.

Josh sent another splash of water at her, forcing her to jump back again to avoid getting her clothes soaked. "If you're going to do it, you have to do it all at once. None of this wishy-washy inch at a time stuff."

Narrowing her gaze, she stared down at him with her hands on her hips. "That means it's cold, doesn't it?"

"It's fine." He wiped the water out of his eyes and slicked his hair back. "Do I not look fine to you?"

He did look fine with water glistening on his bare shoulders and broad chest. *Extremely* fine.

The lure of Josh's naked body was too strong to resist—and enough to overmaster her fears.

Mia pulled her shirt over her head. Then she unbuttoned her shorts and let them fall to her feet as Josh let out a wolf whistle. But after that she hesitated, unsure how far she wanted to take it.

Play it safe by swimming in her underwear? Or go all the way?

"What's it gonna be?" he asked. "Are you going to let me be the only one who's naked here?"

Oh what the hell? If Josh could do it, so could she.

She reached behind her back to unclasp her bra and tossed it onto the blanket. Next went her underwear, down to her feet. She couldn't believe she was naked in the middle of a state park. At any moment, someone could come upon them and see her like this.

She found the prospect simultaneously terrifying and oddly thrilling.

All her life, Mia had been a rule follower. A good girl. Never one to get in trouble or do anything naughty. And while she might not technically be breaking any rules by getting naked at a publicly sanctioned nude swimming hole, it didn't change the fact that it *felt* naughty.

And exhilarating.

And sexy.

"Get in here," Josh said, his eyes glinting darkly. "Before I come over there and make you."

Mia bit down on her lip, took a deep breath, and jumped into the water.

HOLY MOTHER SHITTING FUCK.

It was so cold it sucked all the oxygen out of her lungs. So cold it felt like it was burning her skin. Her fingers and toes went completely numb. Her nipples tried to invert and retreat inside her body. Worst of all, the cold water went straight up her cooch.

She spluttered to the surface with a screech of agony and outrage. Before she'd even cleared the water from her eyes, Josh's arm was encircling her waist, pulling her against his warm body.

She clung to him with one hand, trying to absorb some of his body heat, while the other hand pummeled his chest. *"HOW COULD YOU DO THAT TO ME OH MY GOD IT'S FREEZING!"* she shouted in his face.

"It's better this way. I promise." He was clearly trying not to laugh at her, which only made her yell even more.

"You know what would have been even better than this? *NOT JUMPING IN THE FREEZING FUCKING WATER!*"

And yet, infuriatingly, she had to admit he was right. Now that the initial shock had passed, the water already felt more tolerable.

And hey, after all her yelling and splashing, there couldn't possibly be any snakes still hanging around. Right?

Nevertheless, at the thought of snakes, she shimmied even closer to Josh.

"You okay?" He bobbed as he treaded water, moving his arms and legs to keep them both afloat. "It's not so bad once you get used to it, right?"

"I guess now I know why they call it the Holler," she said, and he snorted a laugh. Untangling herself from him, she paddled her arms and legs so he wouldn't have to keep swimming for both of them. "How deep is it here, anyway?"

"Pretty deep." He jerked his head to the side. "Let's swim over this way. There's a ledge where we can stand."

She followed him to the far side of the swimming hole, where time and the elements had carved the rock formations into a series of narrow stair-step-like ledges. Josh seemed to know exactly which one was the perfect height for standing so nothing but their heads were above the water.

"I get the sense you've spent a lot of time here," Mia said, inserting herself against him and slipping her arms around his waist.

His eyes gleamed in the growing darkness. "Maybe."

"Naked time?" she asked, arching her brows.

He shrugged. "I used to come here with some of my friends in high school."

"I thought it was eighteen and up."

"It's supposed to be, but they didn't use to police it much." His hands stroked over her back under the water, and she rested her head against his while he talked. "There's a back road you can use to get in without paying for a state park pass—or there used to be. The bridge got washed out by a storm a few years ago, and they never replaced it. Since then, I guess the place has fallen out of favor with the younger generation."

"But this was your place?" It was almost comfortable in the water now, snuggled up against Josh like this with her bare breasts pressed against his chest. She could imagine how nice it must feel in the height of summer. How thrilling it would be to come here with your friends as a teenager to prove you were daring enough to bare it all.

Not that Mia ever would have done anything like that. She'd been neither daring nor reckless enough, even in her teenage years. Especially in her teenage years. Her greatest act of rebellion had been the math tattoo she'd gotten on her eighteenth birthday with her mother's blessing.

Josh rubbed his nose into her hair. "Me and Wyatt and a bunch of our friends, yeah."

Her arms tightened around him. "Guy friends or girl friends?"

"Both." His hands dropped to her ass and squeezed. "Otherwise, what's the fun?"

"What about Andie?"

"Hell no. I wouldn't let her. I didn't want my little sister seeing all my friends naked, and I sure as hell didn't want my friends seeing my little sister naked."

Mia smiled, wishing she'd had a big brother to watch over her. "It sounds like maybe she used to come here anyway."

"Yeah, I guess sometimes she'd sneak off on nights she knew I wouldn't be here. And then once I left for college there wasn't much I could do about it." He touched his thumb under Mia's chin and tipped her head up to frown at her. "I really don't want to talk about my sister right now."

"Fair enough," she agreed.

When he kissed her, it warmed her down to her toes. The last rays of sunlight danced on the surface of the water as she pressed her body into his, the cold all but forgotten.

He moved farther down the ledge, tugging her along with him. Then he backed up against the edge of the pool and hopped up onto a narrow jut of flat rock so only the tops of his shoulders broke the surface of the water. Pulling her against him, he kissed her again, then spun her around. With her back to him, he picked her up, settling her between his legs.

Mia leaned back against his chest, his thighs bracketing hers, and sighed as his hands smoothed over her belly. His mouth dropped to her neck as he cupped her breasts, and she tilted her head to give him better access.

"I suppose it's probably against the law to actually have sex here," she said, digging her fingernails into his thighs.

He nipped her earlobe as his thumbs flicked her nipples. "Definitely."

"Not to mention unhygienic."

"Possibly." His tongue traced the curve of her ear, and he stroked his hands down her body, over her hips to her thighs. "Do you care?"

She rubbed against him, unable to help herself. "Not if you keep doing that."

One of his hands slid between her thighs as the other spread over her stomach, holding her against him. Not that she needed the encouragement. His caresses already had her quivering and writhing against him.

"Oh my god, are we really doing this?" Her head dropped back against his shoulder as his fingers stroked her with leisurely circles.

"Why not?" His breath was hot on her neck, his voice a low murmur in her ear.

"I thought with the cold water you might have a little trouble with . . . shrinkage."

He pressed his very obvious arousal into the cleavage

of her ass cheeks. "Does it feel like I'm having any trouble right now?"

"No." Her chest hitched as his strokes grew less leisurely. "No, it does not."

"But I can stop if you want."

Her hand clamped on his wrist. "Don't you dare."

A low, rumbling laugh reverberated through his chest and into hers. "Then I guess we're doing this."

She let out a surprised squeak as he lifted her up. The buoyancy of the water rendered her nearly weightless in his hands as he lowered her onto him. Her surprised squeak quickly morphed into a gratified moan, and she reached back to tangle her fingers in his wet hair.

Oh yeah.

They were definitely doing this.

Reptiles had life figured out. That was what Mia decided as she stretched out on the sun-warmed rock beside the swimming hole.

She and Josh had stayed in the water until twinkling stars had pierced the last watery rays of sunlight in the sky overhead, and then they'd gotten out and dried off, rubbing warmth into each other's chilled bodies with the towels he'd brought.

At first she'd been skeptical when he told her to lie down on the blanket. But as soon as she sat her bare butt down on the thin quilt, the stored heat radiating off the stone began to seep into her body. Lying back, she stretched her hands over her head with a deep, contented sigh.

No wonder reptiles lay on rocks to warm themselves. This was heavenly.

Josh draped another blanket over her before flopping down beside her. He twitched the edge of the blanket over his legs and lay back, propping his hands behind his head.

"The term 'cold-blooded' is a misnomer," Mia said. "Ectothermic animals don't actually have colder blood than endotherms."

Josh swiveled his head to look at her, and she realized her mental leap had only made sense inside her own mind.

"Sorry, I was just thinking of how lizards sun themselves on rocks." She shook her head. "I'm trying not to do that so much."

"Do what?"

"Blurt out conversational non sequiturs. According to my ex it makes me sound like a freak."

"He said that to you?" Josh's eyes narrowed with murderous intent.

She tried to shrug it off, not wanting to make a big deal out of it. "He said a lot of things. That's why he's my ex now."

One of the things he'd said was "we should break up," which was the only reason he was her ex now. If Paul hadn't dumped her, she might still be trying to hold on to him from a thousand miles away. And then she wouldn't be with Josh right now.

"That guy sounds like a real asshole," Josh growled. She turned her head to look at him and he reached for her hand, holding it between them. When he spoke again his tone was much softer. "The way your mind works is what makes you special. The fact that your brain is always five steps ahead, making connections no one else can see, is why you're so good at math. Just because the rest of us can't keep up doesn't mean there's anything wrong with you."

She squeezed his fingers, smiling at the dim outline of his face.

No man she'd ever dated had understood her so well. Or been so willing to accept her exactly as she was. Her past boyfriends had always wanted to improve her. Or compete with her. Or they'd simply been puzzled by her. Whatever the case, eventually they'd all wound up so frustrated they'd left.

Would Josh end up frustrated with her too? It was hard to imagine, with his easygoing personality. He was so patient. So perceptive. So kind.

He was exactly the sort of man Mia could imagine herself loving for the rest of her life.

The thought froze her for a second before reality intruded, reminding her she wouldn't have the chance. Not with her leaving Crowder as soon as her contract was up—and with Josh inextricably tied to the farm.

He'd never leave this place, and she could never stay. They were a paradox. A mathematical impossibility.

Her throat tightening, Mia turned her face to the sky so Josh's sharp eyes wouldn't discern her change of mood.

She'd never seen so many stars in her life. They spread across the sky like a great, glittering blanket, so thick in some places it was impossible to pick out the spaces in between them. It made her feel small and insignificant, but also somehow reassured that the universe would continue to produce wonders, regardless of the relatively minor struggles of the tiny organisms living on the surface of an inconsequential planet orbiting an unremarkable yellow sun in a forgotten arm of one spiral galaxy lost among hundreds of billions of others.

"Why's the water here so cold?" she asked, thinking of the coldness of space.

Josh took her abrupt change of subject in stride, as he always did. "It's spring-fed. All the swimming holes along Cooper Creek are."

"It must feel great in the summer. Not just the Holler, I mean, but the non-nude swimming holes too."

"Yeah, we spent about as much time up here as we could manage every summer. We were always nagging our parents, begging someone to drive us. We'd pile as many kids as we could into one car and spend the whole day up here."

"That sounds nice." Idyllic, actually. Josh's childhood sounded like something from a novel. Mia had always been proud of where she was from, but she found herself a little envious of him.

"What'd you do in the summers growing up?" he asked her. "I have this image in my head of kids in Brooklyn playing stickball in the streets and splashing around in open fire hydrants."

Mia laughed. "I think you're confusing Captain America's childhood with real life. It certainly wasn't like that for me."

"What was it like?"

"A lot of families in my neighborhood would leave during the hottest part of the summer and go to the beach or somewhere upstate. My parents couldn't take the time off work though, so we always stayed. My sister and I were usually enrolled in some kind of summer school or camp. Math and science for me, and art or dance for her."

"So you didn't get to hang out with your friends?" Josh asked.

"There were other kids in the camp with me. But we didn't

really hang out. Our au pair would always be there to meet me when the camp let out so she could walk me home." Mia pulled the blanket up higher on her chest, beginning to feel self-conscious about her public nudity. She'd almost forgotten it wasn't normal to lie outside under the stars without any clothes.

"Sounds like you didn't have a lot of freedom," Josh said.

"Not really." She turned on her side, tucking her hands under her cheek. "Not until I was older, and my mom decided we didn't need an au pair anymore. Then my sister and I were on our own a lot. We'd pack our own lunches, get ourselves to and from our summer programs, and order takeout for dinner most nights."

Josh snorted softly. "That explains why you eat like a teenager."

"Yes." Grinning, she sat up and stuck her tongue out at him. "Speaking of eating, what's in the cooler? Please say food."

"Of course it's food." He pushed himself upright. "I take it you're hungry." She could hear his smile better than she could see it in what was now full dark. Though between the starlight, the gibbous moon that had begun to rise, and the way her eyes had adjusted to the darkness, she could see much better than she would have expected.

"Ravenous," she said, smiling back at him. After swimming and . . . other activities, she'd worked up an appetite.

Because Josh thought of everything, he'd brought a couple battery-operated lanterns, which he turned on so they could see to eat. He set out paper plates and plastic cups. Mia bounced with glee when he unpacked a container of his feta cheese, and she lunged to grab it out of his hands.

He arched an eyebrow, the expression made more dramatic by the stark underglow cast by the lanterns. "I'd have thought you'd be tired of eating cheese after a month with me."

Grinning at him, she popped a piece of feta in her mouth. "You seriously underestimate my affection for cheese."

"Is that the real reason you like me? Because of my cheese?"

"You have a great many fine qualities," she said, waggling her eyebrows, "only half of which have to do with your cheesemaking abilities."

Josh blinked, then burst out laughing. "I guess I'll take that as a compliment."

"You should." While he was popping the tops on two aluminum cans from the cooler, Mia leaned over and pinched his ass for good measure.

"Woman, you better behave," he growled. "You're gonna make me spill this fancy canned wine."

She sat back on her heels, affecting the posture of a well-behaved angel. "We can't have that."

"Sorry we couldn't have a nice bottle of wine," he said as he filled their cups. "Glass and swimming holes don't mix."

"This is more than nice enough for me." She leaned over again, this time to press her mouth to his. His tongue slid against hers for one perfect, romantic moment.

He pulled away and lifted his cup. *"Prost."*

"Salute," she said, and tapped her cup against his.

They sipped their wine and then dug in to eat. In addition to the feta, the cooler contained pasta salad, cold ham, and grapes, which they jokingly fed each other like Antony and Cleopatra—until that devolved into a contest to see who could catch the most grapes in their mouth. Josh won, unsurprisingly, but Mia's throws were so bad he had to work hard for his victory.

After they'd eaten—and played—their fill, they put away the leftover food. Then they switched off the lanterns and sat together under the stars, listening to the sounds of the woods around them as they sipped the last of their wine.

For once, Mia relaxed and let herself enjoy being outdoors without thinking about snakes or bugs or mountain lions. It was impossible to think about anything unpleasant when she was sitting with her back nestled against Josh and his arms enfolding her. Her own protective little shell.

"I should probably get you home," he said eventually. "We've both got work tomorrow."

Right. *Work*. The thing that had brought Mia to Crowder in the first place—and the thing that would eventually take her away from all this.

Apparently it was possible to think about something unpleasant after all.

Josh ran his lips along the side of her neck. Despite his stated intention to take her home, he didn't seem in a hurry to move from their comfortable position. "I hope tonight wasn't too boring."

She twisted in his arms to look at him, sank her fingers in his hair, and said, "Of course it wasn't boring. It was perfect."

His mouth curved in that sweet half-smile she adored so much. "Really?"

"You better believe it." She yanked him close and kissed him. As her tongue slipped into his soft, welcoming mouth, his cool fingers pressed against her flushed cheeks. The air seemed to shimmer around them like the star-speckled sky above. A perfect, priceless moment.

If only it didn't have to end.

But maybe it was better that way. They could go out on a high note like a television show canceled before its time. Let each other go before the shelf life expired and the relationship turned sour. Before the illusion of perfection was punctured by their yet-to-be-revealed shortcomings, leaving them both resentful and embittered by the disappointment of their unrealistic romantic ideals.

It was inevitable, wasn't it? A simple matter of geology. The inexorable effect of pressure and time. There was no reason to think this relationship would be any different.

Chapter Seventeen

"Dr. Ballentine?"

Mia looked up from her laptop and smiled when she saw the student standing in her doorway. "Hi, Antonio."

His knuckles whitened as he squeezed the strap of his backpack. "Do you have a minute?"

"Sure. Come on in." Gesturing to the room's only other chair, she tabbed away from the email she'd been sending.

Or not sending, more precisely.

After two rounds of feedback and polishing, her former advisor at UCLA had declared her paper ready for submission to the *Annals of Mathematics*. The Annals was not only the Holy Grail of math journals, it was published by Mia's father's beloved alma mater, Princeton University—which also happened to be the school where Mia had received her undergraduate degree, the top math school in the country, and where she'd spent most of her life dreaming of one day joining the faculty.

No big deal or anything.

Her submission was as ready as it was going to get. There was no reason not to go ahead and hit send. The only thing holding her back was imposter syndrome. A nagging fear that she'd somehow gotten it all wrong and would be exposed as an incompetent. That she wasn't good enough for the Annals, like she hadn't been good enough for any of the postdocs she'd applied to. Inadequate. Unqualified. Useless. A pretender who'd wasted everyone else's time along with her own by thinking she had anything of value to offer the field.

So yeah. That was what had been going through her head, and why she hadn't yet summoned the courage to hit send on her submission.

Mia turned to Antonio, relieved to have an excuse not to think about her paper for the moment. "What can I do for you?"

"Um . . ." His tongue darted out to wet his upper lip. "I've been thinking about my major and what I want to do with my life."

She gave him an encouraging nod. "Great. That's what college is for."

"I was leaning toward a business major?" It sounded as if he was asking for her permission.

"Okay." She nodded again and waited, sensing there was more he wanted to say. Mia wasn't his academic advisor, so there was no need for him to come to her and declare his major—unless there was a specific reason he wanted her insight.

Antonio squirmed in the ancient metal office chair, which let out a squeak of protest.

When he didn't speak up again, Mia tried prompting him with a question. "Why business?"

"Um, I guess it seemed the most practical." He paused. "And the most realistic."

"I see."

"That's why I'm in your calculus class. It's the one recommended for first-year business majors."

"It is." There were a lot of business majors in her calculus class, just as there were a lot of humanities majors in her Math in Society class.

"I've never really liked math." Antonio darted a guilty look at her. "No offense or anything."

Mia smiled. "None taken." She'd heard similar sentiments plenty of times before. It wasn't something she took personally, even in one of her students, although it was certainly an indication she had her work cut out for her.

Antonio seemed to take encouragement from her lack of displeasure at his candor. "I kind of hated it, actually. I always felt like I was bad at it. Until I started taking your class this semester. For the first time, it feels like it makes sense to me, like I actually understand what I'm doing. It's like a switch flipped inside my head or something, I dunno. And now I kind of . . . like math?" He looked up at her uncertainly.

Mia's smile grew wider as a lump of pride formed at the back of her throat. It was what every teacher hoped to hear. She'd gotten through to someone. Overcome a student's aversion to math and infected them with her love of the subject.

"I'm glad," she said, her voice coming out a little hoarse. "I'm really glad."

"The thing is . . ." Antonio scratched his chin as he seemed to consider his next words. "I never really *wanted* to do business. It was just this thing I thought I *should* do, you know?"

"Is there something else you think you might want to do?"

Mia kept her voice neutral, not wanting to influence him with her obvious enthusiasm for her own field.

He leaned back in his chair, seeming more relaxed. "I always had this idea in the back of my head that I wanted to be an engineer. Build things, you know? Like a mechanical engineer, I guess. But since I wasn't good at math, I always figured it was out of the question."

"Mechanical engineering is definitely a challenging major, and it does involve a lot of math and science."

"The science isn't so bad," he said, sitting forward again. "I liked physics in high school. It's what made me think I might want to be an engineer."

"There's a lot of math involved in high school physics," she pointed out.

"Yeah, but it was different somehow? I didn't mind it as much when I understood what I was doing the math for."

Mia nodded in understanding. It was a complaint she'd heard from a lot of people. The math they'd learned in high school had felt pointless, because it had seemed to exist in a vacuum. That was what happened when you taught rote regurgitation of rules, equations, and functions without any grounding in real-world applications.

"So anyway," Antonio continued, "now I'm wondering if I could handle engineering after all. But I don't know. Maybe it's crazy. I just don't know if I'm smart enough to do all that math." He sat back with a doubtful look, clearly hoping she'd tell him what to do.

"First of all," Mia said, "there's no such thing as smart enough to do math. Your perception of your own mathematical abilities is a product of your education and your environment, not a reflection of your innate intelligence."

His expression remained dubious, which didn't surprise her. A secondary education geared toward standardized testing tended to brand students with labels they wound up internalizing. Gifted or not-gifted. Honors or remedial. Passing or failing.

It wasn't until college and grad school that Mia had fully appreciated what an advantage she'd been given by her private, Montessori-based education—not to mention the resources and implicit support of her parents, even if they hadn't always been around to help her with her homework at night. Their high expectations hadn't allowed room for any question of her not being capable or smart enough, and had driven her to push herself in a bid for their approval.

Antonio had likely been told by the state's standardized tests that math wasn't his best subject, a message that had been reinforced by his grades in classes that were organized around the material that would show up on those tests. And like most students, he hadn't had access to additional resources that might have helped him realize his potential. So he'd simply accepted that he wasn't good at math.

"From what I've seen this semester, you're more than capable of doing the work," Mia told him, and he sagged with relief. "The more important question you need to ask yourself is if you like mechanical engineering enough to pursue it seriously. Is it work you want to do for the rest of your life?"

Antonio opened his mouth to respond and she cut him off with a raised hand.

"I don't expect you to know the answer to that yet, and you probably won't until you've taken some engineering courses. But if you're asking me if I think you can handle it, my answer is an unqualified yes."

"Really?" Hope brightened his expression for the first time since he'd entered her office. "You think I should go for it?"

"If it's what you think you want, absolutely. The most important determiners of success are motivation, persistence, and hard work. Everything I know about you says you're capable of all three. But finding a vocation you love makes all the difference. Once you have that, the motivation follows naturally, greasing the wheels to make the persistence and hard work less painful. Enjoyable, even."

"Is that the way it is for you?"

Mia thought about it. "Most of the time."

She grimaced, remembering how long she'd struggled over a single proof, and the stress and dread she'd felt over the pressure to get something published in time to beef up her CV. It had sucked a lot of the joy out of her work. Almost all of it, in fact.

"But I don't always believe in myself either," she admitted. "Everyone has moments of self-doubt and crises of confidence. But you shouldn't let imposter syndrome hold you back." She was conscious of the irony as she lectured Antonio about the exact same thing she'd been battling herself. "There's always going to be a voice in your head whispering that you're not as good as other people—and maybe even some people in your life will tell you the same thing. But you've got to find a way to shut all of that out. Tell that voice in the back of your head to shut up and let you do your work."

Antonio laughed. "I'll have to remember that when I'm doing my calculus homework." He bent over to pull a piece of paper out of his backpack. "I looked up the math requirements for a mechanical engineering degree. Do you think you could go over them with me so I know what I'm getting myself into? Everything makes way more sense when you explain it."

For the second time in just a few minutes, Mia's heart swelled. And maybe her head did too a little. But why shouldn't it? One of her students had just paid her the highest possible compliment. It was a vindication of all the effort she'd put into developing her lesson plans, not to mention every minute she'd spent agonizing over her lectures and practicing them in the mirror.

She stuck out her hand and wiggled her fingers. "Hand it over." Antonio passed her the paper and she laid it on the desk in front of her before saying, "Hold on a second. I need to do something really quick." She turned to her laptop and brought up the email she'd composed with her submission to the Annals attached.

Before she could lose her nerve, she hit send.

There. It was done. Out of her hands and out in the world. Subject to the judgment of strangers. It was a little terrifying, but also exhilarating.

Mia turned back to Antonio with a smile. "All right. Let's see what your future holds."

And then she started to explain why he was going to love linear algebra.

"It was the most amazing feeling," Mia told Josh later that night. "I don't know how to describe it. Like winning the lottery or something. Only not really. It's hard to explain."

It was Friday night, so they'd made spaghetti and meatballs together at the farm. Josh had made the sauce from scratch with the last of the fall tomatoes, and Mia had made the meatballs from Birdie's recipe—under Josh's supervision.

As they sat down to eat the meal they'd cooked together, Mia had relayed the gist of her conversation with Antonio without revealing the name of the student who'd come to talk to her. Since Josh knew both Antonio and Antonio's father, Mia didn't want to betray his confidence, in case he hadn't shared his career aspirations with his father yet.

Josh grinned as he sprinkled Parmigiano-Reggiano over his spaghetti. "Was it as good as cracking a math problem that's gone unsolved for decades?"

"Kind of, actually." Mia accepted the cheese from him and spooned a thick layer over her spaghetti. "It's a more immediate sort of gratification. More personal."

"I seem to recall you felt pretty gratified the day you finished working out your proof." He was cutting up his spaghetti with his knife, a habit that Mia found endearing but would have mortally offended her Italian-American friends back home. She'd teased him about it the first time she'd seen him do it, and he'd shrugged unselfconsciously and said it was the way he'd always eaten his spaghetti.

She shot him a knowing smile. "And I seem to recall you were directly responsible for a lot of that gratification."

He snorted. "I was talking about before that. Didn't you text me something about being so happy you were shaking?"

"I guess I did." Mia tried to remember that feeling, which had faded so quickly after the initial high. "It didn't last though. I remember going back to class the next Monday feeling like nothing had changed, except I had more work ahead of me."

"That's always the way it is, isn't it? Triumphs only last until the next challenge comes along."

"I suppose."

She wound her spaghetti around her fork as she thought about it. Somehow she suspected she'd still feel good on Monday when she walked into class. More confident. More energized, knowing that what she was doing was actually working.

She set her fork down and reached for her glass of wine. "I submitted my paper today, by the way." She hadn't told Josh that she'd been putting it off. She hadn't wanted him to know how much she'd been doubting herself.

"How long before you hear anything?"

"I don't know. Weeks? Months? It depends if they reject it outright or send it for peer review. If they send it for review, it depends on the schedules of the reviewers. And then I might be asked to revise and resubmit, which will drag the whole process out even longer."

It was exhausting to think about. She knew she should be excited, but she was actually sort of dreading hearing back from them. Unable to let herself believe she wasn't just inviting another rejection.

"So it'll be a while," Josh said.

Mia nodded. "That's what I mean. It felt good to share my work with a few close colleagues and have them respond enthusiastically, but now I'm just going to be sitting around waiting for something to happen. It's kind of anticlimactic. And it hasn't changed anything about my day-to-day life. It might eventually, but that's going to take time. I don't feel any different because I hit send on an email."

"You don't feel a sense of accomplishment? Or relief to have it off your plate?"

"I guess. But it's not much of a high."

In fact, it brought a whole new source of anxiety. Because now, not only was she waiting for a possible rejection, she needed to start working on the next paper she planned to submit, not to mention making a list of alternate journals to submit this one to as a backup.

She pushed her plate away and picked up her wineglass again. "You know, it's funny. I never thought I liked teaching before. I was pretty anxious about how much I'd have to do when I took this job. I thought I wasn't any good at it." *Just like Antonio had thought he wasn't good at math.*

Josh frowned at her. "Clearly you are good at it, just like you're good at everything else."

She smiled at the compliment. "It's funny how your perception of something can completely change. I've really started to enjoy teaching since I've been here. I like the students at Bowman, how engaged and motivated they are. I like working with undergraduates, finding ways to connect with them. Engaging their critical thinking skills and awakening their curiosity . . ." Pausing, she sipped her wine as she reflected on it. "I think I might actually—"

She broke off, surprised by the thought as it formed in her mind.

Josh glanced up at her with his fork suspended halfway to his mouth. "What?"

"What if I like teaching as much as research? Or *more* even?"

It wasn't something she'd ever imagined herself saying. And yet, looking back on the past couple months, it was the moments in the classroom and the time she'd spent with her students that stood out to her as the most rewarding. Not the hours she'd spent agonizing over a proof or perfecting it for publication.

"I think that's great," Josh said.

"Is it? I've always thought research was what mattered most. Your contributions to the field. Everything I've done the last ten years, every goal I've set for myself, was based on that assumption."

Did this mean she'd been approaching her career like Antonio, who'd chosen a business major simply because he'd thought it was what he was supposed to do? It was an unsettling thought.

Josh shrugged. "Obviously I'm no expert, but it seems to me that molding young minds is a pretty important contribution to the field. Teachers have the power to change people's lives. That's not an accomplishment to be discounted." He paused, adding, "Although I'm sure research is important too."

Mia nodded, letting the idea sink in.

It was a lot to think about. This could mean she needed to reassess parts of her twenty-year plan.

But she needed to figure it out soon, before she started applying for her next job.

Chapter Eighteen

Mia chewed her thumbnail as she squinted at the screen of her laptop. "What's a pastry cutter?" Next week was Thanksgiving, and she was spending it at Birdie's with Josh and Andie. To say thank you for being included in their family celebration, Mia had insisted on contributing a dish and—perhaps unwisely—volunteered to make a pie.

"You're not making the crust from scratch, are you?" Josh pulled open the refrigerator and got out the coffee creamer. He was wearing her favorite blue plaid shirt tonight, the one with the snaps she liked to rip open. Barefoot and completely comfortable moving around in her tiny kitchen, he looked like something out of a dream. A fantasy boyfriend come to life.

Except he wasn't her boyfriend, Mia reminded herself. Neither of them had used the word yet—or any other words that might put a label on them. They'd both been careful to avoid that particular minefield.

Mia frowned at him. "Of course I am."

Could you call someone a boyfriend when there was an expiration date on your relationship? Could you even consider it a real relationship when it was just a temporary arrangement?

Josh gave the creamer a suspicious sniff and shrugged before pouring it into the two mugs in front of him. "Why don't you buy a crust at the store?"

"Are you implying I can't handle making a scratch crust?"

"Perish the thought."

"I'm detecting sarcasm in your tone."

"All I'm suggesting is there's no reason to make it more complicated than it needs to be. There's no shame in taking a shortcut." Josh brought the two coffees over and set one on the coffee table in front of Mia before settling down at the other end of the couch with his.

Swiveling to face him, she pulled her feet up under her before gesturing at her laptop screen. "It says here, and I quote: There's nothing quite as good as a pie made completely from scratch."

"Don't food bloggers make their money from page views and advertising revenue? Of course they want everyone to use their recipe instead of buying a premade crust that tastes just as good."

"Do they taste just as good though?" Mia eyed him over her laptop. "Do they?"

He shrugged and blew across his coffee. "Probably."

"I'll bet you've never had a premade crust in your life," she said as she copied ingredients to her shopping list. "Admit it. Everyone in your family makes their pie crusts from scratch."

He rubbed his hand over his jaw. "I don't think my dad's ever made a pie that I can recollect."

"Okay, but I know Birdie makes scratch crusts." Birdie made everything from scratch. Even the suet she put out for the birds, and the nectar in her hummingbird feeders. She could probably make a pie crust in her sleep.

"She's not going to judge you if you buy a crust at the store," Josh said. "I promise."

Mia ignored him. "And I'll bet your mom does too, doesn't she?"

"Oh yeah, she makes this apple crumb pie with cream cheese every year." His eyes got a faraway look as he lounged against the couch cushions, sipping his coffee. "It's incredible. Best pie I've ever had."

"Should I make that instead?" Why was she making a pumpkin pie if apple was his favorite? And why hadn't she thought to ask him what his favorite pie was before starting her list?

"You can't," he said. "Mom guards that recipe like her life depends on it. She won't share it with anyone—even Birdie. She says she'll leave it to Andie in her will, but until then we're out of luck." He smiled to himself. "But you'll get to taste it at Christmas when they're here."

Mia's head jerked up. "Your parents are coming for Christmas?"

She didn't know why it hadn't occurred to her that they might. Maybe because they weren't coming for Thanksgiving. Or because her own parents had almost never bothered to visit her. But of course normal parents would want to see their kids—not to mention their old friends and the rest of their family—and Josh couldn't very well leave the farm to visit them in Maine.

"They usually come back twice a year. Once in the summer and again at Christmas. So you'll get to meet them." He looked down at his mug, his brow crinkling faintly. "I mean, if you want. Assuming you're around over the holidays."

He was asking her to meet his parents. She should have been flattered, but instead she felt panicky.

Stalling, she reached for her coffee mug and brought it to her lips.

It shouldn't be a big deal, should it? She was already friends with Josh's sister and his aunt, who practically treated her like a member of their family.

But maybe that was the problem. She wasn't a member of their family. She was only passing through their lives on her way to somewhere else. A tourist, basically.

Meeting Josh's parents carried implications. They'd assume any girlfriend he introduced them to was potentially serious. A possible future wife to help him run the farm and give him the children he undoubtedly wanted.

That wasn't Mia.

It seemed wrong to get their hopes up—not to mention a waste of everyone's time—and go through the harrowing social ritual of getting to know each other when she wouldn't even be around next Christmas. Or next Thanksgiving. Or even Labor Day. Mia would be gone before the end of the summer.

She was intimidated to meet the woman who made Josh's favorite pie in the world and had crocheted the blanket on the back of his couch. How was she supposed to look his mother in the eye, knowing she'd be leaving him in a mere matter of months?

Mia still hadn't responded, and Josh was waiting for her to say something. The silence had grown awkward. Weighty.

She swallowed a mouthful of coffee, which burned all

the way down her throat. "I'll probably go home, actually. I haven't seen my sister in almost a year, and she'll kill me if I leave her on her own to deal with our parents over Christmas."

"Sure," Josh said, unable to completely hide his disappointment. "Yeah, of course."

Mia stretched out her leg to nudge his thigh with her big toe. "If it's any consolation, I would definitely have a better time here with you than with my family."

He laid his hand over the top of her foot. "You don't have to console me. You should spend the holidays with your family. That's what the holidays are for."

His words twisted in her belly. Other than Holly, she didn't have any great desire to see her family. Christmas with her parents was a dismal affair. Her father usually hosted a big gathering on Christmas Eve that Mia and Holly were expected to attend, even though he'd be so busy mingling with his guests he'd barely have any time for them. Christmas Day they always spent with their mother, eating a reheated takeout meal she'd ordered from a local restaurant—assuming she didn't get called in to the hospital, leaving Mia and Holly to eat on their own and watch TV all day.

It was a far cry from the warm, traditional holiday gathering she imagined Josh's family having at the farmhouse every year, full of laughter and home cooking and old-fashioned Christmas traditions. Mia's mother didn't even bother to put up a Christmas tree anymore.

"Hey." Josh gave her foot a squeeze. "You okay?"

"Yeah." She smiled for him. "Fine. Just thinking about Christmas shopping. My mother's impossible to shop for, and it'll be here before you know it."

Time had seemed to pass so slowly at the start of the semester, but now it felt like it was flying by. Before she knew it, she'd be halfway through her contract.

Creases sprouted across Josh's brow. "You know, I didn't mean to put you on the spot by suggesting you meet my parents."

"You didn't." Mia's cheeks hurt with the effort of maintaining her smile.

"Okay." The creases in his brow deepened into a full-fledged frown as his fingers traced the tattoo on her foot. "Do you think maybe we should talk about the elephant in the room?"

Mia blinked, her smile freezing in place. "What elephant is that?"

His gaze met hers. "What we're doing, given the fact that you'll be moving on next year."

"Oh." She swallowed, clutching her coffee mug tighter. "*That* elephant."

"I understand the reality of the situation, you know. I'm not trying to pressure you into anything more than you can offer."

"Right. Well . . . that's good I guess." Her throat felt dry. She tried to soothe it with a sip of coffee.

"You're only here temporarily, which means this . . ." He slid his hand over her ankle and up her shin slowly. ". . . is only temporary."

"True." It was the first time they'd explicitly acknowledged it out loud since they'd become more than just acquaintances.

His index finger traced the bones in her knee. "I'm okay with that. I don't want you to think I'm not."

But what if she wanted him to be a little not-okay with it? Did that make her a bad person? Not that she wanted him to be hurt—she could never, ever want that—but it might be nice if he at least wished she could stay.

Not that she'd ever admit anything of the sort—to him or anyone else.

"Whew." She passed her hand across her forehead in a jokey show of relief and let out a chirpy laugh.

His expression remained serious as he met her gaze again. "When that paper's published, it's going to be huge for you. You'll be swimming in job offers."

Mia made a scoffing sound. "I don't know about that."

She'd received an email from the editor informing her that the paper had been assigned for peer review, which meant she'd cleared the first hurdle in the lengthy submission process. But there were still a lot of hurdles to go. It was too soon to get her hopes up.

"I do." Josh's eyes shone with certainty. "I Googled that knot you were working on, you know. I don't need to know anything about higher math to understand what a big deal it is that you solved something everyone else thought was unsolvable. You're way too smart to hang around here. You deserve so much more than this."

A lump formed in her throat. It was such an unexpected gift to have someone so completely in her corner. How did he always know exactly what kind of support she needed? He had more confidence in her than she had in herself, and he wasn't shy about expressing it. It was exactly the validation her self-esteem craved.

If only she could take him with her when she left.

"You know—" She cut herself off before she blurted out the words *you could always come with me.*

Because he couldn't, and she knew that. It wouldn't be any more fair to ask him to leave his home than it would be for him to ask her to stay someplace she didn't belong. He'd already said he wouldn't try to hold her back. The least she could do was return the favor.

"What?" Josh asked.

"Nothing. I was just . . ." As her mind flailed to provide an excuse for her aborted utterance, her phone buzzed on the table, providing a convenient distraction. She swung around, setting her coffee and laptop aside as she reached for her phone. "Oh." Her stomach dropped when she saw it was her dad calling.

He almost never called her. Not unless he wanted something. And since he'd had little use for Mia since she'd proven herself a largely unemployable disappointment in her ill-advised chosen field, she hadn't heard from him in months. Since she'd told him she was moving here, in fact.

"Who is it?" Josh asked. "Is everything okay?"

"Yeah, it's just my dad." She set the phone down on the table again, where it continued to vibrate against the wood.

"Shouldn't you answer it?"

"No." Flicking her finger, she dismissed the call and the buzzing stopped. "It's fine."

"You don't want to talk to your dad?"

"Not especially."

Josh probably found that unrelatable. His parents called regularly, and he always seemed happy to talk to them. As far as Mia could tell, he had an ideal relationship with both of them.

He leaned forward to set his coffee on the table and scooted closer, letting his knee bump against hers. "You don't talk about your parents much."

"There's not much to say."

"Pretty sure that's not true." His hand stroked up her back.

She let her eyes fall closed, enjoying the sensation. "There's no great hardship or tragedy in my past. We're just not a very close family."

"I'm sorry about that."

She shrugged her shoulders. "Neither of my parents were really into the whole parenting thing. My mom did the best she could while juggling her career, but my dad mostly lost interest in us after the divorce."

Not right away, but certainly after he remarried. There'd been a brief, happy window between her parents' divorce and her father's second marriage. The fights and frigid silences had ended, replaced by alternate weekends at their father's new apartment in Manhattan. He'd tried to make their limited time together fun, like he was trying to make up for his absence the rest of the time. Those weekends were some of Mia's best memories from her childhood.

But then he'd started dating, and it had no longer been convenient to have two kids on his hands every other weekend. He'd started canceling. Putting them off more and more frequently, so they were only seeing him once a month, and then once every other month. Within a year he'd given up the pretense altogether so he could spend his weekends with his new fiancée.

It was the first time Mia's father had disappointed her, but certainly not the last. After years of no-shows and broken promises, she liked to think she'd hardened herself to it. But inside her still lurked that brokenhearted little girl who'd wanted to believe she was important to her dad.

She didn't tell Josh any of this though. She didn't like to talk about it, and she certainly didn't want to admit that it bothered her. Her whole life she'd been acutely aware of her privilege. Never once had her parents let her go without food, shelter, or supervision. They'd given her the financial support she'd needed to succeed in life. She didn't even have student loans to pay off. So if she'd sometimes wished she'd had a little more of their attention, it was hardly worth complaining about in the grand scheme of things.

Josh draped an arm around her, pulling her close so he could press a kiss to her temple. "That must have sucked."

"It's not like I'm the only kid whose parents ever got divorced." She pushed him back on the couch so she could snuggle against him. "What's your mom like?"

"She's a lot like Birdie. The two of them look enough alike they could almost be mistaken for twins. Their personalities are similar too—although my mom's a little less free-spirited than Birdie."

His fingers combed through Mia's hair and she closed her eyes, imagining having someone like Birdie for a mom. How amazing must it have been to be surrounded by that kind of warmth and affection all the time? To be accepted just how you were, without needing to prove anything to anyone.

"What about your dad?" she asked, snuggling closer.

"He's a lot quieter than Mom. Some people might call him gruff, but really he's a big softy on the inside."

Mia gave his chest a playful tweak. "Like you."

He swatted her hand away with a grunt. "I guess."

Her phone gave a single, short buzz on the table, and she

leaned forward to check her notifications. It was a new voicemail. Her father had left a message.

She tapped the screen and held the phone to her ear.

"Mia. This is your father." As if she could mistake that stentorian voice on the recording for anyone else. "Your sister said you're not coming home for Thanksgiving this year."

It was so like him not to wonder about her holiday plans until the week before. As always, she was an afterthought.

"I'm sorry to hear you won't be in town next week. There are some things I'd like to talk to you about. I've got room in my schedule after the holiday, so I was thinking I could come to you. See where you're living now, catch up a little. And you could tell me about your work."

Mia's mouth fell open. Her father wanted to come see her? To catch up and hear about her work? Had he been possessed by body-snatching aliens? Replaced by an android with updated firmware? There had to be some kind of catch. An angle she couldn't see. Like he was dying and needed a kidney.

"How does the Saturday after Thanksgiving look for you? It'd just be for one night. I'll stay in Austin and drive down to see you for dinner. Call me back and let me know if that works for you."

Oh crap.

Her father was coming here.

Chapter Nineteen

Mia waited to call her father back until Josh had gone home to do the evening milking. She hadn't told Josh what he'd said in the voicemail, because she was still trying to process it.

It was probably moot anyway. She couldn't believe her father would actually come here to visit her. Experience had taught her not to take him at face value.

Her father picked up on the second ring. "Hello, Mia."

"Dad?" She was so shocked he'd actually answered her call that she almost forgot how to speak.

"Thanks for calling me back, Ace."

She bristled every time he used his old nickname for her, because it implied a closeness that hadn't existed for a long time. "Is everything okay?"

"Of course. Why wouldn't it be?"

Because you haven't shown this much interest in me since I was eleven.

"I don't know. When you said you needed to talk it sounded like it might be something serious. You're not sick, are you?"

"God no. Fit as a fiddle. Why do people say that anyway? Are fiddles known for being unusually fit?"

"I don't know," Mia said. "I never thought about it."

"Neither had I until just now. Anyway, what do you think about the Saturday after Thanksgiving? Can you spare a little time for your father?"

"You really want to come here?"

"Why not? It's where you live. I want to see how you're doing out there in flyover country. Make sure you're okay."

"I'm fine." If he'd really wanted to know how she was doing, he could have simply called her at any point over the last three months and asked.

"You sure you don't want to change your mind and fly home for Thanksgiving? I'll pay for the ticket. I hate the thought of you spending the day all alone in a strange town."

"I appreciate the offer, but I've got plans for the holiday, actually. Some friends here have invited me to join their Thanksgiving dinner."

"Do these friends include that farmer you're dating?"

"Who told you about that?" As if she couldn't guess. It had to be Holly, who she was going to murder the next time she saw her.

Her father chuckled. "Your sister, of course. She said he works in some kind of dairy? My god, the pickings must be slim there."

"Josh owns a goat dairy," Mia said through gritted teeth. "He makes artisan cheeses that he sells to high-end grocery stores and restaurants in Austin."

"Well, well, a young entrepreneur." Her father didn't try to hide the sarcasm in his voice. "I guess I'll have to come to you, then. Does that Saturday work with your busy schedule?"

"Um . . . sure." She couldn't think of a reason to say no. And even though she knew better, she was curious to find out what her dad wanted. Because it wasn't just to get to know her better.

"Perfect. I'll take you out to dinner at whatever passes for a nice restaurant down there. You can even invite your farmer friend to join us if you want."

The thought of subjecting Josh to her father's pretentious judgment was horrific enough on its own—but dragging Josh out to a restaurant was something she would certainly *not* be doing.

No way in hell.

"I should come to dinner with you," Josh said when she told him about her father's impending visit.

"I'm not asking you to do that." Mia shook her head as she scrubbed the baseboards in her apartment. She only had a week and a half to get the place spotless before her father arrived to pass judgment on her life, which meant she was in a full-on cleaning frenzy.

Would her father even notice her baseboards? Almost certainly not—unless there was something wrong with them. Whatever she managed to overlook, that was what he'd home in on like some kind of imperfection-seeking missile. She could only imagine what he'd think when he pulled up in front of Birdie's house and saw the couch on her front porch. Or when he encountered her chickens in the yard.

But there was nothing Mia could do about any of that, so she was focusing on the things that were within her control, like the dirty baseboards inside her apartment.

Josh came over and stood behind her, looming at the edge

of her peripheral vision. "Because you don't want me there, or because you don't think I can handle it?"

"Neither." She threw a frown over her shoulder, disturbed he'd ascribe either motivation to her. "Because my father isn't worth your time and there's no reason to let him make both of us miserable when I can save you the trouble."

Josh crossed his arms, arching an eyebrow as he stared her down. "Wouldn't it be easier for you if I was there to act as a buffer?"

Scowling, she went back to scrubbing the baseboard. "That's not the point."

He bent to take the sponge from her and pulled her to her feet. His hands squeezed her shoulders. "That's not an answer to my question."

"Of course I'd love to have you on my side, but—"

"Then I'm going." His tone left no room for argument.

Still, she tried to talk him out of it. "Josh, please don't—"

"Unless you can look me in the eye and say you'd rather not have me there, I'm coming to dinner."

Mia sighed in defeat. She wasn't above lying to protect him, but it was useless when Josh could see right through her. Damn him and his uncanny emotional perception.

Smiling, he leaned in to kiss her cheek. "That's what I thought."

Mia pulled her phone out to check the time again. Her father was late. Which shouldn't be surprising, since he always found a way to make her wait on him. At least she knew he'd actually made it to Austin—which had frankly shocked her. She'd half expected him to cancel the whole trip at the last minute the way he'd done so many times before. But he'd texted two and a half hours ago to say he'd landed and would be headed her way as soon as he got his rental car.

So where was he?

It didn't take two and a half hours to drive from the Austin airport to Crowder. She could only assume he'd made some sort of detour. One he'd neglected to mention was on his agenda when he'd claimed to be headed her way. Typical.

While she had her phone out, she texted Josh.

> **Mia:** He's still not here. Maybe he's not coming after all.
> **Josh**: Are you worried? Do you want me to come over and wait with you?
> **Mia**: No it's fine. This is what he always does.

As she was hitting send, she heard a car door slam outside. Peeking out the window, she saw her father standing beside a steel-gray Range Rover, his posture rigid and disapproving as he surveyed the property.

Never mind, she typed out to Josh. *He just got here.*

Mia took a deep breath and tried to manifest serenity and restraint as her father's heavy tread made its way up the stairs. A sharp, impatient rap sounded at the door, and she went to admit him.

Her father took up most of the doorway, his imposing frame smartly clad in a tailored sport coat, dress shirt, and slacks. As always, his appearance was impeccable, though she noted more gray at his temples than the last time she'd seen him.

"Quite a place you've got here, Ace." He strode over the threshold without waiting for an invitation, giving her cheek a brisk kiss as he walked past her into the apartment.

"Hello, Dad." She watched his lip curl slightly as he surveyed her modest but perfectly nice living space. "I was starting to wonder if I should call out the state troopers to send a search party for you."

Two seconds in her dad's presence and she'd already given up on serenity in favor of passive aggression. *Fuck it.* She'd never gotten the hang of all that positive manifestation stuff anyway.

He flicked his hand, dismissing the inconvenience and potential worry he'd caused her. "Oh, I stopped on the way to meet an old friend for a drink. You know how it is."

Unfortunately, she knew too well.

At least it helped explain her father's mysterious presence here. Either his "old friend" was some sort of professional contact he needed something from, or it was a woman he was seeing behind his current wife's back. Mia didn't care to know which explanation was the correct one, but she considered them equally likely.

When he'd completed his visual inspection of her apartment, he rounded on Mia with a smirk. "Nice flock of chickens you've got out in the yard there."

"They belong to my landlady."

"Well, I certainly didn't think they were yours."

Mia felt the need to stick up for Birdie. "She shares some of the eggs with me. And some of the vegetables from her garden too."

"Charming." His tone clearly indicated he considered it anything but.

At least he hadn't mentioned the couch on Birdie's porch.

"Is she having some sort of rummage sale?" he asked.

"Or is that old denim couch a permanent fixture in her front yard?"

Mia's molars ground together. "She's been extremely kind to me since I moved here, so I don't really care what her yard looks like."

Her father offered an unctuous smile. "Lucky you."

Mia *was* lucky to have Birdie in her life, but she knew better than to expect her father to understand that.

"I suppose this is the best you can afford on whatever they're paying at that place," he observed sourly. "Thank god it's only a one-year contract."

Hearing her dad articulate so many of the same thoughts she'd had herself when she first came here made Mia feel sick to her stomach. Had she been this stuck-up and shallow? So contemptuous of everything around her?

It pained her to realize how many of her father's attitudes she'd internalized. Although at least she'd had the courtesy to keep her negative opinions to herself.

"The salary happens to be quite decent," she informed him. "I've actually enjoyed the experience of teaching at a smaller school. I like Bowman and I like living in Crowder, believe it or not."

"I'm glad to see you're making the best of a bad situation."

"I was thinking I'd drive you around and show you the campus and some of the sights before dinner," Mia said.

"Oh, I don't think that's necessary. I got enough of an eyeful on my way here."

She should have known her father wouldn't be interested in seeing where she worked. It shouldn't hurt to hear him dismiss the suggestion out of hand. And yet, here she was, feeling hurt anyway.

Mia forced a flat smile, refusing to let her father see her disappointment. "Well good. Because there isn't time if we want to make our reservation."

"Reservation?" Her father's eyebrows shot up. "Who knew there was a need for reservations in a town of this size?" He let out a condescending little laugh as his gaze focused on her outfit, taking in her simple slacks and blouse. "Is that what you're wearing? I hope I'm not overdressed."

"You're always overdressed, but I doubt anyone will notice." Before he could respond, she snatched her purse off the counter and said, "Shall we go? I could use a cocktail before dinner."

Or five cocktails. Anything to take some of the edge off before her father gave her a rage stroke.

"By all means." He gestured magnanimously toward the door. "After you, Ace."

They were forty-five minutes early for their reservation at the steakhouse that Mia had chosen for dinner. Not only was it the nicest restaurant in town, but according to Andie it was also the best, since they sourced their selection of steaks and wild game from local ranches.

Not that it mattered. As soon as they walked through the door, Mia sensed her father's disdain for the outdated and slightly kitschy hunting lodge decor. She happened to find the rough-hewn log ceilings and antler chandeliers charming, but to her father, who was accustomed to dining at the trendiest restaurants in Manhattan, it must have seemed pathetically provincial.

Fortunately, the restaurant boasted a full bar where they could kill time while Mia got quietly and determinedly drunk. She squirmed on her animal-pelt barstool, sipping vodka tonics while her father bragged about the large gathering he and Mindy had hosted for Thanksgiving and his recent successes at the hedge fund he'd joined last year as a senior executive.

By the time Josh arrived, Mia was on her third drink and desperate for a buffer. As soon as she caught sight of him standing uncertainly in the doorway, she jumped up to wave him over.

"Oh thank god you're here," she murmured in his ear as she leaned over to kiss his cheek in greeting.

He gave her arm a squeeze before turning to her father, who'd gotten to his feet and was gazing down at Josh with an expression of cool appraisal. "Hi, I'm Josh Lockhart," he said, extending his hand.

Her father grasped it in his usual crushing grip. "Dr. Richard Ballentine."

"Pleasure to meet you," Josh said, his smile never faltering.

Mia enjoyed seeing her father wince a little as he let go of Josh's hand. It served him right for trying that hypermasculinity handshake crap with Josh. Her father might be able to intimidate pasty businessmen that way, but he was no match for someone who worked outdoors with his hands for a living.

"Shall we go see about our table?" Mia said, grabbing her drink. "They should have it ready by now."

When she'd made the reservation, she'd requested the most private seating they had, in order to try and make Josh more comfortable. To her relief, the hostess led them to a table tucked away in the far corner of one of the smaller rooms off the main dining room.

"Shame we couldn't be somewhere a little brighter," her father grumbled. "At least the view out those windows wasn't so bad."

"I like this better." Mia smiled her approval at the hostess before her father could ask to change tables. "Thank you."

She'd felt the tension radiating off Josh as they walked through the restaurant, but he seemed to relax a little once they were seated. Her father proposed they order a bottle of wine, then proceeded to spend the next five minutes deriding the wine list before ordering a bottle of champagne he grudgingly deemed drinkable.

"Have you had a chance to see much of Crowder?" Josh asked him once the lengthy wine ordeal had ended.

Her father snorted as he perused his menu. "Hardly any at all. But I must have driven through half a dozen towns like this one on my way down from Austin. These rural hamlets are all the same no matter where you are. There's always a Walmart and a Dairy Queen and a crumbling Main Street where the shops are going out of business because they can't compete with the Walmart and the Dairy Queen."

Josh didn't say anything in response, but from the muscle that ticked in his jaw Mia guessed he was already regretting his decision to meet her father. She was certainly regretting her decision to let him.

"The rib eye sounds good," she announced to fill the silence that had fallen after her father's diatribe. "I think I might get that."

"I don't know if it's worth getting a steak at a place like this," her father said. "I might just have a salad."

"It's a steakhouse in the heart of cattle country, Dad. I'm sure they know how to make a good steak."

"If you say so, Ace." Her father gave her a patronizing smile before setting his menu aside. "So, Josh. My daughter tells me you own a dairy. Is that right?"

Apparently the interrogation was about to begin.

Josh seemed perfectly calm and confident as he told her father about his acreage and herd size. A casual observer would probably think he was doing fine. But Mia knew him better than that. She could see his fingers rubbing against his thigh under the table. She also noted the uncharacteristic rigidity of his posture and detected a faint note of strain in his voice. All of which meant he was uncomfortable and struggling not to show it.

A surge of tenderness tightened her chest, even as she ached for him deep in her bones. She tried to send him a look communicating how much she understood and appreciated him, but Josh's attention was fully on her father.

"How many employees does it take to run a place like that?" her father was asking.

"I've got one full-time and one part-time helper," Josh answered. "But I do a lot of the work myself."

"You're the kind of man who likes to get his hands dirty, I'll bet." Coming from someone else, it might have been a compliment, but her father's tone communicated clear disdain.

Josh's spine grew several degrees straighter. "I'm not afraid of hard work, if that's what you mean."

"What's your educational background?"

"He's not on a job interview," Mia interjected with an uncomfortable laugh.

Josh ignored her, continuing to address her father. "I've got a BS in animal science with a minor in agribusiness entrepreneurship from Texas A&M, one of the top agricultural schools in the country."

"Cow college, isn't that what they call it?" Mia's father turned on her. "That must be what it's like at that school you're at. Trying to teach calculus to farmers' kids."

Mia didn't even know what to say to this incredibly insulting statement. Josh had fallen icily silent beside her, but he was radiating fury. She suspected it was taking all his self-control to hold his tongue.

"I'm just wondering how much you two have in common," her father went on blithely. "A dairy farmer and a PhD mathematician? Do you talk about Gödel's incompleteness theorems or the latest techniques for goat manure disposal?"

Incandescent rage burned in Mia's chest, but she kept silent, not wanting to make things worse for Josh by causing a scene. Drawing more attention to them wouldn't make this any easier.

She threw a pleading, apologetic look at Josh, hoping he wouldn't hate her after this night was over. His gaze met hers with an unsettling blankness. It was impossible to read anything in his shuttered expression, but she knew it was a defense mechanism to hide what he was feeling.

Desperate for connection and unable to reach his hand under the table, she slid her foot across the floor to bump against his. He didn't react, but at least he didn't move away from her. That was something.

Fortunately, before her father could say anything else, the waiter appeared with their champagne. They sat in silence as champagne flutes were distributed and the bottle was opened with a loud *pop* that made Mia flinch.

Once everyone had a full glass in front of them, Mia's

father lifted his portentously. "Now that we're suitably equipped, I can share the news that motivated my trip today."

Oh god, Mia thought, hunching her shoulders in apprehension. *Here it is.* The real reason for her father's visit. Because of course he hadn't just come to see her. As always, he had a hidden agenda.

Her mind raced through possibilities but couldn't find one to explain why he'd felt the need to come in person. On the bright side, her father's news was unlikely to have anything to do with Josh, so at least it would serve to pull focus from him.

Her father turned to address her directly and she braced herself. "I ran into an old grad school friend several weeks ago. I won't give away his name, but he sits on the editorial board of the *Annals of Mathematics*."

Mia froze as her father paused to allow the implication of that to sink in. Josh's gaze snapped to her, and she swallowed as her stomach twisted itself in knots.

"He happened to mention the paper you submitted to them." Her father's eyes narrowed, affecting disapproval. "Shame on you for not sharing it with your old dad, by the way."

She'd never even considered sending it to him. It wasn't like he'd have read it. He didn't give a crap about pure mathematics or anything she might publish on the subject.

"We were talking over drinks—you know how it goes." Her father was grinning like the Cheshire cat now. "And he may have let slip that your paper's passed peer review. It's going to be published in the Annals next year."

"*What?*" Mia's mouth fell open.

Her father looked as proud as if it had been his own

achievement. "The committee's still deliberating over one or two reviewer comments, but my friend assures me you're a lock for acceptance with minor editorial revisions."

"Oh my god." Mia looked at Josh. "Oh my god."

His eyes brimmed with warmth as he broke into a smile. "I knew it."

He had known. He'd always believed in her, no matter how much she'd doubted herself.

"My daughter's going to be published in the Annals." Her father lifted his glass with a flourish, commanding attention as he directed his gaze at her. "I can't tell you how proud this moment is for me. Congratulations, Mia."

Josh lifted his glass, and Mia numbly followed suit.

She couldn't believe it. This was real. Her father might mislead her about a lot of things, but never about something like this. Not about the Annals.

The champagne prickled as it slid down her throat. Slowly, she allowed herself to smile. To revel in her accomplishment. And the fact that for once in her life, her father was actually here to share it with her.

"This is huge," he said, looking as proud as she'd ever seen him. "I'm not sure if you appreciate what this means for you."

"I've got an idea," Mia said, her voice shaking a little. She took another drink of champagne.

"You've solved a problem that mathematicians have been trying to crack for fifty years. You're going to have your choice of jobs. All the top departments are going to be courting you. You'll be able to write your own ticket. Maybe even step right into a tenure-track position."

It was everything she'd ever wanted. Her twenty-year plan

was back on track. Not only on track, but possibly ahead of schedule.

This time next year, she might even be on the faculty at Princeton or somewhere equally as good.

Her gaze flew to Josh, but if he'd considered the ramifications, he didn't seem bothered by them. The only emotion she detected was happiness on her behalf.

Their entrées arrived, and her father continued to chatter about the opportunities that lay ahead of her as they dug into their food. Mia's steak was sublime, but her appetite had abandoned her in all the excitement. She forced herself to eat a few bites before giving up and reaching for her champagne again.

Her father was talking about the Fields Medal now, and how he thought she might have a shot at it. They only awarded it once every four years, and only one woman had ever been the recipient, but maybe he was right. Maybe she did have a shot. She could almost believe anything was possible at this point.

"You'll need to play your cards right for something like that, of course." Her father's brow furrowed as he chewed his salad. "We should start strategizing now. Every decision you make from this moment on could affect your chances. Have you decided on the subject of your next paper yet? Because there's going to be a lot of pressure on you to follow this up with something equally big."

"I haven't figured that out yet," Mia admitted and took another large gulp of champagne. She didn't want to think about that. The thought of having to churn out another paper was bad enough, but the realization that now everyone would be paying close attention to her choice of research, watching to see if she lived up to her potential or fell flat on her face, filled her with a new brand of anxiety.

"That's okay," her father said. "We can come up with a game plan for you. If you want the Fields Medal, it's going to take some big-picture planning. We'll need to make sure all the pieces on the board are aligned to your advantage. Which means we should coordinate your next area of research with the right job—the one that's going to get you what you want. I can advise you on all of that. Help you make the best decisions. Give you a leg up on your competition."

Mia set her champagne glass down slowly as a sour feeling settled in her stomach. She didn't want to think of research as a competitive play in some big football game. It was supposed to be about the search for greater understanding. A way to express truths that were independent of the physical world. Like poetry. That was what she loved about it.

But a businessman like her father could never understand that.

"Of course, we'll need to boost your profile," he said as he crunched on a large piece of lettuce. "It's not enough to simply be good. You've got to be the best, and you have to make sure other people know it. These things are mostly about PR when it comes down to it. Lucky for you, I've got a wide network of contacts that we can utilize. I'm going to set you up with a publicist—don't worry about the cost, I'll foot the bill."

He picked up his champagne and knocked back the last of it. Before he'd even set it down again, a waiter scurried over to refill everyone's glasses.

Her father flicked his hand to simultaneously acknowledge and dismiss the server. "Jennifer—that's the publicist I know—you're going to love her. I'll have her start pitching stories to some of the more mainstream science magazines. We need to get you on people's radar and make sure you stay there. You'll need headshots, of course. And someone to manage your social media too. It's important to make the most of your online presence. That's where it's at these days. You need a Twitter following to get people's attention. But don't worry, Jennifer's people can handle all that for you."

Mia's shoulders hunched as she stared at her plate, her appetite completely evaporated now. Everything her dad was saying sounded . . . awful. The exact opposite of what she wanted. A publicist? A social media manager? Headshots? She wasn't Taylor Swift. She just wanted to teach and do research, not all this other stuff.

"I'm thinking we should start with a human-interest angle," her father went on, oblivious to Mia's growing listlessness. "A joint interview with the two of us—the math prodigy and her mentor." He smiled, but instead of pride Mia saw opportunism in his expression. "A legacy of math passed on from father to daughter."

Now, at last, she understood. This was why her father was here. Why he'd flown down to deliver the news in person. To share her success, yes. But not simply as a proud parent—he was an attention parasite looking for a host. That was the agenda she hadn't been able to deduce before.

Now that she'd finally done something worthy of his notice, he intended to angle her into the spotlight so he could bask in the glow that bounced off her and reflected back onto him.

Mia barely spoke for the rest of the meal. Josh kept throwing her questioning looks, clearly sensing that something was wrong, but she couldn't explain with her father sitting right there. Not until she'd decided what she wanted to do about it.

Her father paid the check when it came, basking in his own magnanimity as he received their thanks. Mia snuck a twenty-dollar bill out of her purse and left it under her napkin. For all he liked to make a great show of his largesse, her father was a notoriously bad tipper.

They stepped out of the restaurant into the chilly November night, and Mia shivered as she struggled with her jacket. Josh moved to help her, sliding the sleeves up her arms and straightening the collar for her. His gaze met hers as she spun to face him, and his brow creased with an unspoken question. *Are you okay?*

She forced a smile for him as her father huffed impatiently, eager to be on his way.

Josh swiveled to extend his hand to her father. "Thanks again for dinner, Dr. Ballentine." Only someone who knew him well would have sensed the lack of warmth in his voice. "It was good to meet you." This was a bald-faced lie, Mia was certain, but Josh was too polite to say anything less. He'd been raised better than that.

Her father shook Josh's hand, this time without attempting to crush it, and replied with a far less gracious, "Likewise," before starting toward the car.

Josh looked at Mia, and she pressed a kiss against his cheek, murmuring, "I'm sorry my dad was so awful to you."

"I don't care about that." His hands grasped her shoulders, his eyes softening with concern as they peered into hers. "Is everything okay with you?"

Nodding, she slid her arms around his waist and rested

her head on his shoulder. "I get stressed around my dad, that's all."

His arms encircled her. "But you're happy, right? This is exciting news."

"Yeah, of course." She squeezed her eyes shut, burrowing into the soft warmth of his shirt. "It's great. I'm thrilled. Just . . . still trying to process it all."

He nuzzled her hair. "Text me when he leaves and I'll come over."

"Mia!" her father shouted across the parking lot. "Say good night to your boyfriend so we can get out of here."

She drew back, giving Josh an apologetic look. "It might be late. Honestly, I'll probably be exhausted and just go to sleep."

"Okay." He tried to hide it, but she saw a flash of hurt in his eyes before he managed to shake it off.

Was this a preview of how he'd feel when she left for good? A glimpse of the pain she was going to cause him? He'd said he was okay with her leaving, but had he only been trying to make her feel better?

For the first time, regret twisted inside her as she looked at Josh. He'd already been hurt enough to last a lifetime. Maybe he'd have been better off if she'd never come into his life.

Cupping his face in her hands, she stared into his warm brown eyes, trying to express all the things she wanted him to know but didn't know how to put into words—and didn't have time to say in a cold parking lot with her father waiting on them. "I really am sorry about my dad, but thank you for coming tonight. It meant a lot to me."

Josh studied her, frowning. "Did it?"

"Of course." She kissed him again, more tenderly this time,

wishing she didn't have to leave him here. It was an effort to drag herself out of the secure comfort of his arms.

But she forced herself to do it.

"We'll talk tomorrow," she told Josh regretfully before going to join her father.

"You're awfully quiet," her father observed on the drive back to her apartment.

Mia was surprised he'd even noticed. He'd been going on about his grand plans for her nonstop since he pulled out of the restaurant parking lot. The photoshoot he was going to schedule while she was home for Christmas. The people he planned to consult for advice about what her next paper should be. The schools he thought would be vying hardest to snap her up.

Shifting in the passenger seat of the rented Range Rover, she turned her face to the window. "I'm just processing still. It's a lot." The car smelled strongly of leather cleaner and that fake new car smell deodorizer they used at car washes. It was giving her a headache.

"You're right, it is a lot," her father said pointedly. "It's a huge opportunity. I hope you won't waste it."

The implication that she'd already wasted opportunities by rejecting the path he'd laid out for her graduate studies hung heavy in the stifling air of the car.

And in a way, he'd been right. She'd insisted on making her own choices and they'd backfired on her. That was how she'd ended up teaching at an unremarkable school in the middle of nowhere.

Hadn't she had enough of a taste of failure to teach her a lesson? She could still remember how it had felt to receive rejection after rejection, laying all her hopes to waste. Maybe she should follow her father's advice now. She might not like him or his methods, but he had a proven track record and ironclad instincts when it came to success.

Didn't she want to succeed?

Her father cleared his throat. "That Josh seems like a nice young man."

Mia cut a knife-edged glare at her dad. "Don't pretend you liked him. It was obvious you didn't."

"All I mean is that I can see what it is *you* like about him. Simplicity can be attractive. There's comfort in the uncomplicated. But I wouldn't want you to get too comfortable."

"What does that mean?" she asked irritably.

"I'd hate to see you settle for less than you deserve." Her father glanced over at her before returning his gaze to the road ahead. "Challenges are what keep us sharp. You need intellectual stimulation and the company of like-minded people if you want to stay at the top of your game. It's admirable that you seem to have made the best of your time in this godforsaken place." His lip curled slightly as he glanced out the window. "Maybe you've even grown to like it here." He slid another look at Mia and shifted into an admonishing tone. "Complacency is the enemy of excellence. Don't delude yourself into thinking that you could be happy in a place like this. It would be foolish to let your emotions get in the way of your career or prevent you from realizing your potential."

Swallowing the bitterness and resentment churning in her gut—along with a disconcerting feeling that there was at least some truth to the things her dad was saying—Mia turned her face to the window again. "I'll keep that in mind."

Chapter Twenty

TO: Dr. M. Ballentine
FROM: Madison Tate
SUBJECT: New STEM student group

Hi Dr. Ballentine!

I've gotten approval from the Student Activities Office to create a new organization on campus with the goal of encouraging and retaining diversity among science, technology, engineering, and mathematics majors on campus. The Diverse Voices in STEM Network will provide resources, programming, community support, and networking opportunities for members of underrepresented groups, including but not limited to women, BIPOC, LGBTQIA+, and disabled students. (See attached mission statement.)

I'm writing to you because I'm hoping you'll agree to sign on as a faculty sponsor. I promise it won't take up much of your time, and I think you'd be a terrific asset to the organization. I'd be happy to provide more information or answer any questions if you have them.

Best regards,
Madison

Before she'd found out about the Annals, Mia would have been thrilled by Madison's request. She was still pretty thrilled about it, but she'd also been hit with a bittersweet feeling.

The idea itself was terrific, and she had no doubt Madison was the right person to put something like this together. Beyond that, she was touched Madison had come to her for help. Mia's eyes had prickled unexpectedly as she'd read the email.

She would have loved to be a part of something like this. Helping the students get it off the ground and watching them take off with it would have been incredibly rewarding.

But Mia wouldn't be here long enough to do that. That had always been true, but now it felt more real. Harder to ignore.

She didn't answer Madison's email. Instead, Mia decided to break the bad news in person. But she did forward the email to her non-university account, because she wanted to have a copy of it to keep after she'd left Bowman.

The next time her calculus class met, Mia approached Madison as she took her usual seat in the front row.

"Did you get my email?" the girl asked hopefully.

Mia nodded. "Let's talk after class, if you have a minute."

She was extra conscious of Madison's attention on her as she went over the homework problems and then walked the class through a lesson on definite integrals. Fifty minutes later, she sent the students on their way with a new set of homework problems, and waited for Madison to pack up her things. Antonio had also hung back as the rest of the class filed out, and Madison waved him over as she got up and slung her backpack over her shoulder.

"Antonio's going to be one of the club's officers," Madison explained as he joined them at the front of the classroom.

Well that doesn't make this any easier. It was hard enough saying no to Madison, but the prospect of letting Antonio down sat about as well as curdled milk.

"Did you have any questions for us?" Madison asked, shifting her overloaded backpack to her other shoulder.

Mia sucked in a breath and offered Madison a smile as she prepared to deliver the speech she'd been reciting in her head for two days. "Your email and mission statement explained everything extremely well. I think it's a wonderful idea, and I wish you both the best of luck." Mia directed an approving look at Antonio, who she was pleased to see taking on a leadership role and embracing his interest in STEM. "I'm honored you'd ask me to be a part of it, and I'd love to say yes, but I'm only a visiting lecturer. I don't think I'm allowed to sponsor a student organization."

She wasn't entirely sure, to be honest. Some schools allowed visiting professors to take on extracurricular advisory roles and some didn't. She couldn't remember if it had been covered in her orientation sessions, and she hadn't actually looked it up in the faculty handbook. But it seemed like a gentle way of letting Madison down.

"I wondered the same thing," Madison said brightly. "I already checked with the Student Activities Office and they said you're allowed to act as an auxiliary advisor as long as we also have a full-time faculty member as our primary advisor. Which Dr. Hussain in comp sci has already agreed to do. So you're fine."

Leave it to Madison to think of everything. As Mia looked into her two students' hopeful faces, it struck her what an odd team they made. But also an oddly perfect one.

The Madisons of the world were a force to be reckoned with. If you could get enough of them together and harness the force of their color-coded to-do lists, aggressive optimism, and unflagging confidence, they could probably solve world peace in a matter of days.

Someone like Madison could do a lot for someone as shy as Antonio. But Mia had no doubt Antonio had plenty to offer in return. His maturity, reliability, and determination would be an asset to anyone, but a little of his empathy and humility might help temper some of Madison's sharper edges.

"What do you say, Dr. B?" Antonio tilted his head. "Does that mean you'll do it?"

"The thing is . . ." Mia hesitated. "I'm only here on a one-year contract." She tried to avoid looking at Antonio, but his disappointment was palpable even in her peripheral vision.

"But—" Madison frowned as her unswerving optimism hit a wall of hard reality. "That doesn't mean you'll be leaving for sure at the end of the year, does it? Isn't there a chance they'll renew your contract?"

"Well . . ." Mia searched for a diplomatic answer. "They could offer me another year, but it's far from certain. But even if they did . . . I'm not sure I'll be able to accept." As she said the words, she felt Antonio's gaze on her with discomfort. Although they'd never spoken of it, he'd seen her at the farm enough to know about her relationship with Josh. She could only imagine what he must be thinking.

"Oh." Madison's lips pressed together. "I see." She fell silent for a moment before her persistence kicked in again. "But you'll be here through the end of the school year, right? You can still act as an advisor until then."

"I could, yes." Mia spoke slowly. "But it might be better for you to find someone else who's able to stick it out with you over the long haul, instead of having to start over with someone new next year."

"We don't care about that," Antonio said, lifting his chin stubbornly. "We'll take you for as long as we can get you." He cast a glance at Madison. "Right?"

"Absolutely." Madison's head bobbed, causing her neat ponytail to bounce. "We'd still love your input—if you're willing, that is."

"In that case," Mia said, smiling as a warm feeling filled her chest, "how can I say no?"

> **Josh**: How's your day going? Feeling any better?
> **Mia**: A little better, but still not great.
> **Josh**: Do you want me to bring you anything? I could come over tonight.

Mia rubbed her chest as she stared at her phone's screen, weighing her answer. She and Josh hadn't seen much of each other the last week. Her period was ostensibly to blame, although she knew he was happy enough to hang out even without the prospect of getting laid. Last month he'd brought her chocolate-covered pretzels and rubbed her back, patiently listening to her whine about the unfairness of biology while she clutched a hot water bottle to her wretched abdomen.

She could seriously use some of that TLC about now, but guilt kept her from begging for the company she desperately longed for. Distance felt like the safer choice for both of them.

> **Mia**: Thanks, but I'll probably just go to bed early. I'd be terrible company anyway.
> **Josh**: OK. Feel better.

And then, a moment later:

> **Josh**: Let me know if you change your mind.

There was no obvious reproach in his words, but Mia felt it anyway.

Even though she technically wasn't doing anything wrong. This was how their relationship had always worked—one of them would offer company and the other would be free to accept or decline. No obligation, no pressure, and no hard feelings on either side. It had been an ideal arrangement that suited both their busy schedules.

But in practice they'd almost always accepted each other's company unless there was a concrete reason they couldn't. Mia enjoyed Josh's companionship—both in her bed and out of it—and he seemed to feel the same way about her. Which meant they'd ended up spending more and more time together over the last couple months.

But now Mia was reconsidering the wisdom of that.

Ever since her father's visit, she'd been doing a great deal of thinking. About her future, and about all the things her dad had said—both the shitty things and the things that had made an annoying degree of sense.

Most of all, she'd been thinking about Josh, and how unfair all this was to him. She was basically using him as a distraction while she bided her time here. And even though he'd claimed to be fine with that, she wasn't sure *she* was.

In addition to the period pain plaguing her this week, she'd developed a chronic, dull ache in her chest. Although it could be acid reflux or perhaps some kind of terrifying cardiac condition, she suspected the cause was more likely to be Josh. More specifically, guilt over the fact that she was using him in a way she was afraid would end up hurting him.

He'd been extremely sweet to her after that awful dinner with her dad. He was always extremely sweet to her—far more than she deserved. He'd insisted on celebrating her accomplishment without once showing any hint of resentment, despite what it meant for her future—and theirs.

But she'd begun to suspect Josh was better at hiding his feelings than she'd given him credit for. Lately, when he thought she wasn't looking, she'd occasionally glimpse a shadow of sadness around his eyes. And she couldn't help thinking she was the cause.

The problem was she didn't know what to do about it. He might have been better off if he'd never met her, but she couldn't change the past any more than she could change the future.

But should she change the present? Should she end things sooner rather than later?

She wasn't convinced that would make anything better. And it could make them significantly worse if she broke it off while she was still in town and still living above his aunt's garage, where he might be forced to see her or hear about her.

No, breaking up with him now seemed unnecessarily heartless. What was the harm in continuing to enjoy each other's company while they still could? It wouldn't make the inevitable end any worse.

As long as neither of them developed any more of an attachment than they already had.

Which was where Mia's new distance strategy came into play. From now on, instead of spending every spare minute with Josh, she'd only spend some of her spare minutes. Maybe half of her free time instead of all of it. That way she'd still get to see him, but it would reenforce the idea that they both led separate lives. It would prevent them from growing too dependent on each other or developing unapproved feelings.

It would help to remind them that they weren't actually a couple. Not a real one with a future.

Mia needed that reminder, because when she was with Josh, her feelings had a tendency to run away with her. It was too easy, when he focused the soft intensity of his gaze on her and revealed that rare smile he saved just for her, to let her affection for him fill her up, crowding out all common sense. And when he touched her in ways that left her breathless and shaking, it exposed something raw deep inside her. Something that scared her a little, even as it warmed her inside and out.

Because it was something she'd never felt before. Not with any man.

So no, she couldn't afford to see too much of Josh. For her own sake as much as his.

Mia rubbed her chest some more as she stared at his last text. The ache of guilt had been joined by an equally potent ache of longing. After another moment's deliberation she typed a reply.

> **Mia:** How about tomorrow? I could bring over BBQ from the place you like.

She was only capable of so much self-restraint. And anyway, she didn't want him to think she was giving him the cold shoulder.

Mia chewed her thumbnail as she waited for Josh's reply, staring at the screen until the energy saver kicked in and it went dark.

He was probably busy working. He'd answer when he had a chance.

"Yo, you ready for lunch?"

Mia looked up and smiled as Andie approached the bench where she'd been waiting. "Always." Dropping her phone in her bag, she got to her feet. "Why is it that no matter how much breakfast I eat, I'm always starving for lunch by ten thirty?"

"I don't know, but I'm the same way and it sucks butts." Andie checked the sports watch on her wrist. "You weren't waiting long, were you?"

"Nope. Just enjoying the sun."

December had brought a long streak of gray, overcast days as the weather had shifted into something approximating winter. But this morning the gloom had finally burned off, leaving behind a gloriously crisp, sunny day that reminded Mia of Los Angeles.

"Let's jet." Andie jerked her head toward the faculty parking lot. "I can't wait to wrap my hands around a giant-ass burrito."

The two of them had been meeting for lunch regularly on days when Andie was on campus and could spare the time. Sometimes they'd eat at the student union, but more often lately they'd been venturing off campus.

Mia had come to appreciate the convenience of living in a small town where nothing was farther than a twenty-minute drive and rush hour meant it might take her nine minutes to get home instead of the usual six. It was an unexpected breath of fresh air after battling bumper-to-bumper traffic in both LA and New York City. She'd never realized how much of her life she'd wasted trying to get from one place to another.

Andie drove them to Groovy's Tacos, one of their favorite go-tos not far from campus. As they walked into the modest establishment and got in line, Mia returned the waves of a few of her students who were stuffing their faces with Groovy's gargantuan burritos.

Despite the name, almost no one ever ordered the tacos at Groovy's. Rita's down the street offered a far superior choice for anyone craving authentic Mexican tacos. The burritos were the draw at Groovy's, stuffed near to bursting with carnitas and your choice of fresh ingredients—including a house-made salsa so addictive Mia was half convinced they laced it with opioids—and wrapped in a fresh, fluffy flour tortilla still warm from the griddle.

They ordered their usuals and made their way to a small table that had just been vacated by two men who waved Andie over as they cleared away their trash.

"All yours," the larger, bearded man said, holding his chair out while the other man gave the table a quick swipe with a napkin.

"Thanks, y'all!" Andie beamed at them as she dropped into the offered chair.

"Enjoy," the slimmer of the two men said, his gaze briefly landing on Mia as he nodded a goodbye. Something about him looked familiar, but Mia couldn't put her finger on what, exactly.

The bigger man, who had red hair and looked like he could probably squat a Prius, gave them a friendly mock salute on his way out the door.

"Do you know them?" Mia asked, watching through the window as they got into a large silver pickup truck. They were both extraordinarily good-looking, and she hadn't seen a wedding ring on either of them.

"Yeah, they're two of Wyatt's brothers, Ryan and Tanner."

That explained the familiarity and the good looks, then. The genes in that family were a marvel of nature. Mia couldn't remember exactly how many brothers Wyatt had told her he had altogether, only that it had been a lot.

She watched Andie unwrap her straw and shove it into her iced tea. "I know you told me you've never dated Wyatt—"

"God no." Andie scrunched her face up as if the very thought stank like month-old egg salad.

"But what about his brothers?"

"Nope."

"Have you ever wanted to? They all seem to be ridiculously attractive." Mia couldn't imagine growing up around the multitudinous King brothers and not at least doing some pining from afar.

Andie pursed her lips. "Not really. I guess I've heard too many stories about them from Wyatt. I just think it would be weird, since I'm friends with him."

"Right." Mia found Andie's friendship with Wyatt slightly puzzling. Sometimes it seemed as if she was even closer to him than Josh was. She certainly talked about him more than Josh did. And she hung out with him more regularly too.

Maybe that was just a by-product of their personalities and current circumstances. Andie had a lot more friends than Josh in general, and obviously socialized and went out more than he did. She was also more naturally outgoing, as was Wyatt.

All Mia knew was that she'd never been anywhere near as chummy with any of her sister's friends as Andie was with Wyatt. But then again, she hadn't grown up in a small town where everyone went to the same schools and had known each other's entire extended families their whole lives.

Still, the last time she and Josh had been to dinner at Andie's house, it had struck Mia as odd, not just that Wyatt was there, but the way he and Andie interacted. If she hadn't known better, Mia would have assumed they were a couple from their playful banter and easy manner around one another.

"Hell yeah, there's our food." Andie had been watching the counter like a hawk hunting prey, and she jumped up as their order numbers were called. "Sit tight, I'll get 'em."

While she was gone, Mia checked her phone. Still no reply from Josh.

Now she was worried she'd accidentally overplayed the distance thing. She read back over their recent exchanges, wondering if she'd inadvertently come off cold or disinterested. She'd only meant to maintain a little space, not drive him away altogether.

Or maybe he was simply busy, and she needed to stop overthinking it.

Mia sighed and shoved her phone back in her purse as Andie returned with their burritos.

"Everything okay?" Andie asked, carefully picking apart the foil wrapper on her burrito.

"Just waiting for a reply to something I sent earlier." Mia took a big bite of burrito, reaching for a napkin as guacamole dripped down her chin. Somehow, as hungry as she'd been, it didn't taste as good today as it usually did.

Andie watched Mia as she chewed her burrito. "You sure that's all it is? You were kind of quiet on the drive over."

"Cramps," Mia said, knowing that would be enough of an explanation for her moodiness.

Andie nodded in sympathy. "I've got Advil if you need it."

"I took some already, but thanks."

"I'm just glad it's not some kind of problem with my brother," Andie said before taking a huge bite out of her burrito.

Mia froze with her own burrito halfway to her mouth. "Why would you think it's a problem with Josh?" She had to wait for Andie to finish chewing, and it was enough time for her imagination to run away with itself, speculating about Josh telling his sister all sorts of things he might have been hiding from Mia.

Finally, Andie swallowed and wiped her mouth. "No reason." Her eyes narrowed as she reached for her tea. "*Is* it a problem with my brother?"

"No. Everything's fine." *Mostly. Probably.* As far as Mia

knew. Unless the unhappiness Josh had been hiding from her was a lot worse than she'd suspected.

"Right," Andie said. "Glad we cleared that up."

They both concentrated on eating their burritos, which didn't allow for much conversation. Mia gave up halfway through, by which point Andie had nearly finished hers.

"Are you excited about your parents' visit?" Mia asked as she wrapped up her leftovers to take home. Since she wasn't seeing Josh tonight, this half-eaten burrito would have to be her dinner.

Andie shrugged as she popped the last bit of burrito in her mouth. "Yeah, sure. It'll be nice to see them again." She tilted her head as she wiped her fingers with her napkin. "Although . . . it's also a little weird when they're here."

"How so?"

"Having them here always triggers this weird arrested development thing." Andie's fingers smoothed the foil her burrito had been wrapped in, flattening it into a wrinkle-free square on the table. "It's like we all revert back to younger versions of ourselves when we were still living in the same house. As soon as they show up, they start treating me and Josh like we're kids and it's still their house instead of his."

Now that her foil square was perfectly smooth, Andie began carefully folding it into a new shape. It was something a lot of the patrons did with their leftover foil wrappers, and it had become a tradition at Groovy's. Every available surface around the restaurant displayed the foil art—little rows of animals, flowers, monsters, vehicles, and elaborate abstract shapes that reminded Mia of the three-dimensional spheres she studied. Everywhere you looked, they decorated the windowsills, counters, tops of the cabinets, and even dangled from the ceiling.

"I guess that would be weird," Mia said as she watched Andie work on her foil creation. She'd been wondering what it was like when Josh's parents came back to stay in the house he was used to having to himself now. But whenever she asked him about it, he shrugged and said it was fine.

Andie nodded, her brow wrinkling as she concentrated on her sculpture. "Yeah, and in response Josh and I start *acting* like kids, bickering with each other and our parents like we're teenagers again. It's this stupid vicious cycle none of us can break out of."

"I'm sorry."

"Eh." Andie shrugged. Her sculpture was starting to resemble a dog. Or maybe a duck. "It's not so bad, really. Just the usual dumb crap families do."

It was the first inkling Mia had ever had that Josh's family wasn't perfect. To hear him talk, his parents could do no wrong. And she'd never seen him bicker with his sister beyond the playful sort of teasing Andie did with everyone.

"When do you leave for Christmas?" Andie asked.

"The morning of the twenty-second."

"Too bad. Our parents are getting in that same afternoon, so you'll just miss them."

Mia kept her gaze on the table. "Yeah, it is too bad."

And not accidental. Mia had asked Josh what days his parents would be in town and then purposely booked her flights so she'd miss them. And *then* she'd lied and said her dad had insisted on those particular dates, so Josh wouldn't suspect she was avoiding meeting his parents.

Yes, fine, she was a bad person for lying to Josh. But it

was worth it to spare his feelings—and to spare herself an awkward encounter with his parents.

"Are you and Josh exchanging Christmas gifts before you go home?"

The question caught Mia completely off guard. "Yesssss?" She dragged the single-syllable word out into four syllables. She hadn't given it any thought until this moment. *Shit.* Now she had to come up with a present for him.

Andie looked up, lifting an amused eyebrow. "You don't sound sure about that."

"Well, we haven't specifically talked about it. But I guess we probably will. Unless you think he won't want to?"

"I don't know shit about y'all and I don't want to presume. I just thought, if you were stumped for ideas, I could probably throw a few your way. He's not exactly the easiest person in the world to shop for."

"That's definitely true." What did you even get a man who never went anywhere? He seemed to have everything he needed already. His whole life was ordered exactly the way he liked it.

Mia felt her phone buzz in her purse and she pulled it out to check it.

Josh had texted her back, finally.

Josh: You're on. Don't forget to ask for extra BBQ sauce.

"Hey, so how's the STEM student group going?" Andie asked. "You guys had your first meeting the other day, right?"

"It's going great," Mia said, smiling to herself. "Really great."

Chapter Twenty-One

TO: *Dr. M. Ballentine*
FROM: *Dr. W. Walker*
SUBJECT: *New assistant professorship*

Mia,

I wanted to let you know how pleased I am that you're helping the students start up this new Diverse Voices in STEM networking group. It's something the campus has sorely needed for a while, and I believe it will be a real benefit to our department's efforts to recruit and retain minority students.

I'm impressed with the connection you seem to have forged with your students during your short time on campus. Enrollment numbers are up for all three of your classes next semester, which indicates you've made quite the positive impression.

In light of that, I wanted to give you a heads-up that we've just gotten funding approved to open up a new tenure-track assistant professorship in the department for next fall. While I obviously cannot make any promises about how a job search would go, we feel you're a great fit for our department and I very much hope you'll consider applying for it.

Best,
Bill

William Walker, PhD
Chair of Mathematics, Bowman University

Mia's stomach did an unexpected barrel roll as she scanned the department chair's email. A permanent, tenure-track position here at Bowman was up for grabs if she wanted it.

Which she didn't.

Staying at Bowman wasn't part of her twenty-year plan.

Especially not now, when she had reason to expect better offers would soon be coming her way. Last week she'd received an email from the editor she'd been assigned at the Annals, letting her know her revisions had been accepted and her paper would be published in the new year. She could officially add it to her CV as a forthcoming publication, which would give her a huge leg up in the job market. She might even find herself able to choose between multiple offers.

It was her dream come true.

So why wasn't she more excited about her new prospects? The few times she'd mustered the will to browse the job listings on the AMS website, she'd experienced an unsettling feeling of detachment rather than the enthusiasm she should be feeling now that her future was looking up.

And yet she'd reacted with elation to the news of a job opening here at Bowman. What was wrong with her?

She must be gun-shy after her disappointing job search earlier in the year. That was probably all it was. A minor case of PTSD. Her brain was trying to wimp out, afraid of facing rejection again. So naturally it had latched onto the Bowman job as an easy way out.

Of course it was gratifying to have the department chair encouraging her to apply, especially since Bill didn't even know about her paper for the Annals. He didn't want her because of her big research breakthrough. He was impressed by her teaching. It was normal to feel flattered by that. But it didn't mean she actually wanted to stay at Bowman.

Except for the small part of her that had been fantasizing about doing exactly that.

There was an undeniable appeal to the idea. She'd gotten used to Crowder. Gotten to like all the people she knew here. Saying goodbye to this place would be more difficult than she'd anticipated, and not just because of Josh. Obviously leaving him would be hard. But he wasn't the only one she'd miss. She'd miss Andie and Birdie too. And then, of course, there were Mia's students. She got wistful every time she reminded herself that she wouldn't be around to see them graduate.

So maybe sometimes she imagined what her life would be like if she could stay. Getting to teach upper division classes, seeing the STEM diversity network grow and thrive, helping some of her students with their grad school applications in a couple years.

She'd even fantasized about living on the farm with Josh. Waking up with him every morning to the familiar sounds of the chickens and goats, cooking together in his kitchen, watching sunsets from his porch. Spending holidays with his family every year and being welcomed as one of them rather than feeling like an outsider.

It was a silly fantasy, of course. Mia wasn't meant for a place like this. She was a city girl. A New Yorker at heart. She could never truly be happy somewhere like Crowder.

The idea of her living on a farm for the rest of her life was as absurd as her girlhood fantasy of marrying Prince William and living in Buckingham Palace.

"I'm dying," Mia fell back onto her mattress, her chest heaving as her lungs strained for oxygen. "Holy shit."

"Dying, huh?" Josh shot her a smile as he rolled onto his side. "Wow, I must be even better than I thought."

Flopping over onto her stomach, she folded her arms under her head and twisted her neck to stick her tongue out at him. "Very funny."

His eyebrows arched as he propped his head up on his hand. "Obviously we need to work you out more often."

"Aren't you tired?" She felt like she'd just had the workout of her life—not that it wasn't worth it, but *damn*.

He shrugged, looking smug. "I can go again whenever you're ready."

"Come on." She knew he was superhumanly fit and energetic, but surely he needed at least a few minutes to recharge before the next round.

"Try me." His heavy gaze dragged down her body, so pointed she felt it like a physical caress. "I'll be ready by the time you are."

Despite her exhaustion, Mia's whole body tightened in anticipation.

Josh stretched out his arm, slowly trailing his fingers down her lower back and over the contour of her ass. When he got to the curve at the top of her thigh, she drew in a sharp, hitching breath.

He paused, watching her, and licked his lips. "Sounds like you might be ready sooner than you think." His palm glided over the back of her thigh until his fingers dipped between her legs.

A burst of heat erupted in the pit of her stomach. He was so close to where she wanted to feel him, but not close enough. Her body twitched, aching for contact.

His eyes darkened, and he squeezed her inner thigh, his fingers digging into the flesh hard enough to make her gasp. Hard enough to leave a bruise, which wasn't something she'd ever expected to find sexy, but she shuddered as a hot flood of desire surged through her veins.

Loosening his grip, he slid his hand a little higher, and Mia's ass flexed as she fought the compulsion to writhe with yearning.

Josh smiled, clearly enjoying himself.

His hand inched higher . . . but still not high enough.

So close—

Mia nearly jumped out of her skin as her phone started shrieking a Beyoncé song on the nightstand next to her.

"Shit, it's my sister." Groaning, she banged her forehead against the mattress. "She left a voicemail the other day and I totally forgot to call her back."

"You better take it, then." Josh dropped a kiss on the small of her back before rolling away and sitting upright on the edge of the bed.

"Hey, Holly!" Mia chirped into the phone as she sat up.

"Thanks for calling me back, bitch."

"Sorry, sorry, sorry. I've been distracted the last few days."

Mia's gaze jumped to Josh, who was walking bare-assed around her apartment in search of his underwear.

Her distance strategy was proving more challenging than she'd anticipated, and she'd failed pretty hard this week. It was difficult to say no to Josh's invitation of company when every part of Mia longed to say yes.

"Yeah, I'll bet," Holly said. "How are things with your hot farmer?"

I'm gonna take a shower, Josh mouthed, cocking his head toward Mia's bathroom.

She gave him a thumbs-up. "Great. Er, fine. It's fine."

Holly cackled. "He's there, isn't he? You're with him right now."

"Yes." Mia watched Josh disappear into the bathroom. "He's taking a shower."

"Oh my god, tell me I didn't interrupt anything. You're not naked right now are you?"

Mia snagged Josh's T-shirt off the floor as she heard the water turn on in the shower. "I wouldn't answer the phone if I was naked," she said as she struggled into the shirt.

"You know I can always tell when you're lying, right? I'd make you put me on video, except I have no desire to see your tits."

"Was there an actual reason you called?" Mia asked, grabbing her underwear off the floor. "Or did you just feel like hassling me?"

"I do enjoy hassling you, but I'll be able to get my fix in a few days when you're here. Which was actually why I was calling. Do you have any plans while you're in town?"

"Um, well, Dad's scheduled this photo session for me on the twenty-eighth, and I guess I'm also getting my hair done that morning." Their father had gone so far as to have his PA make Mia a hair and makeup appointment at one of the best salons in Manhattan. Because apparently he didn't trust her to do it herself. "And he's trying to set up an interview with some reporter from . . ." She tried to remember which magazine while she wrestled her underwear up her legs, nearly falling over in the process. "I forget. One of those New York culture magazines."

"Jesus, he's really got his claws into you, hasn't he?"

"He's helping me," Mia shot back. "I mean, yes, he's obviously enjoying the attention for himself, but I'm letting him because it's going to help me get what I want."

"If you say so."

"Why are you asking about my plans, anyway?"

"Because I want to schedule some one-on-one sister time," Holly said.

"Don't we always have plenty of sister time? Since when do we have to schedule it?"

"Since Dad started pulling your strings like his little puppet."

"Don't start," Mia snapped. "I'm doing two whole things for dad while I'm home, plus his Christmas Eve party, which you will also be attending. It's not like he's monopolizing all my time."

"Maybe I've got plans of my own and I'm trying to figure out how to squeeze you in. Have you considered that, hmmm?"

"What kind of plans do you—oh!" Mia said when she realized what Holly probably meant. "Do your plans have a penis? Are you trying to work me in around your current slam piece?"

"That's a crude way of putting it," Holly said archly.

"That I learned from you," Mia reminded her.

"Well . . . now that you mention it, there is someone I've been spending time with lately."

Mia wandered over to the couch and sat down. "Come on, then. Tell me about this one."

"I'd rather not."

"No fair. You're supposed to let me live vicariously through you."

"You don't need to live vicariously through me," Holly said. "You've got your own slam piece, remember?"

"Josh is not a slam piece."

"What is he, then?"

Mia got up again and paced across the floor of her small apartment. "I'm not sure there's a word for what we are."

"Mia." Holly's voice softened. "Are you sure you know what you're doing?"

"Not really." Mia threw a glance at the bathroom door, which was slightly ajar, letting steam and the scent of her shampoo spill out into the studio apartment. "But we can talk about all that when I'm there. We were talking about you and your latest gentleman friend. What's his name?"

"I'm not telling."

"Why not?"

"Because I don't want you to judge me."

"Why would I judge you?" Mia's pacing came to an abrupt halt. "Oh god, is it someone I know?"

"Maybe."

"Who? It's not someone I dated, is it?"

"Jesus, no. I wouldn't have anything to do with any of those losers."

"Thanks very much."

"You know what I mean."

Mia did, actually. Holly was fiercely loyal, which meant that once Mia's boyfriends had moved themselves into the "ex" column, they were officially dead to Holly.

"So who is it?" Mia asked. "Spill."

"Noah," Holly mumbled.

Mia rubbed her temple. "Oh Holly, no."

Noah was someone Holly had dated on and off through high school. He was a skater she'd met at the park where she used to go to smoke with her friends, and Mia had never liked him. Not only was he the first boy her little sister had ever had sex with, but he was the one who'd first introduced her to weed.

"I knew you'd judge me!"

"There's a reason you broke up with him. Three times, if I remember correctly." Mia heard the water in the shower shut off and sat on the couch again, crossing her legs underneath her.

"There's a reason I dated him in the first place," Holly said. "He's mega hot. And he's gotten even hotter since high school."

"Okay, sure, he's pretty, but he's so dumb, Holly. He thinks a double helix is a sex position." That particular misunderstanding had led to an uncomfortable conversation during which Noah had apparently thought Mia was talking about some sort of orgy when in fact she had been talking about differential geometry.

Holly cackled. "Dude. It *is* a sex position. Also, since you brought it up, he's *really* good in bed now. Much better than he used to be. Like, mind-blowingly good. Just for your information."

Mia made a face. "Meaningless sex is fine and all, but come on. There's more to life than sex. What about being able to have a conversation with someone? Sharing common interests?"

"We share plenty of interests and manage to have conversations just fine."

"He's barely civilized," Mia said. "He is exactly who the phrase 'raised in a barnyard' was invented to describe."

When Noah used to come over to the house to hang out with Holly, he'd drink their milk and orange juice straight out of the cartons and then leave the half-empty containers sitting out on the counter to spoil. He'd also had an unpleasant habit of leaving the bathroom door partially open when he peed.

"Now you're just being mean," Holly said. "He's not the same person he was when he was sixteen. None of us are. He's grown up a lot. You might actually like him now, if you could quit being such a snob for five minutes."

"You're right, I'm sorry. I am being a snob." Talking to her sister seemed to bring it out in her. Like what Andie had said about her parents' visits bringing on arrested development. Interacting with her family made Mia backslide into some of the elitist attitudes she'd been trying to shed.

"You should talk, you know. It's not like you and your dreamy goat farmer have a lot in common on the surface. Do the two of you have trouble thinking of things to talk about?"

"No, we don't." Mia glanced over her shoulder as Josh

came out of the bathroom, his hair wet and disheveled, and snatched his jeans off the floor.

"There you go," Holly said.

Mia bit her lip. "I just want you to be happy."

Something about Josh's manner seemed off. He had his back to her, but his movements were stiff and jerky as he dragged his pants up his legs.

Holly sniffed. "I am, actually. Believe it or not."

Josh's face was hard when he turned around. Something was definitely wrong. Anxiety prickled over Mia's skin as she watched him stalk across the apartment toward her. "I need my shirt," he said in a weirdly flat voice.

"Holly, I've got to go," Mia said as she looked up into his cold expression. While she was saying goodbye to her sister, he walked away and started putting on his socks and shoes. Mia set down the phone and got to her feet, approaching him warily. "Is everything okay?"

"Fine." His voice cut sharper than a knife. "Can I have my shirt?"

"You don't have to go." Mia reached for him, but he jerked out of her grasp.

She was so surprised, all she could do was stare at him. Something had obviously happened to upset him, but she had no idea what. He'd seemed fine when he went to take a shower. What could have happened while he was in the bathroom? Had he gotten a call or a text from someone?

A spike of panic stabbed through her gut. "Josh, what's wrong?"

He refused to look at her. His gaze stayed locked on the hardwood floor between them as he spoke. "Is that what you really think of me? 'Pretty but dumb'?" He spat the last three words out like venom.

Mia blinked in confusion. "I don't—"

"There's no use denying it." His eyes flashed with anger as they locked on hers. "I heard every word you said."

"I have no idea what you're talking about." She started to reach for him again, but the cold fury in his face stopped her. The air around them felt spiky. Like there was barbed wire everywhere and if she moved the wrong way she'd get cut.

"Just now. Talking to your sister on the phone."

Oh. Okay. Now she understood. He must have overheard her talking about Noah and thought she'd been talking about him. Which was ridiculous; she'd never say all those things about Josh. As soon as she explained that, they'd both have a big laugh over it and everything would be fine again.

"Josh, no." She shook her head, smiling in relief. "I wasn't—"

"Meaningless sex?" His voice shook with a mixture of raw pain and restrained anger. "That's all you think I'm good for?"

"Of course not. I wasn't talking about us."

"I guess I shouldn't be surprised," he bit out as if he hadn't even heard her. "You never bothered to pretend any of this meant anything to you."

She recoiled at the harshness of his accusation. Was that how he felt? When she'd been agonizing for weeks over how she was going to give him up and trying to figure out how to spare him pain?

The unfairness of it left her shaken. She thought he knew

her better than that. He'd always been so good at reading her. At understanding her. How could he believe he didn't mean anything to her?

"That's not fair." It took all her effort to keep her voice steady. "I swear I wasn't talking about you." She was trying to stay calm and be patient, even though it hurt that he would say that about her. Or that he could even think it.

Josh dragged his hands through his wet hair as he paced away from her, his footfalls heavy on the wooden floor. He wore shoes but no shirt, and she saw his back muscles contract just before he spoke. "Did it really not occur to you that I'd overhear everything you were saying? Or did you want me to hear it?"

"Why would I want you to hear something like that?" Mia trailed after him as he stalked around the apartment like a caged tiger. "Why would I talk about you when I know you're in the next room?"

Nothing he was saying made any sense. It was like he'd been possessed. Whatever had gotten into him had turned him into someone she didn't even recognize.

He rounded on her, his face twisted with a bitterness so strong his whole body seemed to vibrate with it. His voice came out like a snarl. "Did you get off on humiliating me by trash-talking me to your sister where you knew I'd hear it? It's not enough that you're using the dumb redneck to scratch an itch while you're slumming it in Hicksville—you've got to make sure I know that's all I am to you, so you can watch me squirm."

"Hey!" she snapped, losing her composure as his words ripped through her. "That's not me and you know it!"

The way he was talking to her—the way he was looking

at her—it was like he thought she was someone else. Like he was looking at her and seeing his vindictive ex-girlfriend.

Mia didn't know what to do. Obviously, what he'd heard—what he'd *thought* he heard—had dredged up his old trauma. He wasn't in control right now, that much was clear. The emotions he kept so tightly locked down had flared up and detonated all over both of them. How was she supposed to get through to him when he wasn't being rational or thinking clearly?

She sucked in a shaking breath and tried again, swallowing her own hurt feelings. "I wasn't talking about you, Josh. I was talking about some goon my sister's sleeping with."

He heaved out a harsh, mocking laugh. "Oh come on. You expect me to believe that?"

His sneering tone cut deep into her heart, bleeding away the last reserves of her patience. When she spoke, her voice was as hard and cold as the look in his eyes. "Actually, yes. I do. Why wouldn't you believe me? What have I ever done to make you think I could be so callous and cruel?"

For a second, some of his anger seemed to seep away as he let out a long, ragged breath. A knife-edge of hope flared inside her, but it only left another laceration when his expression slammed shut, all trace of emotion replaced by a terrifying blankness.

"You think I don't know what you think of me? What your whole family thinks of me?" The perfect flatness of his tone was betrayed by a heartrending tremor. "Why wouldn't you make fun of me to your sister after you let your dad practically call me an ignorant hick to my face? Did you think I was too stupid to notice the way you've been pulling away from me since that night? It's obvious you're embarrassed by me. I'm just some dumb redneck, not smart enough or sophisticated enough for you. I'll do well enough to pass the time while you're stuck in this shithole town, but that's all."

Mia stared at him, stricken. There was enough truth in his words to gnaw at her. She had hated the idea of being stuck here. And he was right that she hadn't defended him to her father. And lately she had been pulling away.

Even though she'd had what felt like good reasons for all of it, she hadn't appreciated how it must have made him feel.

"I realize I'm just a pit stop," he ground out, "but you could at least treat me with a little respect while you're enjoying my bed."

"I knew it," she fired back. Her throat burned as her eyes prickled with hot tears. "I knew you weren't fine about all this."

"Of course I'm not fine with it!" His voice grew rough as it gained volume. "But what am I supposed to do? Be the asshole who makes you feel bad about the success you're about to have? Complaining about it isn't going to change your mind about leaving."

Mia reeled as this latest revelation sank in. Everything she'd thought about them was wrong. She hadn't understood Josh any more than she'd understood any of her other failed relationships. Her legs felt weak underneath her. She made her way to the couch and sank down. "You could have at least been honest about how you felt."

"What, the way you're always so honest about your feelings?"

It was a direct hit. A shot of acid that burned its way down her throat and left her stomach churning with shame.

"You know," he continued, sounding almost calm now,

"I've been consoling myself with the thought that at least you liked me enough to spend this time with me. Even if that's all I ever get of you, at least I had that much." Pain lashed his face, twisting his mouth into a bitter shape. "But I was kidding myself, wasn't I? You never cared at all."

"That's not true." Her voice cracked on the last word. "I wish you'd believe me."

"I don't think I can."

She couldn't even blame him. Not after everything he'd been through.

In the end, that was what made her decision for her. He'd already been hurt enough for one lifetime. She couldn't stand the thought of causing him even more pain. It was too much to bear. Josh deserved to be happy, and he'd never be happy with her.

Why try to fix something when you knew it was only going to get broken again? Better to let them stay broken so Josh could at least start to move on.

Mia marshaled her strength and got to her feet. Forced herself to look him in the eye as she spoke, slowly and decisively. "I think it's better if we don't see each other anymore." An iron band tightened around her chest as the words hung in the air.

Josh didn't react, but whether it was shock or indecision that froze him in place, she couldn't tell. She'd never been able to read him, she realized now. He was too good at hiding. As good as she was.

For a long moment they stared at each other while the strained silence swirled around them. Then his shoulders sagged, his jaw clenching as a look of resignation crossed his face. His head jerked in a nod. "I think you're right."

Without another word he turned and strode out of the apartment. The door slammed so hard behind him it rattled the windows.

Mia's legs gave out and she sank to the couch again. Pulling her knees up to her chest, she listened to his footfalls move down the stairs. The slam of his car door and the engine roaring to life. The crunch of gravel as he backed out of the driveway.

In the silence that fell when he was finally gone, she broke down and cried.

Two hours later, long after Mia had finished crying and gotten into bed, her phone rang. She'd been staring at the ceiling trying to will herself to sleep, even though she knew there was no point. Insomnia would be her only company tonight.

Rolling over, she reached for her phone, and her stomach turned over.

It was Josh.

Panic bubbled up inside her as she fumbled to answer. Was he okay? He'd been so upset when he left. So unlike himself. Had he done something foolish in his heightened state? What if he was hurt?

"Josh?" Her voice sounded thick and woolly after all the crying she'd done earlier.

There was a pause, long enough for her panic to ramp up a few more notches before he said, very quietly, "I wasn't sure you'd pick up."

"Are you okay?"

He made a sound that could have been a laugh but sounded more like he was breaking apart. "No, not really.

I—" He cut himself off, and she heard him suck in a shaky breath. When he spoke again, he sounded steadier. "I should have believed you."

A ragged gasp of relief tore its way out of her throat as fresh tears stung her eyes.

"Are you crying?" His voice was so gentle it brought even more tears.

She sniffled and rubbed her eyes. "A little."

"Shit."

Mia sagged back against the bed and closed her eyes. "It's okay."

"It's not okay. I freaked out on you, and you didn't deserve that."

"Josh, I swear I wasn't talking about you when I said those things. I would never say anything like that about you, because that's not how I feel about you. I don't think you're stupid. I hope you know that."

"I do. I believe you."

He sounded like he meant it, and it lifted some of the weight that had been sitting on her chest. But she had more to atone for. "I'm sorry I didn't defend you when my dad said those awful things. I didn't agree with him. I was just trying not to make a scene."

At the time, she'd thought she was doing it for Josh, but in hindsight she realized it had been as much for her. She'd been a coward. Afraid of conflict. Willing to swallow the hurt to avoid a fight, and expecting Josh to do the same.

"I know," he said. "I get it."

"What about the rest of it? Do you really think I don't care about you?"

There was the slightest hint of hesitation before he

answered. "No, of course not. I overreacted, okay? I heard you saying those things and I just lost it. I couldn't think straight. It was like I was trapped in some kind of nightmare, like my mind and my body belonged to someone else and I wasn't in control anymore." He blew out a nervous breath. "That probably sounds crazy."

"It's not crazy." She rolled over on her side, pulling her knees to her chest. "I understand. I really do." He'd been hiding his trauma—and hiding from his fears—instead of confronting it. Which meant it had never properly healed.

"Mia, I'm so sorry." The anguish in his voice tore at her heart. "Please let me come back so we can fix this."

She knew exactly how that would go. They'd both apologize and fall into each other's arms and then into her bed. It was exactly what she wanted. Desperately. But they'd only end up right back here again. And she couldn't go through that—or bear to put him through it. She needed to save them both.

Forcing conviction into her voice, she said, "I don't think that's a good idea." The words burned on the way out, leaving blisters that threatened to choke her.

He made a raw, desperate sound. "Please, Mia . . . just give me a chance. I know I fucked up and I'm so sorry."

She could picture his face right now. His mouth twisted, his lower lip betraying a slight tremble. His dark eyes hollow and bloodshot, blinking hard to fight off tears. The thought of it nearly undid her. But she needed to be brave. For once in her life, she needed to have a spine.

"It's not you," she said, realizing too late how trite that sounded.

"Right." The bitterness in his voice pricked at her already aching heart.

"It's not." She squeezed the phone until it bit into her fingers. "This isn't about tonight. Not directly. It's something I've been thinking for a while. You were right that I've been pulling away lately, and it's because I'm afraid."

"Of what?"

"Of what happens when I leave." Her mouth tasted like it was full of ashes, but she kept going. "I think we should quit while we're ahead. Before anyone gets hurt."

"Little late for that, don't you think?"

Mia flinched at the sting of truth in his words but refused to back down. "The longer we're together, the worse it will be when I have to leave."

"I don't care. We'll figure it out when the time comes."

Something cold clamped around her spine, extending icy tendrils into her limbs and leaving a numb, pins and needles feeling in its wake. It was the exact same thing Paul had said to her. And the way they'd "figured it out" had left her broken and reeling.

With a little more distance, she might have found it darkly humorous that after things had ended with Paul, she'd run straight into the arms of a man who was his opposite in almost every way—unassuming, empathetic, down to earth, and at peace with his place in the world. The two men couldn't be more different. And yet she'd still ended up in the exact same situation.

Which meant the problem wasn't them; it was her. If she'd been hoping for a sign she was doing the right thing, this was a giant Buc-ee's billboard by the side of the highway pointing the way to clean bathrooms thirty miles ahead.

Mia's resolve hardened even as her heart broke a little more. "No, we won't," she said, finding it easier to keep her voice firm. "There's nothing to figure out because there's no future for us. We need to acknowledge that instead of pretending it will magically work itself out somehow."

"I acknowledge it, okay? Is that all you need? Are we good now?"

Her lips itched with the urge to say yes, and she clamped them together, before speaking through gritted teeth. "Josh—"

"We've still got months left," he said, interrupting her. "That's time we could be spending together instead of alone. We've got a good thing going. Why shouldn't we enjoy it while we can? I promise I'll let you go when the time comes. You don't have to worry about me."

She did have to worry about him though. He wasn't as okay as he was pretending to be. What happened tonight was enough evidence of that.

Mia squeezed her eyes shut, knowing he wouldn't like what she was about to say. "Do you remember before, when I said you should talk to a therapist?"

"Not this again." His defensive walls slammed down like clockwork. "I just lost my temper, that's all."

"It's more than that. I don't think you've ever dealt with the trauma of what Kayla did to you. It's like this gaping wound that you've been trying to cover up, but it's been festering all this time. It doesn't mean you're weak. But when you've got a wound that won't heal, you need to see a doctor. You need therapy. Please, will you at least consider it?"

There was a long pause before he spoke. "If I say yes, can we go back to the way things were?"

Mia rolled over and stared at the ceiling. If this was the only way to get him the help he needed, maybe . . .

No.

It'd be manipulative. She couldn't blackmail him into getting help. He had to make the choice for himself. Otherwise he'd just be going through the motions. Unless he accepted that he actually needed help, it wouldn't take.

"No." She shook her head even though he couldn't see her. "I want you to get help, but you need to do it for yourself, not for me."

"So that's it. Just like that. We're over."

"Yes."

"Don't do this."

"I'm doing it for both of us. It's better this way. We need to end this now before it goes too far and one of us falls in love."

The laugh he let out was harsh and hollow. "You really think that's a possibility?"

His words shuddered through her like an icy blast. This was exactly why she had to do this. She couldn't bear to go through this a second time. It hurt too much. And they'd already gotten through the hardest part. If they fell back into each other now, it would all be for nothing.

"I'm sorry," she said, knowing he'd thank her eventually.

"Me too." He hung up without another word.

Chapter Twenty-Two

Mia knew she'd done the right thing. Unfortunately, that didn't stop her heart from aching every time she thought about Josh. It didn't fill the cold hollow his absence had left behind. It wasn't enough to stop her eyes from trying to tear up whenever they saw something that reminded her of him.

Which was everything.

Every inch of her apartment had been tainted by their first and final fight. Everywhere she looked she saw his face cracked apart by pain, or she heard the echo of his voice flinging accusations at her.

She was terrified of running into Birdie in the yard, so Mia took to sneaking in and out of her apartment like a nervous trespasser. When she drove through town, she was confronted by all the places she used to pick up takeout to share with Josh, or the Rusty Spoke where he'd risked so much just to see her, or the goddamn steakhouse where she'd let her dad insult him and the town he loved.

Even at work, where she ought to be safe, she was reminded of Josh every time she saw Antonio. And as she walked around campus, worried about bumping into Andie.

Mia hadn't heard from her since the breakup, which was just as well, since she lived in fear of Andie's sisterly wrath. Even seeing Cody sit for his calculus final made Mia think of Wyatt, which made her think of Josh, which made her chest constrict as she fought the urge to cry.

She felt like she'd been pulled apart and put back together with some of the important pieces missing.

She hadn't only lost Josh, she'd lost every friend she'd made here in Crowder. They were all tied to Josh somehow. All loyal to him. She was back to where she started—completely on her own. She told herself it was better that way. Letting people get close to her here was only setting herself up for heartbreak. She didn't need anyone. She'd always been fine on her own.

At least it was finals week. She could distract herself with the stacks of exams she had to grade and the comforting monotony of calculating and inputting final grades. Then she could fly home and leave this place behind for a little while. Hopefully when she came back after Christmas, the pain wouldn't be so fresh anymore and everything would be easier.

"Anything you want to add, Dr. Ballentine?" Madison's question jerked Mia out of her self-pity fest.

She was sitting in on the STEM student group's final planning meeting of the semester. As soon as they came back from break, they'd be launching their recruitment drive in advance of their first general meeting at the end of January.

Mia forced a half-hearted smile. "No, it sounds like y'all have thought of everything."

"You just said 'y'all'!" Madison pointed a triumphant finger at her. "That's the first time I've ever heard you say it."

"Is it?" Mia flushed. "It's a very useful word."

"You're one of us now," Antonio said with an approving nod.

Mia's heart squeezed, but she didn't say anything. It was too difficult to explain to her students why that wasn't true. A year from now, she'd not only be gone from their lives, but they'd probably have forgotten she was ever there.

She doubted she'd be able to forget them so easily, however. This group of determined undergrads had wormed their way into her heart in a single semester.

When the meeting let out she shouldered her bulging messenger bag, which was stuffed with all the exams she planned to spend the weekend grading, and made a beeline for the door. But before she could complete her getaway, she was intercepted by Madison.

"You're coming to Christmas on Main Street, aren't you?" Madison thrust a flyer into Mia's hands. "I'll be selling pies to raise money for the animal shelter."

Of course she is, Mia thought with a little envy. Where did Madison find the time and energy to take on so much? And the pluck to recruit anyone and everyone around her to assist her endeavors.

"I don't know," Mia hedged. "I've got a lot to do before I fly home next week."

"You could stop by for a few minutes and pick up a pie from our booth. You deserve a sweet treat while you're grading our exams." Madison flashed a brilliant smile, showing off her perfect teeth.

"You have to come check out the Christmas fair, Dr. B." Antonio sidled up alongside Madison. "Everyone dresses up in costumes like it's Halloween."

"Why?" Mia frowned at the flyer, which didn't mention anything about Halloween costumes.

Antonio scratched his chin. "I guess originally the idea was for people to dress up in Victorian costumes or something."

"Like *A Christmas Carol*," Madison said.

"Yeah." Antonio nodded. "But most people don't have any Victorian clothes lying around, so they started showing up in whatever they had."

"As if Disney princess dresses or Renaissance festival outfits were the same thing as period Victorian attire," Madison added with a sniff. "But I guess some people thought it was close enough."

"People just wanted to get in on the fun," Antonio said, shooting Madison an eye roll. He'd really come out of his shell the last few weeks while they'd been working on the student group. Taking on a leadership role had done wonders for his confidence. "And now everyone shows up dressed like whatever they want. Anything goes. It's pretty cool."

"Mask-wearing and playacting were part of the Roman midwinter festival of Saturnalia that was eventually displaced by Christmas," Mia said.

Antonio grinned. "There you go. Plus there's food and music and all kinds of stuff for sale. The whole town comes out for it. My dad's gonna have a booth to sell these Christmas ornaments he's been making along with some of his bigger metalworking pieces."

"Oh." Mia's chest tightened at the mention of Antonio's father, who worked with Josh every day. "That's nice."

"So you'll come, right?" Antonio looked so hopeful, she couldn't bear to turn him down outright.

"I'll try," Mia said, with no intention of doing any such

thing. "But if I don't see you on Saturday, I hope you guys have a Merry Christmas."

She'd almost said "y'all" again but stopped herself in time. She wasn't one of them and wasn't ever going to be. The sooner everyone—including her—accepted that, the better.

On Friday evening there was a knock on Mia's apartment door. Since no one ever came to her door except Josh and occasionally Birdie, apprehension coiled in her belly as she disentangled herself from the nest of pillows and blankets she'd made on the couch. She hadn't moved for hours, and her back popped in protest as she stiffly made her way to the door.

Birdie stood on the doorstep in a purple-patterned caftan and Santa hat. "Merry Christmas!" she announced cheerfully and held out a gift bag.

Mia stared at it in surprise. "You didn't—but—I didn't expect anything."

"Oh good." Birdie pushed the bag into Mia's hands and walked past her into the apartment. "Presents are always better when they're not expected." She took in the blankets on the couch and the collection of dirty mugs on the coffee table with a raised eyebrow.

Mia cast around hopelessly for something she could give Birdie in return, but the only thing that sprang to mind was the gift she'd bought for Josh and subsequently hidden in the recesses of her closet. It was a ruffled gingham apron she'd picked up at the farmers market with "Kiss the Cook" printed on the front of it, which she'd thought at the time would be cute, but now just made her depressed.

She could give that to Birdie, she supposed, and pretend

it had been meant for her all along. But Mia couldn't bring herself to do it. She wasn't ready to let go of it yet, even if she'd let Josh go. Plus, she'd only end up feeling sad every time she saw Birdie wearing it.

"I didn't get you anything," Mia confessed. "I'm sorry."

"Pish, don't worry about that. The pleasure's in the giving." Smiling, Birdie nodded at the gift bag. "Go on, open it up."

Mia picked through the green tissue paper sticking out of the bag and pulled out an embroidery hoop. The fabric it held had been embroidered with a pattern of cross-stitch roses surrounding the words SMASH THE PATRIARCHY.

"I love it," Mia said, blinking back unexpected tears.

"Well goodness, it's not that nice." Birdie tilted her head as her eyes narrowed. "Are you okay, honey?"

Mia assumed Birdie didn't know about her breakup with Josh, or else she wouldn't be here right now giving her gifts and calling her "honey." Until Birdie came into her life, no one had called Mia "honey" since her grandmother had died, and it was one of the things she was going to miss most.

"I'm fine." Mia tried to offer a convincing smile, but her lip betrayed her by trembling a little.

Birdie tutted and opened her arms, gathering Mia up in a hug. "I'm sorry you and Josh are having troubles."

"You know about that?" Mia sniffled as she clutched Birdie's waist. She hadn't realized how badly she'd needed a hug after the last week. And the fact that Birdie still wanted to hug her after she'd broken her nephew's heart only made Mia even more wibbly.

Birdie patted her shoulder. "All I know is that he stormed out of here the other night looking like someone had run over one of his dogs and hasn't been back since."

"We broke up," Mia mumbled.

"Oh that's a shame. It's none of my business, but I thought you two were good for each other."

Mia let go of Birdie and wiped her eyes. "It's for the best, since I'll be leaving in a few months anyway."

Birdie regarded her for a long moment before saying, "I'm sure you're right. You'd know better than me." Birdie's arched brow, on the other hand, seemed to be saying, *I know you're full of shit, but I'm too polite to say it out loud.* "Anyway, I've got twelve dozen cookies to bake for Christmas on Main Street tomorrow." She started for the door, then stopped halfway there and rounded on Mia. "You're coming to the Christmas fair, aren't you?"

"I don't think so." Mia waved her hand at the stacks of exams next to the couch. "I've got a lot of grading to do."

"But you have to come to the fair!" Birdie looked aghast. "It's not Christmas until you've had some of my snickerdoodles with hot mulled wine."

"I'll try." It was becoming Mia's go-to lie, just as it had been her parents' frequent refrain.

The difference was that Mia really was trying. She was exhausted with trying so hard to do the right thing—for herself, for Josh, for her students.

Ever since her paper had been accepted to the Annals, she'd felt nothing but an increasing sense of anxiety. She hadn't expected it to feel this bad to get everything she wanted.

When did she get to start being happy?

On Saturday afternoon Mia looked at the stacks of grading, dirty dishes, and empty takeout containers that had built up around her, realized her apartment had acquired a funk that matched her mood, and decided she needed a break.

The first thing she did was take out the trash. The second was shower. Once she emerged from the bathroom, feeling fresher and slightly more energetic, she found herself with an unexpected urge to get out of the house and into the world.

And so, even though she hadn't intended to, Mia went to Christmas on Main Street.

The fair took up all of the grassy town square. The surrounding streets had been closed for the occasion and were lined with booths selling food, drinks, and other assorted items. Rides and other activities for the kids surrounded the big Christmas tree that had been erected in the middle of the green, with a stage off to one side where live music played. Mia recognized Wyatt's voice belting out a rock version of "Holly Jolly Christmas" and immediately headed in the opposite direction.

Antonio had been right about the costumes. Almost everyone around her was dressed up, some sweating in festive Christmas sweaters despite the seventy-degree weather, a few in full Victorian attire looking like they'd stepped out of a Dickens novel, and most of the rest in a variety of random costumes ranging from elaborate cosplay to drugstore Halloween costumes. All around her strolled superheroes, fairies, witches, a variety of animals, and the odd vampire.

Mia found Birdie's booth first and purchased some snickerdoodles to help pay for renovations to the community center. Birdie had dressed up like a Greek goddess in a flowy white caftan paired with a gold laurel wreath headpiece. She tutted over Mia's lack of a costume and insisted on giving her a unicorn headband with fuzzy ears and a rainbow-colored horn, before pointing her toward the booth selling mulled wine.

Mia armed herself with a cup of the unseasonably hot beverage before seeking out Madison's booth and allowing herself to be talked into buying a buttermilk pie. By the time Mia caught sight of Ray's metalworking booth, the wine had supplied her with enough courage to stop by and say hello to Antonio and his father.

They both greeted her warmly, and Ray was kind enough not to betray any hint that he'd noticed she wasn't coming around the farm anymore or that he knew anything about why that might be. Mia admired his intricate metalwork ornaments and bought a holly leaf for her sister, a snowflake for her mom, and a dove to give Birdie later.

After that, Mia wandered aimlessly for a bit, figuring she'd go back home as soon as she got bored. Only instead of getting bored, she wound up perusing all the booths and buying a few more gifts to take home to her family, along with another cup of the mulled wine and a bag of spiced nuts to nibble on.

She was in the middle of deliberating whether to buy herself a kebab for dinner or try the Polish dill pickle soup served in a bread bowl—or maybe get both—when she nearly ran smack into Andie. She was dressed as a pirate, and between the eye patch and tricorn hat, Mia didn't recognize her until they were face-to-face and it was too late to avoid the encounter.

"Hey." Andie drew back a little, regarding Mia with a look of surprise. "I didn't expect to see you here."

Mia bobbed her head and lowered her gaze to the ground,

overcome with guilt for being out enjoying herself while Josh was probably home all alone feeling miserable because of her. "I didn't expect to come."

"So," Andie said. "This is weird and awkward."

Biting her lip, Mia braced herself to face Andie's fury. "I guess that means you heard about—"

"You and my brother breaking up?" Andie flipped her eye patch up to better level Mia with a penetrating look. "He didn't go into any detail. All he'd tell me was you two weren't together anymore."

It sounded so final.

It *was* final. Mia had made that choice, but hearing that Josh had said it like that drove home the fact that it really was over. He wasn't trying to get her back. He'd given up on them.

"Is it true?" Andie asked. "Did y'all break up?"

Mia swallowed. "We did, yeah."

"Damn. I was hoping maybe it was just a bump in the road. Josh has a tendency to blow things out of proportion. He can be oversensitive sometimes."

"He's got a right to be."

"I guess."

The weight of Andie's gaze was too much to bear. Mia looked down at her shoes again. "The winter solstice is the longest night of the year, regarded by many cultures as a time of death and rebirth."

Andie ignored the tangent, having long since grown used to Mia's nervous tic. "I really want to ask you whose fault it was, even though I know I probably shouldn't."

"It was mine," Mia said without hesitation.

"Did you—" Andie stopped herself, pressing her mouth

closed. "Look, whatever happened between you and my brother is between you and my brother. As long as you didn't, like—I don't know—cheat on him or record him without his consent and publicly humiliate him."

"I didn't." Mia met Andie's gaze, hoping she'd believe her. "I would never do either of those things."

Andie seemed to consider this. Eventually, she nodded. "Then we're square. You and me are still friends, okay?"

Mia blinked. "We are?"

"Like I said, whatever happened between you and my brother is between y'all. It doesn't have anything to do with you and me."

"That's awfully big of you." Mia didn't think she'd be able to stay friends with anyone who'd hurt her sister, even inadvertently.

Andie shrugged. "Relationships are hard and complicated. I'm in no position to judge anyone for messing one up."

Mia opened her mouth to reply, but before she could say anything else they were accosted by Wyatt. He draped his tattooed arms around both of them, drawing them into a vigorous three-way hug. "There you are! I've been looking all over for you!"

He was shirtless, clad only in a Santa hat, a pair of fuzzy Santa pants that hung low on his hips, and the small gold medallion he always wore. Although it wasn't the first time Mia had been confronted by the spectacle of Wyatt's bare chest, it was the first time she'd found herself pressed up against it. She noticed several pairs of jealous female eyes turn their direction as he continued to hold her and Andie in a tight clench.

"You smell like beer." Andie wrinkled her nose but didn't disengage herself from Wyatt's grasp.

"Did you hear us play?" Wyatt asked, steering them toward the green.

"I did," Mia said. The music had carried over the whole square, so it had been impossible not to hear. "You were great."

"Thank you!" Wyatt grinned, looking pleased, and kissed the side of Mia's head.

"Where are we going?" Andie asked.

"To sit down, of course. I'm exhausted." Wyatt led them to an empty spot at the end of one of the long picnic tables on the grass and collapsed onto the bench. Andie slid in next to him and Mia took the bench across from them.

"Is that wine?" Wyatt licked his lips as he stared at the cup in Mia's hand.

"You can finish it," she said, pushing it toward him.

"Have you eaten anything?" Andie asked and Wyatt shook his head as he downed the rest of Mia's wine. "You need some food in your stomach. I'll get us turkey legs." She got to her feet, glancing at Mia. "You want one?"

"Thanks, but I'll pass." She'd never enjoyed tearing meat off a bone with her teeth, and anyway she was still thinking about the pickle soup. She might go get some for herself in a bit.

Andie pointed at Wyatt. "Stay with him and make sure he doesn't wander off or get into any trouble."

Mia wasn't sure exactly how she was supposed to manage that, but she gave a thumbs-up.

Wyatt regarded her across the table, his expression

growing abruptly sober and accusatory as soon as they were alone. "Josh told me y'all broke up."

Mia felt ambushed after his friendliness a few minutes ago. He'd lulled her into complacency with his drunken geniality. She stared down at her lap, twisting her hands together under the table. "Did he tell you why?"

"He didn't want to, but I wheedled it out of him."

She actually felt relieved that Josh had opened up to someone. It wasn't healthy for him to keep everything inside. "Is he okay?" she asked, looking up at Wyatt.

He tipped his Santa hat forward and scratched the back of his head as he considered his answer. "He's not great, but . . ." He paused while he repositioned his hat squarely on his head. "I guess he will be. The damage *probably* isn't terminal."

"That's something, I suppose."

"Are you okay?" Wyatt asked in an unexpected show of sympathy.

Mia nodded, her throat growing tight. "Do you think I did the right thing?"

Wyatt's jaw clenched as his mouth pulled into a flat line, all traces of sympathy gone. "You broke my best friend's heart, so no, not really."

She had that coming. But it was almost a relief to hear someone say it. Wyatt was the only other person who knew what had happened. The only person Mia could talk to about it, and the only one who would give her his unvarnished opinion.

"But do you understand why I had to do it?" she asked him. "Don't you think it's better, if I'm leaving next summer, to end things now, before he gets even more hurt?"

"I don't know." Frowning, Wyatt squeezed the medallion around his neck, rubbing it between his thumb and forefinger. "I'm not sure there's a way to make any of this better. The whole situation sucks. I know it's not really your fault that it sucks . . ." He dropped the medallion and lifted his gaze to Mia, his eyes soft and grave. "But I'm not sure he's actually any less hurt now than he would be next summer."

That definitely wasn't what Mia had wanted to hear. She swallowed around a painful lump in her throat as Andie returned with two giant turkey legs.

"Eat this," she told Wyatt, thrusting one into his hand as she slid back onto the bench next to him.

Mia got to her feet, gathering her bags of purchases. "I should get back home." She couldn't be here anymore, pretending to be fine when she wasn't.

"Are you okay?" Andie asked, her face clouding with concern. She turned on Wyatt with a glare. "What did you do?"

"Nothing!" he protested with his mouth full of roasted turkey. "Why do you assume I did something wrong?"

"Because I know you." Andie turned back to Mia. "Don't go. Stay and hang out."

"He didn't say anything wrong." Mia's gaze met Wyatt's in a silent apology before shifting back to Andie. "I just have a ton of grading left to do before I go home. I didn't mean to stay this long, but I'm glad I got to see you before I left."

"Me too." Andie got to her feet and gave Mia a hug. "I'll see you after Christmas."

"Sure." Mia muttered into her hair.

Turning, she made her way through the crowd, walking faster and faster, desperate to get back to her empty, silent apartment.

Chapter Twenty-Three

Predictably, Mia's Christmas holiday was turning out to be a big, fat bust.

Her mother's house felt even more empty and lonely than usual. Holly was so busy between her advertising job and her current boyfriend—the infamous Noah, who had indeed matured into a perfectly respectable adult—that Mia had been left largely to her own devices while her mother worked her usual long shifts at the hospital.

Mia had gone to dinner once with Holly and Noah, after which she'd admitted to her sister that she'd been wrong about him and taken back every mean word she'd said.

Remembering the things she'd said about Noah inevitably caused a fresh surge of guilt over her terrible last fight with Josh. She'd hoped to forget him while she was home, but instead the hollow in her chest only seemed to grow larger.

Wyatt's words had haunted her ever since the Christmas fair. She'd thought she was minimizing Josh's pain by letting him go now. But what if Wyatt was right and she'd already waited too long? What if sooner wasn't any better than later, and she'd given up their last months together for nothing?

Mia wondered how Josh was coping with his parents'

visit, and if he was managing to enjoy his holidays more than she was. At least three times a day she took out her phone to text Andie and ask how Josh was, but so far she'd managed to talk herself out of it every time.

The annual Ballentine family Christmas Eve was even more excruciating than usual. She and Holly always spent the evening with their father, who always hosted a party for his fifty closest friends and business associates. Traditionally, he gave his daughters fifteen distracted minutes of his time before the party to exchange gifts, then more or less ignored them the rest of the night in favor of mingling with his guests.

This year, however, he'd practically handcuffed himself to Mia, parading her around so he could boast about her upcoming paper in the Annals. She spent the whole night smiling and nodding at people she didn't know, largely left out of the conversation yet unable to excuse herself from it. Meanwhile, Holly was left alone to shoot Mia smirking looks while she guzzled martinis.

Christmas Day had been pleasant enough, at least. Her mother actually had the whole day off, and she and Holly and Mia had spent it on the couch watching their favorite holiday movies and eating the takeout holiday meal her mother had ordered in advance. Mia had even told her mom a little about Josh and about their breakup, and her mother had given her a sympathetic hug and handed her another cookie.

But now Mia was back at her father's ostentatiously decorated apartment for the photo session he'd set up for her, followed by an interview with a writer from *New York* magazine. As she struggled to maintain a pleasant expression under her thick layer of makeup, she was reminded why she'd chosen to go to graduate school on the opposite coast from her father.

While she acknowledged the practicality of having professional headshots taken, she'd had to grit her teeth all morning as her father issued instructions to the photographer, offered "helpful" suggestions on everything from the wardrobe to the lighting, and criticized Mia's smile for being too strained. It had left her in a sour mood for the interview that followed.

The interview that turned out to be the last straw.

As she sat there listening to her father take credit for her interest in math as an excuse to ramble endlessly about himself—during an interview that was ostensibly meant to be about *her* accomplishments—Mia began to reevaluate her willingness to go along with the rest of his plans.

Who was she kidding? She hated this shit.

She'd gotten a taste of it before, when she'd been applying to college. At first she'd been thrilled that her father actually wanted to escort her on her campus tours. She'd let him schedule all her campus visits for her, deciding which schools were worthy of her consideration. But it had quickly become apparent he wasn't there to support her. As he dragged her to a series of private meet and greets he'd set up with university faculty and administrators who played no part in the admissions process, Mia realized her father was using her college application process as an opportunity to network and show her off like a fashion accessory.

She felt a creeping sense of déjà vu as her father hijacked yet another question from the *New York* writer to tell a longwinded story about his work as a quant. When he finally wound down, the interviewer turned to Mia and asked what had drawn her to the field of knot theory. She started to explain her affinity for puzzles and spatial reasoning, but before she got very far, her father interrupted with an anecdote about the wire and string puzzles he'd given her to play with as a child, and how he'd introduced her to the Seven Bridges of Königsberg problem, which had been her first taste of topology.

The irony of him crowing about his influence over her field of study was rich, considering how much he'd disapproved of it.

By the time Mia had started thinking about her graduate studies and formulated her twenty-year career plan, she'd grown more of a backbone and ceased to care so much about pleasing her father. There were a lot of reasons why she'd been drawn to pure math instead of applied math like her father wanted, and why she'd chosen to do it at UCLA. But a big factor had been a desire to break out of his shadow. To prove she could make it on her own without his influence and connections aiding her. To chart her own path instead of blindly adhering to the one he'd laid out for her.

Mia had followed her heart once before, and it had been the right choice. Why was she letting him lead her around like a show pony again? She hated it when he pushed her into the spotlight to feed his own ego. She'd always detested being the center of attention. So what was she doing all this for? Was it even worth it?

Maybe he was right, and this was the way to get the tenure-track job she'd always dreamed of in a top ten department. Maybe it would even help her get the Fields Medal.

But how much did she actually care about those things?

Did she even still want them that badly? Enough to build her life around getting them?

"So Mia," the interviewer said when her father had finished his monologue, "what's next for you?"

Her father started to answer for her, but Mia cut him off. "I don't know yet," she said. "I've actually been rethinking what's important to me and what I want from my career."

Her perspective had changed dramatically over the last few months. She'd learned a lot about herself in her short time at Bowman—and realized she wasn't the person she'd thought she was. She was more adaptable than she'd expected, less concerned with status and appearances than she used to be, and far better with people than she'd given herself credit for.

"How so?" the interviewer asked as Mia's father frowned beside her.

"Well," Mia said, "I used to think I was mainly interested in research, but I've recently begun to realize how much I enjoy teaching."

Maybe even more than she liked research. In fact, she might not even like research all that much. She still enjoyed thinking about problems as an intellectual exercise, but she didn't love the constant pressure to perform and publish.

The interviewer smiled, leaning forward a little in her chair. "Teaching's certainly a noble profession."

Her father's frown had turned into a glower, but Mia ignored him as she continued. "Right now I'm teaching at a small, regional university in rural Texas, and I've enjoyed the opportunity to work one-on-one with the undergraduates there. There's something that appeals to me about teaching students fresh out of high school who haven't yet figured out their path in life. Helping them construct knowledge and understanding. Opening their eyes to the possibilities available to them, whether their futures lie in mathematics or other fields entirely."

"Rural Texas?" The interviewer chuckled. "That's got to be a big change for you after growing up here in New York."

"It is." Mia smiled. "But I love it there. It's been absolutely wonderful."

"Of course, Mia's going to be looking at all kinds of opportunities," her father cut in. "She's got a bright future ahead of her. We're all excited to see what that mind of hers comes up with next. Right now she's looking for a research postdoc, and I like to think one of our East Coast schools will snap her up. But I'm sure there will also be plenty of opportunities for seminar talks, guest lecture series, colloquia . . ."

The more her father described the future he envisioned for her, the more Mia realized it wasn't what she wanted for herself.

She'd always assumed she needed to be at some big, impressive university to prove her worth, but now she knew she could be perfectly happy at a smaller, less renowned school and still feel good about herself. A school where there was more emphasis on teaching and less institutional pressure to "publish or perish." And she'd already proven she could do research just as well there as at any tier one school.

Despite thinking of herself as an inveterate city girl, she'd loved living in a small town. She didn't miss trendy restaurants or shopping malls or freeways. She'd gotten comfortable around livestock, learned to appreciate the utility of cowboy boots and hats, and developed a soft spot for country music.

Did she really want to start over in a new place at a new

job and have to make new friends? Why? When she already had friends and a job she liked in a place she loved. A place where she was wanted. Where she fit in. Where she'd been accepted and welcomed when no one else would have her.

Why would she want to leave all that? For what? Prestige? Money? Acclaim?

That was the stuff her dad cared about. It wasn't what would make Mia happy. Not as much as being somewhere she felt like she was making a difference in her students' lives. A place where she was part of a community, not just of academics, but of people. Students. Neighbors. Friends. That was what she longed for. To be someplace that felt as much like home as Crowder did.

Mia let her father take the lead for the rest of the interview, because she realized she didn't care anymore. Let him have this moment of reflected glory, because it would be his last. The interviewer wrapped things up soon after and asked if they'd mind posing for a few photos to accompany the article.

"What was that?" her father hissed, positioning his arm around her shoulders as they stood in front of his fireplace. "All that stuff about teaching high school kids and constructing knowledge?"

"The truth," Mia said with her first genuine smile of the day.

That evening, she accosted her sister as soon as she got home from work.

"I want to run something by you," Mia said, handing Holly a glass of wine. "I need you to tell me if you think it's nuts."

"Walk with me." Holly gulped down a mouthful of wine as she headed for her bedroom. "I have to take this bra off."

Mia sat down on Holly's bed, cradling her own glass of wine while Holly disappeared into the closet to change clothes. "You know all that stuff Dad wants to do for me to help my career?"

Holly leaned her head out of the closet long enough to roll her eyes. "Yes."

"What if I didn't do any of it?"

Holly reemerged in a pair of black leggings, pulling a faded NYU hoodie over her head. "Good for you?" Her brows drew together as she picked up her wine again. "Isn't that basically what I've been saying all along? That you shouldn't let Dad pull your strings."

"There's a tenure-track job opening up in my department at Bowman and . . . I think I'm going to apply for it."

Holly's eyes widened, and she sank down on the bed opposite Mia. "What about finding a postdoc? What about your twenty-year plan?"

"Maybe I don't care about the twenty-year plan anymore. Maybe it's a bad plan." Mia stared at her sister's *Hamilton* poster as she took a swig of wine. "Maybe I'm happy where I am."

"Are you?"

"Maybe? I think so. Is that nuts?" Mia looked at Holly, terrified she was going to say yes.

"I mean . . . shit." Holly chewed her bottom lip as she studied her through the heavy, long lashes Mia had always envied. "Are you doing this because of Josh? So you can stay with him?"

Mia had been asking herself that exact same question all day.

Did she want to stay with Josh? *Abso-fucking-lutely.*

Was she sacrificing everything else she wanted in order to do that? She genuinely didn't think she was—or that she'd even be tempted to do something like that.

She was pretty certain she wanted this, not because of Josh, but in addition to him. Even if she didn't get to have him—if he was so hurt and angry he refused to take her back—Mia felt confident saying she'd still rather live in Crowder and teach at Bowman than anywhere else she could think of. It was a place she knew she could be happy, even if she couldn't have Josh.

But *god* wouldn't it be amazing if they could actually be together?

"I don't think this is about that," she told Holly finally. "Obviously being able to stay with Josh would be great, but . . . I think I want this even aside from that. I like it there, and if I can get a permanent job there, I think that's what I want." She took another drink of wine and shook her head. "It all kind of hit me while I was doing that stupid interview today. The more Dad talks about my future and all the possibilities waiting for me, the more I want to stay right where I am." Sighing, she shot a look at her sister. "Have I finally cracked? I'm counting on you to tell me the truth."

Holly was quiet for a moment. "There's absolutely nothing wrong with prioritizing your own happiness, and it's okay if you decide that staying where you are is the best way to do that." She paused. "Just make damn sure that's why you're doing it and not for some other reason."

Mia shook her head. "I told you, I don't think I'm doing this for Josh."

"Okay." Holly's eyebrows lifted as she pinned Mia with a pointed stare. "But are you doing it to get back at Dad for his perpetual dickishness?"

"This isn't about Dad."

Holly snorted into her wineglass. "Everything's always a little about Dad."

"Not this time," Mia said, feeling defensive. "That's the point. I'm done trying to please him."

"Forgive me for being blunt, dearest sister, but I've heard that before." Holly stabbed a finger into Mia's arm with the force of a power drill. "And if you're making this decision to piss Dad off, that's way worse than doing it because you want to stay with your goat farmer boyfriend. At least Josh seems like a great guy who makes you happy. Pissing Dad off doesn't win you anything worth having."

While she rubbed her bruised arm, Mia considered her sister's words.

Making a major life decision to spite her father would be foolish and pathetic. But she didn't think she was doing that. She had been willing to go along with him for the sake of her career. She would suck it up and let her father work his publicity magic—regardless of how much she hated it—if it would get her something she actually wanted.

The point was that she didn't want those things anymore. The twenty-year plan she'd made in college was for someone else's life. It didn't fit the person she was now.

"This isn't me giving Dad the finger," she told Holly firmly. "This is about what *I* want."

Holly regarded her, as if she was weighing the truth of this statement. Breaking into a grin, she slapped Mia on the leg. "Good for you. In that case, I say go for it."

"I think I'm going to." Mia smiled to herself as she rubbed the painful mark Holly's slap had left on her leg.

Holly clinked her wineglass against Mia's and they both drank. "Can I ask you something?" Holly said, cocking her head to one side.

"Shoot."

"Do you love Josh?"

The question startled Mia. She hadn't ever allowed herself to consider the possibility or even think about the word *love* in proximity to the word *Josh*. Not when there was no hope of a future for them.

But now . . .

Now there might be a hope.

Could she fit *love* and *Josh* into the same sentence? Did she *love Josh*?

The answering starburst of bright, giddy excitement that filled her chest was all the proof she needed.

"Yes," she said, surprised at how sure she sounded. "I do. I love Josh."

"Wow." Holly's eyes were wide as saucers. "*Wow.*"

All Mia had to do now was figure out how she was going to get Josh back.

Chapter Twenty-Four

Two days later, Mia was back in Texas.

A palpable sense of relief overcame her as she took the exit off the highway for Crowder. The familiar sights that greeted her as she drove through town felt more like coming home than anything in New York had the past week.

She'd submitted her official application for the Bowman job yesterday after emailing the department chair to informally express her very great interest in the position. Being back in Crowder only reinforced the rightness of that decision. This was where she wanted to be. It was where she belonged.

Once she got back to her apartment, however, she paced around the small space, phone in hand, feeling shaky and far less certain than she had a few minutes ago.

She wanted to fix things with Josh, but she wasn't sure of the best way to approach it—and she couldn't afford to screw this up.

How could she convince him to give her a second chance when he had so little faith in her? She needed to find a way to show him what was in her heart. Give him a reason to trust her. Which meant laying bare all the feelings she'd worked so hard to repress.

A nauseating stew of fear and doubt churned in her stomach. She wasn't good at this kind of stuff. She might be getting better at understanding people, but she still didn't have a lot of experience with emotional honesty.

She sank down on the couch and rubbed her chest, thinking about Josh. Missing him. Aching for him.

What if he wouldn't take her call? What if he was so upset with her he didn't want to hear anything she had to say? It would help if she had some insight into his current state of mind. A better idea of where his head was at now that some time had passed.

What she needed was advice from an expert. Someone who knew Josh even better than she did.

She just had to hope her woman on the inside would be willing to help.

Her nerves jangling, Mia called Andie and held the phone to her ear.

"Hey!" Andie's voice came through the phone like a ray of sunshine. "Are you back?"

"I am," Mia said, feeling herself smile. "How was your Christmas?"

"Good. We missed you though."

The smile slid from Mia's face. Did that "we" include Josh? Or just Andie and Birdie? Mia swallowed as a lump formed in her throat. "I missed y'all too. I wish I'd stayed here. I'm sure it would have been a lot better than my Christmas at home."

"You didn't have a nice holiday?"

"It was okay. Nothing special."

"I thought Christmas in New York was supposed to be magical or something. Are you telling me all those movies have been lying to us?"

"It was cold," Mia said, thinking of more than the weather. "I guess I'm not used to it anymore."

Andie laughed. "Funny how fast a person can acclimate to a new place, isn't it? A few months in Texas, and we've got you saying y'all and complaining about the cold when the temperature drops below sixty."

"Yeah, it is funny." Mia squeezed the phone. "Listen, I want to ask for your advice about something, but I also want you to feel like you can say no if it's not something you're comfortable with."

"Sounds ominous." Andie's voice deepened with amusement. "You've got me intrigued."

"It's about Josh."

There was a moment of silence before Andie spoke again. "What about him?"

"The thing is . . ." Mia stood up and paced as she tried to gather her thoughts.

This was good for her. It was like a trial run. If she could tell Andie what she was thinking, it would be easier to open up to Josh.

"The thing is, I've decided I want to try and stay in Crowder." She felt better as soon as she said the words.

"Okay." Andie still sounded cautious.

"There's an open tenure-track position in the Bowman math department, and I've applied for it. I can't be sure I'll get it, but I think there's a decent chance."

"That's great." There was a heavy pause before Andie added, "If that's what you want."

"It is. I thought about it a lot while I was home. This is where I want to be—for a lot of reasons."

"Is one of those reasons Josh?" Andie's tone was flat, revealing nothing.

"One of them," Mia admitted. "He's not the only reason, but he's a pretty big one. I—" *I love him. I need him. I can hardly breathe, I miss him so much.*

Mia pulled herself together before she got carried away. Andie didn't want to hear all that. She just needed the basics.

"I want to fix things with him," Mia said instead. "But I don't know how. I don't know if that's something he even still wants and—" She swallowed as the words got stuck in her throat. "I'm scared, I guess."

An unnerving moment of silence passed before Andie responded. "And you want me to tell you what? How to woo my brother back?"

Mia sank down on the couch and pressed her forehead into the palm of her hand. "That's weird, isn't it? I'm sorry, I shouldn't have dumped this on you."

"No, it's okay. It's fine, actually."

Mia sat up, squeezing the phone. "It is?"

"Yeah, why not? If you need someone to talk to, I'm your girl. Even if it's about my brother—as long as you don't go into any gross detail or anything. Hearing about my brother's sex life is where I draw the line."

"No," Mia said quickly. "Definitely not."

"I'm kind of with a friend right now though."

"Oh gosh. Sorry." Mia was mortified. "We don't have to do this now. It can wait."

"It's cool," Andie said. "I'm working tomorrow, but why don't I swing by when I'm done and we can go for a drink?"

"Er . . . isn't tomorrow New Year's Eve?" Even in Crowder, she assumed the bars would be crowded and not exactly conducive to conversation.

"Is it? Even better. We can talk and celebrate at the same time."

"Okay," Mia said. "Sounds good."

Andie was doing her a favor, so if she wanted to go out on New Year's Eve, it was the least Mia could do. Her conversation with Josh could probably wait another day or two. It wasn't like he was going anywhere.

And neither was Mia.

Hopefully.

Andie insisted on going to the Rusty Spoke. On New Year's Eve. Mia had gently tried to suggest somewhere a little quieter, but Andie seemed to have her heart set on it.

So to the Rusty Spoke they went.

The place was packed. And deafening. Wyatt's band was on stage, blasting out a cover of "Jessie's Girl." According to the retro-style decorations and large banner that had been tacked up behind the stage, the theme for the night was "Back to the 80s."

Andie dragged Mia behind her as she moved through the crowd, determined to find them a spot close to the stage. "How's this?" she shouted, pushing her way into a space next to a noisy gaggle of women who waved an enthusiastic greeting at Andie while they danced and sang along with Wyatt's Rick Springfield impression.

"It's kind of loud," Mia shouted back. They were dead center in front of the stage, in the middle of the noisy crowd.

Andie grinned as if she hadn't heard and turned back to

the stage. Wyatt's gaze lit on them and he nodded his head in greeting. Andie flashed him a thumbs-up before leaning over to say something to one of the women next to them.

Mia gave up on the idea of having any sort of meaningful conversation tonight and decided to try and enjoy herself instead. It was New Year's Eve, after all. She was back home where she belonged and in the company of friends. Everything else could wait until tomorrow. It would be the start of a new year and a brand-new chapter of her life. That was worth celebrating.

"I'm going to go get us some drinks," Mia shouted in Andie's ear.

"Not yet." Andie clamped onto Mia's arm, holding her fast to keep her from going anywhere. "In a minute."

"Okay . . ." Mia was a little confused by Andie's behavior tonight. But it felt nice to know her company was wanted, at least. She could think of worse ways to end the year.

If only Josh were here too, it would be perfect.

But Mia knew better than to look for him in the crowd. Even if he accepted her apology and they worked things out and she was offered the job at Bowman so she could stay here—which was a lot of ifs—Josh would never want to come out to someplace this crowded. He'd never be able to relax and have a good time listening to his best friend's band play.

Which was okay—even if it made her a little sad for him—as long as they were together. Next year, if things worked out like she hoped, she and Josh would be spending a quiet New Year's Eve together at the farm.

Assuming he wanted her back, of course.

"Hey." Andie gave Mia a shake.

"What?" Mia blinked, coming out of her daze.

Andie grinned at her. The song had ended, and as the applause died down a buzz of conversation rippled through the crowd. People around them were whispering and murmuring, reacting to something. The music started up again, and Mia recognized the intro to the song from *Dirty Dancing*.

But it wasn't Wyatt's voice that started singing. It was a deeper, warmer voice. A beautiful voice. One she knew intimately . . .

Every muscle in Mia's body froze in place.

It can't be.

Andie grabbed her and spun her toward the stage. Mia lifted her gaze—

It *was* him. The last person she ever expected to see standing up there crooning into the microphone.

"Josh," she breathed, not quite believing it was real.

He was looking right at her. Singing *to her*.

Josh. Her Josh. Was up on a stage. Singing "The Time of My Life" in front of a crowd of people.

Mia stared in open-mouthed shock. Unable to look away. Barely even able to breathe as she drank in the sight of him ablaze under the lights in her favorite blue plaid shirt—looking a little nervous, but not as much as you'd expect. His chestnut eyes were shining and locked onto hers as he sang both parts of the duet, every word imbued with meaning directed straight at her.

As her surprise wore off she started to smile, and it seemed to banish the last of Josh's nervousness. His voice grew more confident, and his lips curved in a smile of his own as he belted out the last note of the intro.

The tempo picked up as the bass and drums came in.

Wyatt pumped his fist at the side of the stage. Andie used her thumb and forefinger to let out an ear-piercing whistle as the crowd hooted and hollered in response, cheering as Josh started singing the first verse.

Mia blinked back hot tears as the song enveloped her, sinking into her heart before bursting inside her chest. She'd never paid attention to the lyrics before. She'd never been this moved by *any* song—or known this sort of happiness before. She'd never even imagined she could feel this way. She wouldn't have been able to stop smiling if her life depended on it.

The music seemed to shimmer in the air, infecting the crowd with a delirious excitement. She was vaguely aware of people whooping and whistling around her, but it was the words Josh was singing to her that glowed like starlight in her mind.

This could be love.

The women next to Andie practically collapsed to the floor in a collective swoon when he launched into the chorus. By then Mia was openly crying, rubbing away tears with the heels of her hands as the music swelled. She wasn't the only one tearing up either. People around her were hugging and swaying. Dancing. Losing their minds when Josh pointed at her at the end of the chorus and shouted, "Hey, baby!"

The crowd parted, opening up a path between Mia and the stage, and she felt a hand on her back, pushing her toward Josh. "Go on," Andie shouted in her ear. "What are you waiting for?"

Mia stumbled forward as people around her shouted encouragement. Wyatt grabbed the microphone from Josh and gave him a shove off the front of the stage. She came to an unsteady stop as Josh jumped down onto the gravel a few yards in front of her.

Then she started running, straight into his waiting arms.

Mia's breath caught in a joyous gasp as he picked her up—*not* over his head like the movie, thank god—and spun her around. The crowd went nuts around them as the band kept playing, with Wyatt taking over the vocals.

But all Mia cared about was Josh, who was holding her like he never wanted to let her go. She smelled the warm, familiar scent of his skin, and her stomach swooped like he *had* lifted her over his head, and she knew she never, ever wanted to be anywhere else but with him.

"I love you," she said, the words tumbling out of her on a gust of pure happiness.

Josh set her down, frowning slightly. His eyes searched hers, wide with surprise and full of uncertainty. "What did you say?" His words were nearly drowned out by the crowd noise and the music, so she mostly had to read them on his lips.

She reached up and cradled his face in her hands. "I love you," she said, louder this time and looking right at him so he could see her saying it.

The corners of his lips tilted in a heartbreakingly beautiful smile. And then those lips pressed against hers, still smiling as he kissed her, inspiring the crowd to erupt in a fresh bout of cheers and wolf whistles.

Heedless of their audience, Mia sank her fingers into his hair, her tongue parting his lips hungrily as their bodies pressed together.

After an indeterminate number of dreamy, intense, lustful seconds, she felt Josh's chest rumble with a growl, and he pulled back, panting. "Come on." Wrapping a protective arm around her, he guided her toward the exit.

People made space for them to pass, clapping, cheering, and slapping Josh on the back along the way. When they reached the gate, he turned and offered a sheepish wave to the crowd before pointing up at the stage and giving his old bandmates a heartfelt salute.

Then he took Mia by the hand and led her away.

Chapter Twenty-Five

They only ended up making it as far as Josh's truck at the back of the gravel parking lot. That was as long as Mia could stand to wait before she grabbed the front of his shirt and dragged him in for another kiss. His hands cupped the back of her head as his lips caressed hers, his tongue dipping into her mouth with a sweetness that made her knees go weak.

He caught her when she stumbled backward, his arms strong and steady as they held her. Music drifted over to them from the bar as he gazed down at her, his eyes shining bright in the moonlight. "Say it one more time."

Mia didn't need to ask what he wanted to hear her say. She smiled up at him, happy to say it as much as he liked. "I love you."

His mouth curved in that beautiful smile again. "I love you too."

Something brittle and heavy inside her softened, growing lighter as his words washed over her. They soaked into her pores and flowed through every nerve in her body before finally settling in her chest where they curled around her heart.

Josh lifted an eyebrow, his forehead crinkling slightly. "Is that okay?"

"Better than okay." She felt like she could fly. Like her feet were hovering a few inches off the ground. She reached up to cup his face, loving the way his frown smoothed out at her touch. "I can't believe you're here. I can't believe you got up on stage like that. *How?*"

"Andie called me last night. She told me what you said. Is it true? Are you really staying?"

"If I get the job at Bowman, I am." It wasn't guaranteed, even if she did have reason to think her chances were excellent.

Josh's frown came back. "You don't have to do that. I don't want you to give anything up for me."

"I'm not. Not anything I want, anyway. I thought about it a lot while I was home, and I realized this is where I want to be. Here in this town, at this university . . ." She stroked her thumb over his lower lip. "With you."

He still looked doubtful. "Are you sure?"

"I haven't been this sure about anything in a long time."

His doubt melted away and he kissed her again, so softly and tenderly it felt like Mia's heart would overflow with everything she felt. When her lip trembled against his, Josh picked her up again, holding her tight. He carried her around to the back of his truck, lowered the tailgate, and set her down on it.

She made a space for him between her knees and wrapped her arms around his waist, pulling him close. Luxuriating in the scent of him. Burrowing into his warmth.

"Mia . . ." His breath hitched as he cradled her against

his chest. "I'm sorry I freaked out on you. You didn't deserve that."

Pulling back to look at him, she touched his cheek. "I'm not sure that's true." He opened his mouth to argue, but she shook her head. "I'm not always good at expressing what I feel."

His lips tugged into a smile. "I don't know, you did pretty well tonight."

A laugh bubbled out of her. "I guess I did." She grew serious again. "I don't ever want to give you reason to doubt me. I want to be someone you can trust, the way I trust you."

His eyes fell closed and he bent his head, brushing his nose against hers. "You are."

"I know trust isn't easy for you. I should have been more mindful of that."

"That's not on you." He pressed his forehead against hers. "Yes, it's hard for me to trust people after what Kayla did. But what's even harder is figuring out how to trust myself again after my gut instincts failed me so spectacularly. And that's something I have to work on."

"I still don't understand how you got up on that stage tonight."

He pulled back, his eyes softening as he gazed at her. "When Andie told me you'd said you wanted me back but you were scared . . ." A crease wrinkled his brow. "I had to do something to show how much you meant to me, so you'd know you didn't have to be scared."

Her heart gave a painful lurch. "You didn't have to do that for me. I never want you to feel like you have to do something that makes you uncomfortable in order to please me. I don't need you to be anything but who you are."

"I don't regret it," Josh said. "It helped me realize how much I've given up. That man who got up on stage tonight, that's who I used to be. And I miss it. I miss being able to enjoy going out and being around people. I'm tired of being afraid all the time." He paused, his mouth and jaw tightening. "That's why I've started seeing a therapist."

Mia had some idea how hard that must have been for him—both to admit it and to make the decision to do it in the first place. She wrapped her arms around him, holding him to show how much she meant it when she said, "I'm so proud of you."

He cleared his throat. "I've only had one appointment so far. I don't know how much difference it'll make, but I guess it's worth a shot."

"Does this mean you might start singing with Shiny Heathens again?"

Josh snorted. "I don't know about that . . ." He tipped his head back, his eyes crinkling at the corners. "Why? Did you like seeing me do that?"

She gave his shoulder a shove. "Are you kidding? You were amazing up there! I knew you had a great singing voice, but I had no idea you were such an incredible performer." She narrowed her eyes in mock disapproval as she poked a finger into his chest. "I feel cheated that you've been hiding that side of you from me."

He smiled, but his expression grew somber as he stroked his hand down her neck. "I've been doing too much hiding. It's something I'm trying to fix." His eyes twinkled as his smile warmed again. "But maybe I could manage to get back on that stage every once in a while. I sure didn't mind the way you looked at me when I was up there."

"That's because I liked the way you looked when you were up there." She dug her fingers into his hips, pulling him into the cradle of her legs and enjoying the flush that crept up his throat. "It was *hot*."

She hadn't imagined it was possible for Josh to be any more attractive to her, but the way he looked on that stage . . . her ovaries had definitely melted. The effect of it still surged through her, heating her blood despite the cool night air.

He rocked into her, exhaling a ragged breath. "Even if I don't get up on stage every week, I've been thinking I should probably try to get out more. I think I might be able to do that if you're willing to do it with me."

"Of course." Cupping his face in her hands, she brushed her lips against his. "I'll be here for whatever you need. You don't have to do anything alone anymore."

His eyes burned into hers. "Neither do you."

The truth of those words reached inside her and filled up a hole she hadn't even known was there. An unquenched yearning she'd carried all her life vanished in a burst of incandescent happiness. Suddenly the world seemed a lot less daunting.

It's going to be okay. We're going to be okay. Both of us. Together.

"I missed you," she said softly, feeling her lip tremble again. "I want you with me. Just to be super clear about that. I always want you, any way you're willing to let me have you."

He cocked a provocative eyebrow at her. "*Any* way?"

"Yes." She smiled, wondering if it was possible to actually die of happiness. "That's what I said."

"I like the sound of that." He lowered his head and kissed her, hard and deep. Using his lips and his tongue to say *you're mine* in a way that left absolutely no room for doubt.

A shimmer of electric heat danced through her body, and her stomach swooped like a bird whirling through the sky. When he finally pulled back it left them panting and clinging to each other for support.

"But maybe not here in this parking lot." His voice sounded strained and hungry. "I think we should go home."

Home. She liked the sound of that.

Mia closed her eyes. Nodded. "Yes, please."

Happy New Year, indeed.

Epilogue

Three months later

"Sorry about your feet," Mia said as Josh led her off the dance floor.

He squeezed her hand and threw a grin over his shoulder. "That's the good thing about boots—I barely even feel it when you step on me."

"Even when I'm wearing boots too?"

Past Mia would probably recoil in horror to learn that she now owned not one but *two* pairs of cowboy boots—one pair for mucking around the farm and another, nicer pair for going out. Not only that, but she was at a boot scootin' country-western dance hall, surrounded by men wearing cowboy hats and giant metal belt buckles listening to a honky-tonk band play . . . and she actually liked it.

It was the third Saturday night in a row she and Josh had come to King's Palace dance hall. He was teaching her how to two-step while practicing the desensitization techniques he'd learned in therapy. They were both a work in progress, but so far he was doing a lot better at managing his anxiety than Mia was at country-western dancing.

They reached the bar table where they'd left their drinks, and she tipped back her now-lukewarm beer. Swallowing, she wiped her sweaty forehead with the back of her hand. "I think I'm getting better though. I only stepped on you a couple of times during the last song."

Josh smiled indulgently. "You're doing great, sweetie."

Her lips formed into a pout. "That bad? Really?" She'd lived in Texas long enough to know that "sweetie" was only slightly less condescending than "bless your heart."

"No." He reached for her hand and brought it to his lips. "You're coming along fine."

"I think my problem is that I have a negative sense of rhythm."

His palm cupped her cheek and he leaned toward her, his voice lowering to a husky murmur as his lips skimmed hers. "I know for a fact your rhythm is impeccable."

Mia smiled against his mouth, slanting her head as her tongue sought his.

"Gross." Andie slammed a fresh bucket of ice-cold beers on the table. "Are y'all trying to give me nightmares? Quit with the PDA."

"I'm going to the bathroom," Josh said, rolling his eyes at his sister. "I'll be back."

Mia reached for a fresh beer and twisted the cap off as she swiveled to face Andie. "Have I mentioned I really like that dress on you?" It wasn't often that Andie wore dresses. When she wasn't in her park service uniform of khakis and polo shirts, she tended to favor shorts or jeans and T-shirts.

"Thanks." Andie offered a perfunctory curtsy before grabbing a beer for herself. "Hey, what's the name of that sunscreen you were telling me about?"

"Facial or body?"

Andie's nose wrinkled. "Both, I guess. Can you text me the links?"

"Does this mean you're finally going to take my advice?" Mia had been on Andie's case about the fact that she didn't wear a daily SPF formula, which was especially egregious given how much time she spent outdoors. You couldn't be too careful with your skin when it came to the sun.

"Maybe." Andie shrugged as she flicked her bottle cap into the bucket. "I've been thinking about it."

"I'll send you a link to the cleanser I use too. If you're going to be wearing sunscreen every day, you'll need to start washing your face with something more than water."

She'd been flabbergasted to learn Andie's entire skincare routine consisted of splashing water on her face. Andie never wore makeup, so she'd said she didn't feel the need to give her face any special treatment. And yet somehow her skin still looked fabulous. Some people were just blessed with great genes, while others required ten-step skincare routines to make up the difference.

Andie rolled her eyes. "Fine."

"Just wait, I'm going to have you addicted to serums before you know it."

"No way. I'm not doing all that shit. All I'm trying to do is not get cancer."

"I'll send you a link to my moisturizer too. It's got just the slightest bit of tint to it, to give you that glowy, makeup-free look." Sunscreen was a gateway drug. From there it was a slippery slope to hydrators, toners, and exfoliants. Soon she'd be able to talk Andie into driving up to Austin with her for regular visits to Sephora.

"I get my makeup-free look by not wearing makeup, thanks." Andie pursed her pink, shiny lips.

"Hang on . . ." Mia took her by the shoulders and studied her face. "You're wearing lipstick!"

"No, I'm not." Andie's cheeks reddened as she clamped her lips together and pulled out of Mia's grasp. "It's lip balm."

"*Tinted* lip balm!" Grinning, Mia pointed a triumphant finger at her friend. "Wow. What's the occasion?"

"Chapped lips. That's the only occasion." Andie turned away and chugged her beer.

"I don't buy it," Mia said, studying her more carefully. "The dress, the lip balm—and your hair's down too." Andie almost always wore her hair in a ponytail, braid, or bun. Thoughtfully, Mia tapped her index finger against her lips. "Could it be . . . are you trying to impress someone special? Maybe someone who's here tonight?" She peered around the dance hall, trying to guess who the lucky man might be. "Is it Tanner King?" she asked, spotting Wyatt's brother by the bar.

"God, no," Andie said.

"What about Ryan?" Mia asked, pointing at another of Wyatt's brothers.

"Stop that." Andie grabbed Mia's finger and shoved it down under the table. "There's no one."

"No one? Really?"

"Really." Andie set her beer down. "I have to pee." She walked off, brushing past Josh as he returned to the table.

"Why do they put ice in urinals?" he wondered aloud, reaching for a fresh beer. "Is it just to give us something to aim at?"

Mia ignored his urinal inquiry. "Is it possible your sister has a secret boyfriend?"

Josh made a scoffing noise as he lowered his beer. "I seriously doubt it. Why would she keep a boyfriend a secret?"

"Or maybe it's a secret crush."

"That doesn't sound like Andie."

Wyatt pushed his way between them to snag a bottle out of the bucket. "What about Andie?"

Mia's gaze traveled around the room. "I think a special gentleman's caught her eye."

Wyatt coughed and wiped his hand across his mouth as he leaned forward, trying to see what Mia was looking at. "Who?"

"No one," Josh said. "She's imagining things."

Mia reached around Wyatt to give Josh's shoulder a shove. "I am not. Haven't you noticed how pretty she looks tonight?"

Josh shrugged and said, "No" at the same time as Wyatt said, "Yes."

Mia swiveled her head to look at Wyatt, but his attention was occupied by a group of women who'd come in the door.

"The thing about Andie," Josh said, "is that when she wants something, she usually just goes for it. Secrets and pining aren't her style."

"Oh fuck." Wyatt ducked his head, pulling his cowboy hat down over his eyes.

"What?" Mia turned to see what he was reacting to.

"Nothing. Don't look." He grabbed her arms, spinning her around to face him while using her as a shield to hide himself. "It's just someone I don't want to talk to."

"Gee, could it possibly be another woman you've pissed off?" Mia guessed as Josh snickered into his beer. It seemed as though Wyatt was always trying to avoid some poor woman he'd recently spurned.

"Shit, she's coming over here," Wyatt hissed. He seized Mia's hand. "Dance with me."

As he jerked her toward the dance floor she threw a desperate *help me* look at Josh, but he only offered an amused shrug as he let his best friend drag her away.

Mia sighed in resignation, turning back to Wyatt as he pulled her along beside him. "I'm warning you right now, I'm terrible at this."

"That's okay." Flashing a cocky grin, he twirled her onto the dance floor and into his arms with Gene Kelly-esque smoothness. "I'm good enough for the both of us."

Indeed, she was forced to admit he was an even better dancer than Josh. While Josh had impressive agility and technical proficiency, Wyatt moved with more casual flair and a loose-limbed grace that made everything he did look effortless. Alas for Wyatt's excellent dancing skills, Mia's lack of rhythm proved challenging even for him.

"You're too tense." Wyatt smoothed his hand down her back with a frown. "You need to relax and let me lead."

"You do know women hate it when men tell them to relax, right?"

Wyatt's eyes crinkled as he winked at her. "Not when I do it."

Mia let out an amused snort. If anyone else had said something like that to her, it would have raised her hackles. But she'd grown accustomed to Wyatt's flirtatiousness by now and figured out that most of his swagger was an act he put on. Birdie had been right—his bark was worse than his bite. The cocksure attitude he presented to the world was a defensive facade—though exactly what he was defending himself from, Mia hadn't sussed out yet. In the same way Josh used to hide in his house, Wyatt hid himself away by pretending not to care about anything.

But Mia knew better. By now she'd seen for herself how much Wyatt cared about Josh, and how much he cared about Birdie and Andie too. They were essentially his adoptive family. Which was sort of strange, considering he had such a large and powerful family of his own. The very dance hall they were in right now bore his family name and was run by one of his uncles.

"Why aren't you playing up on that stage?" Mia asked as they danced past the band. She was getting a little better at matching Wyatt's footwork after a couple of revolutions around the floor.

He laughed as he whirled her around a slow-moving older couple. "Because that's a real band up there."

"Shiny Heathens is a real band."

"No, we're a bunch of amateurs having a good time, which is the way I like it." His gaze drifted to the six-piece swing band, and Mia could swear his blue eyes looked wistful. "Those are real musicians up there."

"I'll bet your uncle would let you play here if you asked. Didn't you say he was your favorite uncle?"

Wyatt shook his head, a faint smile curving his lips. "He wouldn't give me anything I hadn't earned, which is one of the reasons he's my favorite uncle." His smile turned wry. "That and the fact that he hates my dad's guts."

She squeezed his shoulder as he led her through a turn. "Your family's like a soap opera."

"More like *Game of Thrones*," he replied in gruff amusement.

"*Game of Thrones* is just a soap opera with swords," she pointed out.

Wyatt's eyes crinkled in a smile. "Fair enough."

"Who are you using me to hide from?"

His smile slipped a little. "Just some girl who's looking for a boyfriend and didn't like it when I told her it isn't going to be me. Same old story."

"Don't you ever want something more?"

Wyatt lifted her hand over her head, leading her into a surprise spin. Miraculously, she managed to follow his signals and mostly keep step with him. He smirked as he spun her back into his arms. "What's better than having great sex with lots of beautiful women? What more could I possibly want?"

Mia clutched his hand, feeling pleased with herself but also a little dizzy from the spin. "What about love? Partnership? Commitment?"

He made a face. "No thank you."

"Come on, don't you ever get lonely playing the field?"

He spun her again, twice in a row this time, before pulling her back to him once more. "You're getting pretty good at this."

"And you're trying to distract me."

"Do I look lonely to you?" he asked with another smirk.

She looked him in the eye. "Yes."

"Not me," he said lightly, shaking his head. "I'm allergic to commitment." His smirk faded as his gaze focused on something behind her. His expression seemed to freeze in place for a second before he shifted his attention back to Mia with a shrug. "Seriously, I dated someone for a whole month once, and I got this scratchy throat I couldn't kick, and my skin started feeling itchy all over. Eventually it got so bad it felt like I couldn't breathe. But then we broke up, and the very next day I felt fine. All cured." He shrugged again. "What can I do? It's a medical condition."

"You're so full of shit," Mia told him, and he laughed and spun her again.

"Congrats on the job, by the way." He glanced over at the table where Josh stood watching them. "I'm glad you're staying."

"Me too," Mia said, smiling.

She'd gotten her official offer letter from Bowman that week. Josh had insisted she apply for other jobs and give them serious consideration before making up her mind. He hadn't wanted her to compromise her aspirations for him, and had promised her they'd figure it out if she decided to take a job in another city.

But unlike Paul, he'd actually meant it. Josh's way of figuring it out involved serious conversations about bringing on an apprentice cheesemaker and handing over day-to-day management of the farm to Ray.

Mia was deeply touched that Josh was willing to even consider doing something like that for her, but she wasn't the slightest bit tempted to take him up on it. She was glad he'd insisted she go on other interviews though, because they'd cemented her decision to stay in Crowder. Since her paper had been published, she'd become rather famous in her subfield. Several prestigious programs had been interested in her, which was certainly flattering. But none of them could beat what she already had here.

Wyatt lifted his arm and spun her all the way back to their

table and straight into his best friend's waiting arms. Josh grabbed her around the waist, pulling her up against him.

"Thanks for the dance." Wyatt touched the brim of his hat and helped himself to another beer before strolling away.

Josh slid Mia's beer closer to her and kissed her temple. "You looked great out there. You really are getting the hang of it."

She leaned against him, grateful to be standing still again and back in his arms where she belonged. Someone at a nearby table let out a loud peal of laughter and she felt Josh stiffen against her. She glanced at him, checking for signs of stress. "Are you doing okay?"

He gave her a nod as he did one of the diaphragmatic breathing exercises he'd learned to help manage his anxiety.

She waited, watching while he took a few long, deliberate breaths. "We can go whenever you want to."

"I'm okay." He rolled his shoulders, shaking out the tension. "I can do this."

Mia cupped his cheek, forcing him to look her in the eyes. Making sure he was telling the truth and not trying to put on a brave face. He'd gotten better about admitting when he was struggling, but sometimes he still fell back on old habits and tried to play the stoic.

He covered her hand with his. "Really," he said. "I'm good."

"I'm so proud of you," she said. "You're amazing, you know that?"

"You're pretty great yourself." His eyes took on a playful glint. "One might even say you're sweet as pi."

Mia laughed and pressed a light kiss to his lips. "If you were a triangle, you'd be acute one."

When he smiled at her, the force of the love in his eyes turned her inside out—just like it did every time. But then she saw a flicker of uncertainty cloud the warm brown depths.

"What's wrong?" she asked.

He shook his head. "Nothing." His thick, rough fingers intertwined with her thinner, softer ones. "I've been thinking . . . now that it's definite you're staying—"

"It was definite before," she told him. She'd been telling him all along, even though he'd insisted she keep her options open. He'd refused to accept her decision as final until it really was final. But now it was. She'd formally accepted Bowman's offer of a tenure-track position. Starting in the fall, she'd be an assistant professor.

The corner of Josh's mouth twitched. "Now that it's definite you've got a job here beyond the summer . . . what do you think about moving in with me at the farm?"

Mia thought it sounded like heaven. She'd already been spending as much time there as she could because Josh's farm was her favorite place on earth. There was nowhere else she'd rather be. And no one she'd rather be with. All she'd been waiting for was an invitation.

"I'd love that," she said, light-headed with happiness.

His smile spilled over her like sunlight. "Good, because I'd love it too."

"My lease isn't up until the end of the summer," she pointed out. But whatever. She didn't mind paying rent for an empty apartment if it meant she could wake up in Josh's bed every morning.

His eyes crinkled. "I've got an in with the landlord. I think I might be able to convince her to let you out of that lease."

"Only if she can find a new tenant to take my place. I'm

not going to leave Birdie in the lurch." Birdie was Mia's family now, just like Josh was her family.

"We won't," he promised. "We'll figure it out."

She knew they would. Whatever life threw their way, they'd handle it.

Together.

Thank you for reading! I hope you loved meeting Mia and Josh. If you'd like to find out what's really going on between Andie and Wyatt, don't miss My Cone and Only, *the first book in the King Family series.*

Acknowledgments

Thank you to Lisa Seger at Blue Heron Farm in Waller County, Texas, not only for answering all my questions about raising dairy goats and running a farm business, but for making lots of good trouble (and also the best damn goat milk feta cheese I've ever tasted in my life). Follow Blue Heron Farm on Twitter (@BlueHeronFarmTX) or Instagram (@BlueHeronTexas) for photos of their spoiled goats and foster dogs.

My undying gratitude goes out to all the mathematically inclined people who double-checked my math work for me, including Jo, Dave, and Mikaela. Extra thanks to Mikaela for sharing her knowledge of publishing and hiring in academia. Special shoutout to my friend Tammy for supplying me with lots of excellent math puns.

As always, this book wouldn't be half as good without the contributions of my wonderful editor. Don't ever leave me, Julia.

You may also enjoy the first book in
the Chemistry Lessons series . . .

The Love Code

Read on for an extract now . . .

Chapter One

Three Years Ago

Melody Gage checked her phone for the tenth time in five minutes.

Nothing.

Sighing, she reached for her pint glass and took a swig. It was warm inside the bar, and she was still wearing her leather jacket, which she couldn't take off because there was a hole in her shirt, right at the seam running across her shoulder blades.

Besides, taking off her jacket would imply she was staying more than another few minutes—which she wasn't.

She couldn't believe she'd actually made an effort tonight. She'd worn her favorite leather jacket, even though the weather was too warm for it. It was the nicest thing she owned, despite the fact that it had come from a thrift shop. She'd even exchanged her usual Doc Martens for a pair of cute ballet flats. And for what? A no-show.

Melody felt someone jostle her arm as they slid onto the barstool beside her. She looked up hopefully, but it wasn't Victor.

The guy who wasn't her date leaned toward her, grinning. "How you doing tonight?"

He was young, college-age like her, and like a lot of the other patrons at the Cask 'n Flagon, he was sporting a Red Sox cap. He was also wearing a T-shirt for a fraternity "Pimps & Prostitutes" party, which earned him a few demerits. He wasn't bad looking, though. In fact, she might even be tempted to call him attractive.

Too bad she was waiting for someone . . . who was fifteen minutes late. Not exactly a promising start to a first date.

Melody offered her new seat mate a polite but guarded smile. "I'm doing okay."

"You're really fine, you know that?" he said, leaning in closer.

Gross. She had always despised that word in that context. *Fine.* Had a man ever described a woman as "fine" without sounding like a sleazebag? Also, his breath smelled like garlic. No thank you.

"Thanks, but I'm waiting for someone." She stared down at her phone again. Still no text.

"You know, I'm not usually into chicks with short hair," her companion said, gesturing at her brunette pixie cut, "but I might be willing to make an exception for you."

Ugh. That was what she got for venturing outside her comfort zone. She probably should have known tonight was going to be a bust when Victor had a) picked a sports bar near Fenway for their date, and b) suggested they meet instead of coming together.

She'd only agreed because she'd been desperate to break out of her routine. Desperate to do something—anything—other than spend another Saturday night studying in her dorm room or working in the computer lab.

And look what it had gotten her.

"I bet you know you're fine," the wannabe pick-up artist said, undeterred by Melody's unwelcoming body language. "You probably have guys telling you that all the time, right?"

WHERE ARE YOU??? Melody texted Victor, mashing her thumbs against the screen of her phone.

She didn't even like Victor all that much. They were chemistry lab partners, but the only sparks between them were the ones they used to light the Bunsen burner.

The biggest thing he had going for him was the fact that he'd actually asked her out, which was more than anyone else had done lately. He was the only guy who'd shown any interest in her all year.

As her roommate had helpfully reminded her, Melody hadn't been so much as kissed since that guy with the butt chin during orientation week—and he hadn't remembered her the next day when he'd sobered up.

Not that she'd been putting herself out there. Almost all her time had been divided between studying and working to pay the portion of her tuition not covered by scholarships.

MIT was *hard,* in a way school had never been for her before. Her whole life, she'd always been at the top of her class. But everyone else at MIT had been at the top of their classes, too. She'd had to work twice as hard just to stay in the middle of the pack.

Melody didn't like the middle of the pack. She wanted to be at the top again. Or at least close to the top. And if that meant missing out on a few parties, so be it. No big loss.

Only . . . now that her freshman year was almost over, it had occurred to her that everyone else had been going out, meeting new people, sleeping around, falling in love, breaking up, and falling in love again while she'd been buried in her books. They'd been having *experiences*.

If Melody wasn't careful, she'd be heading out into the world with a bachelor's degree and the social maturity of a high school student in three years. She figured she ought to devote some effort to leveling up her life skills along with her academic skills.

Which was how she had ended up in this bar, being negged by a frat boy who reeked of Axe body spray and desperation.

Her new friend leaned in even closer, pressing his shoulder right up against hers, and blew another cloud of garlic breath in her face. "What's a girl like you doing here all by herself, anyway?"

"I'm waiting for someone," Melody repeated through gritted teeth. She craned her neck, scanning the crowd milling by the door on the off-chance Victor had shown up.

"A girl like you shouldn't be all alone. How about I keep you company until your friend gets here?"

"How about no?"

"What are you drinking? Lemme buy you another one."

"I don't want another—"

"One more of whatever she's having," the creep shouted to the bartender, ignoring her. It was like talking to a brick wall.

"Don't bother," Melody told the bartender. "I'm not staying."

Seriously, screw Victor. She was not waiting around one second longer.

"Hey, where you going?" Creepy Guy protested, making a grab for her arm as she slid off the barstool.

Melody twisted out of his grasp, spinning around to make her escape—and crashed face-first into a male chest. Startled, she looked up into a pair of dazzling blue eyes belonging to a *very* tall, very *cute* guy. "Whoa," she blurted.

"I'm so sorry I'm late, babe!" The cute guy beamed a dimpled smile at her and squeezed her arm like he knew her.

Melody stared at him, open-mouthed. She was positive she'd never laid eyes on him before in her life. *What was happening right now?*

When he stooped to kiss her cheek, she was so stunned, she couldn't move. Only, instead of kissing her, his lips hovered near her ear, and he whispered, "Play along if you want to get away from this guy."

Oh. *Hell yes,* she would play along if it got Creepy Guy off her back.

She threw her arms around Cute Guy's neck and hugged him with exaggerated enthusiasm. Wow, his back was muscly. And he smelled fantastic, like a really expensive redwood forest. She may have hugged him a smidge longer than necessary, just to get an extra sniff in.

"Where have you been, Boo Bear?" she demanded in her best bubbly girlfriend voice.

He tilted his head, his eyes crinkling in amusement as his mouth curved into a smirk. "Well, *Schmoopy Pants,* I guess I got mixed up about where we were supposed to meet."

"Oh, you big silly, it's a good thing you're so pretty." She let out a tinkly fake laugh and punched him playfully in the arm. Then she wrapped her hands around his biceps—his *very firm* biceps—and dragged him off toward the hostess stand.

As they were retreating, Cute Guy shot a pointed, don't-mess-with-my-girl glare at Creepy Guy, who was already backing away with his hands up in the universal sign for *hey, man, sorry, I didn't mean anything by it.* Figured. The jerk hadn't been willing to take *her* no for an answer, but the second another guy staked his claim—like she was a piece of property—he threw up the white flag and fled the scene. Asshole.

Not that she wasn't grateful for the intervention. But it was also possible she'd just leapt out of Jabba the Hutt's barge and into the sarlacc pit. So, as soon as they were out of sight of the creep at the bar, Melody let go and took a big step back, putting a few feet of distance between them.

Her benevolent savior shoved his hands into the pockets of his madras shorts, sidestepping a party of four as the hostess led them to their table. He was wearing boat shoes and a polo shirt with the collar popped, like he'd stepped out of a Ralph Lauren ad. "Are you okay?" His brow scrunched in concern as his eyes dropped to her arm. "That guy didn't hurt you when he grabbed you, did he?" He had unusually kind eyes for someone who dressed like a prep school douche.

"No, I'm fine." Melody clenched her hands into fists, resisting the urge to rub her forearm where the creep had touched her. "Thanks for the assist, though."

"Do you need a ride home?" As if he'd just realized how that sounded, he added, "I mean, I can call you a cab if you want."

She shook her head. She was a girl with a hole in her shirt and a thrift-store jacket—no way could she afford cab fare on her work study salary. "Thanks, but I'm good." She'd get herself home on the T—the same way she got there.

"All right," he said. "If you're sure."

"I'm sure."

He nodded and sauntered off toward the back of the restaurant, without even hitting on her or expecting anything in return for his good deed. Huh. Apparently, chivalry wasn't dead after all.

Melody's phone buzzed in her hand. It was a text from Victor.

Sorry got hung up and can't make it.

Great. Wonderful. Perfect.

"Hey!" she called out, hurrying after the Cute Guy. "Wait."

He turned around, eyebrows raised. His sandy hair flopped across his forehead, and he reached up to push it back, smiling at her. He had cute dimples when he smiled. She'd always been a sucker for dimples. They were her kryptonite.

Melody took a deep breath, ignoring the hamsters running nervous laps in her stomach. All she had to do was talk to him. She could do that. It wasn't like it was rocket science or anything.

No, it's way worse. Rocket science, she could handle. Talking to cute guys, on the other hand—*that* was intimidating. Especially heavenly smelling, well-muscled paragons of kindhearted chivalry.

Flo Rida blared from the bar's speakers as a group of people in Sox jerseys pushed through the space between Melody and the cute dimples, trying to get to the bar. She elbowed her way past them, giving dirty looks as good as she got, until she was standing right in front of him.

"What's your name?" At five-foot-six, Melody was hardly what you'd call short, but he was tall enough she had to tip her head back to look at him when they were this close.

"Jeremy."

"Well, Jeremy, I think I owe you a drink."

He shook his head, and his hair flopped onto his forehead again. "You don't owe me anything." He paused, running his hand through his hair. "But if you're propositioning me of your own free will . . ." There was that smirk again. How dare that kind of sass be so sexy? A smirk like that had no right to make her feel so swoony, but it did. It really, really did.

"Let's not get carried away," she said, unable to control the smile on her face. "I'm offering to buy you a drink. That's all."

He did that head tilt thing again, which she was starting to love. Then there was the matter of his eyes, which were outrageously blue, now that she was looking at them up close. Cerulean blue, like that *X-Files* episode about the guy who hypnotized people.

"You didn't tell me your name," Jeremy said, gazing at her with his preposterously blue eyes.

"Melody," she said, trying to pretend like this was totally normal for her, like she went around offering to buy drinks for cute guys with hot smirks and adorable floppy hair all the time.

He grinned. "In that case, I accept your offer, Melody."